The Glass Devil

The Glass Devil

Helene Tursten

Translated by
Katarina E. Tucker

First published in the English language in the United States in 2007
by Soho Press, Inc.
853 Broadway
New York, NY 10003
All rights reserved.

Library of Congress Cataloging-in-Publication Data
Tursten, Helene. 1954–
[Glasdjävulen. English]
The glass devil / Helene Tursten; translated by Katarina E. Tucker
p. cm.
ISBN-13: 978-1-56947-452-5
I. Tucker, Katarina Emilie. II. Title.
PT9876.3.U55G5313 2007
2006052205

10 9 8 7 6 5 4 3 2 1

To Hilmer and Cecilia

Many thanks to Magnus Tuneld at Mactun Data in Karlstad for all his helpful information about computers; Peter Jernfalt for his corrections as to weapon specifications; and both the active and retired police officers whom I have been able to consult.

Everything had seemed perfect. Maybe too perfect; he realized that now. He had been lulled into a sense of security, believing that it would never catch up with him. It really hadn't seemed like it would. Not until now.

It was, quite simply, terrible bad luck. Nothing else.

In the big city, he was anonymous; he could live in peace. That was the only thing he wanted: to be left alone.

The long walks in the surrounding countryside had helped heal his spiritual wounds. He had started going to the gym again. He'd spent this evening at the gym and given his body a real workout. It felt good. He was on his way to building a new body and a new life.

Everything had been going in the right direction. Then she came into his life.

She was everything he had dreamed about. Long dark brown hair, brown eyes, and a fantastic smile. Her warm, supple body against his when he held her in his arms. . . .

They had known all along that they had to keep it a secret. If her family found out about their relationship, anything might happen. Her father and brothers were capable of taking the law into their own hands. He had asked her several times to be very careful, not to tell *anyone* about them.

And now it had all fallen apart. She hadn't had the strength to hold out against her family's questions. In the end, she had told them everything.

It would be best to move from his house for a while and hope that things would calm down. He would have to live with Mom and Dad for the time being. In reality, he knew that this wouldn't help. Her family would refuse to understand how much they had loved each other.

He feared retaliation. It would surely come. It was their custom and culture when they believed the family's honor had been stained. He knew this and didn't fool himself. Vengeance would come.

HE TURNED in on the small gravel road that led up to the cottage. For what must have been the thousandth time, he swore because there were no streetlights. The municipality saw no reason to spend money on them, since the remaining three houses along the road were also summer cottages. He parked in the little gravel-covered area inside the gate. When he turned off his headlights, he was surrounded by impenetrable darkness. It was after eleven o'clock on this cold night at the end of March. Black clouds had gathered in the sky and it looked like it would rain or snow during the night. There was no light at all here in the forest. The tall trees grew thickly. The small lamp that hung over the front door was lit, but failed to illuminate the parking area.

He got out of the car and stretched. As always, he took a deep breath and filled his lungs with clean forest air. Despite the fact that he should be used to it by now, he felt the silence press against his eardrums. But it wasn't completely quiet: A gentle breeze swished in the tops of the trees, and a dog barked in the distance. The cars on the highway could be heard like a faint roar, if one really strained to listen. The sound of an approaching airplane could be heard in the distance, coming in for a landing at Landvetter Airport.

His earlier thoughts caught up with him, and he looked around nervously. Everything appeared normal, calm and quiet. He focused his attention on the small Falu-red house, painted the color of baked bricks. It was a winterized summer cottage that his parents owned. He had felt completely safe and secure here. Now he scanned the house nervously. Nothing seemed out of place. Everything looked as it had when he had left it that morning. Then, he hadn't known how the day would turn out. It had been a complete catastrophe! What wasn't allowed to happen, had happened.

He removed his gym bag and lunch box from the back seat, as well as a grocery-filled plastic bag, locked the car, and walked toward the front door. Then he took the key ring from his jacket pocket, unlocked the door, and stepped into the small hallway. The light from the outside lamp silhouetted him in the doorway.

God, I really must be visible, he thought. Then he became aware of a faint movement in the deep darkness.

"Who is it? No! Not this way!" he tried to scream. But not a word crossed his paralyzed lips.

The only thing he could make out in the sparsely lit hall was the black hand that held a rifle. The rest of the figure was concealed by darkness. "Gloves," he had time to think for a second, irrationally pleased with his own deductive ability.

He stared as though hypnotized into the round black eye.

There was a thousandth of a second's flame.

Then darkness.

Chapter 1

THE INTERCOM ON DETECTIVE Inspector Irene Huss's desk beeped.

"It's Sven. Is Tommy there?"

"No. He's interrogating a suspect in custody in the Speedy murder case. He probably won't be back before five at the earliest."

Criminal Superintendent Sven Andersson snorted into the intercom. "He'll have his hands full if he's going to try and soften up Asko Pihlainen. He may not be back until five *a.m.* tomorrow!"

Even though the superintendent couldn't see it, Irene Huss nodded her agreement.

"Is there anything I can help you with?" she asked. She began to hope that she might be able to leave the piles of boring reports which, for some unexplainable reason, had the tendency to pile up on her desk. The fact that she loathed paperwork and gladly put it off may have had something to do with this.

"Come to my office and we'll talk."

The superintendent hadn't finished his sentence before Irene hopped up. If the boss called, she didn't have to be urged to respond. That she would have to stop writing reports was simply an unfortunate side effect.

Andersson looked contemplative. He leaned back in his chair, which whined under his weight, nodded at Irene, and motioned her to the visitor's chair. He sat quietly, seemingly at a loss as to how to begin. The silence started to become oppressive. His asthmatic breaths seemed to echo in the room. He pressed the palms of his hands together; his knuckles popped; he rested the lower of his double chins against the tips of his fingers and stared blankly at a point above Irene's head. Finally, he slapped his hands on the desktop, rose with difficulty, and said, "It'll have to be you and me. We'll have to go."

Without providing any more details, he took his coat from the hook near the door. "We're leaving immediately," he called over his shoulder.

Irene went to her office to get her jacket. I'm just like Sammie: Jingle the leash and say the magic word *out*, and I'll come running eagerly without asking *where to*, she thought, ironically.

"First, I was thinking about sending a patrol car, but it's so damn difficult to get ahold of a free one. And to send it out into the woods around Norssjön. . . . No. It's better that I take care of it myself," Superintendent Andersson told her as they drove toward Boråsleden.

Irene was about to point out that he actually wasn't alone, but she knew her boss and remained silent. She didn't want to tease him because she really liked him.

"Maybe I should explain," Andersson said.

"Yes, please," Irene replied.

She tried not to sound sarcastic. Apparently, she didn't, because he continued. "My cousin called me. He's the principal of a charter school here in the city."

Irene was surprised to learn that Sven Andersson had a cousin. They had worked together for almost fifteen years, and she had never heard about any of his relatives. She had always thought of him as being completely alone. Divorced, no children, no close relatives, no friends. A lone wolf: that was the phrase that popped up when she thought about her boss.

"Georg, my cousin, is very worried. One of the teachers hasn't been seen at work since yesterday. He doesn't answer his telephone when they call. No one answers at his parents' house either. Georg is concerned because apparently this teacher has had a difficult time and may be depressed. It seemed as if he is afraid the guy may have committed suicide."

"But that's not a reason to dispatch two inspectors from the Crime Police. Your first idea, to send a patrol car, seems more appropriate," Irene said.

She cast a sideways glance at Andersson and saw a flush rise from his neck and flare over his round cheeks.

"I'll decide what's appropriate," he snapped.

He turned his head and looked out the side window. Irene cursed her big mouth. Now he was sulking and wouldn't say another word.

The silence in the car felt heavy. Only the metronomic scraping of the windshield wipers could be heard. Snow mixed with rain had been falling since last night and showed no signs of letting up. Finally, Irene said, "Do you know where we're going?"

"Yes. Turn down toward Hällingsjö, and after a kilometer* or so there will be a sign for Norssjön. That's where you turn in, and then I'll show you the way."

"How come you know the roads so well?"

"I went there once, for a crayfish party."

"To the teacher's home?" Irene asked, surprised.

"No, it was at his parents' cottage."

Her sense that something was fishy was confirmed. There were probably several reasons for her boss to have reacted the way he did, but one of them was clear. In some way, he was personally mixed up in this.

A crayfish party at his parents'.... Suddenly even *friends* of the superintendent's were popping up! He spent time with people and attended their parties. Wow! Irene decided not to let the conversation end.

"Then you don't know the teacher at all?" she continued.

"No. I've never met him. Only his sister."

"Is she also a teacher?"

---

*A kilometer is almost exactly .625, five eighths, of a mile.

"I don't know. She was little then."

He took a deep breath and turned his face toward Irene. "I know what you're wondering. It was seventeen years ago. I was recently divorced, and my cousin thought that I needed to get out and meet people. That's why I ended up at the parents' crayfish party. They're acquaintances of Georg and his wife, Bettan."

Irene pondered. She had to admit that this unexpected trip woke her investigatory instincts. But it wasn't concern over the teacher's fate that had stirred them up, but rather sheer curiosity about the superintendent's personal life. They had known each other so long, and she had never supposed that he had one.

"Have you ever seen them again?" she asked.

"No."

So, no lasting friendship had developed.

"What do the teacher's parents do?"

"The father is a pastor. The mother is probably a housewife. Pastors' wives probably have a lot of work to do at home. Church coffees and stuff like that," Andersson said, evasively.

Irene decided to try to find out as much as possible about Andersson's newly discovered social life. "How was the party? I mean . . . it was held at a pastor's house. There's usually quite a bit of drinking at crayfish parties."

The superintendent broke into a smile. "You can say that again! It ended with the pastor passing out drunk as a skunk in the porch swing. His wife had thrown in the towel several hours earlier and gone to bed inside the house. She seemed to have no tolerance for alcohol at all. The rest of us in the group were pretty drunk."

"Were there many people there?"

Andersson thought for a moment before he answered, "Nine—no, ten including me. This is where you turn off."

He pointed, Irene turned off, and Andersson directed her to take another left just after that. "Go straight for a few kilometers, and we'll reach Norssjön," he said.

Irene had been driving on autopilot while her brain processed the information she'd received from Andersson.

"Is it a large summer cottage?" she asked.

"No. Pretty ordinary. Georg and Bettan had a camper, so we slept in that. Bettan's a teacher and works at Georg's school. She was probably the one who thought of inviting me to the party. It's better these days since we don't see each other as often, but she used to try to fix me up with all her boring teacher colleagues."

"Did it work at that party?" Irene asked.

Andersson just chuckled softly.

The road to Norssjön appeared. Snowy woods lined both sides of the narrow asphalt-paved road. Now and then they glimpsed a small glade with a house, or a small gravel lane snaking its way into the vegetation.

"Slowly, now. It's here somewhere," Andersson said.

As far as Irene was concerned, everything around them was underbrush and it all looked the same. She was impressed that Andersson had such a good memory after so many years.

"There. Turn," he said.

A hand-painted sign placed by the main road pointed toward a narrow gravel trail. "Luck Cottage" was written on it in faded blue letters on a white background. There was a barely discernible flower border around the sign.

Irene turned onto the gravel. The road was bumpy and poorly maintained. A thick forest of spruce hemmed them in. Three small cottages popped up between some trees a short distance down the road. Irene started slowing, but the superintendent told her to continue. They drove for about another hundred meters* until the road ended. Irene saw a fence surrounding a

---

*A meter is 39.37 inches, about one and a tenth yards, so a hundred meters is about 110 yards.

house that was painted brick-red. Irene parked the unmarked police car outside the gate.

They got out and stretched. Everything was quiet aside from the rattle of the falling sleet. A relatively new black Skoda was parked inside the open wooden gates. It was remarkably dirty, and there was a star-shaped crack in the windshield. They started toward the cottage on a path of slippery snow- and moss-covered stones. No sign of life could be seen. The superintendent tried the door handle, but the door was locked.

"The outside light is on," he remarked loudly.

Irene started to walk around the house in order to look through the mullioned windows.

When she looked in through the first window, she spotted him right away.

"Sven!" she called.

The superintendent lumbered over to her. She pointed.

They were looking into a simple kitchen. Through its open door, they could see a man's body lying on its back in the hall. His legs and lower body weren't visible, but his upper body and head were. Or what was left of his head. It was enough to determine that he was dead. Under his open jacket, the front of his light-colored shirt was covered with rust-red blood. One hand was resting on the threshold to the kitchen. Inside the threshold was a plastic bag with food. Some of the items had rolled out onto the kitchen floor.

Andersson turned toward Irene with a grim face. "Call for backup. This is no suicide."

Chapter 2

LATER THAT AFTERNOON, IRENE and Superintendent Andersson told the remaining inspectors in the unit about the murder in the cottage. Irene began. "The body we found was that of Jacob Schyttelius. We've not succeeded in reaching his parents for a positive identification, but his boss gave us a description which matches the victim's exactly. He was thirty-one years old. Sven and I found him at twelve thirty, shot, in a summer cottage. We found the key to the front door under a large plant on the steps and unlocked the door. The body was lying in the hall and didn't didn't appear to have been moved after the murder. A gunshot wound to the chest near his heart had been inflicted by a large-caliber weapon, and the head was partially blown away. We didn't find a weapon. We made a quick survey of the area while we were waiting for the technicians. The house has two small bedrooms, and apparently he used one of them as an office. He'd squeezed a desk into it, and there was a computer on top of the desk. Someone had drawn a symbol on the monitor, probably in blood."

"What kind of symbol?" Fredrik Stridh interrupted to ask.

"A star inside a circle. Svante says that it might be a magical sign, the kind that witches and Satanists use during their rituals. He has come across similar ones in past investigations of church fires and the like. The technicians are still working out there."

"Satanists! What a bunch of shit!" Jonny Blom snorted.

Irene shrugged and nodded at Hannu Rauhala, who had raised his hand.

"Why was the victim living in a summer cottage?" he asked.

"According to the principal of the school where he worked, he had recently been divorced and moved back to Göteborg after spending a few years up north. It's hard to find housing, so he borrowed his parents' cottage, which is winterized. He's lived there all fall and winter. The last time he was seen was yesterday afternoon when he left work at around four thirty. Some damp gym clothes were in a bag, so he may have worked out at a gym. We found a membership card to a gym in his wallet and will check with them to see if he went there after work. He had bought food at Hemköp on Mölndalsvägen, and we're also going to check there to find out if someone remembers him. His school was somewhere near Heden. His parents don't live far from the cottage but, as I said, we haven't been able to reach them yet. The father is rector of the church in a small community called Kullahult. We're thinking about how to tell the parents that their son has been murdered. I mean, after all, normally we take a pastor with us when we deliver the news. But what do you do when the recipient of such news *is* a pastor?"

Irene stopped her report and looked at her colleagues around the conference table. It was just after five in the afternoon. As usual, Jonny Blom was half asleep in his chair. When his head nodded, Irene noticed that his bald spot had become larger. The careful comb-over and fix with hair gel from that morning had lost its hold. The unit's youngest man was sitting next to him and looked alert—as well as thick-haired: Fredrik Stridh was becoming as skillful as he was energetic, and Irene had begun to appreciate him. Hannu Rauhala sat quietly on Irene's right, but she knew that he was registering everything. His wife, Birgitta, was the unit's other female inspector. She was on maternity leave and wouldn't be back for a few more months. When she started working again, Hannu was planning on taking paternity leave to care for their son. This information had been leaked a few days earlier, and Superintendent Andersson's mood had darkened considerably. Amid his furious mumbling, some phrases like "babies need their mothers" and "men shouldn't be nannies" could be discerned. Tommy Persson was also absent but might show up at any moment. He had devoted a large part of the day to questioning a suspect in the murder of a drug peddler, Ronny "Speedy" Olofsson. Speedy had embezzled some money from his connection. Since the sum was large, his punishment had been execution.

Speedy had been shot in the head early one Saturday morning. The only witnesses were some ornithologists in a car. Two of the birdwatchers had seen the murderer's face. He had had a large scar, running from the bridge of his nose down his right cheek. With this description, the investigators knew right away who they should look for. The suspect, Asko Pihlainen, had already served several sentences for aggravated assault as well as narcotics violations, threatening witnesses, and grand theft auto. It was, however, the first time he had been connected to a murder. According to Asko, he wasn't connected to it; he'd never set foot at the scene of the murder. And, incidentally, he had witnesses to state that he had been at a neighbor's playing poker at the time of the murder.

That's where the problem was: The neighbor, and two women, stated that Asko had been playing cards with them at five o'clock on Saturday morning. They stuck to their statements, and the investigation had come to a halt.

Irene didn't envy Tommy's task. Asko Pihlainen was notorious for always proclaiming his innocence. Those who testified against him almost always recanted. Asko hadn't discovered the birdwatchers' identities yet but it was only a matter of time. Irene sighed, but she had to concentrate on her own case.

She repeated her question. "Do you think that we should take another pastor along to Jacob Schyttelius's parents'?"

"Aaah. If he's a pastor, he can manage on his own," said Jonny Blom.

Hannu asked permission to speak. "It's one thing to provide assistance professionally. But when it comes to yourself, it's something completely different."

Fredrik Stridh nodded in agreement. "Exactly! And as he's a pastor, one has to assume he's religious." He stopped when the others started laughing, but quickly continued his line of thinking: "I mean that a religious person may have a greater need than others to speak with a pastor."

"Fredrik has a point there. I agree that we should take a pastor with us to the Schytteliuses'," said Irene.

Superintendent Andersson spoke for the first time. "His name is Sten. Sten Schyttelius. I don't remember what her name is."

Fredrik Stridh arched his eyebrows. "Do you know them?"

"Not really. Friends of friends." His tone of voice said that this subject was closed. Fredrik got the message and didn't ask any more questions. He gave his boss a long contemplative look.

Andersson cleared his throat and said, "Irene, you'll have to find a pastor and drive out to the Schytteliuses'. Take someone else with you."

Fredrik volunteered. With a teasing look in Hannu's direction, he said, "It's right to help out a friend, and Hannu is going for training tonight. Guess in what."

He looked so mischievous that Irene became curious. Certainly, the white-blond Finn with ice-blue eyes was slender and in good shape, but she had never thought about what sport he trained in. His colleagues suggested strength training, weight-lifting, hardening for the Finnish championships in sauna, the last-man-standing Koskenkorva championship, but no one was right.

"Baby swimming!" Fredrik announced.

A faint blush could be detected on Hannu's cheeks, but there was no emotion in his voice when he asked, "How did you know?"

"We're detectives, aren't we? Seriously though, Birgitta called a while ago. You weren't in, so she asked me to remind you that you were going to baby swimming tonight. I must admit that I had forgotten about it, but now I can give you her message: Don't forget baby swimming!" Fredrik laughed.

The superintendent said, "Okay. Get the address and drive out to Schyttelius's parents'. I'll stay at the station. The press will probably be in touch soon."

IRENE WAS lucky: The pastor of the neighboring parish was home. His name was Jonas Burman, and he had a friendly voice. When he understood what it was about, he offered to accompany them and provide support when they delivered this news of the death of a son. He gave them detailed directions to his home. He would direct them from there to the rectory in Kullahult, where Rector Schyttelius lived.

They found Burman's house in Slättared without any problems. A tall figure bent against the biting breeze stood outside the gate. The wind had picked up during the last few hours and brought with it a great deal of whirling snow, though the flakes melted as soon as they touched wet ground. Irene pulled in and put the transmission in park. Both she and Fredrik got out to greet Burman.

He was much younger than he had sounded on the telephone. His hair was light and rather long and kept blowing in his face. When he took Irene's hand in greeting, his was cold but his handshake was firm. His slender fingers reminded Irene of a musician's. Enlarged by the lenses in his rectangular, thin-framed glasses, the friendly look in his blue eyes was comforting.

The three of them drove off in the police car. During the ride, Fredrik informed him of what they knew of Jacob Schyttelius's death. Jonas Burman listened without interrupting. When Fredrik was finished, the minister said, "I've met Jacob several times. He is . . . was . . . a very nice guy. It's completely incomprehensible that someone would want to shoot him. Why? Could it have been a burglary?"

"No idea," Fredrik replied. "We're going to try to find out both why, and who. But right now we don't have the faintest lead. His parents may know something."

"You aren't going to question them tonight, are you?" Jonas asked, concerned.

"Only if they are up to it. Otherwise we'll wait," Fredrik said.

The minister pointed at a sign. "That's where we turn off."

The sign read "Kullahult 2."

IN THE growing twilight, the floodlit church could be seen from far away. It was situated on a partly snow-covered hill and towered over the small town of Kullahult.

"The rectory is located right next to the church. Just steer toward it," said Burman. At the foot of the hill, he directed them onto a gravel road. Irene could see the cemetery wall a short distance above them. They left it behind as the road went straight ahead instead of continuing around the hill.

They could see a large white house down a driveway in a park-like, snow-covered yard. Irene drove in through the open gates. Coarse gravel crackled under the tires.

"Strange that—" Jonas started to say. He looked around after they had parked the car. They could hear the rattling of the wind and sleet in the tops of the trees.

"Sten and Elsa usually light the garden lamps and turn on out-door lights and a lot of lights in the house as soon as it gets dark. It's very isolated here at the back of the church hill," he continued. "They like to illuminate the house."

Wet snowflakes slapped them in the face when they stepped out of the car. Darkness wrapped the big trees and bushes. A tall, depressing spruce hedge circled the garden impenetrably. The black windowpanes of the house seemed rejecting.

"Could they be out of town?" Fredrik asked.

"No. We always tell each other if we're going to travel," Jonas answered.

"Even if it's only for the day?"

"Yes. There's only one pastor in each parish, so we have a schedule for the pastor who's on call . One of us is always available on weekdays in case something urgent comes up. But we always inform each other if we're going to be out of town, even if we aren't on call. There are two other parishes that are part of this system. Four pastors in all. It works well."

Irene remembered to take the flashlight, which was in the glove compartment, before they started toward the house's grand entrance. Four wooden columns held up a roof which protected the steps and the entry from rain and snow. It enhanced the feeling of an old country estate. The front door consisted of two beautifully decorated half-doors. Irene reached for the heavy knocker, but stopped herself halfway there.

One of the door halves was ajar.

She turned on the flashlight to inspect the door, which appeared to be undamaged. She carefully pushed it open with the flashlight.

Before they went in, she said to the minister, "The fact that the door is open doesn't mean anything. Just as it doesn't necessarily mean anything that the house is dark and appears to be empty. But under the circumstances, I don't want you to touch anything in the house. No light switches, no hand railings, and so on. Just stay close to us. Can you guide us through the house?"

Jonas Burman said "Yes" and stepped behind Irene, following her over the threshold. Irene let the flashlight swing around the interior to locate the light switch. She turned it on with a light push of the flashlight's handle.

A small crystal chandelier illuminated the large downstairs hall. A rag rug in bright colors covered the floor. Just inside the door was a wooden chest with a vaulted lid. The year "1796" was barely visible on it, among painted flowers and butterflies. The chest was beautiful and might very well be as old as the date indicated. The mirror that hung above it hardly appeared newer. It had a heavy golden frame, and the glass was divided into sections. A grandfather clock stood next to it, beating out the time with heavy ticks.

Jonas Burman made a funnel with his hands and yelled into the house, "Ho! Ho! Sten and Elsa! It's Jonas!"

The three of them listened tensely. An unbroken silence ensued.

With a resigned sigh, Burman went to the center of the room. "There's a bathroom under the stairs that lead to the second floor. There are several bedrooms and some other smaller rooms on that level, a bathroom and a separate toilet as well. To our right, on the first floor, there's a dining room and a living room. But out here in the country, we use the old-fashioned word 'hall' for the living room. Since this estate is old and the room is large, there is a reason for this usage."

He turned a hundred and eighty degrees and pointed at the door opposite. "The kitchen is in there. The door next to the stairs leads to a work room. If you walk through that room, you come to the library."

They decided to inspect the kitchen first. It was large and airy. At first glance, Irene felt as if she had been transported back in time but then she saw that the refrigerator and stove were new. There was also a dishwasher. Other than that, the cabinet doors were made of a dark wood, country style. Beams in the ceiling were visible, and a large table stood in the middle of the polished wooden floor. Irene counted twelve chairs around the table. Everything looked old and well-built. She couldn't keep from asking the pastor, "Are there only two people living here?"

"Yes. That's the problem with these old rectories: They're terribly expensive to heat and a normal modern family doesn't fill the house with life. In the old days, pastors often had large families, as well as servants. The pastors' homes were also fellowship halls. That's why they were built on such a grand scale."

Irene had very vague ideas about what the function of a fellowship hall was, but decided not to ask. They opened the doors at the other end of the kitchen and found a very small room which had probably been a maid's room and, behind the other door, a laundry room with modern conveniences. A large box freezer buzzed monotonously in a corner. In the laundry room, there was also a door that led to the back yard. Irene determined that it was locked. She carefully lifted the lid to the freezer. It was half-filled with neat packages and plastic containers. They went back through the kitchen, turning the lights on as they went.

A quick tour of the Schyttelius work room and library revealed that they were large and the furniture very old. The walls of the library were covered with bookshelves full of old books. It smelled of dust and old leather.

The dining room and the so-called "hall" were adjacent: It was necessary to walk through the dining room to reach the hall. The rooms were big with high ceilings, but they were also very cold. Irene understood why the door from the front hall had been closed. The heat in these two rooms had been lowered considerably. Capacious tile stoves on either side of the hall looked as if they hadn't been used in a long time. The furnishings were sparse. There were a very long settee and a single Windsor chair in the floor. The settee might have seated as many as ten people if they had squeezed together. Chairs matching the settee were ranged along the walls. A large rug covered the center of the floor. It was worn, the colors faded, but it had probably been magnificent once upon a time. A long white painted table with just six chairs furnished the dining room. Irene concluded that the family sat in the kitchen when they had company.

Reentering the front hall almost felt warm and cozy. They climbed the stairs and entered an open room off the landing which was surprisingly modern, containing brown leather sofas and a large TV. With expressionless eyes of glass, three stuffed moose heads stared down at the visitors from the walls.

"The TV room," Jonas Burman said superfluously.

They split up. Irene went to the left half of the second floor, and the men took the right. To her surprise, the first room Irene entered was a billiard room. The central table dominated the space. Stuffed animal heads and birds also adorned these walls. Some chairs stood at one end. The next surprise was that there was a well-stocked bar cart next to the chairs. Irene took a closer look at the cart and determined that the liquor bottles were foreign brands. Apparently, the Schytteliuses traveled quite a bit and returned with souvenirs.

Irene crossed to the door on the opposite side of the room. There was a key in the lock but the door was unlocked. She used the flashlight handle again to push it open and to turn on the light switch. The ceiling fixture held a weak bulb behind cracked frosted glass. The room was remarkably cold. Some modern office cabinets and a large desk were the only furniture. There was an open computer on the desk so Irene circled it to look at the screen.. At first, her brain refused to register what she saw. She started backing away. A star in a ring appeared to have been smeared onto the screen in blood.

Chapter 3

"PASTOR JONAS BURMAN AND I found Sten and Elsa Schyttelius in their bedroom. I tried to keep him from seeing anything, but unfortunately he's tall and managed to peer over my shoulder. He collapsed on the spot. It was a bloodbath," said Fredrik Stridh.

He paused and looked around the conference room. In addition to himself and Irene, Superintendent Andersson, Tommy Persson, and Hannu Rauhala sat around the table. Jonny Blom had already gone home when the call about the double murder at the rectory reached the police station. Hannu had just been on his way to baby swimming but when he heard what the call was about he decided to stay put.

"When I pushed Burman down on the couch, Irene appeared. She had found a computer with one of those star symbols painted on the monitor, like the one she and Sven had seen at Jacob Schyttelius's," Fredrik said.

"Did the star look exactly the same?" Andersson interrupted. She nodded. "Exactly."

Fredrik cleared his throat. "Sten and Elsa Schyttelius were shot at close range with a large-caliber firearm. Sten Schyttelius hunts."

"How do you know that?" the superintendent interrupted again.

"Jonas Burman said so. And the walls of the rectory are covered with stuffed animal corpses. Burman has worked in Slättared parish for two years, so he knew quite a bit about the family. They also have a daughter whose name is Rebecka; she lives in London. He's only met her once. It was at a Christmas dinner or something like that."

"We have to give her protection right away!" Irene burst out.

"Why?" said Andersson.

"Because of what's happened to her family. She's the only one still alive. We don't know the motive for the murders yet, but it seems as if someone wants to wipe out the Schyttelius family."

"But she lives in London—" the superintendent began. He was interrupted by Tommy Persson.

"The Schytteliuses seem to have died at about the same time as their son. The murderer has more than a day's lead on us. He could be in London right now."

The superintendent muttered something inaudible, but then nodded. "Okay. You're right, we'll have to find her address and get in touch with our colleagues in London. Can you do it, Hannu?" This was clearly an order, not a question. Superintendent Andersson nodded at Fredrik to continue.

"There were no signs of a struggle in the bedroom. Both Irene and I believe that they were shot in their sleep. Each body lay with its head on a pillow. What's left of its head, I should say. And both of them were shot from the front."

"Did the neighbors hear anything?" the superintendent asked.

"We have the same problem there as we did at the cottage: There *aren't* any neighbors near the church. The rectory is located on the back of the church hill, so it's in an isolated area," said Irene.

"We've found a possible murder weapon," Fredrik put in.

This was news to the superintendent, who said, impatiently, "And you're only mentioning it now! What was it?"

"A Husqvarna 1900. It was lying under the bed. I saw the barrel sticking out, but of course I didn't touch it."

"I see. Our dear old Husqvarna," the superintendent sighed.

Irene understood why he sighed. When it comes to firearms in

Sweden, Husqvarna, with its various types of shotguns and sporting rifles, is the most common brand for homicides, and in particular suicides. The explanation is simple: They are the most common sporting weapon.

"Svante Malm called me just before we got back to the station. The technicians have found an unlocked gun cabinet, brand name Zugil, in the rector's work room," said Fredrik.

"The work room on the second floor, or the one on the first floor?" Irene asked.

"The one with the computer on the second floor. Svante says that he'll come to morning prayers and make a report about what they've found. Two technicians are still at the cottage, but they should be finished late tonight."

"How old were the Schytteliuses?" Tommy asked.

"He was sixty-four and she was sixty-three. He was going to retire this summer," Fredrik answered. He looked down at his papers. "I asked Jonas Burman how old Rebecka is, but he isn't sure. He thinks she's about twenty-five."

"What does she do in London?" Irene asked.

"She works as a computer consultant, according to Burman."

"He was informative, that Burman," the superintendent muttered.

"Yes. He was in shock but tried to answer my questions. Nice guy."

"What else did he say?" Tommy asked.

"Not much. He thought that we should speak with the deaconess. She has worked with Schyttelius for several years. Her name is . . ." He flipped through his pad of paper until he found what he was looking for. ". . . Rut Börjesson. Then there are people at the parish registration office who we can question."

"Okay. I already have four guys going around Kullahult knocking on doors. And two other guys have been at it out by Norssjön since this afternoon. They'll call me if something comes up. Tomorrow after morning prayers, the three of you are going out to Kullahult to start questioning those people. Hannu and Jonny will head for Norssjön," the superintendent said, ending the meeting.

THE CLOCK on the old Saab's instrument panel showed 22:41 when Irene stopped in front of her garage. The row-house garages created their own rows in the outskirts of the area. She opened the heavy garage door and parked the car inside, not out of fear that the thirteen-year-old automobile would be stolen but for fear that it would be freezing when she got into it the next morning.

When she had closed the door, she felt the fatigue in her back and shoulders. She decided to try to work out the next day. Then she realized that there would hardly be any time for working out; the questioning would probably take the whole day and part of the evening. She would have to settle for an early-morning jog, even though early mornings were not her strong suit. In truth, she was terribly tired early in the day. But if that was the only time available, it would have to be a morning run.

If you've turned forty, you have to be disciplined about exercising. She was proud of being in good shape, and she worked out whenever the opportunity arose. Twenty years ago, she had won the gold at the European Ju-jitsu Championship, which had given her high status at the police academy in Ulriksdal. About a year later, she met Krister and had almost immediately become pregnant. The birth of twin girls had meant a temporary setback for her figure, but she had gotten into training again pretty quickly. These days, she did strength exercises once a week, jogged a few times, and trained a group of female cops every Sunday in ju-jitsu.

Keeping in shape was harder on her as the years passed. Old injuries started making themselves known. She had to wear a knee brace now when she ran. But she didn't feel well mentally or physically if she didn't work out. So morning jogs, the only type of exercise she could do during heavy periods of work, were essential.

When she opened the door to their row house, she was enthusiastically greeted by Sammie. He bounced with joy and tried to lick her face when she bent down to pet his golden-brown coat. The best thing about dogs is that they're happy no matter what time you get home; they never reproach you for being late, thought Irene.

A note from Krister was lying on the table informing her that there was vegetarian lasagna in the fridge. Irene sighed. The Huss family diet had been perfect, as far as Irene was concerned, until Jenny had become a vegan a few years ago. At the same time, Krister had decided to go on a diet, and after a while he adopted their daughter's new food habits with enthusiasm. These days, the Huss family ate vegan food three times a week and meat and fish the rest of the time. On those days, Jenny lived on leftovers or fixed her own food. Irene sighed loudly again and thought longingly about a large bloody steak with a creamy garlic-scented potato casserole.

She microwaved a slice of lasagna and drank a glass of milk standing at the kitchen counter. After a quick shower, she went up to the second floor. When she opened the doors to the girls' rooms, she saw that they were sleeping in their beds. Only a little more than a year left of high school, and then they'd probably move away from home as soon as possible. Irene felt a pang in her heart at that thought. Then it would just be her and Krister left in the house. And Sammie.

When she padded into the bedroom, she could hear Krister's heavy breathing. He would start snoring any minute. Naturally, Sammie had placed himself in the middle of Irene's side of the bed. He was lying on his back with his paws in the air, pretending to be asleep. Irene was too tired to coax him down. Instead, she resolutely put him on the floor. Deeply insulted, Sammie went out and lay down on the rug in front of the TV.

When she closed her eyes, she saw alternating images of the bloody scenes from the cottage and the rectory. Who wanted to wipe out the Schyttelius family? And why? Was Rebecka Schyttelius also in danger? Reason said that she was. But maybe the threat was local and she was safe because she lived in London. Why had the murderer written the symbol in blood on the computer screens?

Questions swirled around in Irene's head before she fell into an uneasy sleep.

Chapter 4

SVANTE MALM LOOKED AS if he hadn't slept a wink during the last twenty-four hours. His usual happy, horse-like face was ashen with exhaustion, and even his freckles looked faded. He blinked and ran his fingers through his salt-and-pepper red hair several times. If it was in an attempt to give some shape to his nonexistent hairstyle, it was completely in vain: He looked even more like an over-aged punk.

We're all starting to get older and more worn down, thought Irene. Lucky that we have Fredrik. She glanced at him. He sat upright and, as far as Irene was concerned, seemed almost brazenly alert. His thin light-blue cotton shirt matched his eyes, and he smelled nicely of body lotion and aftershave. Even though she might be newly showered after her morning jog, she never managed to achieve that bright-eyed and bushy-tailed look.

Svante Malm began to show signs of wanting to get started. He cleared his throat and said, "I've spoken with Åhlén. He'll be here at any moment and will give an account of what has materialized out at the cottage. I'll go through what we've found so far at the rectory. Professor Stridner was actually nice enough to come out last night to look at the bodies. She said that they had probably been dead less than twenty-four hours. It was cold in the bedroom, not more than seventeen degrees,* and that, of course, impacts the process. She promised to give these autopsies priority this morning."

He stopped to take a gulp of coffee. Irene noticed that his hand shook slightly as he brought the mug up to his lips.

---

*One Celsius degree is 9/5 the size of a Fahrenheit degree, and zero Celsius is 32 degrees Fahrenheit, which means that 17 degrees Celsius equals 63 degrees Fahrenheit.

Forensics was more understaffed than usual since this year's flu season was still reaping victims. Two of them worked in the Forensics department of the Göteborg Police Department. There were no substitutes for those positions.

"The victims were shot at point-blank range with at least one shot each, right in the forehead. You don't get a small, neat little hole when you shoot someone between the eyes with large-caliber ammunition. The back of the skull is torn away. They died immediately. No signs of a struggle. Based on the injuries, the rifle which was lying under the bed is probably the murder weapon. There were no fingerprints on the rifle. It had been wiped carefully. The murderer probably wore gloves."

"How did he get in?" Superintendent Andersson interrupted.

"The door was open when Irene and Fredrik arrived at the crime scene, the key in the lock."

Tommy whistled softly and said, "So the murderer had a key to the house."

"That's not certain," Andersson replied. "Irene and I found a key to the cottage under a flower pot on the outside steps. Was there one like that on the steps to the rectory?"

Irene tried to remember but before she could answer, Fredrik beat her to it.

"There was a large white ceramic pot with pine needles or something like that on the outside stairs. The key may have been under it."

The superintendent nodded and shrugged at the same time. No one could know for certain but the family may have been in the habit of putting an extra key under potted plants, the most common place for Swedish families to leave a spare key.

"There is no apprarent damage in the rest of the house. Which brings us to the computer. The lab did a quick test; the symbol on the monitor was written in human blood. We'll know whose blood a little later. But when I tried to start up the computer, it was completely dead. It beeped when the power was turned on, but the monitor remained blank. We've brought it in to the station. Ljunggren is good with computers. Åhlén brought in the other computer, from the cottage. The last thing I did before I came up here just now was to try to boot it up. Exactly the same thing happened: It beeped but wouldn't start up."

Svante pulled out some Polaroid photos from an envelope and handed them to Tommy Persson. "Here are pictures of the symbol."

The photos were divided quickly among the officers present. Irene felt uneasy when she saw the five-pointed star surrounded by the ring. Svante had written "the cottage" and "the rectory" in one of the top corners. From what Irene could make out, the symbols were almost identical.

"These stars are called pentagrams. A pentagram is a five-pointed star that can be drawn in one pass with five straight lines. One point faces up, two down, and two to the sides."

Svante stood. He pulled down the white screen from the ceiling and turned on the overhead projector. He drew a five-pointed star in blue ink.

"This is a pentagram. Compare it with the pictures. Do you see any differences?"

"Yes. On the computer screens, they're upside down," Fredrik said quickly.

"Exactly. Now I'll turn my picture as well."

With a quick movement of his hand, Svante rotated the picture a hundred and eighty degrees.

"Do you see that the appearance of the star changes? Now it has two points going up and one down. Drawn this way, it becomes a magic symbol. I've come across it a few times in the past. And now I'll fill in the two top points and the lower one."

He quickly colored in the three points and the space in the middle of the pentagram with a red pen. The spectators saw a triangle with two points facing upward. Svante took a new gulp of coffee before he continued: "This is the Devil's face, with two horns and the goatee."

He paused to see the effect of his words. All the officers looked surprised, but Superintendent Andersson suddenly woke up. "What kind of crap is this? The Devil's face!? Are you messing with us?" he asked angrily.

Svante attempted a smile. "No. As I said, I've come across this before, twice at church fires and once at a murder. The murder was never solved, but everything pointed to it being a Satanic sacrifice. I'm thinking of the Purple Murder. Do you remember?"

Everyone but Fredrik nodded. Svante looked at him and said, "You are too young: It was more than twenty years ago.

"We found the victim in an apartment. The neighbors called the police when they began smelling him in the summer heat. When we got there, it appeared to be a completely ordinary apartment. The hall, kitchen, and living room looked normal. But the bedroom was a house of horrors. The floor, walls, and ceiling were painted black. The window was covered with a thick black curtain. He had covered the walls with a lot of symbols. Different whips and masks were hanging in there too. There were candleholders everywhere, but all the candles were black and made of wax. A large ceramic basin, which he had filled with strange objects, had been placed in the middle of the room. There were pieces of bone, tufts of hair from humans and animals, a snakeskin, and I can't remember what all. He was lying on top of the bed with his throat cut. The murder weapon was never found, but it must have been a hunting knife with a large blade. Extremely sharp. The murderer had drawn a pentagram on his stomach."

"Why was it called the Purple Murder?" Fredrik wondered.

"The man was only wearing a purple cloak. Underneath, he was naked."

"Why was it purple? Did the color mean something in particular?" Irene asked.

"Black, white, and red are the colors used during black masses. Sometimes they may have a little silver as well. When they use red, it's a purplish red. Also, the ring around the pentagram symbolizes a snake which is biting its own tail. Exactly what the significance of that is, I don't know."

"Hadn't the neighbors heard anything?" Irene asked.

When the Purple Murder happened, she had been an alternate in the field and had been driving a police car in Angered. All she'd known about that murder was what she had read in the papers.

"Nothing. But the murder occurred during vacation time, when most people were out of town. And this fellow was pretty odd and kept to himself. He rarely said anything to his neighbors, but he didn't bother anyone either. Not until he started smelling."

"So you mean we're going to be chasing Satanists? . . . who murder pastors? But why did they murder the son? He was a teacher, not a pastor. And why Mrs. Schyttelius?" Jonny asked.

Svante gestured tiredly. "I'm not saying that the murderer is a Satanist. I'm saying that the symbol on the computer screens is supposed to be magical and is common in occult and Satanic contexts." He pointed his finger at the blue star with the three red-colored points that was projected on the screen and continued. "I've also seen it painted on church doors, churches burned down by Satanists. In one case, we caught the perpetrators. When Kålltorp's old church burned down, two guys and two girls had set the fire. They said they were confirmed Satanists and had done it in the Devil's honor. The existence of an older leader surfaced during the investigation; he was the one who had ordered the fire set. We never got our hands on him. The kids didn't know his real name or what he looked like."

"They must have seen what he looked like," Jonny objected.

"No. He always had a silver mask over his face when they met him. They had a 'church,' as they called it, an old storage facility out on Ringön. A perfect remote location. The congregation consisted of about ten youths, and these four were given the honor of an assignment to burn down the church in question. Neither we nor his 'congregation' saw any trace of the leader after the fire. It was as if he vanished from the face of the earth. The kids were taken care of by Social Services, and this specific congregation dissolved. But a new one may have been founded; maybe the leader came back and started over again. What do we know?"

"Was the pentagram written in blood?" Tommy Persson wondered.

"Yes. The kids had killed a cat and drawn the symbol before they started the fire. They had used hamster blood at the other church fire."

"Which was the other church where you saw the pentagram?"

"Norssjön's summer church."

"Norssjön! That's where Schyttelius's summer cottage is located!" Irene exclaimed.

Svante Malm nodded. "Exactly. But the church was on the other side of the lake and burned down almost two years ago. It was a small wooden church that was only used during the summer since there wasn't any heating or electricity in it."

"So it couldn't have been an electrical fire," the superintendent concluded.

"No. A witness who was out that summer night rowing on the lake heard voices from the church around midnight. He thought it sounded like chanting. A little while later, he saw flames shooting up from the building and supposedly he saw shapes moving around the fire. According to him, they were dancing. The witness was in his seventies and had heart problems, so he realized that he wasn't going to be able to do anything about the fire. Instead, he hurried home and called the fire department.

But by the time they got there, the building had practically burned to the ground. Strangely enough, the door had survived, and I saw an upside-down pentagram for the second time."

"Drawn on it with hamster blood," the superintendent added.

"Yes. Animal sacrifices are common during their rituals. There's one additional item at the crime scene in the rectory that has Satanic connections: A crucifix is hanging upside-down in the Schytteliuses' bedroom. Satanists often use upside-down crosses during their black masses. The crucifix may well have hung in the bedroom before the murders, but the killer took the opportunity to turn it around."

Irene tried to pull together the items of information they had just received. It wasn't yet possible to combine them into a pattern. She raised her hand and posed her question when Svante nodded at her: "Do you think it's plausible that someone would shoot his victims as part of a Satanic rite?"

Svante shook his head. "No. Rituals using knives are important elements in such murders. Swords are not uncommon. Nor is poison. There are usually different symbols painted or carved on the victims. They're marked to show that they belong to the devil. Satanists have a strong belief in the power of blood. They drink blood and sacrifice blood. Of course it was bloody at the crime scene yesterday, but nothing points to these deaths being the result of the performance of a Satanic ritual."

"Except for the pentagrams and the cross," said Tommy.

"Exactly."

Svante hid a yawn with his hand. A tap at the door was followed by its opening. Svante's colleague, Bosse Åhlén, stuck his bald head into the room. He lumbered over to where Svante sat. Irene knew that Åhlén was a few years younger than herself but his early hair loss and chubbiness made him look much older. Otherwise, the most notable thing about Bosse Åhlén was that he had seven kids, the youngest only a few months old. Maybe that was the main reason he looked tired, but the night's work had left its mark as well.

He took off his glasses and rubbed his eyes. He wiped his glasses on his not-so-clean lab coat. When he had returned them to their place on his round potato nose, he started speaking. "Report from the cottage at Norssjön. The victim was shot at close range with a large-caliber weapon. One round in the chest near the heart, and one through the head. He had his jacket and shoes on when he was found. These and his other clothes were in order. A plastic bag from Hemköp, a bag with gym clothes, and a lunch box were lying next to him. Everything points to the victim having been shot just as he stepped through the front door. It opens outward and he fell inward, so the murderer didn't need to move the body in order to close the door. There are no signs of a struggle. No weapon was found in or around the crime scene. We're going to make a thorough search of the property today."

"Has Ljunggren looked at the computer?" Svante Malm asked.

"Yes. It's completely dead, not functional. According to Ljunggren, someone formatted the hard drive using the Pentagon method."

"The 'Pentagon method'? Explain!" Andersson commanded.

"You can burn, crush with a sledgehammer, or pick apart a computer to try to destroy information on its hard drive. It's useless, according to Ljunggren. It's always possible to piece together at least a part of the contents again."

"Who the hell is able to do that?" Andersson asked.

"A few really skilled hackers. Ljunggren says that there's a company in Norway which is expert at it. Of course, it costs a lot of money, but in some cases it's worth it. Usually, computers get sent there after a fire.

"So, basically, it's very difficult to get rid of information stored on hard drives. According to the Pentagon, which obviously has top-secret material on its computers, there's only one surefire way: You run a formatting program which actually writes random ones and zeros to the entire drive, replacing the information that was previously there. And you run it several times, just to be sure. That makes it impossible to reconstruct the files. Ordinarily, when you erase or even format a disk, the actual information, the non-random ones and zeros, is still there; what the erasing or formatting does is simply to destroy the 'map' to where all the information is located on the disk but it's still theoretically possible to retrieve that information if you know what you're doing."

"And where does one get their hands on such a formatting program?" Tommy asked.

"You can buy them in computer stores. You can probably download them from the Internet as well. Anyone who has this software can replace everything on the hard drive with ones and zeros, which again totally destroys all the information that was there; and then just reinstall the system software so the computer will function, but with an otherwise empty hard drive."

"How long does it take to erase an entire hard drive?"

"According to Ljunggren, about one to two hours on average, depending on its capacity."

Tommy wrinkled his brow in concentration. Suddenly he brightened up and asked eagerly, "Did you find any kind of disk or CD containing formatting software at the cottage?"

"No."

Tommy turned toward Svante Malm. "Did you find such a disk at the rectory?"

The technician shook his head.

"So the murderer must have stayed with his victims for an hour or two, running the formatting program."

"Or maybe he had time to run it before the murders. Jacob Schyttelius was shot when he came home in the evening. The murderer could have gotten into the house during the day, and then he would have had plenty of time," Fredrik Stridh objected.

"And he may have downloaded the program directly from the Internet rather than carrying it around with him," Åhlén put in.

"So all we know is that the murderer effectively destroyed the computers at both crime scenes," Irene thought out loud.

"And marked them with the Devil's face," Tommy added.

"The Devil's . . . !" Andersson exclaimed, irritated. "That is just a dead end. A pastor wouldn't have anything to do with Satanists!"

"Don't say that. The summer church at Norssjön was burned down by Satanists. And Schyttelius had a house by the lake," said Irene.

"Do you mean that Schyttelius himself was a Satanist and burned down that church?" Jonny Blom asked.

"Of course not. I just think it's strange that the church was located in the vicinity of the Schyttelius family, and that the symbol which had been painted on the church doors was also on the computer monitors."

"Except that it was written in hamster blood, not human blood," the superintendent muttered.

"The question is whether there is any relationship. According to Svante, pentagrams are commonly drawn during different rituals. It's possible that the person who drew the pentagrams on the computer screens didn't know about the symbol on the church door," Irene continued thinking out loud.

"I say it's a dead end! To hell with the computers and the bloody symbols and that crap, and concentrate on the murders!" Andersson exclaimed.

Irene became worried when she saw how red his face was. She knew how much he hated not having even the smallest definite lead to start with. Here, everything was just a guess. In certain complicated cases like the Schyttelius murders, there were no obvious leads or motives and it gave the investigators the feeling that the murderer was playing games with them. Irene wasn't sure that that was the case with this investigation. Maybe the murderer was trying to say something? But that was contradicted by the fact that the murderer had silenced the only witnesses who could have provided any clues: the computers.

Andersson took a deep breath in order to regain his composure and get his blood pressure under control. "It's been settled with the police in Borås that we will undertake the investigation of the murders. Most of the parish lies within our jurisdiction, not to mention that it's a large complicated case. Irene, Tommy, and Fredrik will drive out to Kullahult and question the church personnel and the neighbors. Jonny and Hannu will speak with the people who live in the vicinity of the cottage. It will go faster out at the cottage, and when you are done you can join the others at Kullahult. Canvassing the neighborhood has apparently not given rise to anything concrete yet, but you'll have to speak with the officers who have been making inquiries.

"We'll meet here at the station around five o'clock. Personally, I'm going to speak with the press in an hour. After that, I'm going to contact Georg . . . the principal at the school where Jacob Schyttelius worked. Then it would probably be a good idea to pull out the reports from the Purple Murder and the fire at the church by Norssjön. And I'm going to try and get ahold of Yvonne Stridner."

A heavy sigh escaped him with the last sentence. The others nodded in understanding. Professor Yvonne Stridner, the head of Pathology, was not easy to deal with.

Chapter 5

THE SLUSHY SNOW FROM the day before had transformed itself into an annoying freezing drizzle. The temperature during the night had risen to seven degrees above zero, Celsius, but it was premature to start feeling giddy about spring warmth. Veils of rainy haze obscured Landvetter Lake and erased the division between air and water. Everything was obscured by a single wet gray mist.

The unmarked police car turned toward Kullahult. The streets were noticeably empty. It seemed as though everything and everyone huddled indoors because of the tragedy that had befallen the small community. After driving around the church hill, they found a sign reading "Fellowship Hall." It pointed at a low yellow brick house with a flat roof in the style of buildings from the late 1960s.

Irene had called the Kullahult Church Association before they left. Deaconess Rut Börjesson had answered. She seemed articulate and efficient, despite the fact that her voice shook with suppressed tears. She promised to gather all the association's employees in the Fellowship Hall to make things easier for the officers. Irene had informed her that three investigators would arrive, so the questioning would go quickly. She imagined that there could hardly be very many people employed by the church; therefore, she was surprised when they entered the hall and counted ten people waiting.

A small, thin woman dressed in mourning clothes came forward. Her thin gray hair was cut in a short bob, untouched by dye or a permanent. Her eyes, behind thick glasses, were red-rimmed and tear-filled. The woman stretched out her ice-cold hand to the officers one by one and told them that she was Rut Börjesson, the deaconess. Then she introduced her colleagues.

First was a tall woman with mahogany-colored hair. She was probably over fifty, but her figure was slender and her face still beautiful. "Well-preserved" was a good adjective for her. Rut Börjesson introduced her as the church accountant, Louise Måårdh.

"With two 'å's." Louise smiled and held out her cool hand.

Irene was one hundred and eighty centimeters* tall in her stocking feet, and Louise Måårdh was almost as tall. She was surprised to meet a woman who could have once been a photographer's model working as a church accountant in a country parish. This was explained when a dark man in a pastor's shirt next to her introduced himself as Bengt Måårdh, the assistant rector of Ledkulla parish. Still, Louise Måårdh didn't look like a clergyman's wife to her. My assumptions are probably at fault, thought Irene. She'd pictured a round and happy woman who smelled of newly baked rolls, smiling, serving the women in the church sewing circle. Louise Måårdh looked as if she spent her spare time on the golf course rather than in front of an oven.

The same could have been said for her husband. He was tall and slender, with clean-cut features. His dark hair, just beginning to be streaked with gray, contrasted nicely with his tanned skin. After a glance at Louise's face, Irene concluded that the Måårdh family had recently been on a ski trip and had had good weather.

The look in Bengt Måårdh's brown eyes was sad and serious. He took Irene's hand in both of his, and for a confused second Irene had the impression that he was planning on extending his condolences to her. Instead, he mumbled a few words about how incomprehensible it was that Mr. and Mrs. Schyttelius were no longer with them. Not to mention their son . . . the assistant rector's voice broke as he shook his head without letting go of Irene's hand. She had begun to extract it from his grip when he released it with a mumbled apology.

---

*A centimeter (a hundredth of a meter) is .3937 inches, which means that an inch is 2.54 centimeters. So 180 centimeters is almost 71 inches, or five feet eleven.

Jonas Burman stood next to Bengt Måårdh. They greeted each other briefly. Irene noted that the young assistant rector looked pale but resolute.

The short, dark-skinned woman at his side was Rosa Marqués. She was not quite middle-aged and spoke very good Swedish, though with a distinct accent. The deaconess explained that she cleaned both the Fellowship Hall and the rectory.

There was yet another married couple in the room. They looked to be in their sixties and introduced themselves as the church sextons, Siv and Örjan Svensson. They took care of the custodial duties in Kullahult and Ledkulla parishes. He was short and slender; she was also short, but plump. There we have the cinnamon roll maker, Irene thought.

A man in a checked shirt and carpenter's pants stepped forward energetically and introduced himself. "Stig Björk, cemetery caretaker," he said, and smiled. The smile created rays of wrinkles around his blue eyes. His white teeth gleamed in his weather-beaten face. Obviously, he spent a lot of time in the fresh air. There was a trace of gray here and there in his dark hair. Irene estimated his age to be around forty. He must have realized that his smile was inappropriate, because it quickly faded and he peered nervously at the man behind him.

The latter had been leaning against the wall, but now he stepped into the light. Like Bengt Måårdh, he wore a black shirt with a white pastor's collar, but over the shirt he wore a short black coat, similar to a blazer. He introduced himself as Assistant Rector Urban Berg of Bäckared.

His handshake was dry and cool. His entire person radiated self-control verging on stiffness. His gray-speckled blond hair was perfectly combed. A bald spot on the very top of his head was barely perceptible. He and Bengt Måårdh seemed to be about the same age.

Now there was only one woman left who hadn't been introduced. She was small and dainty. It was hard to guess her age,
probably between twenty-five and thirty-five. Her long blond
hair was held in place by a leather headband which showed off
her beautiful features. Her large violet-blue eyes were shadowed
by long eyelashes. Not the slightest trace of makeup could be
seen on her face. She wore a dark-blue linen dress with puffed
sleeves, and low black boots. The cemetery caretaker gave her
a look, and Irene could see that it was one of admiration. And
maybe something else. Even the restrained Urban Berg's eyes
gleamed a bit when he let his gaze sweep over this woman.

"My name is Eva Möller, and I am the cantor and organist,"
she said in a soft, melodic voice.

Irene had thought that a cantor always was also the church
organist, but the way Eva phrased this showed that it wasn't the
case.

The portly man seated on a loudly creaking chair by the door
was Nils Bertilsson, sexton part of the time in Bäckared parish
and the other half at Slättared. His worn black suit was tight-
fitting, and he wiped his forehead and bald spot with a large
handkerchief. When he rose to be introduced, Irene saw that he
was almost as tall as she was but certainly weighed more than
twice as much.

Irene was assigned to question deaconess Rut Börjesson, the
Måårdhs, and the housecleaner, Rosa Marqués.

"You can use my office," Louise Måårdh offered.

She opened a french door which led into a pleasant office
space. Two pots containing miniature Easter lilies stood on the
window sill, framed by sun-yellow curtains. Combined with the
bouquet of red tulips on the desk, they evoked a feeling of
spring, even though it might as well have been November outside. A framed poster from the Göteborg Theater's production
of *Les Misérables* hung on the wall.

Irene decided to start with the deaconess. She asked Rut

Börjesson to follow her into the room. The black-clothed woman sat in a comfortable-looking visitor's chair and gripped the armrests with both hands.

Irene began with routine questions. She determined that the deaconess was fifty-eight years old, married with no children, and that she had worked in Kullahult parish for seventeen years.

"Did you work here before Pastor Schyttelius came to this congregation?" Irene asked.

"Rector. Sten Schyttelius came here as the rector exactly twenty years ago. So he was here three years before me."

Irene realized that she had a very poor understanding of the titles bestowed by the Swedish church. Cautiously, she asked, "Was he the boss of the other pastors?"

"Yes. Ledkulla, Bäckared, and Slättared each have an assistant rector. Because Kullahult is the largest parish with the largest church, the rector has always had the church here."

The deaconess answered all questions put to her but she hugged the armrests of her chair so hard that her knuckles turned white. Irene put it down to indignation. She must have known her boss well after having worked with him for so many years. That's why Irene shifted her inquiry. "I assume you knew Elsa Schyttelius?"

"Yes. We've spent some time together over the years."

"What kind of person was she?"

Uncertainty was visible in the deaconess's face. "She was very nice . . . reserved. Very pleasant and friendly, when she was well."

"So when she was feeling well, she was kind. What kind of illness did she have?"

"It was unpleasant . . . she suffered from depression. It came and went. Apparently, she had had it since childhood, and the illness worsened after she had her children."

"What was she like when she was sick?"

"When she was sick, she became withdrawn. Didn't want to

see people and didn't have the energy to do practical things. She just stayed in bed."

"Did you know Jacob and Rebecka?"

"Of course. When I came here, Jacob was a teenager and Rebecka had just started school. Such wonderful children. Well-behaved. In appearance, Jacob is most like his mother, but his personality is probably more like his father's. It's the opposite with Rebecka."

"Does she also suffer from depression?"

"No, but she is also a bit reserved. Jacob is . . . was as open and happy as Sten. And now someone has . . . Sten and Jacob and Elsa. . . ."

Her self-control cracked and she started sobbing. Irene waited for her to calm down, then asked, "Are you able to answer a few more questions?"

Rut Börjesson nodded and blew her nose in her wet handkerchief. In a thin, trembling voice she said, "I would so very much like to help if I can."

"Do you have any suspicions whatsoever as to what could be behind these murders?"

The deaconess seemed to be thinking intensely before she shook her head. "No. It's incomprehensible!"

"Did anyone in the Schyttelius family say anything that would make you think that he or she felt threatened?"

Again Rut Börjesson hesitated before answering. Finally, she said, "The only things I recall are Sten's words last summer and fall. After the Satanists had burned down the summer chapel in Norssjön, he tried to find out who was responsible for that atrocity. You could almost say that he was obsessed with it."

She stopped in order to dry her eyes and nose again. Irene could see that her hands were shaking.

"One afternoon, I was forced to speak with him about an important matter. Sten hadn't come to the Fellowship Hall, so

I went over to the rectory. Elsa let me in, and I remember that it was obvious that she was in the middle of one of her episodes. In any case, she pointed up to the second floor when I asked where Sten was. She said that he was in the office behind the billiard room. Actually—"

She stopped and looked uncertainly at Irene before she continued. "Actually, I didn't know that he had an office on the second floor as well. But, of course, the one downstairs is large and old-fashioned. When I knocked, the door was locked. Sten called 'One second,' and then he unlocked the door. He pointed at the computer and said that he was on the trail of the Satanists. From what I understood, he had found some clues on the Internet. And he said that he had to be very careful so they didn't become suspicious, because that could be dangerous."

"Did he say in what way it could be dangerous?"

"No, just that it could be dangerous. I thought it sounded nasty. Who knows what those fools might come up with?"

"Did it seem as though Sten Schyttelius was afraid of the Satanists?"

Again Rut Börjesson looked hesitant. "'Afraid' . . . I don't know . . . he said that one had to be very careful."

"Was the computer on?"

"Yes. I went up to the desk in order to lay out some papers that he was going to sign, and I remember that there was a very beautiful picture on the screen. There were a lot of colorful fish swimming around a coral reef."

So Sten Schyttelius had put on the screen saver before he opened the door for the deaconess. Was the information on the Internet really dangerous? Irene made a mental note to contact someone who could help her find out.

"Do you know if he continued searching for the Satanists?"

"Yes. Jacob knows . . . knew a lot about computers, and he was here about a month ago helping Sten—"

"Sorry for having to interrupt. But were they using the computers here in the Fellowship Hall?" Irene asked, pointing at Louise Måårdh's computer on the desk in front of them.

"No. No, they were using the computer over in the rectory. I was invited there for afternoon coffee. Elsa was feeling quite well at that time and asked me to come. When I arrived, Jacob was also there. Elsa said something about them having spent the whole morning with the computer, and then Sten said that he and Jacob had something big going on. I asked if they were on the trail of the Satanists, and Sten nodded."

"He nodded? He didn't say anything?"

"No. But he and Jacob exchanged a look, as if they were . . . conspirators."

Conspirators. Father and son were on the trail of Satanists, who had burned down the chapel. According to Rut Börjesson, the rector had been obsessed with the idea. Despite their caution, had they gotten too close? Even if the murder method was not typical of Satanism, the symbol on the computer screens and the upside-down crucifix pointed to a connection. As Sten and Jacob Schyttelius had hunted the church arsonists via the computer, it might explain why the computers had been marked with the pentagrams.

"Were there many people who knew that they were seeking the Satanists via the Internet?" Irene continued.

Rut Börjesson shook her head. "I don't think so. Right after the fire, he spoke of catching the guilty ones and punishing them severely. But as time went on, there were more important things to take care of. I was actually quite surprised when he said that he was still looking for them."

"And was it a complete coincidence that you found out about it?"

"Yes."

There was a short silence while Irene reflected. Finally, she decided to move on to something else and let go of the Satanic angle for a while.

"What kind of a person was Sten Schyttelius?" she asked.

The deaconess's sorrowful expression vanished. Her face lit up. "Deeply pious, good-hearted. He hadn't had an easy time through the years with Elsa's illness, but he never complained. He took care of the kids and did his job. They've always had help with the cleaning, but otherwise he did most things himself. He enjoyed mealtimes and was a good cook and a wine connoisseur. He was an avid hunter as well. Each year, he took a break from work for the moose hunt."

"And Jacob was like his father?"

"Yes. Except maybe not quite as good at cooking, but he was also a hunter. Very nice and friendly. The last few years, both of them became heavily involved with Sweden's Ecumenical Children's Villages. Mostly it was Sten, but last fall Jacob also started working actively."

"What would they do?"

A blush suffused Rut Börjesson's pale cheeks as she described the absorbing work of father and son Schyttelius. "They traveled with aid groups to war- and catastrophe- stricken countries in Africa to help needy children. Various Christian organizations in Sweden have set up several villages for orphaned children, about ten in all. For the most part, all work is done by volunteers, and both Sten and Jacob helped wholeheartedly. The expense of the trip and room and board was paid by the parishes, but otherwise they weren't compensated."

"Did Rebecka also help?"

"No. She has lived in London for the last two years, where she works as a computer consultant, or whatever it's called. I don't think she's active in the church."

"Was Elsa Schyttelius involved in the children's villages?"

"No. Elsa had more than enough to occupy her with her illness."

Irene saw that Rut was exhausted and decided to end the questioning. She followed her to the door and asked the cleaning woman, Rosa Marqués, to come in.

* * *

ROSA WAS short and rather plump. Her dark hair was gathered in a thick braid hanging down her back. Her face was pretty, dominated by a wide mouth which looked like it broke into a smile readily. Right now, neither her mouth nor her dark brown eyes were smiling; rather, they mirrored grave sorrow.

She seated herself on the edge of the chair with her hands folded in her lap. Irene started with personal information. It turned out that Rosa was thirty-eight years old, married, and had four children. She had not had close contact with the Schytteliuses during the four years she had cleaned their house once a week. She had never met their children, because they were both adults and had moved away from home before she started working at the rectory. She spontaneously mentioned Elsa Schyttelius's periods of illness, during which Mrs. Schyttelius had locked herself in the bedroom and Rosa wasn't allowed to clean in there.

"Do you clean the whole house every week?" Irene asked.

"No. I only clean the large fancy rooms on the first floor every week. When it's needed, I do some of the rooms upstairs."

"How do you know when it's needed?"

"The rector tells me."

"Have you ever cleaned the office upstairs?"

Rosa raised her dark eyebrows in surprise. "The office is on the first floor."

"Sten Schyttelius has a smaller room with a computer on the second floor. It's located behind the billiard room."

Now Rosa frowned. Finally, she shook her head decidedly and said, "No. I've never cleaned in that room. The door is always locked."

Over a period of four years, Rosa Marqués had never cleaned the computer room. Irene recalled that there was a gun cabinet in the room. It would be interesting to know what kind of weapons had been kept there. Is that why the room had always been locked? But if the cabinet had been kept locked, according to law, then locking the door to the room itself would have been unnecessary.

"Do you remember if anything was hanging on the wall in the bedroom?"

"The crucifix. The beautiful cross," Rosa said.

"There was a cross hanging on the wall?"

"Yes. I always look at it when I'm cleaning the room. It's so beautiful. Mrs. Schyttelius says that it's very old. From Italy."

"How big is it?" Irene asked, mostly out of curiosity.

"About like this," said Rosa, indicating about a foot and a half in height and a few inches less in width. "And Jesus Christ is in silver," she added.

This was the antique crucifix from Italy that had been turned upside down during or after the murders. Was this completely irrelevant, or was it important? Irene was unsure. But maybe that was the murderer's intention.

THE FIRST of the Määrdhs whom Irene interviewed was Louise, the church accountant. She sat down in the armchair across from Irene and smiled faintly. "I can hardly remember ever sitting in this chair."

"It doesn't matter to me which chair I sit in. Do you want to trade?" Irene asked.

"No, no! I just meant that sometimes you become a little blind to your own surroundings. This chair is actually really comfortable."

Louise Määrdh leaned back and crossed one slender leg over the other. Irene observed her. Her expression was serious and her gaze sorrowful, but she wasn't nearly as distraught as the deaconess had been. Her black pinstriped suit, worn with a white silk blouse, was formal and appropriate. A necklace of large pearls shimmered at her throat.

She was actually quite attractive. And she had become the wife of a pastor in a country parish. Amazing.

Here, too, Irene commenced with general personal questions. Louise and Bengt Måårdh had two sons, twenty-five and twenty years old. The family had lived in Kullahult for almost ten years and Bengt had been the assistant rector in Ledkulla parish the entire time.

"And have you worked as the church accountant the whole time?" Irene asked.

"Yes. Earlier, I had handled the finances at a small company in the town where we used to live. But when we came here, this position was open and Sten asked if I was interested. I thought that I could always try it out and, well, I'm still here."

"A thought just struck me. If your oldest son is twenty-five, then maybe he knows Rebecka Schyttelius?"

"Of course. They were classmates in high school."

"Did they spend a lot of time together?"

"They are far too different. My Per is an outgoing boy who always had a large group of friends. Rebecka is more reserved. Even in high school, she preferred to spend time with her computers."

Suddenly she stood. "Wait. I'll show you. . . ."

She walked around the desk and pulled out a drawer. Two thick colorful envelopes were lying on top.

"Pictures from two Christmases ago. I dropped off the film, picked up the pictures and brought them here, and they're still here." She started flipping through the photos. At regular intervals, she would place one on the desk. When she had gone through both piles, ten pictures were lying on the desk.

"Rebecka wasn't home this Christmas. She had apparently come down with the flu. But she was here the Christmas before. Our tradition is that all the pastors' families eat breakfast together after Christmas Day services here in the Fellowship Hall. Of course, the rest of the staff is also welcome to join us, if they want. Both of my boys were home, so I brought the camera with me to the Christmas breakfast."

As she was speaking, she laid out the pictures in a particular order. When she was satisfied, she said, "In the first pictures you have the Schyttelius family. And there is our family. And in the later ones you can see the rest of the staff."

For the first time, Irene saw what the Schyttelius family had looked like when they were all intact and alive. Sten Schyttelius was smiling in three of the four pictures. In the fourth, he was laughing as he raised a schnapps glass to Bengt Måårdh in a toast.

"Is the early service the only thing a pastor does on Christmas Day?" Irene asked.

"No. Then there is High Mass and Evening Service. Why?"

"Sten Schyttelius and your husband are drinking schnapps in the morning."

"Just a small one, to go with the herring. Don't worry, it would have worn off before High Mass. The service is divided among the pastors and the churches. It would be too much otherwise."

Sten Schyttelius had been a tall, impressive man. His large hand which grasped the foot of the schnapps glass looked more as if it belonged to a day laborer than a clergyman. His face was powerful, dominated by a large, meaty nose. His hairline had receded, but his steel gray hair was thick, worn *en brosse*. His smile in the pictures seemed warm and heartfelt. His eyes almost disappeared in laugh lines in the photos where he was beaming at the camera.

Next to the rector was his wife. She looked plain next to her sparkling husband. A dark-blue suit jacket and a high-necked gray blouse added to that impression. Her thinning gray hair was cut short and lay flat on her head. Irene thought that she looked a bit like Rut Börjesson, but the deaconess had at least some sense of life about her. Elsa Schyttelius had none. She was looking straight into the lens in one of the pictures. Her gaze was empty and her facial expression stiff. Had she been sick during that Christmas season?

A young woman was seated next to Elsa. It had to be Rebecka.

She was also big, and the contrast made Elsa look even smaller and more colorless. The similarity to her father was apparent. Rebecka wasn't heavy like him, but her large bone structure was like his. She wore a light-brown suit jacket, under which a yellow turtleneck could be seen. Her thick hair was dark and shoulder-length. Loose curls softly framed her face. Based on what Irene could make out, she wasn't wearing makeup, but her own coloring was strong enough to accent her distinct features. When she saw Rebecka's face, Irene thought of a Mediterranean movie star from the fifties. She didn't fit the twenty-first century ideal of anorexic good looks, but she was a beautiful woman.

"She must be tall," Irene said, looking up at Louise Måårdh.

"We are exactly the same height: One hundred seventy-eight centimeters," Louise responded.

She smiled faintly when she saw Irene's surprise at this exact reply.

"We started talking about it during breakfast. She had bought that nice brown jacket at a London shop. Long Tall Sally, I remember it was called. You, of course, will appreciate how difficult it can be to find clothes," she said.

Irene nodded. She knew the problem well. The church accountant placed a long well-manicured index-finger nail on one of the photos and said, "Jacob is sitting there next to my Per. Jacob and Rebecka were the same height."

Jacob Schyttelius smiled at the camera and looked happy and relaxed. He had light hair and a slender build. Irene couldn't see the slightest resemblance to his father or sister, but it was possible to see some similarities with his mother. The only thing the siblings had in common were brown eyes and dark eyebrows.

In the last three photos, Irene saw the people she had met a little while ago in the hall, but also a number of others whom she hadn't met.

"Who are these people?" she asked.

"The church association's employees. The secretary of

information, the parish hostess, parish assistants, childcare workers, activity director, youth director, and our three preschool teachers." Louise pointed at each as she identified them.

"Childcare workers? Secretary of information? Are all of them employed by the church?" Irene asked.

"We have a Christian preschool and a good youth program. The church is a large employer here in the municipality. And I'm the one who tries to find the money to pay for it all. The churches themselves also need renovations, as well as the fellowship halls, the rectories, and other properties. I'm in charge of paying all the bills and salaries, and I do the bookkeeping as well."

Irene had never thought of the church as an employer with a large economic impact, but that's apparently exactly what it was. And Sten Schyttelius had been in charge of it all, the commander of the parish or association or whatever it was called. She said out loud, "So you're financially responsible, but Rector Schyttelius was the boss. What was he like as an employer?"

For the first time, Louise thought before she answered. Then she said, hesitantly, "Sten was a pleasant person, but as a boss he had certain . . . bad sides. He was actually ready for retirement, so you can understand that he was relatively old-fashioned and authoritarian. He was difficult to deal with sometimes. He had a short fuse and could get very angry. He saw women as personal assistants, not as colleagues. We had some clashes. . . . The woman who held this position before me actually quit. There was a lot of talk about harassment, but it didn't come to anything. Not to mention his controversies with the vestrymen! The new director and Sten never got along."

While Louise was speaking, one of the envelopes slipped from her lap and fell on the floor. The photos fell out, and Irene bent to help pick them up. She stopped at the first photo.

In the far left of the picture, Sten Schyttelius was raising a generously filled schnapps glass. Bengt Määrdh was seated in the middle, half turned away from the rector. He had one of his arms around Cantor Eva Möller's shoulders and was leaning over to whisper something in her ear. She looked enchanting in a red dress with embroidery around its square neckline, and she was smiling at what he said. It appeared to Irene that the assistant rector was taking the opportunity to peer down the neck of Eva's dress.

Louise Måårdh saw that Irene had examined the photo of her husband and the lovely cantor, but she didn't say anything. She held out her hand to take the pictures Irene had gathered together. "Thank you," she said.

"Do you know if anyone in the Schyttelius family felt threatened?" Irene asked.

Louise shook her reddish-brown hair. "No. I never heard anything like that."

"Did Sten Schyttelius ever talk about Satanists?"

"Yes. After the summer chapel burned down; he was terribly upset."

"Did he speak about Satanists during the last couple of months?"

"No, not that I remember. It was mostly in the months following the fire."

"Did you hear that he was trying to trace the Satanists via the Internet?"

"Internet? No, that's news to me," Louise said with sincere surprise in her voice.

"Then I don't have any more questions at the moment. Would you be so kind as to ask your husband to come in?"

BENGT MÅÅRDH'S face bore a troubled expression as he seated himself in the visitor's chair. He folded his hands and rested his elbows on the armrests while his serious gaze focused on Irene. Again she felt that a priest was here to console her, as if she was the one who needed comforting. The feeling was absurd, yet it was there. Maybe it was evoked by his sympathetic brown eyes behind frameless glasses.

Then it struck her that she was simply being exposed to a basic tool of his profession. This was the way Bengt Måårdh had learned to act in times of grief: He displayed compassion. It probably worked with a person who actually needed it, not least with women. And who doesn't need compassion nowadays? Our need for comfort is immeasurable.

She was pulled from her thoughts when the pastor said, in a low voice, "I am prepared to answer your questions. If there's anything I can do to catch the person who murdered Sten and Elsa and Jacob, then I want to do everything within my power to help." He leaned against the backrest of the chair with his hands still folded.

"Have you ever heard any of the three murder victims say that he or she felt threatened?" Irene began.

"No. Never. Who would want to threaten them? The world's nicest people and—"

"Did Sten Schyttelius ever speak with you about Satanists?" Irene interrupted.

"He spoke about them a lot directly after the fire. Dear Sten was actually pretty hot-tempered, but he never held a grudge. He was very angry with the Satanists and their followers. You'll have to forgive me, but he didn't think that the police cared enough. Sometimes it sounded like he was thinking about going after them himself." He smiled almost imperceptibly.

"Did he speak about chasing Satanists in the last few months?" Irene asked.

His surprise was obvious. "No. Not at all! I was referring to last summer and fall, right after the fire. During the last six months, I haven't heard a word about Satanists. Sten had other projects that took up most of his time. He was very involved in Sweden's Ecumenical Children's Villages. That project was close to his heart, and he was thinking about working even more closely with it after retirement."

"I heard something about Jacob also being involved in this work."

"Yes. He became interested through Sten. They took a trip together last fall. Sten wasn't as young as he used to be, so it was probably a good thing that he had Jacob with him."

"Could Jacob take off from work right in the middle of the semester?"

For the first time, the pastor was uncertain. "He was apparently free during the fall. I don't know if he was on sick leave. As you probably already know, he got divorced last summer."

This was news to Irene, but she satisfied herself with nodding as if he had confirmed her information.

"While he was married, Jacob and his ex-wife lived in Norrland somewhere. She's also a teacher."

"Did they have any children?"

"No. They were only married a few years."

"Did he move down here because of the divorce?"

"Yes. He didn't have a support system up there. His family was here, of course."

"Had he already moved to the summer cottage at Norssjön by the fall?"

"Yes. Jacob has always been considerate and probably didn't want to burden his parents, especially because of Elsa and her condition. I don't know if anyone has told you that Elsa suffered from depression, but unfortunately that was the case."

"I'm aware of it. What was Elsa Schyttelius like as a person?"

At first, Bengt looked as though he hadn't understood the question but after a while he frowned in contemplation.

"Well . . . she was nice, but she didn't draw much attention to herself. Sten was a real social butterfly and liked parties. Elsa loathed that sort of thing. She showed up at parties sometimes, but always sat quietly."

"She never spoke?"

"She spoke, of course, but she was taciturn."

Suddenly he bent forward toward Irene again and looked her straight in the eye. Both his voice and his eyes revealed sincere concern when he asked, "Have you gotten hold of Rebecka?"

"Yes. An English police officer and a pastor from the Swedish Seaman's Church informed her of what happened. It took some time to find her because she had recently moved."

"That's right. Sten actually said that she was going to move, last fall."

"Do you remember if he said anything else?"

"He said that things were going very well for the company. Rebecka works for a computer firm which undertakes assignments for different clients. I'm not very knowledgeable about computers, but I understood that much. Then he said that her new apartment was big, considering that it was located in central London. But she was happy about having rented it."

"It must have been expensive?"

"Probably. But money doesn't seem to be a problem in the IT business. It's good to know that she's doing so well."

"You've known her for ten years. Did you expect that she would have such success?"

"Honestly, I wouldn't have. She did well in school but kept to herself for the most part. She wasn't bad-looking, but she was . . . serious. Distant. During high school, she was probably pretty lonely; but when she moved to Linköping—or was it Lidköping—I always mix them up . . . in any case, when she moved away from home and started working with computers, it was as if she loosened up. I think she blossomed. We only saw each other for any length of time at a Christmas Breakfast but I've noticed that she changed during the last years."

"In what way did she change?"

"She seemed happier and more talkative. You could also see how her appearance altered . . . clothes and that sort of thing.

She spoke about her friends, and Elsa confided to Louise that she had a boyfriend. But that apparently ended before she moved to London. Maybe that's why she moved? I know that Sten and Elsa never got a chance to meet him."

"How do you know that?"

Bengt arched his eyebrows in surprise.

"Naturally, I asked Elsa. She said that neither of them had met the boyfriend. And then she said that it was over. A few months later, Rebecka moved to London. But there was a rumor that she had a new guy in London. According to Louise, he was here at Kullahult over the summer last year, but I don't know if it's true."

"Did Louise meet him?"

"No. This was just something she heard. It's best if you ask her yourself."

Irene nodded and was about to ask her next question when a new thought suddenly struck her. "Do you know if Rebecka had helped her father to trace the Satanists over the Internet?" she asked.

Bengt Måårdh looked at Irene in surprise. "I really don't know! Certainly Sten had a lot of ideas about how he was going to find those responsible, but I've never heard him talk about tracking them via the Internet."

But others have, thought Irene. If Rebecka was involved in her father's investigation in some way, maybe she would have some information to give them. Was she threatened as well? That couldn't be ruled out. Thankfully, the English police had promised to keep an eye on her.

Irene decided to change the subject. "Who will become rector now?" she asked.

"The position has been open for a few weeks since he was about to retire anyway, and both Urban Berg and I have applied for it. Of course, there are other applicants, but it will probably be one of us. We have the age and experience needed. But Urban has some problems that may count against him."

Irene asked the obvious question: "What problems?"

"Unfortunately, he has a drinking problem. He has been arrested for drunken driving twice. It is, of course, very tragic. Urban became a widower a few years ago, and after that his drinking became worse."

Bengt Måårdh looked sympathetic when he spoke about his colleague's problems, but Irene thought she heard an undertone of satisfaction. If Urban had this blot on his resumé, naturally Bengt's chances of getting the position increased. And Louise would become the rector's wife. Something told Irene this was better than being the wife of the assistant rector.

"Jonas Burman hasn't applied for the position?" Irene said, mainly to have something to ask about.

Bengt smiled broadly, and Irene could see that he had a very pleasant smile. "Oh, Jonas is far too young to apply for a rector's position. And—" He stopped himself for a second before following through with what he had been about to say. "There has been some speculation . . . Jonas is thirty-one, but there doesn't seem to have ever been a woman in his life. Someone murmured that he may be homosexual, but I don't think so. Honestly, I think he's just prudish and moralistic. Moreover, he's a member of the synod."

For a second, Irene wondered if the synod might have something to do with Satanism, but she realized that it was hardly possible. "What is the synod?" she asked, feeling foolish.

Bengt Måårdh didn't seem surprised at her lack of knowledge, and said, with a meaningful smile, "It's a group of pastors within the Swedish Church who see themselves as more orthodox than the rest of us. They're best known for their categorical opposition to female pastors."

"Are you opposed to female pastors?"

"No."

"Was Sten Schyttelius?"

"No . . . not directly. But he preferred male colleagues. He had an old-fashioned view toward women in the church."

"So he wasn't a member of the synod?"

"No."

"How would Sten Schyttelius have reacted if he had learned that Jonas Burman really was homosexual?"

Again Bengt contemplated the question before answering. "He wouldn't have approved of it. He was very fixed in his opinion of homosexuality: It was completely unacceptable. We had a discussion last year. There were two women who wanted to be blessed in Kullahult's church after they had entered into a domestic partnership, but it wasn't even a possibility for Sten. He declared very clearly that all forms of homosexuality are a crime against God. The Lord made man and woman in order to be of joy to one another and to take care of their children."

Irene could hear in the priest's voice that he shared his late rector's opinion. She decided to leave the topic for the time being. "I've heard that Sten and Jacob Schyttelius were hunters. Are you also interested in hunting?"

"No."

"Do any of the other pastors hunt?"

"Not that I know of. I'm almost certain that none of the others do."

Irene couldn't come up with any more questions and thanked Bengt Måårdh for his assistance. He rose and took her hand in a firm grip. His handshake felt dry and firm. He wished her luck with the investigation, adding that he sincerely hoped that the repulsive murderer would be caught.

THE THREE officers found a pizzeria right across from Konsum. The inspectors had their choice of the four tables inside, since most of the other customers appeared to want to take their pizzas out. They chose a table as far away from the counter as they could get, not because they were afraid the pizza maker would be able to overhear their conversation but so that they would be able to have one at all. The employees had a flower-covered boom box behind the counter which was pounding out Turkish pop songs at the highest volume.

They were hungry and ate their pizzas in utter silence. The volume of customers had slowed after lunchtime, but the tape player's volume remained unchanged.

Irene leaned forward over the small table, making sure she didn't put her elbows in the leftovers. Tommy and Fredrik also leaned forward to hear what she had to say.

"The picture I've gotten of the victims is pretty clear. Sten Schyttelius was a happy, extroverted, sociable person. Like his son, he was interested in hunting. He took care of the family during Elsa Schyttelius's periods of depression. He was authoritarian and old-fashioned as a boss and had a biased view of women. But since he was going to retire before the summer, he got away with it. By the way, Bengt Måårdh said that he and Urban Berg had applied for Sten's position. And Bengt 'mentioned' that Urban has a drinking problem; he has been arrested for drunk driving twice."

Tommy smiled broadly. "What petty gossipers! Urban Berg told me that Bengt Måårdh is a notorious womanizer. According to Urban, he can't leave any woman alone."

"And according to Måårdh," Irene continued, "there are suspicions that Jonas Burman is gay. Sten Schyttelius would never have tolerated that, because he was against allowing homosexuals into the church community. Oh, and Jonas Burman is a member of the synod."

"Don't you mean the sewing circle?" Fredrik laughed.

"It's obvious that you don't know what it is either. I asked. According to Bengt Måårdh, it's an association of pastors who are more religious than others. 'Orthodox,' I think he said. Mainly, they're against women pastors."

"Yuck, what beasts!" Tommy said and rolled his eyes.

"Since when did *you* become a feminist? Elsa Schyttelius seemed to just be a small gray shadow trailing after her husband because of her depression. I'd like to know what Hannu found out about the Schytteliuses and if there are any living relatives we can speak with."

"On the topic of relatives, Jacob appears to have been a nice guy but no one knew him very well. He spent most of his time with his parents since he returned to Göteborg after his divorce. Wouldn't one want to go out and have some fun if he was suddenly free again?" Fredrik the bachelor asked.

"Maybe that's what he did. But before he got divorced," Irene said dryly.

"Possible. We should speak with his ex-wife," said Tommy.

"And Rebecka," Irene added.

"Exactly. But that may not be very easy. We don't dare ask her to come here and if she does come, she'll need to be given protection," Tommy said seriously.

His colleagues nodded. Irene continued, "I asked Louise Määrdh about the rumor that Rebecka has a boyfriend in London who visited Kullahult with her last summer. According to Louise, it was only a rumor. Neither she nor anyone else saw the guy. Someone supposedly said that Rebecka had shown up at the rectory with him, but no one has been able to confirm it. And Rebecka didn't have anyone with her when she came home for Christmas last year."

"Someone really needs to speak with her. Maybe she knows something, consciously or unconsciously, that will provide a clue to the motive for the murders," Tommy said.

"Based on the pentagrams and the upside-down cross, the motive is Satanic. About a month ago, the deaconess heard Sten Schyttelius say he was chasing Satanists on the Web, but that it might be dangerous," said Irene.

"Dangerous? Well, maybe. A computer always leaves electronic traces. A few years ago, you couldn't follow them, but now you can," said Fredrik.

"Is it easy?" Irene asked.

"I don't think so. But some specialists and hackers know how to do it."

They contemplated the situation. Irene said, "Strange. Only the deaconess heard the rector mention Satanists, and that only by chance. The others said that Sten Schyttelius had only spoken of the Satanists right after the fire last year, but not since."

"I spoke with that cantor, Eva. She described Sten Schyttelius as a man with hidden depths. When she said that, could she have meant that he was conducting a secret investigation?" Tommy speculated.

Neither of the other two had a better guess.

"Maybe we should go back to the rectory before we leave. The technicians are probably done now," said Irene.

They went out to the car.

"I want to go into the library on the first floor first," said Irene.

They entered the large room lined with full bookshelves. The smell of dust and musty old books was intense; Fredrik sneezed. Irene stood for a moment, thinking. Finally, she was certain. Out loud, she said, "This doesn't feel like a room someone has worked in recently. This is a museum. Sten Schyttelius used the office upstairs."

They went up to the second floor. Svante Malm emerged from the bedroom. "Can you wait ten minutes?" he asked.

"No problem," Tommy answered.

The billiard room was untouched. Irene unconsciously bent when she passed the stuffed animal heads. She thought that they looked at her accusingly with their eyes of glass.

Fredrik stopped at the well-filled bar cart and whistled. "Wasn't it that guy Urban who has a drinking problem?" He grinned.

"If that cart had belonged to Urban, the bottles would probably be bare, if what Bengt Måårdh intimated is true," Irene replied.

They entered the office. The desk was bare. The computer had been removed, leaving its outline in the dust on the desktop. The doors to the gun cabinet were wide open, and Irene could see that while it was now empty, there was room for six rifles.

"Was the cabinet full?" she asked.

"I don't know. We'll have to ask Svante," said Tommy, and he left the room.

There were some books and bibles and piles of papers called "Our Church" and "News from Kullahult's Church Association," paper, stamps, a hole punch and other office materials on shelves, and a box marked "Sweden's Ecumenical Children's Villages." Irene started flipping through the papers but was interrupted by Tommy's return.

"They found five rifles and a lot of ammunition in the cabinet and took everything to the lab. The cabinet originally held six rifles, including the murder weapon. The interesting thing is that the cabinet was unlocked when the technicians found it and the key was in the lock. Just like the front door," he said.

"Weren't the guns broken down?" Irene asked.

"No. It's not necessary if weapons are stored in an approved gun cabinet, and this one was, aside from the fact that it was left unlocked."

"The murderer seems to have known where all of the keys were," Irene thought out loud.

"Or the Schyttelius family kept their keys in places that were too obvious. Remember the key under the plant at the summer cottage," Tommy reminded her.

Irene nodded and continued to flip through the contents of the box that contained informational brochures about the different villages. The children were orphans and received room and board and schooling at the villages, as well as a hefty dose of old-time Swedish religious education, Irene thought, examining a picture of a group of dark-skinned children with bowed heads and folded hands in front of an altar. The young, blond pastor stood with one hand held in a gesture of blessing. His gaze was directed at a point above the children's heads. The text under the picture read: "The children are inquisitive and gratefully accept God's word."

The buildings were described as simple but well cared for. The children received food, healthcare, and access to education at the cost of various associations. All the workers were volunteers.

Irene considered. Both father and son had become involved in this worthy work. Why had these nice idealistic men been brutally murdered? Not to mention the timid wife and mother who seemed to have been incapable of hurting anyone?

"We're done in the bedroom," Svante shouted through the door to the billiard room.

Irene replaced the contents of the box and put it back on the shelf. Before she left the room, she turned on the threshold to view it. It had been used a great deal but was impersonal, aside from the stuffed birds on the walls. No paintings, no photographs or anything else decorated the walls. Even the bedroom was relatively impersonal, almost Spartan, she noted. It was a big airy room, dominated by a double bed with a nightstand on each side of it. There were only two straight-backed wooden chairs in the room, a small dresser, and a worn rag rug in light blue and beige on the floor. There were no paintings or pictures on the walls here either.

All the bedclothes, including the mattress, had been taken from the bed, but large bloodstains were still visible on the light-colored wallpaper above the headboard. The crucifix was still hanging upside-down between the two windows. The cross was made of some black wood; the Christ figure was silver. With outspread arms and a hanging head, Jesus looked more helpless than usual.

As if he had read her thoughts, Tommy said, "My impulse is to put it back, right side up."

Irene nodded but let the crucifix stay as it was. "The Satanists want to scare us by stealing the symbol of the Christian church."

"I don't think that's the whole truth. They have their own symbols. Where in the Christian church are pentagrams used? Symbols have exactly the power and the strength we give them.

The image of the crucified Jesus, the strongest symbol for Christians, naturally has the greatest power. A Hindu who saw an upside-down cross probably wouldn't even react."

Uncertainly, Irene said, "But I'm not particularly religious. I almost never go to church. The twins didn't want to be confirmed, so they weren't. But you're right. I react with . . . discomfort."

"Exactly. And then you realize why the Satanists use religious signs turned the wrong way around in their rituals. Their aim must be to make the Christian rituals and symbols look ridiculous. To dare to disgrace and mock the most sacred symbol is to tell us 'We don't give a damn about the Establishment,' in this case the Church. But they also steal the power of the symbols they mock."

When Irene looked at the cross, an involuntary shiver ran through her.

Chapter 6

SUPERINTENDENT ANDERSSON SEEMED TIRED during the evening meeting. Irene became concerned when she saw bags under his eyes and wrinkles that seemed to have deepened in just a few hours. He was, after all, getting close to retirement age. Maybe it wasn't strange that he looked exhausted.

"The press has been hounding me! I can't set foot outside the station, and I've told the operators not to put through any phone calls from the media. We still haven't any information about the pentagrams and that Satanic crap, and I don't know how long it will be before we do." He drank some warm coffee from a mug that bore the inscription "I'm the boss." He had gotten it as a Christmas present the year before, and he was childishly fond of it. He continued, "I've spoken with Georg again."

At first, Irene didn't remember who Georg was. Then she recalled that the superintendent's cousin was Georg Andersson, and he had been Jacob Schyttelius's boss.

"According to Georg, Jacob Schyttelius was a good teacher and well-liked. He taught computers and physical education and . . . what else was it?"

Andersson started rummaging through the pile of papers in front of him and finally found a wrinkled notepad. His tired features brightened as he flipped through it. "Here! Computers, P.E., and *math*, for grades one through seven. Isn't there a hell of a difference between a student in first grade and one in seventh? In my time. . . ."

He stopped and looked down at the notebook again.

"He started as a substitute at the end of the fall semester and was given a full-time position for the spring. All his reports were good, and Georg said that he was very pleased with Jacob. The school is a charter school with an ecumenical profile, so Jacob's background was an added bonus. And Georg has known his parents for many years."

Fredrik asked, "What does 'ecumenical profile' mean?"

"Oh . . . I asked as well. It takes students from all Christian denominations. Georg said that, for example, there are Christian Syrians, and Russians who are Pentecostal."

Now Irene asked permission to speak. "The reason you and I went out to Norssjön on Tuesday was because your cousin had called and was worried about Jacob: He hadn't shown up at work during the day and didn't answer the telephone. But I remember you mentioned that the principal had said that Jacob might be depressed. Why did he think that?"

"Jacob was on sick leave during the fall for depression. It was probably due to his divorce," Andersson replied.

A divorce might well result in depression, especially with Jacob's genetic predisposition.

"But more than six months had passed, and he had started working again. Why should his depression return?" Irene persisted.

The superintendent's color rose and irritation could be heard in his voice. "I'm no headshrinker, but can't depression return without any particular reason?"

Irene nodded; maybe he was right.

The superintendent stared grimly down at his notebook. "Our pathology professor called me a little while ago. Jacob Schyttelius was first shot in the chest near the heart, with a round fired from a distance of a few meters. The second shot went straight through his brain, and was fired at very close range when he was lying on the floor. The bullet was found in the floorboards. Each shot would have been fatal.

"The pastor and his wife were each shot between the eyes. Those shots were also instantly fatal because large-bore ammunition was used, so the damage was extensive. The bullets have been sent to the lab, but Stridner thinks they are of the same caliber. Ballistic tests aren't complete yet.

"It is interesting to note that Jacob was shot two hours before his parents."

"What did the killer do between the murders?" Irene wondered.

"Erased the hard drives," Fredrik Stridh replied.

"*Bam bam.* One shot in the chest and one in the forehead for Jacob. *Bam bam.* One shot between the eyes for the two other victims. A Husqvarna 1900 is a type of Mauser rifle and can be loaded with five rounds. This killer is familiar with guns. There couldn't have been much time between shots at the rectory, as the victims never stirred," Tommy thought out loud.

"Chambering a round with a Mauser-type rifle takes less than one second for someone who is trained in its use. I think he shot Sten Schyttelius first and then popped Elsa," the superintendent said.

"That sounds plausible. But we don't know for sure," Tommy agreed.

"It's the most likely scenario, since Elsa was full of sleeping pills according to Stridner."

Irene felt some sense of relief. Even if Elsa had been awake in the last few seconds before her death, she would have been too dazed to understand what was happening.

"I've checked the license for the rifles. The ones from the gun cabinet belonged to Sten Schyttelius. The Husqvarna under the bed is registered to Jacob Schyttelius," said Hannu.

"Is there a gun cabinet at the cottage?" Irene asked.

Hannu shook his head.

"Then he must have left his weapon in his father's cabinet. It was just coincidence that the murderer chose that particular rifle," said Tommy.

"Very possibly. But that would mean that the murderer took

the rifle and ammunition from the rectory, then headed over to the cottage to shoot Jacob. Then he returned two hours later to shoot Sten and Elsa. My question is why didn't they see the murderer take the weapon, since they were alive and we know that both of them were in the rectory all afternoon and evening," Irene objected.

"Could he have taken the weapon earlier? Maybe several days ago?" Tommy suggested.

"But I think that would have been a big risk. Sten Schyttelius might have discovered that the weapon was missing. He—"

Irene was interrupted by a knock at the door. Åhlén stuck his round head in.

"Interesting find at the cottage," he informed them as he entered.

In one hand he held a simple cloth bag made of unbleached cotton. He took a thick clear plastic bag from it. Inside was a book.

"This is a book about Satanism. Written in English. We found it behind some loose boards in the wall of the bedroom. Along with a tin of ammunition."

He set the book on the table in front of the superintendent and took out another plastic bag. Irene glanced at the tin in the bag and recognized it. Norma 30-06 is the most common type of large-caliber ammunition.

"Was the space behind the panel big enough to hold a large rifle?" Tommy asked.

"Yes. But not several. It wasn't that big."

"But there was room for the book," Irene commented.

She took the thick plastic-wrapped book. The title was *Church of Satan* and the author was Anton LaVey. Åhlén pointed at the book and said, "Ljunggren recognized that name. He's a leader of a Satanic cult in the USA. Svante may know a little more, but he has gone home. He hadn't slept in a day and a half."

You probably haven't either, Irene thought. But maybe it was more peaceful at work than at home with all the kids.

"Fingerprints?" the superintendent asked.

"Yes. Jacob Schyttelius's and a few others. But they are smudged and could have been acquired at the bookstore before it was purchased. Schyttelius left a lot of prints on it. He must have read the whole book; several passages are underlined."

"Can we keep it?" Irene asked.

"No. We aren't done with it yet. I'll bring it back as soon as possible."

The investigators had to be satisfied. The technician replaced the two plastic bags in his cotton sack and left.

The room was silent after his exit. Then Andersson cleared his throat and said, "This changes things. Jacob may have had a rifle and ammunition hidden at the cottage, as well as a hidden book that some damn leader of Satanists in the USA wrote. Why?"

Hannu was the first one to break the silence. "The rifle may mean that he felt threatened."

"Yep. Otherwise, according to law, he should have stored the weapon and ammunition in his father's gun cabinet. You're forbidden to keep them unlocked as he did."

Irene nodded. "Since Jacob was shot first, it seems likely that the murderer found the rifle and ammunition behind the panel and used it to kill him. Then he took the loaded weapon with him to the rectory and shot Mr. and Mrs. Schyttelius. How many rounds were still in the murder weapon?"

The superintendent consulted his notes before he answered. "Three."

Irene went on. "Then he reloaded between the murder of Jacob and the murders of Sten and Elsa."

She turned toward Hannu. "When did Jacob buy his rifle?"

"In June last year."

"The moose hunt isn't until October, right?"

"He may have wanted to practice before the autumn hunt. Or maybe Hannu is right: Jacob might have felt threatened," Tommy said.

"By whom? And how did the killer know that Jacob had hidden the rifle behind the wooden panel?"

"No idea."

"We won't get any farther with the rifle. But I'm sitting here wondering why he hid the book," Andersson said.

"Because it was pro-Satanic? It wouldn't have looked good, since he was said to be helping his father trace the Satanists," said Fredrik.

Irene mused, "Maybe he was trying to understand the Satanists. Maybe it helped him to search."

"Maybe. But I think we need to question Rebecka Schyttelius as soon as possible," Superintendent Andersson said.

"I've spoken with Inspector Glen Thompson of the London Metropolitan Police. He's our contact person and is keeping an eye on her. She's not doing well; after the news was broken to her, she broke down completely. She might be allowed to come home from the hospital tomorrow. Yesterday she told him she had no idea as to any motive for the murders."

"Have you found any other relatives?"

"Sten Schyttelius had a sister fourteen years older than he. She's in a group home for patients with senile dementia in Mariestad. Never married. No children. The middle sister died two years ago of breast cancer. She was ten years older than her brother. The dead sister had two sons. One lives in Stockholm and one lives here, in the city. The one from Stockholm will drive down tomorrow, and then both nephews will come here. I've scheduled a meeting with them at two o'clock."

"And Elsa?"

"She was an only child. There are a few cousins, but I haven't been able to reach any of them. They all appear to be much older than she was."

"Okay. Tommy or Irene will have to go to London to interview Rebecka Schyttelius," the superintendent said.

Tommy looked uncertain. "Could it wait until next week?" he asked.

"Yes. It may be best to let her recover a bit more. Hopefully, we will have more information by then, too. One of you should locate Jacob Schyttelius's ex-wife first and see what she has to say."

Tommy leaned toward Hannu and half-whispered, "Have you found out anything about her?"

Hannu smiled faintly. Some questions were so stupid, they didn't require an answer.

"I've never been to London. Have you?"

"Yes. On a language study trip in '74. The only thing I learned was to drink a lot of beer. And then there was a red-haired girl named Patricia, and she taught me. . . ."

Tommy left the sentence unfinished, raised his eyebrows meaningfully, and formed his mouth into a quiet whistle.

Irene's parents had never had the money to send her on any language study trips; she'd had to work during the summers. If she remembered correctly, she had sold ice cream at Drottningtorget in the summer of '74—off the books, since she had been under fifteen years of age.

Tommy stopped and pointed at the side corridor. "I'm going to pass by Hannu's office. He has the info on Jacob's ex-wife," he said.

Irene continued on to their office to get her coat. It had been a long, tiring day, but they had made some progress. If they could only find a motive for the killings. Could there be several motives? Hardly possible. Everything pointed to Jacob's rifle having been used for all three killings; the hard drives had been erased at both crime scenes; and a pentagram had been drawn with human blood on the victims' computer screens. In addition, a crucifix in Mr. and Mrs. Schyttelius's bedroom had been turned upside-down and the technicians had found a book about Satanic cults at Jacob's.

Irene stopped herself with one arm in the sleeve of her coat. The book was not *about* Satanic churches, but had been *written by* a founder of one. If Jacob had wanted to know more about Satanists and their thoughts and reactions, he should have obtained a book that described them objectively. A book written by a leader of a cult was hardly going to be objective.

Tommy came in waving a paper in the air. "Good news. She moved from Norrland and now lives in Karlstad. Moved before Christmas and resumed using her maiden name."

"What's her name?"

"Kristina Olsson. She was born . . . then she would be . . . let's see . . . thirty-eight years old."

"But that means she's older than Jacob," she pointed out.

"By seven years. That's not so much."

"No. But it's not common either."

"Maybe not. By the way, do you think you can interview her tomorrow? I've got a tip in the Speedy murder case that I need to check out."

"Sure, that's okay. Give me the note."

"HELLO, SWEETHEART," Krister spoke from the living room. The introductory notes of "The Evening News" could be heard in the background, and then a deep male voice reported dramatically on the latest bomb explosion in Spain.

Irene's pet, Sammie, enthusiastically greeted her, trying to convince her that *no one* in the world had paid *any* attention to him *all day*. But his coat was shiny from being newly brushed, his paws were still damp after his recent walk, and his food dish was sitting in its usual place: Some remains of the dry food were lying at the bottom, but the leftovers they usually added were nowhere to be seen. Irene gave him a kiss on the nose. He snorted but realized that he had been found out. Still relatively content with his existence, he went into the living room to his master and lay down on the rug under the glass table.

Irene warmed the vegetable soup that was standing on the stove and made some generous liver paté sandwiches with piles of pickles. She knew that there must be a can of light beer in the refrigerator somewhere; after a few minutes of rummaging around in the far reaches, she found one. She put her dinner on a tray and carried it into the living room. She hadn't liked the idea of having two TV's in the house but if she and Krister wanted to watch anything other than ZTV or MTV, they were forced to use another set. Choosing television programs was the only thing the girls agreed about and their tastes didn't coincide with their parents'.

Krister gave her an absentminded kiss, with one eye trained on the TV screen. Irene was too hungry to care about the lack of passion in his greeting. With a raging appetite, she practically inhaled the soup and all the sandwiches.

Sammie made an attempt at looking undernourished and pitiful, but Irene cold-heartedly refused to give up any of her sandwiches. She brusquely told him to stay put. Grunting, he went back to his place. He lay there staring at her through the glass tabletop with imploring eyes. For what must have been the thousandth time, Irene was sorry they hadn't chosen the rustic coffee table made of thick pine when they bought the couches.

"Nice to see you eating, sweetie."

Krister had lost interest in the news when the business report started.

"I ate pizza pretty late this afternoon and I haven't had anything since, just a few cups of coffee," she responded.

"Lucky for your colleagues that you've had a steady supply of caffeine. Otherwise they would have had to bring in the safety controller and close the station. Warning! Duck, guys and gals! She's reloading!"

Krister spoke in his broadest dialect. Since he had grown up in Säffle and his family was still there, his Värmland dialect sounded genuine.

"Nice!"

Irene had actually tried to cut back on her coffee consumption, but it hadn't gone very well. She had become tired and irritable. As the sum of your vices is said to be constant, and as she didn't smoke and didn't drink much, she had decided that coffee would be her vice.

Krister chuckled at his own joke but then became serious.

"You should know that Katarina barely ate any soup. She ate about ten peas and that many carrot cubes, and that was it," he said.

"Why? Doesn't she usually eat? Her training takes a lot of energy."

"She's got the idea in her head of competing for Miss West Coast."

"Miss . . . ! It sounds like a beauty contest!"

"It is. Apparently she sent in an application, and now she's been chosen for some regional here in the western part of the city. If she wins, she'll go on to the big final."

Irene sat dumbstruck and tried to make sense of what her husband had just told her. The thought of participating in a beauty contest had never occurred to her, and the idea that one of their daughters would do it felt just as odd. She had to admit to herself that Katarina was prettier than she had been at that age. But to enter a beauty contest! Even though she suspected the answer, she asked anyway: "Why can't she eat because she's participating in Miss West Coast?"

"She says that she's too fat."

Too fat! Katarina was just like her mother, one hundred and eighty centimeters tall, but she probably weighed ten kilos*

---

*Ten kilograms is 22 pounds.

less. And Irene herself was slender; Katarina was already on the verge of skinny, in Irene's opinion.

"Where is she now?"

"Ju-jitsu training. She'll be home any minute."

Irene tried to digest both the food and the news about her daughter's new career as a beauty queen. Suddenly, she remembered something.

"I probably need to go to Karlstad tomorrow. But I'll be home in the evening."

"Hmmm," said her husband, deeply engrossed now in the local news.

Chapter 7

IRENE CAUGHT THE SÄFFLE bus at Nils Ericsson Place; it would go on to Karlstad. This was not only much cheaper than taking the car, but much less tiring as well. She had decided to relax and read on the bus. Supplied with that day's edition of GP, the Göteborg newspaper, a newly purchased paperback, a thermos, and two sandwiches, she got on the bus just after ten o'clock. The sun was shining in a clear blue sky. The temperature was only five degrees above zero, Celsius, but the air already felt as if it would warm up. Maybe the first spring day would finally arrive. The birds that were singing in the bushes outside the police station seemed convinced that it was on its way.

She hadn't had time to open either the newspaper or the book when she fell asleep, only awakening when the bus left the Säffle station. With stiff fingers, she poured coffee into the thermos lid and drank. It was almost lunchtime, and the two wilted cheese sandwiches she had packed tasted heavenly. When she sipped the last bit of coffee, she thought back on her recent telephone conversation with Jacob Schyttelius's ex-wife.

IRENE HAD called her at seven thirty. After just two rings, a woman answered.

"Yes?" The voice sounded weak and hesitant.

"I am Detective Inspector Irene Huss. I'm investigating the murder of your ex-husband and his parents. I wonder if you might be able to meet with me today or tomorrow."

There was a long silence. Irene started to worry that the woman on the other end of the phone had hung up.

"I don't want to," Kristina Olsson whispered.

A second later, she started sniffling. Irene was at a loss, but decided to continue.

"I understand that this stirs up a lot of feelings, but I really must ask you to answer some questions. We're investigating a terrible crime, and we don't have any leads as yet. You knew Jacob and—"

"I don't know! I don't know!"

The last part sounded like a desperate scream. Irene wondered if Kristina Olsson was well. She was behaving very strangely. Irene became determined to meet her as soon as possible.

"What would be best for you? This afternoon, or tomorrow afternoon?" she asked.

Again there was a long pause. Then a dejected sigh was heard and the thin voice whispered, "After two o'clock, today."

IRENE HAD been surprised by the poor rail connections between Göteborg and Karlstad. She had already missed the first train, and the next one left too late. But as luck would have it, she managed to catch the Säffle bus. She wouldn't be able to return by bus, since the last one left at two thirty. However, there was a train just before five o'clock that she should be able to catch.

The bus zigzagged forward between the parked taxicabs and stopped outside the central station in Karlstad. Irene took a taxi from the station, since she had no idea where Sundstavägen was. The taxi stopped outside a three-story yellow brick apartment building. The house had a few years under its belt, but the area looked prosperous. Irene pushed the button next to the name "K. Olsson." The call box crackled. Irene leaned forward and said, "It's Irene Huss."

No one answered, but there was a buzz and the lock opened. The stairwell was clean, but it needed to be painted. There was no elevator, so she had to walk up to the third floor.

On the top landing, Kristina Olsson let her half-open door

slide fully open. Irene stopped dead in her tracks when she saw the woman in the doorway. There was almost no resemblance between Jacob and his sister Rebecka in the photos Irene had seen, but Jacob and Kristina, his ex-wife, could very well have been siblings. The same slender build and the same dark blond coloring. Later, Irene realized that it wasn't just Jacob and Kristina who were alike: Jacob had married a younger version of his mother.

Kristina wore her shoulder-length, straight light hair in a neat ponytail at the nape of her neck. There wasn't the slightest trace of makeup on her face. She had beautiful skin, though it was pale. Her pallor was enhanced by the dark circles under her eyes. Or maybe it was the pale, powder-pink sweater set that made her look wan. The straight gray skirt was no more vibrant, but to Irene's surprise she was wearing bright orange crocheted slippers on her feet.

Kristina tried to stand straight and forced a grimace—which was supposed to represent a smile—to her lips. The hand that she held out shook from nervousness. When Irene took it, it felt ice-cold, unpleasant, like the hand of a dead person.

Kristina moved aside in order to let Irene into the small vestibule. The first thing Irene noticed was the faint smell of Ajax floating toward her. A dark-blue wool coat and a forest-green down coat were hanging on the rack by the wall. A pair of sturdy brown walking boots and a pair of semi-high black boots sat beneath the shelf. A black wool beret lay on top.

A rag rug in cheerful colors covered the floor in the vestibule. Irene thought she recognized its type. When she was shown into the living room and saw the rug under the coffee table, she remembered where she had seen one like it. The person who had woven the rugs that lay on the floors in this apartment had also made the rug that adorned the hall floor of Kullahult's rectory.

Irene took a seat on an uncomfortable yellow silk-covered couch. Kristina sat on the edge of the matching chair. These were odd pieces of furniture to find in the home of a relatively young woman, thought Irene.

"It's lovely when the sun shines on your beautiful rug," she began.

"Yes," was the toneless answer.

Irene refused to give up this early, so she continued. "Did you weave it yourself?"

"No. My sister."

"There's a similar rug in the hall of your former parents-in-law. Did your sister weave that one as well?"

"Yes."

Irene suppressed a sigh and got right to the point. "Our investigation is complicated by the fact that we don't have a motive. Can you think of one?"

Kristina shook her head in reply, and Irene saw tears forming in her eyes. Why was she so nervous? Too emotional to talk about her ex-husband?

There still hadn't been anything in the papers about the pentagrams on the computer screens, but it was only a matter of time before someone would leak this tidbit to the press. Irene decided to start with the Satanic lead.

"Were you aware that Jacob was helping his father track Satanists via the Internet?"

Kristina jerked back and opened her eyes wide. She seemed to be about to say something, but instead sadly nodded.

"Can you tell me anything about it?"

Kristina nodded again like a small, well-disciplined girl, but it took quite a while before she started speaking in her weak voice. "His father was the one who came up with the idea. After the fire. They burned down the summer chapel. The Satanists, I mean. . . ."

She left the sentence unfinished and there was a helpless, desperate look in her gray blue eyes. For the first time, she had uttered enough syllables for Irene to be able to make out her

Norrländsk dialect. How can she work as a teacher? Irene wondered. As if she had read her thoughts, Kristina said, "I've been on sick leave since . . . the murder . . . murders."

"Were you involved in the hunt for the Satanists?"

"No. I don't know anything about computers."

Her voice dropped off, and she looked down at her tightly clutched hands.

"Did you and Jacob have any contact after the divorce?"

"No."

"Did you see Sten or Elsa afterward?"

"No."

It was strange to see how crushed Kristina seemed to be, even though she claimed to have had no contact with either Jacob or his parents during the last nine months.

"When was the last time you spoke with Jacob?"

"Last July. When everything was done . . . after. . . ."

"And when did you hear from his parents last?"

"Last June. His father called and was . . . upset . . . because we . . . we were going to. . . ."

She started sniffling quietly. She was incapable of saying the word "divorce." The crucial point was getting closer, and it demanded an answer. Irene gave Kristina time to pull herself together, and then she asked, "Why did you and Jacob get divorced?"

Kristina straightened her back and took a deep breath. "He didn't want to have children."

It wasn't the answer Irene had expected. Kristina didn't look at her, focusing instead on a point behind Irene's back. She bit her bottom lip hard to keep it from trembling.

"But he was a teacher. He must have liked children," Irene said.

"Yes. But he didn't want any of his own."

Strange. Irene's brain went into overdrive. "He wasn't seeing other women?" she asked vaguely, for lack of anything better.

"No."

Again Kristina sat, her head bowed, looking as if she was waiting for a punishment.

Now Irene became aware of the image in an embroidered wall hanging that was above the television. It was a Christ figure, a figure surrounded by light, raising his palms in a gesture of blessing toward the beholder. When Irene turned her head, she could see through the half-open door to the bedroom. A simple wooden cross in a light wood hung above the headboard of the bed. Otherwise, the walls were bare.

"Did you, or your sister, embroider this beautiful wall hanging?" Irene asked.

"I did. My sister weaves."

"Where in Norrland are you from?"

"Vilhelmina. But we moved around a lot. My father was a preacher."

"A preacher? In the Pentecostal Movement?"

"He . . . we were Laestadians."

Irene had fuzzy recollections from school religious lessons about an ecstatic congregation that had been founded in Norrland in the 1800s. Weren't they the ones who weren't allowed to have curtains? Kristina had beautiful white lattice-woven curtains in her windows.

"You say 'were' Laestadians. You aren't any longer?"

"No. My older sister left the congregation and joined the Swedish church. She's a pastor and works here in Karlstad."

"Is that why you moved here?"

Kristina hesitated but then she nodded.

"Is her name also Olsson?"

"Yes. Kerstin Olsson. She never married."

"Are your parents still living in Norrland?"

"Father is dead. Mother lives near our brother outside Vitangi."

"Are there any more siblings?"

"No."

Irene unconsciously took a deep breath before she asked her next question. "Was it you or Jacob who wanted to get a divorce?"

"It was me."

Kristina looked down at her clenched fists again.

"Because he didn't want to have children with you?" Irene said for clarification.

Kristina nodded without raising her eyes from her hands.

Irene felt that it was impossible to come up with the right questions for her. And even if Irene asked the right questions, getting a real answer seemed hopeless. Was she hiding something? Or just terrified? Irene didn't understand her.

IRENE WALKED back to the center of town. She followed the signs and used her good sense of direction. The shining sun felt wonderful, even if it had started to set and didn't add much warmth. It was a few degrees colder in Göteborg than here. She passed over a glittering watercourse. Quacking ducks and honking Canada geese were swimming and walking along the edges. She didn't know what the stream or river was called. Even though Krister's family lived in Säffle and her own family usually spent several weeks every year in the parents-in-law's cottage outside Sunne, she had been in Karlstad three times at the most. Which was really a pity.

As she strolled and peered into shop windows, she realized how hungry she was. She had an hour and a half before the train left, time enough to eat.

Once, long ago, on one of her three trips here, she and Krister had taken the kids to a cozy restaurant next to Stora Torget. She remembered that it was on the same side of the square as the magnificent city hall, but that you had to walk down one of the side streets. Her memories were fuzzy, but she managed to find the restaurant, which, she remembered now, was named Källaren Munken.

When she walked in through the heavy doors and down the worn stone steps, she recognized the basement with its many passages. It had been freshened up since her previous visit, but the cozy atmosphere still prevailed.

The maitre d' showed her to a table which was covered with a white linen cloth. He recommended the day's special, grilled char with almondine potatoes and chive sauce. Irene decided to take his advice, and ordered a Hof as well. After her interview with Kristina Olsson, she deserved a beer. Maybe two. The home-baked bread she was served was still so warm that the butter melted when she spread it. A feeling of pleasure suffused her, and she stopped thinking about the conversation she had just had. There would be plenty of time on the train.

WAS KRISTINA Olsson mentally ill? The answer would have to be no, but with the reservation that she appeared to be near a nervous breakdown—if she hadn't already had one, which was difficult for a layman to decide.

Was she hiding something? Irene was almost convinced that that was the case. But what was she hiding? And why? What was she afraid of?

Irene realized that she had forgotten to ask Kristina if she had been threatened. How could she forget such an obvious question? Maybe not so entirely obvious, though, since Kristina hadn't had any contact with either Jacob or his parents in more than nine months.

Was there something in Kristina's past that was frightening her? As members of a fundamentalist religious sect, she and her siblings would have had a strict religious upbringing, but it seemed that both Kristina and her sister had freed themselves from the faith of their childhoods. Even so, they might be deeply spiritual. The decor of Kristina's apartment bore the stamp of Christian faith with ascetic elements. Except, of course, that she had curtains.

IRENE PROMISED herself that she would look up Laestadianism in an encyclopedia. Personally, she wasn't very interested in religious questions. The Huss family was about as religious as most of the other people in Sweden. They went to church for baptisms, weddings, and funerals; never otherwise. But she had realized several times, in the course of this investigation, how annoyingly ignorant she was.

And Satanism had popped up as a counterweight to all this Christian faith with Laestadians, synods, and goodness knows what else. How relevant was this negativity toward Christianity? The clues were there, but did they mean anything?

The questions whirled around in her mind; she had no answers.

WHEN SHE got off at the Göteborg Central Station, she was met with the latest edition of the *Götesborg Times,* usually referred to by its initials, *GT:* **"Extra! Extra! Satanic leads in the triple homicide!"**

Chapter 8

"Some idiot leaked!"

Superintendent Andersson was in a terrible mood. He stared grimly at the group during Friday's morning prayers. None of those present looked guilty, and he hadn't really suspected any of them. But it was enormously irritating not to have a specific person to pounce on.

Svante Malm, just joining the meeting with a lab report in his hand, said, "The strange thing is that no one did it earlier."

The superintendent turned around on his heel and hissed, "What do you mean?"

"Spectacular! Pastor's family murdered by Satanists! Candy for the evening papers. Whoever leaked the information was probably well paid."

Still red in the face, Andersson mumbled something unintelligible. After taking a few deep breaths, he asked Svante to review the new information the lab had come up with.

Svante took a seat and looked down at the papers he had set in front of him on the table. "The analysis of the pentagrams is finished. The one on the computer screen in the cottage was, as expected, made with Jacob Schyttelius's blood. We've found the tool that the murderer used: A bloody pastry brush was lying in the wastebasket under the desk."

He paused briefly and took out some new papers, which he laid on top of the pile.

"The analysis of the pentagram in the rectory is a bit surprising. The star itself was made with Sten Schyttelius's blood, but the ring around it was made with Elsa's. The murderer used a pastry brush there as well. We found it inside one of the desk drawers."

"Did the murderer leave any clues?" Irene asked.

"Not that we've found yet. Naturally, there are a lot of hairs and fibers at both crime scenes, but nothing seems suspicious so far. We've found a little bit of soil from the yard on the floor of the bedroom at the rectory. It doesn't have to be the murderer who dragged it in. It could just as easily have been Mr. or Mrs. Schyttelius, or one of you."

"No footprints, or anything like that?" Andersson asked hopefully.

"No. Nor are there any signs of bodily fluids or other foreign substances—"

"What do you mean by 'foreign substances'?" Fredrik Stridh interrupted.

"Substances that are used during Satanic rituals. For example, smoke, different types of narcotics, alcohol, blood from sacrificial animals. There was a lot of blood, but all the blood at the crime scenes came from the victims."

The investigators contemplated the surprising lack of evidence left by the murderer. Irene couldn't explain how he had managed, as so much blood and tissue had to have splashed around the victims. Instead, she asked the technician another question. "Do you know for certain that the same weapon was used in all three murders?"

"Yes. All three were shot with the rifle which was lying under Mr. and Mrs. Schyttelius's bed; and with the same type of ammunition, Norma 30-06. There are no fingerprints on the murder weapon."

Svante gathered his papers together and returned them to his worn canvas bag. He rose, nodded, and disappeared through the door. The superintendent reclaimed his position in front of the audience.

"A man who lives a little farther down the road, right after the turnoff to the Schytteliuses' cottage, phoned. When he was out walking his dog just before eleven on Monday night, he saw a dark-colored car parked on a forest road a little way off."

Andersson turned on the overhead projector but didn't bother pulling down the screen. A hand-drawn map in blue ink was projected onto the wall.

"Here's the gravel road down to the Schytteliuses' cottage. Here's the cottage. The car was parked a little way down the next road. There aren't any cottages along it, because it's an old logging road. The technicians found some blurred tire tracks, but the sleet and rain the last few days washed away most of it. Footprints have been washed away by now as well."

"Does he know what make the car was?" Hannu asked.

"No. He never went up to the car, just stopped on a path forty or fifty meters away from it. The dog was probably taking care of business. The man had a flashlight with him so he could see where he was walking, but the car was too far away for the flashlight to illuminate it enough to make out any details."

Andersson pointed at the dotted line that wound its way in the opposite direction from the cottage.

"This is where the path goes. And the car was here. The witness thinks it was a smaller model car, possibly a small Mazda or something similar. It was either black, dark blue, or dark green. He thinks it had Swedish license plates."

"But he isn't completely certain?" said Irene.

"No. He saw the car at an angle from behind, and apparently it was parked next to a grove of spruce trees. According to him, it wasn't visible from the main road. The car was impossible to see unless you walked in a short distance on the forest path."

"So someone wanted to hide the car," Irene concluded.

"Looks that way, yeah. I've measured on a real map and if you keep to the roads, it's almost exactly a kilometer to walk from the car to the Schytteliuses's cottage. The question about the shortest distance, as opposed to staying on the roads, is whether the undergrowth is too thick to allow someone to walk through the woods. If it's possible, then it's barely two hundred meters as the crow flies from the car to the cottage. Someone should take a closer look."

Fredrik held up his hand and Irene slowly followed his lead. It was the thought of the reports that needed to be written and the piles of paper that. . . . She held her hand a little higher so the superintendent wouldn't miss how interested she was in the navigable aspects of the terrain around Norssjön.

There was a knock at the door, and a head could be glimpsed through the opening. A female voice said, "Telephone for Huss. It's about the pastors' murders."

The door closed again and Irene got up and went to her office. The call was put through, and to her surprise Louise Måårdh was on the other end of the line. Louise went straight to the point: "I've read the papers about the symbols that were written in blood. What are they called . . . ? Pentagrams! It struck me that I've actually seen one of those symbols recently. Namely, in Eva Möller's car."

If she listened for Irene's reaction, she was probably disappointed. Even if Irene was surprised, her voice didn't reveal anything. "In Eva Möller's car? Where?" was all she said.

"The gearshift. She has one of those pentagrams on the knob."

"Are you sure?"

"Yes. I've ridden with her several times to church choir rehearsals. She drives past our house, and I usually catch a ride with her when the weather is bad. After Christmas, I noticed that knob, and I asked her why she had traded the old one in for this strange one and she laughed and said it was a Christmas present."

"What does this knob look like?"

"The knob itself is black, and the pentagram is silver."

"Thanks a lot. I'll speak with her."

When Irene had hung up the phone, she stared blankly in front of her as the thoughts swirled around in her head. A gearshift knob with a pentagram on it? Maybe Eva Möller didn't know what kind of symbol she was driving around with? But the chances of her not knowing were slight. For the first time, they had gotten a lead on a possible Satanic link to the Schyttelius family but this lead had led to a most unexpected place.

TOMMY SWEPT by in the corridor with a cheerful "Things are starting to move in the Speedy murder case!"

Irene vaguely wondered why he had a video camera in tow but when Fredrik came steaming in with the car keys jingling in his hand, she lost her train of thought. She would have to get going if she was going to keep up with Inspector Stridh.

They drove out toward Boråsvägen. Irene said, "Eva Möller can't meet with us until one o'clock. Apparently she's also a music teacher and has lessons until then."

"Should we eat lunch before, or after?"

"Before. It will buy us some time."

Irene had the directions to Eva Möller's cottage in her pocket. She had been surprised when she realized that the cantor lived alone in a house in the middle of the woods. To get there, one had to drive toward Landvetter Church and then wind one's way on some smaller roads. "I'm right out in the middle of nowhere," Eva had said.

They turned off what was now the familiar road to Norssjön, but this time they didn't turn at the little wooden sign with the faded text "Luck Cottage"; they continued a few hundred meters further until they came to the forest road. There was no sign here. Fredrik slowed down and drove onto a narrow road, more like a wide lane. The car lurched over the deep ruts and holes.

"It wouldn't be easy to drive in here, even with a small car," Fredrik noted after the Saab's chassis had bottomed out on the rough road.

The forest stood thick around them on both sides. Tall pines, planted several decades ago at a disciplined distance, now had a tangle of undergrowth between them. Whoever owned the forest hadn't been looking after it properly. Yet a bit farther on, Irene could see that the trees opened up, revealing some deforestation.

The beautiful weather of yesterday still held. When the wind was still, the silence was almost overwhelming. The sun rays fell through the tree trunks at an angle. There was a heavy scent of damp earth and of vegetation that had started coming to life in the first of the spring warmth.

"This must be it," said Fredrik. He stopped a few meters in front of a group of spruce trees growing in a clump, creating an impassable wall.

Irene and Fredrik walked toward the spruces with their gazes fixed on the ground, tracing several old tire tracks from heavy vehicles but also a few barely noticeable ones from regular cars.

"Now we know why he parked here. It's not possible to go any farther." Fredrik pointed at the continuation of the road behind the spruce grove. There it descended into a deep hollow filled with water at the bottom. It was obvious that any car that drove down there would get stuck in the mud.

Irene started walking back to their car. When she reached the path that the witness with the dog had been on, she turned and looked around her. Their Saab could be seen at an angle from behind, since the forest road curved around the spruce grove. The small car that the witness had seen had been parked closer to the spruces. With a sigh, Irene had to agree with him: It was impossible to see the license plate and doubtless difficult to determine a particular make, since all compact cars seemed to look alike these days.

She walked back to Fredrik, who was standing near the water-filled hole, deep in thought. "I think I would try to reach the clearing, rather than force my way through this mass of undergrowth. It must be easier to make one's way along the edge of it," he said.

"If it stretches far enough in the direction of the cottage, then I agree. Let's take a look."

They made a circuit around the mud hollow and trudged forward toward the clearing, stopping at the edge of the woods to look around. The clearing was narrow and relatively long.

"You could walk at least a hundred meters here. Then you'd have to get out your machete," Fredrik concluded.

It was still quite difficult to make their way. The earth's surface was damp and porous, and they sank into it at each step. Irene's suede boots would need to be both washed and brushed before she could show herself in public in them again. Fredrik, who went around in boat shoes, was even worse off. The best footwear would have been rain boots.

They stopped at the edge of the clearing. The vegetation looked impassable.

"What do we do now? I wish we really had a machete," Fredrik groaned.

"I suggest we do what my dog would do."

"And what does your dog do?"

"Follow the game trail."

A short distance away, she had noticed a narrow opening between some spruce trees, a game trail. A large pile of moose dung was lying in the middle of it.

"It probably leads down to the lake, because the animals want to drink after they've grazed. Let's follow the path and see how close to the cottage we can get," said Irene.

They had to bend down and push away hanging branches, at the same time as watching where they put their feet. Irene slipped several times on the slimy roots.

"Good thing it's not tick season yet," Fredrik puffed.

Irene was about to answer, when she felt a thread across her mouth. She spit and sputtered, thinking it was a sturdy spiderweb. Disgusted, she wiped her mouth with her hand and got ahold of the filament. She instinctively glanced at it before she shook it from her fingers. She stopped and held it up to the sunlight that filtered down through the spruce trees.

A spider hadn't produced this thread, but a sheep probably had. A thin forest-green-colored woolen thread, about three or four centimeters long, dangled from Irene's fingers, pinched between her thumb and index finger.

"What is it? Why are you stopping?" Fredrik asked, irritated.

He was busy picking things out of his hair. The hair gel he always used in the morning to get his bangs to stand straight up turned out to be the ideal surface for twigs and pine needles to attach themselves to.

"A thread. Someone has been on this path before us. It hasn't been here very long, because it isn't faded or dirty."

She showed Fredrik her find. He whistled softly. "We'll have to keep an eye out for more fibers."

Irene found a new thread only twenty meters farther up, but this one was bright red. It hung on the outer branch in a patch of thick shrubbery. Irene stopped and pointed. "It's at shoulder height for me. This piece is about as long as the green one. Where could these threads have come from?"

"I think we're looking for a short murderer, max one hundred and sixty centimeters tall, wearing a hat with a tassel or pompom made of green and red yarn."

Irene laughed and took a doggie poop bag from her pocket. She carefully placed the two woolen threads inside. Maybe the technicians could get something out of them.

The path led down to the lake. They estimated that if they walked fifty meters along the edge of the lake and then turned their backs to it and walked into the vegetation, they should arrive at the cottage.

To their relief, the lake shore widened into a small sandy beach, and a narrow gravel path led into the woods from the beach. The path ended about ten meters from the Schyttelius cottage's gate.

"It's probably a community path to the beach for all of the cottage owners in the area," Irene suggested.

"Maybe. But there's nothing keeping someone from turning off the path earlier and climbing over the Schytteliuses' fence at the back of the property. No one would see. Should we check?"

Fredrik had already turned on his heel and was on his way back in the same direction they had just come. Thirty meters away, he stopped and pointed.

Irene could also see a barely noticeable walkway between some raspberry bushes. It followed the rotten wooden fence along the lake side of the Schytteliuses' property. The fence sagged to the ground in the middle from age and poor maintenance.

"We can step right onto the property," Fredrik determined. They did so, taking a good look at where they put their feet.

"If the murderer went this way on Monday, the ground would still have been frozen. It has rained since then, and the frost has started rising out of the topsoil. The murderer didn't have as much trouble getting here as we did," said Irene.

"Think about the position of the car and the trails. He knew he was going to get here without risking being seen. Everything points to familiarity with the area."

Fredrik was right. The murders had been planned, and the murderer had known how to make his way to and from the cottage without being seen.

They walked toward the back of the cottage. The Schyttelius family had built a large glassed-in veranda running the length of the wall. So this was where the superintendent had sat at the crayfish party seventeen years ago. Irene turned her back to the veranda and looked down at the lake. She could glimpse water through the thicket.

"Too bad they didn't own the property all the way down to the lake. Then they could have cleared it for the sake of the view," she remarked.

"Must have been irritating for them."

"Probably."

"Should we take the road back? It's longer . . ."

". . . but it will be faster," Irene finished.

THEY STOPPED at a hot dog stand and ate before heading for Eva Möller's house. It was easy to find Landvetter Church, but trickier to locate the right small road. They were on a gravel road that rose steadily. According to Eva Möller's directions, they were supposed to go over the crest of the hill and then they would almost be there. The coniferous trees didn't grow as thickly up here. Deciduous forest and fields could be seen.

"Turn to the right after the split oak," Irene read from her notes.

"I see it," Fredrik said, indicating the silhouette of a large mangled tree. Most of the crown was gone, and the branches that were left splayed out in all directions. No branches grew at all on one side, since only half of the tree remained. Right after they passed this oak tree, they turned onto an uneven dirt road.

"How can someone live in a place like this?" Irene asked, holding on to the dashboard as they slowly jounced down the rutted road.

After they had lurched forward a good distance, a Falu-red cottage appeared in the back of a glade bathed in sunlight. The forest came up to the eaves on three sides, but there were no woods at all on the western exposure. They parked next to a relatively new bright-red Honda and got out. Because the cottage was located on the crest of the hill, the view to the west was fantastic. Irene and Fredrik stood for a moment to admire it. Irene took the opportunity to look at Eva Möller's car before they walked up to the house. What Louise Määrdh had said was correct: There was a black knob with a silver-colored pentagram on the gearshift lever.

The blue-painted front door opened and Eva Möller stepped out onto the porch. She was wearing a light-blue floor-length dress with wide sleeves, trimmed with beautiful dark-blue embroidery around the neck and on the chest. The dress matched her eyes. Her blond hair, hanging down to her shoulders, glittered like silver in the sunlight.

"You did a good job of finding the place," she said, laughing.

Her hearty smile and the smell of coffee that trickled out through the open door made Irene feel welcome.

They hung their coats from the rack of hooks, pulled off their muddy shoes just inside the door, and stepped right into the kitchen. The sun shone through the light-yellow curtains in the western window, bringing a cozy warmth to the small kitchen. It was decorated country-style with a lot of pine that seemed relatively new, like the kitchen appliances. There didn't appear to be a dishwasher, but the old iron stove had obviously been kept through the renovation. A shelf holding old objects was located above the stove. A three-legged iron pot was enthroned on its center, surrounded by a beautiful glass goblet and a purple stone the size of a fist, cut in half. The crystals on the inside of the stone emitted small flashes of light when the sun shone on it. A half-meter-long glass staff lay in front of the objects, and a small round glass paperweight was located farthest out on the shelf. Sturdy iron hooks were fastened to the wall above the shelf. A double-edged knife with a beautifully carved wooden handle and an old-fashioned table knife with a handle made of bone hung from these hooks. The sun reflected along the sharpened edges, which scintillated in its light.

Eva Möller had set out thin gold-edged coffee cups and a plate with cinnamon rolls by the window. The yellow-and-white checkered cotton tablecloth looked newly ironed. A shallow blue porcelain bowl holding blooming blue windflowers was placed in the middle of the table.

She invited the officers to sit down. The coffee smelled heavenly when she poured it. She told them to help themselves to the rolls.

"Take as many as you want. I have more in the freezer. Unfortunately, I don't have any coffee cake to serve you," she said.

"Wonderful rolls," Fredrik announced with his mouth full.

The cantor flashed him a delighted smile and looked into his eyes. Irene noticed that he stopped chewing for a few seconds. Eva Möller continued to smile as she strolled over to the stove to put the coffeepot back on a burner. Fredrik had a hard time taking his eyes off her, but with an effort he focused on the coffee cup, chewed the rest of the cinnamon roll, and swallowed loudly.

Irene recognized Fredrik's behavior. The caretaker for the cemetery, Stig Björk, and Pastor Urban Berg had displayed exactly the same kind of reactions at the Fellowship Hall on Wednesday, though Berg had shown a bit more self-control. Tommy was the one who had questioned the cantor on Wednesday. Had he also experienced the same kind of attraction? Irene and Tommy knew each other well enough that she could ask him.

"The blue windflowers are so nice," Irene said in order to start the conversation.

Eva Möller smiled. "Yes. I've borrowed them from Mother Earth. When they are done blooming, I will put them back. And then maybe I'll be allowed to take a tuft of cowslips instead."

"Which you will also replant when they start wilting," Irene assumed.

"Yes. Why did you want to speak with me again?" Eva Möller asked.

Since Fredrik had his mouth filled with cinnamon roll, Irene replied. "We need to supplement the introductory interrogations. The picture is starting to take shape, but new questions come up all the time. We hope that you will be able to help us answer some of them."

"I'm happy to help, if I can."

Irene remembered something Tommy had said; she decided to start with it and save the question about the pentagram for later. "Our colleague who spoke with you on Wednesday mentioned that you told him that Sten Schyttelius was a man with hidden depths. Could you explain what you meant by that?"

Eva Möller gave Irene a long, thoughtful look before she replied. "Sten had several sides to his personality, just as we all do. He was a sociable person. He could let loose, and he never turned down a drink. However, he rarely held any parties himself. It was probably because of Elsa's illness. When it came to his job, he was conservative through and through, with respect to his work in the parish as well as his position in the church. During the service, everything was supposed to go according to tradition. There were supposed to be shining chasubles and polished candelabras, and he was happy to sing the liturgy. If he had been allowed to swing censers, then he would probably have done so.

"Those were perhaps the two opposite sides that were most obvious. But sometimes I thought there was something else about him. Something dark . . . secret . . . or maybe sad. I don't know really."

"Did you like Sten Schyttelius as a person?"

Eva Möller took her time before she replied. "I accepted that he was the way he was. He was old and about to retire. We never had any difficulties between us. It was probably because he let me take care of the music and the church choir the way I wanted to. Actually, he never got involved in my work and I stayed away from his."

"How long have you been the cantor in this . . . congregation, is it called?"

"Church Association. I've been here almost exactly four years. It was actually this house that lured me here."

"First you got the house, and then the job?" Irene asked.

"Yes. I was fortunate enough to buy it very cheaply from an acquaintance who had renovated it but realized he would never have the time to stay here. He wanted to use it as a summer cottage, but his new wife couldn't imagine spending her vacation in the woods. But I felt that it was my house the first time I saw it."

"Was it for sale then?"

"No. But I knew it would become mine."

Fredrik didn't seem to have a single question. He chewed on rolls and sat and stared, fascinated by the lovely Eva. Irene was slightly irritated at her colleague's passivity. She decided that it was time to broach the real reason for their visit.

"As I'm sure you've read in the papers we found pentagrams at the crime scenes. At both places the pentagrams were painted directly on the computer screens with the victims' blood."

Eva Möller nodded.

"I spoke with Louise Määrdh this morning. She mentioned that you have a pentagram on the gearshift of your car. Can you tell us why?"

To Irene's surprise, Eva Möller burst out laughing. When she managed to stop, she said, still with restrained amusement in her voice, "I got it at Christmas from a friend. He thinks I have too much fire and wind in me. The pentagram is the tool of the earth. It stands for stability. I got the knob simply so that I would keep my feet on the ground. Or rather on the road."

Irene was disappointed that the explanation was so simple. Or was it?

"Why does a cantor drive around with the devil's face on her gearshift?" Irene asked.

Eva Möller instantly became serious. "Oh. Was the pentagram on the computer screens turned upside down?"

"Yes."

"Then it was used for a Satanic purpose. The pentagram, in and of itself, is a strong tool, but it's only Satanists who turn it upside down. My pentagram isn't turned the wrong way. But...."

Eva pressed her lips together and looked Irene steadily in the eye. She quickly got up and walked over to the shelf above the stove. She took down the paperweight and pressed it hard against her chest as she walked back toward the kitchen table.

"This is my pentagram," she said. She set the glass object in front of Irene and motioned for her to look closer. She could see that it wasn't just a paperweight, but a rounded glass dome with a pentagram engraved in its bottom.

"The pentagram in and of itself isn't a symbol of evil but, like all magical implements, it has strong powers that can be abused. It's easy to turn my pentagram and then—poof—you have the devil's face."

She turned the glass dome so that two of the points faced up and one down.

The devil's face looked up at Irene from the glass.

The glass devil.

The phrase etched itself on Irene's brain, though she didn't really understand why. The pentagram's power depended on how you used it. And if you believed in it. Clearly, Eva Möller believed. Was she nuts, or was she messing about with funny New-Age foolishness?

"How do you reconcile a belief in the pentagram's power with your work in the church?" Irene continued.

The cantor looked sincerely surprised. "They don't have anything to do with each other. Music is my work, and I love it. I love the church as a place of holy energy. But I feel the power of the pentagram as a tool."

Tool? What kind of tool? Suddenly, Irene was irritated with Eva, batting her eyes and trying to make herself interesting with her New-Ageism.

The worst thing was that it worked. Fredrik sat as though under a spell, with a ridiculous grin on his face.

Unnecessarily brusquely, Irene asked, "What are your opinions about Elsa and Jacob?"

Eva was grave as she said, "Elsa was a very tragic person. There was only darkness within her. She carried a grief which she had bottled inside. Periodically, she became better, but I saw the shadow standing right behind her, just biding its time. It had her in its power. Sometimes she was close to taking her life, but she didn't have the strength to do that."

"How do you know she was contemplating suicide?"

"I felt it. For some people, it's the only way out."

Eva sat, calm and relaxed, with her hands loosely folded in her lap. Her long hair shone like a halo around her head, adding to her image as a lovely angel. Irene started to wonder how crazy this cute cantor actually was.

"And Jacob?"

"I didn't know him at all. We only met twice. The association's employees usually eat breakfast after Christmas Mass. . . ."

"I'm aware of that. That's the only place you met?"

"Yes. The first time he had his wife with him. They were newlyweds then."

"What impression did you get from them?"

Eva sat quietly for some time. "There was no energy between them at all. No fire. Only cold."

Irene was surprised. Had it been bad from the beginning of the marriage? She composed herself; that's what Eva Möller was claiming.

"You never spoke with Jacob?"

"I did, at Christmas. But only a few words."

"How did he seem to you then?"

Eva wound a strand of hair around one index finger while she thought back. "Neutral. Low energy. He didn't make much contact."

A look at Fredrik was enough to determine that full contact had been made there. His face was aglow. To finish the questioning, Irene asked, "Have you ever met Rebecka?"

"Yes. At the same time I met Jacob and his wife."

"What impression did you have of Rebecka?"

Again Eva was quiet for some time. "She has a great deal of inner energy. It isn't darkness, like her mother. But she hides it. Inside she is more like her father, but on the outside no likeness is visible."

"Oh, Rebecka is very much like her father in appearance," Irene objected.

"In appearance, yes. I'm not speaking about appearances, but about her spirit. On the surface, she's very reserved. She never lets anyone inside. Not a single person."

Irene started thinking that it was high time to say good-bye. Fredrik still bore a smile that didn't show any signs of fading away.

Irene thanked Eva for the coffee. Fredrik reluctantly got up as well. They walked over to the front door and put on their coats, taking their muddy shoes with them to the porch before putting them on. Irene's zipper got stuck. Sweat broke out on her back while she stood and yanked at it. Fredrik wandered over to the car. Then Eva touched Irene's shoulder lightly and said, "You have the right energy and you can reach your inner being. Contact with your spirit is strong. You can meditate and lose yourself."

Astonished, Irene could only nod. How could Eva know that she used meditation in jujitsu?

"Together we can discover Sten Schyttelius's hidden depths. I can't do it alone, because it requires too much energy. Contact me when you want to try."

Before Irene had time to gather her thoughts, Eva stepped backward across the threshold. She smiled and waved at Fredrik, who happily waved back. Then she closed the blue door.

* * *

"THE GLADIATOR Gym on Mölndalsvägen has confirmed that Jacob Schyttelius was there and worked out from eight to ten thirty on Monday night. No cashier at Hemköp remembers whether he shopped there. But since they close at ten o'clock, he must have been there before he worked out. What did you get from the questioning of Jacob and Rebecka's cousins?" Superintendent Andersson asked Hannu.

"The cousins barely knew each other. Too much of an age difference. The youngest of the brothers is nine years older than Jacob."

"Could they tell us anything about their uncle?" Irene asked.

"Not much. Sten Schyttelius was a surprise child. Didn't spend a lot of time with his sisters as an adult. Their father was a pastor in a small congregation outside Skövde."

"So Sten came from a pastor's family?"

"Yes. Just like Elsa. Her father was a pastor in a neighboring parish. She was the only child. Elsa and Sten knew each other from childhood."

Irene took a bite from her cheese sandwich while she pondered over the new information from Hannu. Aside from the two of them, only Sven Andersson and Fredrik Stridh were present. The sun was setting, and Friday evening began to descend on Göteborg. Soon, happy expectations would be followed by dashed hopes and drunkenness, police sirens would begin to sound, and everything would be as it always is on any ordinary Friday night.

Hannu broke the silence. "I've received Rebecka's telephone number. I've not spoken with her directly. Chief Inspector Thompson has apparently tried to get Rebecka to talk. She says that she isn't up to it. Thompson has been in touch with her doctor, who says that she's very fragile. It's going to take some time before she bounces back."

He handed a note with Rebecka's address and telephone

number to Irene. The street she lived on was called Ossington Street, which didn't mean anything to Irene. In London she'd heard of Carnaby Street and Oxford Street, and of a few famous places: Piccadilly Circus, New Scotland Yard, and Buckingham Palace. That was about it.

"If she works with computers, she should have an E-mail address," said Irene.

"Probably, but Thompson didn't give it to me," Hannu replied.

"I'll wait to telephone her."

Irene folded the note and put it in her jeans pocket.

"How do we proceed?" Andersson asked shortly.

They shared the old familiar feeling of having reached a dead end. Finally, Irene said, "I'll get in touch with Rebecka over the weekend. On Monday, I'm going to meet with Eva Möller again. Alone."

She added the last word when she saw how Fredrik brightened up.

"Why?" the superintendent wanted to know.

"She's some kind of New-Ager, but she's actually the only one close to the Schyttelius family who believes in such hocus-pocus. And she owns at least two pentagrams. Maybe she knows more than she's telling us."

Irene avoided mentioning what Eva had whispered to her when she and Fredrik were about to leave. It was better to keep some information to herself for the time being.

"Okay. Talk to her. Hannu and Fredrik will follow up sum-marizing the door-to-door questioning. Possibly you'll have to make another try," said Andersson.

It was a boring job, but it had to be done. Fredrik nodded and shrugged in dejection. As usual, Hannu provided no clues as to what he was thinking. Hannu and Fredrik were experienced investigators and knew that it was ordinary routine chores like this that often resulted in the capture of a killer.

Chapter 9

"SAMMIE RECEIVED A DEATH threat from the stupid idiot *bajshög*, that shitpile!"

Jenny was standing with her legs shoulder-width apart in the hall, her arms crossed over her chest. The light from the ceiling lamp reflected from her temporarily platinum-blond hair with bright blue highlights. Since she was a singer in a pop band on its way to stardom, she had to do something extra to her appearance: hence the nine gold rings in her left ear and the miniature glass penis which hung from the right.

Irene stopped in the process of hanging up her jacket. She looked down at her happy dog. Sammie didn't seem to have been adversely affected by the death threat.

"Why?" she asked, surprised.

"He killed Felix."

An icy hand clutched Irene's heart. The only Felix she knew was their neighbors', the Bernhögs, fat red cat. Please don't let it be that one!

"You know, *bajshög's* red cat," Jenny continued.

Unconsciously, Irene fumbled for support.

The relationship between the neighbors wasn't good. Truth be told, it was really quite awful. Ever since she and Krister had moved to the row-house area fourteen years earlier, there had been little battles. Since the childless Bernhögs had lived in the area ever since it was built, they felt that everything should be on their terms. To them, two lively four-year-old twin girls had not exactly been the ideal next-door neighbors. The girls attracted the neighborhood children and played wild games and laughed and screamed. Mrs. Bernhög's migraines became worse, and Mr. Bernhög had his well-tended flowerbeds destroyed by the trampling feet of children. He yelled at both children and parents. As a result, all the children suddenly *had* to cut through just those flowerbeds and Mr. and Mrs. Bernhög got the nickname *Bajshög*--excrement.

The Bernhögs had put up a high fence in front and back of their row house. They didn't speak to their next-door neighbors when they saw them on the street. However, they left angry notes in their mailbox when something didn't suit them. Usually the notes were about things like poor snow-shoveling and improper sanding of ice patches on the communal porch in front of the house. But after Sammie had joined the Huss family nine years ago, the battles had stepped up. Now they suddenly complained that there was dog crap everywhere, despite the fact that the Huss family always picked up after Sammie with doggie poop bags.

"Who picks up after all the stray cats?" Irene had ventured to ask Mr. Bernhög one time when she had gotten yet another a note of complaint. A dark red flush had suffused his quivering cheeks, and his small pursed mouth had opened and closed without managing to produce any audible sounds. Irene thought that he looked like a fat, worried goldfish.

Sammie was an Irish soft-coated wheaten terrier, a long and complicated breed name whose last word was the most important: he was a terrier. All terriers are bred for hunting and fighting. They are happy and devoted, while at the same time they have an intense temperament. Sammie loved to chase everything that moved. His absolute favorite prey was cats; he was a notorious cat-chaser. Irene had even spoken with a dog psychologist once. According to him, it wasn't possible to get rid of an inbred hunting instinct; they just had to make sure the dog didn't get loose. That was easier said than done. According to Krister, Sammie could well have been the master-of-escape Houdini's dog: like master, like dog. . . .

The Bernhögs had always had cats. The first one had died of old age a few years ago, and they had immediately replaced him with Felix, who was spoiled, overweight, and infinitely loved.

And now Sammie had killed this cat.

"How . . . how did it happen?" Irene asked weakly.

"We went out for a walk about an hour ago. Sammie was completely calm and well-behaved. Suddenly he yanked on his leash like you wouldn't believe and threw himself into our evergreen hedge, and Felix was sitting inside. I didn't have time to react. It happened in, like, two seconds. Can you believe it? Sammie just shook it a few times and the cat was dead. It didn't even have time to make a sound. Sammie bit him right on the throat and he bled . . . totally gross!"

As a vegan, Jenny was a huge fan of animals; now she looked at her dog accusingly. Sammie didn't seem the slightest bit guilty, but he noticed that the charge in the air was negative and not to his advantage. He did what he usually did in this situation: He quickly headed up the stairs to the second floor and crawled under a bed. He usually stayed there until the storm had blown over.

"Did Baj . . . Mr. Bernhög see Sammie kill Felix?"

"Yes. He was only a few meters away, sweeping outside the gate. When he understood what had happened, he started chasing me and Sammie with his broom, but I ran in here and locked the door. Then he yelled outside that he was going to kill Sammie."

Irene started to get angry. "Did he also swing the broom at you?"

Jenny looked surprised. "Of course. I was holding on to the leash."

Irene didn't bother putting her jacket on when she went out again. She went through the Bernhögs' gate and stepped up to the always freshly painted front door. It was thrown open before she had a chance to ring the doorbell.

"This is going to cost you—" Bernhög started.

Irene interrupted him in an authoritative police voice. "Be quiet! I understand that you're upset that Felix is dead, and I apologize for that, but you are partly to blame. Your cat was running around loose outside, and that always presents a risk. It could have been run over or killed in a fight with other animals. The only way to avoid such risks is to have an indoor cat. My dog was on a leash. It wasn't running and chasing your cat. That Felix wasn't able to keep himself out of Sammie's reach is something neither we nor Sammie can do anything about.

"What is, however, very serious is that you threatened my daughter and chased her with a broom. If this happens again, I'll report you!"

Bernhög did his goldfish imitation again. He looked like he might be about to have a stroke, but at that moment Irene was so angry that she didn't care. His health was supposed to be so bad, yet he was able to chase people and dogs with a broom! After having remained silent and clenching her fists in her pants pockets for so many years, it felt really good to blow off some steam. She stared at him one last time before she turned on her heel and walked back to her house.

SHE HAD overreacted. She had to admit it. At the time, it had felt good to vent many years' worth of pent-up anger, but now the pale ghost of reflection appeared in the innermost corner of her conscience. The poor Bernhögs had, after all, lost their dearly beloved cat. And it was the Huss family's fault. Or, anyway, that of certain members of the family. Irene sent an accusing look in Sammie's direction, but it didn't affect him. He lay under the glass table, snoring loudly and digesting his dinner. Irene had crawled onto the couch with a cup of coffee after dinner. The TV poured out these incessant game shows with the chance of winning millions or nothing at all, but the thought of the dead cat was unavoidable and she paid no attention to the TV.

Jenny had gone off somewhere, and Katarina was expected to be home from her training at any moment. Krister was working late; in the best case, he wouldn't arrive home until after one.

Her thoughts shifted to the Schyttelius case. She was going to try to contact Rebecka the next day, and then she would have to decide when she was going to London. She must not forget to get in touch with Thompson at the Yard. What was the weather like in England this time of year? What should she wear? She couldn't forget her passport. It was new, applied for because of the trip she and Krister were going to take to Greece in August. It would be their first trip abroad since the twins were born. It would be warm and pleasant on Crete. . . .

SHE WOKE with a start. A police car with flashing blue lights was chasing a white van on the TV. The blaring of the police siren had awakened her. Dazed with sleep, she looked at the clock on the VCR; it was almost midnight.

She got up with stiff, creaking limbs and turned off the television. Sammie came jumping up from his place under the glass table and immediately informed her that he needed to go out. There was nothing that could be done about it. He hadn't been out since the cat murder.

Irene put on her jacket and boots with a sigh. The cool night air woke her. It was a clear night with shining stars and a nearly half moon.

They passed the Bernhögs' house on the way back. Through the kitchen window, Irene could see Margit Bernhög sitting at the kitchen table with an untouched glass of milk in front of her, staring out the window with red eyes. It was clear that she had been crying. Irene realized that Margit couldn't see her because of the light over the kitchen table.

Irene felt miserable when she reentered her own house. Sammie ran ahead of her into the bedroom, lay down on the bed, and pretended that he was sound asleep.

Irene peeked into Katarina's room and heard her daughter's steady breathing. The bed in Jenny's room was still empty.

THE WHOLE family slept in on Saturday morning. Just before ten o'clock, Irene awakened because Sammie was licking her right foot, which had ended up outside the cover. He could never resist feet, the sweatier the better.

"Yuck! Dogs are so disgusting!" she hissed at him and slapped him on the nose.

Krister mumbled something unintelligible and turned over. Irene would have to walk the dog. No activity could be heard from the girls' rooms; Irene hadn't expected any.

The sun was shining and it was almost perfectly still. Irene walked down toward Fiskebäck's small boat harbor. Snowdrops and crocuses bloomed in front yards, and Easter lilies were shooting up close to house walls. A slight breeze blew down by the ocean, heavy with the scent of salt and rotten seaweed. Irene filled her lungs and felt revitalized. This was true wealth: having free admission to the ocean.

KATARINA WAS in the process of setting the table and fixing breakfast when Irene came home. As soon as she had taken Sammie's leash off, he rushed into the kitchen to say that a liver paté sandwich or two would be just the thing. One of the other two members of the family was also up; Irene could hear the shower running upstairs.

"Hi, sweetie. Did you see me sleeping on the couch last night when you got home?" Irene asked.

"Couldn't miss it. You were snoring," Katarina replied, smiling teasingly.

"Why didn't you wake me?"

"But hello! I was talking to you, but you were sleeping like you were drugged."

Irene had to admit that she had probably been very tired. She'd had to put in a lot of overtime on the Schyttelius case during the past week. She and Katarina had hardly seen each other for several days; Irene took this opportunity to bring up a ticklish subject.

"Pappa said that you were thinking about participating in a beauty pageant," she mentioned in a casual tone of voice.

Katarina's smile was instantly erased. "Yeah. Fun to try."

"Why?"

"What do you mean 'why'?" Katarina said.

"Why are you competing in a beauty pageant?"

"You get to meet a lot of interesting people and travel. You get to be like an ambassador for your city and a role model for other girls. An anti-smoking role model. And you get twenty-five thousand SEK,* cash. And a chance at a modeling job. It's really well paid."

Irene stared at her in shock. About a year ago, this girl had said that all beauty pageants were degrading. What she was saying now sounded memorized and was not particularly convincing. Irene posed the question again: "Why are you *really* competing?"

Her daughter's face froze in anger but when their eyes met, to her surprise Irene saw that Katarina's were filled with tears.

"To show him that he's wrong," she whispered.

Irene took her in her arms. Unconsciously, she rocked Katarina just as she had done when she was small and had come running to her for comfort.

"'He'? Micke?" she asked.

Katarina nodded and sniffled. They stood like that for a long time.

The sound of the shower upstairs stopped, and Krister could be heard singing in his falsetto bass voice: "*I can't get no da-da-da-da-da-daaa sa-tis-fac-tion, I can't get no bam-bam-bam-bam-bam sa-tis-faction, but I'll try and I'll try and I'll try-haj-aj. . . .*"

---

*One Swedish krona (plural kronor, currency code SEK) equaled 9.8 cents in March 2001.

Irene pushed her daughter a short distance away and made eye contact. Katarina was forced to smile through the tears.

"He always sings Stones songs in the shower," she said.

Mother and daughter burst out laughing. Katarina went to get some tissues to dry her eyes and blow her nose. She stood with her back to Irene. Without turning around, she said in flat voice, "When we . . . Micke broke up, he said I was a fat ugly cow."

"Fat cow! You know that's not true! That's the kind of thing people say when they're upset and angry," Irene said.

Katarina turned around and looked straight at her.

"No. He was ice-cold. Not a damn bit upset."

"That can also be a way of showing your anger."

"He wasn't angry! Just damned mean!"

Irene nodded and tried to calm the tone of the conversation. "Okay. He was mean. But why do you need to start dieting, and compete in—"

"Like I said, to show him that he's wrong!"

"What do you prove by competing in this contest?"

"That I'm beautiful and not some stupid fat cow!"

"You don't prove anything by competing. If you don't get any farther, you'll feel like a failure. But it would almost be worse if you won, because life as a beauty queen isn't the kind of life you really want to live."

"I want to—" Katarina started, but then stopped herself.

"No, you don't. You're good-looking enough, but you're so much more than that. You're athletic and active and do well in school. You have a lot of friends and hobbies and I don't know what all. You're more than enough as it is. You don't need to prove a damn thing to yourself, or to anyone else."

"Who said you're a fat cow?" came a man's voice.

Krister stood in the doorway in the white terry-cloth robe Irene had given him as a Christmas present. Neither Irene nor

Katarina had heard him come down the stairs. His rusty-red hair was sticking out in all directions. Apparently he had dried it with a towel but not taken the time to comb it.

Irene made a frustrated gesture. "Micke. And that's why she's competing in the beauty contest."

Krister nodded. He stroked Katarina's cheek and said, "You are letting yourself be manipulated. We men can be real jerks, and we know exactly what hurts the most. Our society is completely obsessed with appearance, and there's no better way to break a woman than to say that she's ugly."

"How do you break a guy, then?" Katarina asked, gruffly.

"Say with a voice as sweet as honey," Irene volunteered before her husband had a chance to reply, "that he has the world's cutest tiny little dick. And the fact that he's a terrible lover is something he can probably fix, if only he's willing to get help. And then you finish with a beaming smile and add that there's always Viagra."

Both Krister and Katarina started laughing, and Irene's mood improved.

Krister walked over to the stove and poured boiling water through the tea strainer. The coffee had already finished percolating. He opened the refrigerator.

"Anyone else want an egg?" he asked. Without waiting for an answer, he put four eggs in a pot, filled it with water, and turned on the burner. Then he said to Katarina, "For once, I think you really should listen to your mother. As I said, men can be real jerks; but as you just saw, women can be, too. It usually evens out in the end."

Katarina opened her mouth to reply, but quickly closed it. She scrutinized her parents, and then said, "Okay. Can we eat breakfast without discussing this any more?"

Her parents nodded and exchanged a look of agreement.

IRENE PHONED Rebecka Schyttelius after they had finished their weekly marketing at Frölunda Torg. The phone rang several times, and she was about to hang up when a man's voice answered, in English. "Yes?"

Irene was nervous about having to speak English over the phone. Hesitantly, she said, in her stilted English, "Excuse me. I'm looking for Rebecka Schyttelius, but maybe I have the wrong number?"

The man laughed softly. "Not at all. This is Rebecka's number, but she's not home right now. Who am I speaking with?"

At first Irene couldn't remember what her title was in English. When she had finally managed to introduce herself, there was another moment of silence on the line before the man replied, "I understand. Another police officer from Göteborg called for her a few days ago. . . . She's been taken to the hospital again. The shock she received was terrible, and it's only been a short while since she found out . . . the horrific news. But I've spoken with her doctor, and he says that she might be allowed to come home on Monday."

Irene thought for a moment before she asked, "May I ask who you are?"

"Christian Lefévre. Rebecka works for my company."

"The computer company?"

"Yes."

And what are you doing in Rebecka's apartment? Irene was about to ask, but she refrained. Maybe it would be best to ask Rebecka first. She also noted the man's French name, but it seemed to her that he spoke English without an accent.

"Could you tell Rebecka that I called?"

"Of course."

Irene gave him her numbers: work, home, and cell. Then she hung up.

THEY HAD purchased a lot of good food and were preparing for a cozy evening. Krister was actually scheduled to work this weekend; but his colleague, Lenny, needed the following weekend off, so they had traded.

Jenny had disappeared early that afternoon to rehearse with her band. Before the front door closed behind her, she had informed them that she was staying at Martin's.

"Who's Martin?" Irene had called after her but only got the echo of her own question in reply.

Katarina shrugged when she was asked that question a little while later.

"Don't know. They've been seeing each other for a while. I think he's a musician."

It was a guess that Irene could have made herself.

Irene dialed Jenny's cell number and demanded to be told Martin's full name, address, and telephone number. It was a condition for spending the night somewhere. The alternative was to be collected by the police; in plain words, by a detective inspector: in even plainer words, Mom. Irene reacted when she heard the address. Apartments in that neighborhood were not cheap. It seemed Martin was a boy with rich parents.

Katarina left for a classmate's who was having a party. Aside from the clattering of the pots and pans and other kitchen utensils that the master chef used when he created, the peace of the weekend fell over the family home. Irene took Sammie out on an evening walk so she wouldn't be in the way. When she returned, she would set the table. Maybe Krister would, mercifully, let her fix the salad. She didn't complain about this arrangement, since she was a terrible cook. Before she met Krister, she had never learned how and after they had moved in together, she had never needed to.

It was almost eight o'clock and her hunger was sharp. In her imagination, she could already see the scrumptious dishes Krister was preparing. Since they had been together when he had bought the ingredients, she knew what was on the menu. The appetizer was going to be baked goat cheese encrusted in honey, served on a bed of basil on a slice of bread. The main course was grilled cod, vegetables in wine sauce stir-fried in a wok, and home-fried potatoes. The dessert was Irene's favorite: chocolate mousse. Not exactly food for weight-watchers, but incredibly good. The wine was from South Africa and was called, oddly enough, Something Else. Intriguing, because they hadn't had it before.

Reluctantly, she peered in through the Bernhögs' kitchen window when she passed by. Mr. and Mrs. Bernhög were sitting at their kitchen table, with the lamp over the table lit. No candlelight dinner in there, Irene thought. The next second, she saw Margit Bernhög take a handkerchief and dry her eyes. Her husband didn't look at her. He raised his spoon mechanically, up and down. An open can of Bong's meat soup stood on the kitchen counter behind them.

All her joy and anticipation left her. The Bernhögs were so sad over Felix's death that they didn't even have the energy to cook dinner on Saturday night. Because Sammie was strutting around, carefree, on his end of the leash, she, on the other end, was the one who had to bear the feelings of guilt.

She decided not to say anything to Krister, in order not to disrupt the mood at their dinner table. Naturally, though, he immediately noticed that something was bothering her; and before they had finished the appetizer, she told him what she had seen through the Bernhögs' window.

"They are really grieving for their cat," she finished.

Krister nodded. "Seems so. We'll just have to get them a new one."

Irene felt a little twinge of hope. "Do you know anyone who has a cat they want to get rid of? Or kittens?"

"No. But we'll have to explore the options. Maybe someone at work knows some cat people."

Irene's mood began to improve. They would get a new cat for the Bernhögs!

"Sweetheart," Krister said, "this wine is far too light and dry. Shall I go to the wine cellar and get a Drosty-Hof instead?"

Irene thought the wine they had had was good, but Krister was the expert; if he said they should drink the other wine, then it would probably be better.

Krister went to the laundry room and opened the top cabinet of the closet next to the drying cabinet. An almost-empty bottle of Famous Grouse was there, along with two bottles of Drosty-Hof white wine and a small Bristol cream purchased on their last short vacation to Skagen because the blue bottle looked so nice.

DURING JU-JITSU training on Sunday, Irene gave it everything she had. She felt her heart pounding, and a great feeling of well-being streamed through her whole body. She rarely had the chance to attend more than one training session a week these days, and it was far too little.

The female officers she taught were getting to be really good. They would be tested next month. The two beginners were going for orange belts, four would be promoted to green, and three to blue. Irene felt satisfied. But they needed to schedule some extra sessions, which wasn't easy. Most of them already worked out at least once a week with their male colleagues, but they needed to do some intensive training before being promoted. And in the midst of all this, Irene was going to England. A maximum of two days in London was all she could afford, she decided.

WHEN IRENE left the dojo, she drove down Guldheden to pick up her mother, Gerd. Krister thought it was just as well to invite his mother-in-law over for Sunday dinner this weekend, since he was going to be working the next three weekends in a row. It matched Gerd's desires perfectly. Her significant other, Sture, was in Denmark with his poker group.

"I was actually at Pappa's grave yesterday," she announced when they drove past Sahlgren Hospital. Irene's father had died there at The Jubileum Clinic almost ten years ago. The cancer had moved quickly, and he died after only two weeks in the hospital.

"I want to be buried with him and I also want to be cremated," Gerd continued.

Irene cast a glance at her. She asked uncertainly, "Why are you talking about this now? Are you feeling sick?"

"Not at all. My health is superb. I just wanted you to know in case it goes quickly. At my age, it can strike like lightning. You know Stina and Bertil Karlsson in the building next door. . . ."

Irene nodded. She had been friends with their youngest daughter.

"He died on Friday. Heart attack. On the spot! And he's three years younger than me."

So that's why Mamma Gerd was bringing this up. And if Irene thought that what she had heard so far was enough, she was wrong, as Gerd continued, "And I want them to sing 'Day by Day' and 'The Beggar from Luossa.'"

"'The Beggar from Luossa.' But that's not a hymn!"

"No. But it's my favorite song, and it's the one I want. And it would be great if someone could play the trumpet. That part that Arne Lambert usually plays. You know the one. '. . . home to Ukraine's dark blue sky where the scent of. . . .'"

When her mother sang the short verse, Irene recognized it.

"Doesn't it go something like '...hm-hm the little bell rings'?"

"No idea. But I want that one."

Irene nodded in response. She didn't like the way this conversation was going. Even if she didn't have time to visit her mother very often, they both knew that they meant a lot to each other. Her mother had helped out when the twins were small and Irene was working. There weren't any part-time jobs for crime inspectors. And if Krister hadn't reduced his hours to part-time and Mamma Gerd hadn't helped out after preschool, Irene would never have been able to become an inspector.

BOTH KATARINA and Jenny were home. They were both very fond of their grandmother. Maybe it was because they rarely saw Krister's parents, who lived so far away in Säffle. That and the fact that their paternal grandparents were over eighty, and had five children and eleven grandchildren. Gerd only had Jenny and Katarina, because Irene was an only child.

Krister had fixed a spring-theme dinner. The meal started with steamed fresh asparagus served with whipped butter. For the main course, he'd prepared pan-fried chicken with a rosemary sauce, and duchess potatoes. Jenny ate fried mushrooms instead of the chicken. Jenny had made the dessert, a gooey chocolate cake with whipped cream. It was something of a specialty for her, even though she didn't eat whipped cream. (Of course the butter in the recipe had been replaced with vegetable margarine.) Jenny had inherited some of Krister's interest in cooking. Katarina was like her mother: You ate to survive. If it tasted good, that was wonderful; otherwise it would just have to do, as long as you didn't have to fix it yourself.

A little while after dinner, the phone rang. Jenny was the closest and answered. She gave the cordless phone to Irene, whispering, "It's a guy who speaks English. He wants to talk to you."

"If he speaks English, then you don't need to whisper. He won't understand anyway," Katarina remarked.

Irene took the receiver and went into the hall to escape the twins' fussing.

"Irene Huss here."

"This is Christian Lefévre. We spoke earlier today."

"I remember."

"Rebecka asked me to call. She doesn't feel well and hasn't the strength to talk about . . . what has happened."

"She won't speak with me at all?"

"No."

Irene thought feverishly. Finally, she said, firmly, "She has to. We think she can help us with our investigation."

"She says that she doesn't know anything."

"She probably does. Maybe it doesn't seem important to her,

but we've gotten a lot of information and we know that she can help us," Irene said, trying to sound more certain than she felt.

Christian Lefévre asked, "What have you found out that makes you think Rebecka knows something?"

The question surprised her, but she pulled herself together quickly. "I can't tell you that."

It was quiet on the other end of the phone. Then Lefévre cleared his throat. "Her doctor says that she needs to rest. She mustn't get more upset. I didn't know her family, but I know Rebecka and I care about her a great deal."

"Is that why you were in her apartment?"

"Her apartment? It's just as much mine."

"So you live together?"

"No. But almost," he answered shortly.

It was a strange answer. In Irene's opinion, either you live together or you don't. In a tone just as curt as his, she said, "You can tell Rebecka that I'm coming in a few days. I'll be in touch with her and Inspector Thompson before I arrive."

He hung up on her.

Chapter 10

"Let's start with Jacob Schyttelius. Thirty-one years old. Found in a cottage, shot: one round to the chest and one through the head. No weapon was found near the body, but the technical investigation of the bullets shows that he was shot with the same weapon as his parents. The first bullet's point of entry was a few centimeters above the heart, at an angle toward the breastbone. The bullet tore the aorta and became lodged in the spine. No carbon or gunpowder residue was found around the point of entry. The other shot went through the head. The point of entry was between the eyes, just above the bridge of the nose. The remaining portions of the face were covered with large quantities of carbon and gunpowder residue. The whole back of the head was blown away."

That's where Superintendent Andersson stopped his reading of the preliminary autopsy report, which he had received that morning. He peered over the edge of his cheap reading glasses. "There's a lot of stuff here about which parts of the brain were damaged, but I'll skip that. The end result is that the brain was destroyed."

He cleared his throat and continued reading aloud. "The bullet was retrieved from the floor. Each of the gunshot wounds would have been fatal. The victim would have become unconscious and died immediately. At the time of examination, rigor mortis was fully developed. Body temperature indicated that Schyttelius had been dead for about sixteen hours, which means he died around eleven o'clock on Monday night, with a window of an hour before and an hour after."

The superintendent looked up from the paper again.

"We know that he worked out at the gym until ten thirty. Then it took a little time for him to take a sauna and shower. We don't know exactly when he left the gym. The murder most likely occurred between eleven and twelve. We can't get closer than that yet."

He looked down at the paper to find his place.

"The toxicology tests were negative. The absence of a weapon, the appearance of the crime scene, and the victim's injuries make it clear that Jacob Schyttelius was murdered."

Andersson put the paper on the table in front of him and looked at his inspectors gathered there on this Monday morning. Everyone in the division was present except for Jonny, who had called in sick during the morning.

"Any comments?"

"The murderer was cold-blooded. Despite the fact that the shot to the heart hit home, the perpetrator walked up and fired a shot through the head, which would without a doubt be fatal, while the victim was lying on the floor. An unnecessary assault," said Tommy.

The others nodded in agreement. The superintendent also nodded before he read the two other reports.

"Sten Schyttelius. Sixty-four years old. Found dead in his bed. Shot in the head with one round. The point of entry was calculated as being just above the bridge of the nose. The remainder of the face was heavily covered with carbon and gunpowder residue. The weapon was fired from a distance of just a few centimeters. The bullet was retrieved from the floor under the bed."

Andersson looked up again.

"The head injuries of all three victims were the same, so I'll continue reading. Death was most likely instantaneous. Rigor mortis and their body temperature pinpoints the time of death at some eighteen hours before the victims were found, about one o'clock on Tuesday morning. The toxicology tests show that

Sten Schyttelius had been drinking alcohol. His blood alcohol level was one point one. Elsa had high levels of nitrazepam and citalopram in her system, and the pathologist writes in parentheses that these are sleeping pills and anti-depressants. In Sten's case, the bullet's trajectory was slightly to the left. Elsa's bullet veered more strongly to the left. Based on this, the pathologist determines that the murderer stood next to Sten Schyttelius's side of the bed during both shots and that he's right-handed. Comments?"

It was quiet for a few seconds before Irene asked permission to speak.

"The murderer sneaked into the bedroom after Sten Schyttelius fell asleep. He was probably sleeping quite heavily, based on his blood alcohol level. Elsa was also probably already asleep, because she was filled with sleeping pills. That's why he shot Sten, then Elsa. What strikes me is that Elsa was also shot from a distance of only a few centimeters. He must have placed one knee on the bed and leaned over Sten in order to get so close to Elsa.

"Two shots hit Jacob, and one definitely fatal shot each for Sten and Elsa. Perhaps he didn't want to fire more often so as not to risk being heard. One or two shots may pass as a backfire, but three or four will arouse suspicions," Irene continued.

"The fact is that no one heard any shots at all. It was after midnight when they were shot," Fredrik pointed out. "The rectory is in a remote location. The neighbors who might have heard something were probably in bed asleep."

"We also have no reports of suspicious cars near the rectory. In such a small place as Kullahult, people should have noticed if an unfamiliar car showed up during the evening or night," the superintendent said gruffly.

"But we have the car in the woods near Norssjön. And the technicians have confirmed that the woolen threads we found come from the same piece of clothing. Of course, we don't know for sure that the clothing belongs to the murderer, but in any case someone walked between the clearing and the beach below the cottage," said Irene.

Suddenly Andersson left the room. The others looked at each other in surprise. Since the door was open, they could hear him rummaging around in his office, mumbling, most likely swearing. He came back after about a minute, red in the face but with a triumphant smile. In one hand, he held a set of maps of Göteborg and surrounding areas.

"I found it. It's more detailed than the road map," he said while he was flipping through the pages to find the ones covering Kullahult and Norssjön.

"I thought about Fredrik and Irene's walk from the position of the car in the woods to Schyttelius's cottage, and then something struck me. If you drive on the roads, then it's at least six kilometers between the cottage and the rectory. Let me check. . . ."

With a lot of puffing and mumbling, Andersson measured the distance on the map and tried to transform the map's scale into kilometers.

"Twelve kilometers, round trip. Plus two hundred additional meters to the suspicious car in the woods," he determined finally.

He tore out the page for the Norssjön area and placed it next to the map of Kullahult. He placed his fat index finger where the cottage was located and said, "But if the murderer went to Norssjön and then *walked* straight through the woods, the distance would be considerably shorter. Let's see. . . ."

New grunting and measurements revealed that it was four and a half kilometers between the crime scenes, if one took the path through the woods.

"Add two hundred meters to reach the car. A total of nine point two kilometers back and forth. It's not impossible to walk it," said the superintendent.

"But terribly difficult! We were pretty tired after trudging those two hundred meters through the woods," Irene objected.

"But we had on the wrong kind of shoes," Fredrik said. "If this guy is used to being in the woods and had the right gear, then it wouldn't be a problem."

"But it must have been pitch-black in the woods if the murderer set out right after killing Jacob. He'd have to be careful not to break his ankle or get lost. But he might have felt safe if he used a flashlight," Tommy added thoughtfully.

"The murderer seems to be very much at home. He knew where the keys were to the front doors and to the computer room at the rectory, and where the gun cabinet was. He knew of the small hiding place behind the panel in the cottage. And maybe he went through the woods between the cottage and the rectory. What strikes me is the degree of his local knowledge," Irene concluded.

Fredrik glanced at Irene. "We never continued farther than the cottage. Maybe there's a path or a trail there that we missed. Maybe we should go out and look again . . . ?"

"You can go out in the woods and look around," Irene said. "I'm going to see Eva Möller."

She really didn't want to have him accompany her. At the same time, she wondered if she was crazy to take an airhead like Eva seriously. But she couldn't get the cantor's last words out of her head: "Together we can find out Sten's hidden secrets. . . ."

Irene called Eva Möller, and they arranged to meet at Eva's place after two o'clock. That gave Irene a few hours to spend on the files and to write her report. As luck would have it, Tommy came storming in and insisted that she listen to the latest news about the Speedy murder.

"Everything changed when I had the idea of talking to Asko Pihlainen's neighbor across the street, an eighty-year-old woman named Gertrud Ritzman. She has serious heart problems and doesn't have much time left, she says. But her mind is clear as a bell. She was the one who came up with the idea that we should film her testimony, in case she gets worse or dies before the trial.

"When I asked her about the morning in question, when Asko and his neighbors, Mr. and Mrs. Wisköö, claim they were playing cards, she said right away that it wasn't true. She doesn't sleep well and often gets up during the night. She remembered this particular morning really well. At about five thirty in the morning, Wisköö's car pulled up outside Pihlainen's shack, and Asko jumped out almost before the car stopped. He rushed into his place as Paul Wisköö drove the car into his carport. Neither Asko nor Paul Wisköö were playing cards with their wives at around five a.m.

"I did some research on Paul Wisköö, by the way, and, as you've probably already guessed, it's a fake name. Guess what good old Neighbor Paul's real name is?"

"No idea."

"Paul Larson, alias Pepsi!"

Irene thought she recognized the name, but it took a few seconds before she was sure. She exclaimed, "Clark Bertilsson's old buddy! Well, I'll be damned. His resumé must be as long as the road between Kungsbacka and here. If he's involved, then it's definitely about narcotics. Lots of drugs."

"Bingo. He's served time for narcotics violations and bank robbery at various times. And a few years ago, Asko and Pepsi were in the same jail. They hit it off and became friends. They even live next door to each other."

"And they have quite a bit of money. They live in huge new houses near the ocean outside Kungsbacka. Officially, what do they do?"

"Cars. They work at a company which only sells luxury cars, both new and used."

"Is there a lot of money to be made from used luxury cars?"

"Let's put it this way: Rather a used Porsche than no Porsche at all."

"Good point. So, is there suspicion that their income is too big for the car business?"

"Yep. And both Pepsi and Asko have served time for narcotics violations and assault. My thinking is that these guys took a contract on Speedy. Rumor has it that Speedy embezzled money from his distributors. Because Speedy was a big dealer, it must have been a lot of money. The boss decided to get rid of Speedy, to make an example."

"Do you have any idea who the head guy is?"

"Not a clue. The idea is that we begin by investigating Pepsi and Asko. It will be a difficult job to map out the circles these guys move in, but we'll run this investigation together with Narcotics. They've been doing surveillance on the importing of luxury cars to Sweden. There is clear suspicion that the drugs are being smuggled in via the cars. Welded into beams and the like."

"Have they found anything?"

"A Jag which seems to have no owner. It's registered in a fake name and still parked in the garage. Of course, no one is stupid enough to inquire about a car that held five kilos of heroin and twice as much cocaine."

"You'll be very busy now," she realized.

"Yup. You'll have to go to London by yourself. But you have to promise not to do any investigating on your own. We haven't really recovered from your last trip abroad."

It was meant as a joke and Tommy smiled, but for the life of her Irene couldn't join him. The events in Copenhagen more than year ago were still far too traumatic.

IRENE TOOK several wrong turns, even though it had only been a few days since she and Fredrik had located Eva Möller's isolated cottage. It wasn't until she saw the ruined split oak that she was certain she was on the right road. The sun had hidden itself behind a thick layer of clouds during her entire trip from Göteborg, but it broke through just as she pulled up next to Eva Möller's red car and turned off the engine. It warmed and illuminated the property, and Irene had an easier time understanding why someone would want to live like the cantor. The view took her breath away just as it had the first time. Everyone who visited Eva must do the same thing: stop to admire the fantastic view.

When Irene turned her gaze from the valley and the distant blue sky, she saw Eva standing in the doorway. She waved in welcome, and Irene walked over to her.

"I'm so happy that you wanted to visit! Come in," Eva said, and she sounded as if she meant it.

Irene stepped into the cozy kitchen and began to unbutton her coat, but Eva said, "Keep your coat on. We'll go outside, since it's so warm and comfortable near the house. You can help me carry things." Without waiting for an answer, she gave Irene the iron pot and the glass staff from the shelf above the stove. She herself took a wooden box whose contents Irene couldn't see, since it was covered with a blue cloth. Irene, puzzled, followed in her wake. What had she gotten herself into? Now it was too late to back out.

Eva walked up to the western wall of the house, where the sun was broiling hot. She set the box down and spread a well-ironed blue cloth over the table. She pointed at two white plastic chairs, one on either side of the table.

"Let's sit and talk first. Put the things down in the meantime."

Irene did as she was told and sat on one of the cushionless chairs, which felt cold even through her jeans. Eva gracefully sank into the other chair. The dark-blue dress she was wearing was much more dramatic than the ethereal light-blue one she had worn on Irene's first visit. It had long slits in the straight sleeves, and the dress itself was of a narrower cut. The V-neck was deep and revealed her cleavage, where a small silver bell hung. Over the dress, Eva wore a vest made of thin black yarn. It was ankle-length, made of extremely small crocheted stars sewn together.

"I know that you think what we're going to do seems crazy, but it's really very simple magic," Eva started.

Irene didn't reply, because she didn't know what to say.

"Regular magic is something that anyone can perform, but what we're going to do requires much, much more. We're going to try to uncover the deepest secrets of a dead person. It's possible that it won't work, but it's worth a try."

Eva smiled, and her eyes shone with excitement. The sun gleamed on her loose hair, and she looked completely enchanting. Definitely not like the witch she must see herself as. Eva's little speech about magic had opened Irene's eyes; now she wasn't afraid, just curious.

"First we need to create a sacred room, and we couldn't wish for a better room than Mother Earth's sacred temple."

Eva threw her hands out and made a sweeping gesture, encompassing the nature surrounding them. Irene had to agree that it was very pretty, now that the trees and bushes around Eva's house were turning light green. It was warm near the wall of the house, and an early bumblebee buzzed lazily under the overhang of the roof in its attempt to find a good place to live. Irene felt relaxed. Suddenly, a picture of the mangled cat Felix popped up in her mind. It was strange, because she hadn't actually seen the dead cat. She must have made a gesture of aversion, and Eva noticed it.

"Something is weighing on you. Tell me, and you'll be rid of it. If you allow it to remain with you, it will affect your meditation and will weaken us. And we need all the energy we can get," she said.

To her own surprise, Irene explained how Sammie had killed Felix, and described their neighbors' terrible grief. She revealed that she wanted to give the Bernhögs a new cat. Eva stared at her for a moment, then rose and disappeared into the house.

After a few minutes, she came back and, with a sunny smile,

said, "It's been taken care of. We can pick up the kitten when you're ready to go home."

Irene was uncomfortable for a moment. Then she felt as if a knot in her stomach had loosened. She hadn't been aware that it was there, but now that it was gone she felt free. It was easier to breathe. Irene inhaled deeply and, half unaware, noted that she was already ready for *Mukuso*—meditation.

"I have a ring of silicon stones here," Eva said. "When we've entered the circle—the holy room—we must not leave it until we've finished everything we're going to do. It would weaken the power."

Irene nodded.

"Good. I'll put the table inside the ring, so that we'll have an altar."

Eva lifted the table, carried it a few meters away, and set it down again. She straightened the cloth and backed up a few steps, as if to make sure the altar looked neat. When Irene stood, she saw a ring of small white stones lying in the thin grass. A large flat-topped stone lay inside the ring.

"I'll lift my tools, explain to you what they are, and bring them inside the circle. If you know what they are and you understand what their purpose is, your concentration won't be affected later on."

Eva bent and took the glass staff from the grass. She held it up toward the sun. Blinding flashes of light were refracted from the top.

"This, of course, is my magic staff. It represents fire. Fire stands for passion and will, change, cleansing, and sexuality. It belongs to the sun."

She carefully set the staff on the table. Now she took up the double-edged knives. The sharpened blades gleamed in the sun. She held up the largest of the knives. "This is my athame. It is the tool of air. It cannot be used to hurt living creatures, but it is a sharpened weapon. You direct and move energy with it. When I cut herbs, I use this old knife with a bone handle, which is also very sharp. Never my athame."

Eva turned around and floated over to the table. When she came back, she took out an object wrapped in a shiny yellow silk fabric. The cloth package held the beautiful glass goblet that Irene had seen on the shelf in the kitchen.

"My goblet. Symbol of the water's power and of the cardinal direction west. That's why I've chosen to be by the western wall of the house. The goblet is going to help us see."

With her other hand, she raised the small three-legged iron kettle into the air.

"The kettle is the tool of the spirit and doesn't represent any element. It will take us to eternity and give us the presence of God. It will deepen our trance."

Irene's former feeling that the cantor was more than a bit weird returned; but at the same time, she had to admit that she was fascinated. Eva *really* believed that she could work magic.

Eva held up a juice-box of black currant juice, a small plate of Marie biscuits, and the glass paperweight with the pentagram that Irene had seen on her prior visit.

"The pentagram is the tool of the earth, the symbol of all earthly life. It is very strong. That's why the Satanists are so willing to use it."

She walked over to her altar and motioned for Irene to follow. Irene was uneasy, but she decided to pursue this to the bitter end. The possibility existed that Eva knew something about Sten Schyttelius, something that she was planning to reveal during her hocus-pocus. What one wouldn't do to learn the truth. . . . Irene grimaced and then stepped resolutely into the ring.

Eva looked at her and started humming a wordless melody. It was a beautiful melody, and Irene again felt at peace. Sometimes Eva rang the silver bell she had around her neck. The soft sound was more of a sensation, but its presence added to the elevated feeling that was growing inside Irene. Humming, Eva walked up to the table and raised the glass staff. She slowly began to walk clockwise inside the circle of pebbles, holding the point of the staff down toward the stones. When she had completed one circuit, she stopped and raised the staff. A sharp beam of light shot out of its point and caught Irene in the eyes. She closed them involuntarily and sank to the ground.

When she opened her eyes again, she saw that Eva had traded the glass staff for the largest of the double-edged knives, the one she had called the athame. Eva stood with her arms outstretched, her face turned toward the house. She made a quarter turn and stood in the same position facing the woods. After another turn to the west, Irene understood that she was greeting the cardinal directions. Her soft humming could be heard the whole time, and sometimes Irene could make out single words. Suddenly, Eva stopped and turned her face toward the sun. Loud and clear, she said, "Mother Earth. Through the four elements and their four cardinal directions which exist within us and raise our spirit, I invoke you. Blessed be you and welcome."

It became completely still. The light spring breeze died away. The heat increased, and it felt pleasant against Irene's half-closed eyelids.

Eva pulled the plastic stopper out of the juice box and poured the dark-red drink into the glass goblet. She took a photo from the bottom of the kettle and placed it on the table. She turned toward Irene and whispered, humming, "Now we're going to become immersed in a trance. A picture of Sten is on the table, one I cut out of a newspaper. We're going to focus on Sten and ask the Goddess to help us. Hopefully, we'll find out his deepest secret."

She turned toward the altar again, placed the newspaper clipping in the middle of the table, and placed the goblet with its shimmering ruby drink on top. With her hands raised, she sang a short invocation, before she gripped the athame with both her hands and pressed the blade against her forehead. With eyes closed, she stood still and let her consciousness sink inward.

Irene had never before experienced going into Mukuso so quickly. A pleasant warmth and peace spread through her body and she felt as light as a feather. Wonderful soap bubbles in shimmering colors floated through her thoughts, and she was pulled toward The Light. When she was almost there, she tried to focus on Sten Schyttelius.

The change came gradually; at first she didn't notice anything. After a while, she realized that she was on her way away from The Light. She became aware that she was freezing and tried to pull her jacket tighter around her. But it wasn't possible, since she was so deep in the trance. Her limbs were heavy, and she couldn't will them to move. A dark mist began to conceal The Light. She heard a voice that said, "*Keikoku! Mate!*," terms from Japanese combat sports, warning her to stop. She felt endangered. She had to break out of her trance. Something was going terribly wrong.

With an enormous effort of will, she came out of the trance and started working her way up toward consciousness. She finally managed to open her eyes and focused on Eva at the altar.

Everything happened very fast. Afterward, she wasn't sure what she had really seen. Maybe she had still been in the trance.

The sun had gone behind the clouds and the wind had picked up considerably. Eva was staring into the goblet, her eyes wide in terror. Only a moaning sound came from her. As Irene gazed at her, Eva was lifted about a few inches above the ground and then hurled backward in the direction of the house. Her head hit the stone base of the house with a dull thud and she lay there, unmoving.

Irene was wide awake at once and on her feet before she was even aware of it. She rushed over to Eva and felt her pulse. It was strong and regular, and her breathing seemed normal. Relieved,

Irene observed Eva's eyelids twitch. When she opened them a moment later, her gaze was disoriented.

"What . . . what happened?" she asked.

Before Irene had time to answer, Eva screamed, "It was Satan himself!"

Irene put her hand on Eva's forehead and told her to lie still and calm down. Perhaps Eva had suffered a concussion. She carefully felt the back of Eva's head. A large bump was starting to swell. Eva tried to get up, but Irene had to help her because she began to shake violently. Irene supported her up the stairs and into the small living room behind the kitchen. Eva lay down on the comfortable-looking sofa.

Irene gazed around the room. It looked ordinary, filled with a mixture of old and new furniture. Nothing showed that a witch lived here, although the tarot cards on the coffee table and the crystals on the windowsill might cause some suspicion.

"I'll bring the things inside. It looks like it could start raining at any moment," said Irene.

Eva nodded and closed her eyes as if she were very tired.

When Irene came in with the box, Eva was sitting up on the sofa. She looked out through the window, where the first drops of rain had started slapping against the pane. She asked, "What happened? I remember that I saw a face in the goblet and I became terribly afraid but . . . then everything went black. But I remember the feeling of strong evil."

She tore her gaze from the window and looked at Irene. To her vexation, Irene could hear herself stammer when she started to explain. "I . . . I was also in a deep trance . . . it's possible that I wasn't completely awake. . . ." Irene tried to explain what she had seen. A trace of her former assurance glimmered in Eva's violet blue eyes, and she said, almost mockingly, "You don't want to believe in what you saw. It doesn't matter. We managed to find out something very important."

"What?"

"There was a place of darkness in Sten. And it was evil."

Eva carefully felt the bump at the back of her head. "Do you think you could bring me a cold glass bottle or jar from the fridge? I need to ice this bump."

Irene went into the kitchen and took a bottle of Ramlösa from the refrigerator. When she gave it to Eva, she asked, "What do you mean?"

"Wherever Sten may be now, he isn't wandering around in heavenly pastures!" Eva remarked.

"Do you mean that he's in hell?"

"No. There's no place called hell. Do you know what hell is?" Eva looked at her with a steady gaze.

"No."

"That everything is too late. You cannot change anything or make anything better. The person you have been during your life is also the person you will be after death. Nothing that you have said or done can be changed, and that will affect all of the people you have met and everyone who has been close to you long after your death. For generations, centuries . . . yes, maybe for eternity. All religions want to offer you peace, and salvation from your sins, at least after death. The truth is that there can be no salvation from yourself."

It took a while before the true meaning of the cantor's words sank in. Eva placed the bottle on the coffee table.

"Now we're going to go and pick up the kitty."

IRENE DROVE along the wet, bumpy gravel roads as Eva directed her. Good friends of Eva's had a cat that had been on the prowl unusually early this spring. The kittens were still maybe a bit too small to be separated from their mother, but they were pretty much weaned. Since its new family was familiar with cats, this wouldn't be a major problem.

"That's where they live," Eva said, pointing at a small farm.

Irene turned into in at the driveway and sent a sympathetic thought to her shock absorbers. She parked on the gravel drive, and Eva jumped out without asking if she wanting to come inside.

Everything looked very neat at this little farm. The main house itself was white stucco, in contrast to the well-kept Falured wooden outbuildings and the barn. All the flowerbeds around the house were newly dug up and ready for planting.

After a while, Eva came running through the rain. She was carrying a box in her arms. Irene opened the door for her so that she could jump inside. When she had the shoe box in her lap, Irene saw that Ecco was written on the lid, in which air holes had been punched. Eva carefully lifted it a crack and whispered, "Isn't she cute? Her name is Felicia. Remember to tell the new family that they absolutely can't change her name."

Irene glimpsed a small, light apricot-colored ball of fur wrapped in a piece of terry cloth.

"Felicia," she said aloud so that she wouldn't forget.

FELICIA SLEPT in her box the whole way home to the row-house area. The rain stopped just as Irene turned in on Fiskebäcksvägen. The setting sun managed to peer out from under the banks of clouds and tinged their underbellies a glimmering golden red. It was a magnificent display of colors.

When Irene had parked the car, she walked directly to the Bernhögs' door and rang the bell. Margit Bernhög opened the door a crack after the second ring. Irene tried to sound untroubled as she recited the litany she had practiced in the car.

"Hi, Margit. I was wondering if you would like to take care of little Felicia here. A friend of mine asked me to find her a new home with a cat lover. Otherwise they'll have to put her to sleep, and that would be terribly sad."

Margit Bernhög jerked at the last sentence and looked wide-eyed at Irene. Reluctantly, she lowered her eyes to the box. Irene lifted the lid and held the box out to her. At just that moment, Felicia woke up. She stretched her little fuzzy body and yawned so that her cute light-pink tongue stretched out. Margit carefully lifted up the sleepy kitten and gently burrowed her nose into her soft fur.

"So cute . . . little Felicia . . . thank you," she stammered without looking at Irene.

She was totally absorbed in the apricot-colored furball. Then Felicia turned her head and met Irene's eyes with her round violet-blue ones.

Chapter 11

"THAT'S A HELL OF a lot of drivel about Rebecka's nerves!" Superintendent Andersson bellowed. He wasn't at all pleased about the cancellation of Irene's trip to London. "That Frog seems to be determined to delay her questioning," he concluded angrily.

He marched around his office, upset, with strides as long as his short legs would allow. Irene sat in his visitor's chair, waiting for the storm to blow over. Andersson stopped in front of his window and pretended to contemplate the view over Ernst Fontell's Place through the thick layer of dirt. He took a few deep breaths and turned toward Irene again.

"I understand that she had a shock, and a serious one, when she got the news. That's not surprising. But we need to speak with her in person. It's a matter of her own safety! We don't have the faintest idea about a motive. All we have are those damn Satanic stars."

Irene was just about to correct him and start explaining what the pentagram stood for, but she came to her senses at the last moment. She would never be able to explain what had happened at Eva Möller's. Truth be told, she still wasn't sure herself.

The superintendent didn't pay any particular attention to her silence. He continued, "Can she come to Sweden and the funeral without taking a risk, or do we need to protect her? We don't know a damn thing! She must have some clue as to motive!"

Irene nodded and jumped in. "I agree with you. I'll call Glen Thompson again and see what he has to say."

"SHE SAYS she isn't up to talking. I tried to speak with her, but she burst into tears."

Inspector Glen Thompson had a deep voice. Irene tried to imagine what he looked like.

"I understand that you're starting to feel pressured. As you said, you need a motive. . . . Is this tale of Satanic symbols true? There was something in our papers about it. . . . Your murders are spectacular, even by English standards."

"Yes. Symbols were painted on two computer screens with the victims' blood."

"So what the newspapers wrote was true. The last time I met with Rebecka, I asked her if there had been any threats against the family from Satanists, but she just shook her head. Then she began crying. She's very difficult to interview."

"Naturally, the shock was tremendous—" Irene started, but he interrupted her.

"True, but she wasn't well before, either. Psychologically speaking."

"She wasn't?"

"No. Dr. Fischer says that he has been treating her for depression since last September."

Then Rebecka had had psychological problems before the murders. Her brother had been on sick leave during the fall for psychological problems after his divorce. That is to say, everyone *assumed* it was after the divorce. Was there a completely different reason? Her thoughts were interrupted by Thompson's voice. "Maybe as a fellow Swede, you'll have an easier time speaking with her."

"I'll have to make an attempt soon. We're at a complete standstill in our investigation, since we have no motive. We still don't know if Rebecka's life is also in danger."

"She denies that there were any threats, but that may not be true. I have a very strong feeling that she's hiding something. It's only a hunch, but it's there."

"Rebecka is like her father"; "Sten's hidden depths"; Eva Möller's words popped into Irene's memory.

"I need a few days to prepare Rebecka and Dr. Fischer," Thompson continued. "She needs to understand that she'll be forced to speak with you. If worse comes to worst, we'll question her in the hospital."

"I'm very grateful for your cooperation," Irene said, and meant it.

"No problem. Let's see . . . today is Tuesday. If you come on Thursday and stay one night, then we have two days to work in. That should be enough."

She was stung by a feeling of disappointment. She would have loved to stay longer, but then this wasn't a vacation.

"My sister runs a pleasant little hotel in Bayswater. I'll make a reservation for you there for Thursday night. Call me when you've booked your flight, and I'll pick you up. Don't forget to look up which airport you're flying into."

"Thanks," Irene said.

IRENE BOOKED a seat on the Thursday morning flight to London at seven ten, which, according to the friendly voice on the phone, would land at Heathrow. She decided to make her return flight as late as possible on Friday, a seven twenty departure. She might have a chance to see something of London if the meeting with Rebecka didn't take too long.

With a sigh, her gaze fell on the pile of paper before her. It had a strange ability to grow from day to day even though she tried to work on it at every available moment. Could paper reproduce itself? Her depressing thoughts faded when Svante Malm's freckled face appeared at her door.

"Howdy. I thought I'd give you the book we found at Jacob Schyttelius's."

He stepped into the room and lay Anton LaVey's book on her desk. *Church of Satan*. She felt a strong desire to throw it out the window. "Avoid that which comes from evil," as Eva Möller would probably say.

"Lots of Jacob's fingerprints were inside the book, and only his. There were some unidentified ones on the outside, probably from the employees at the bookstore. Jacob had done some underlining and written a few notes here and there in the margins."

"Have you read it?"

"I've skimmed through it. Haven't had time to read it properly, but I'll certainly borrow it again. It's interesting."

"Why do you think it's interesting?"

Hesitantly, Svante said, "It's probably because of the criminal investigations with Satanic connections that I've worked on. At first you think it's absolutely incomprehensible, how people can devote themselves to Satan-worship and strange rituals. Then, in some way, you become interested against your will. You wonder what makes these people tick."

"What is it that makes them tick, then?"

"Power. They want power over other people and power to accept themselves. According to LaVey, nothing limits you more than yourself and your own conscience, until you realize that no one else is allowed to make decisions about you. No one else is allowed to judge your acts. You are free to look after yourself and your needs. As long as *you* personally feel good, then *everything* is okay."

"Everything?"

"*Everything*. It's no coincidence that in the USA in particular, there have been major investigations where they've found that young children have been drugged and used sexually during rituals. Satanism gives people permission to live out forbidden desires. Most of the meetings within the Satanic church end in group sex. Sex with animals is also common. And, as we know, they also sacrifice animals during their black masses. The ultimate sacrifice, of course, is a human sacrifice. It has happened, but it isn't as common."

Irene thought about what Svante had just said.

"Could you say that Satan is the same as God for them?"

Again Svante looked uncertain. "Not really. From what I understand, they have their black masses in order to gain some of the devil's power. That's the power that allows people to free themselves from their upbringing and religious conventions. You dare to let Satan loose inside you. The figure of God in different religions often has a law-giving role. The god says what you are and aren't allowed to do. That's not the case in Satanism. There, you're supposed to accept yourself, and Satan gives you the power to do so."

Irene looked at the book on her desk with distaste.

" ' *I*' is the secret word," she said.

Svante nodded. "And complete satisfaction of one's own desires. I can trace Satanism in most of the crimes we investigate."

Irene was taken aback by his statement. When she had pulled herself together a bit, she said, confused, "What . . . ? Satan in *most crimes*. . . . What do you mean?"

"Most crimes are about satisfaction of one's own needs. Money, sex, power, or as a way of finding an outlet for one's anger. The guy waiting in line to get into the pub, who wasn't let in and then out of anger stabbed the bouncer, may have been inspired by the devil who is in us all."

"Cut it out. Drugs are always involved in those cases. Everyone doesn't knife someone just because they don't get into a club! And to start blaming the devil . . . !"

Irene stopped her angry flood of words when she saw that Svante was mischievously smiling at her.

"Well. Maybe some of us have more of Satan inside than others." He turned around and waved to her before he disappeared.

Irene sat for a long time looking at *Church of Satan*.

Why had Jacob Schyttelius read this book? Was it to learn more about how followers of Satanism think, or did he have entirely different motives? Was that why he had hidden the book? But maybe it was so that Pappa Pastor wouldn't accidentally see it.

The question was whether Satanism really had anything to do with the triple murders.

The only person who might have the answer had been admitted to a psychiatric ward on the other side of the North Sea.

SUPERINTENDENT ANDERSSON'S mood hit rock bottom when he neared Pathology Professor Yvonne Stridner's door. To his relief, he saw that the yellow "Wait" light was on; but as he was just about to leave, it went off. With heavy steps, he walked forward and pushed the visitor's button. An unconscious sigh escaped him when the green light immediately came on.

The head of Pathology was enthroned behind her cluttered desk. Her Dior eyeglasses had slid down her nose, and she looked unusually stressed. A blush was evident on her cheeks.

"Andersson? For once maybe you can be useful. What do you do when the computer has frozen? I can't work on my presentation!"

Irritated, she hit the plastic cover of her IBM.

"I . . . I'm not so good with computers," Andersson stammered.

"But don't you use a computer for work?" Stridner stared the superintendent in the eye with her sharp gaze, and he felt himself shrinking. He always became a nervous, sweaty schoolboy when he was around her, a blithering idiot.

"Yes . . . yes, of course," he said, but he could hear how unconvincing he sounded.

Stridner pursed her lips and mumbled something about "technology-hating bosses in middle management."

This made Andersson angry, and he said stiffly, "I haven't come to repair computers, but to find out if the tests have been able to pinpoint the exact time of each death."

Stridner's eyes were frosty, and her voice tinkled like icicles when she replied, "I could have looked it up if my computer hadn't been out of order."

Back to square one. Andersson glared at the pathologist with the flame-red hair. Resigned, he was turning to go when he heard her say, "But I can use the other computer."

Without waiting for a reply, she clattered past him on her stiletto heels and disappeared down the corridor.

Andersson sank onto the uncomfortable visitor's chair. It was both lumpy and covered in vinyl. Andersson suspected that most people who sat in this chair soon found themselves in varying states of nervousness and general dissolution. From his own experience, he knew how quickly one began to perspire on a vinyl chair. Medical students or police officers, it didn't matter: Everyone broke into a sweat during a meeting with Professor Stridner, the superintendent continued his gloomy train of thought.

He was interrupted when the clattering of the professor's heels in the corridor grew closer. She rushed in and stepped up to her ergonomically designed office chair, which was covered in Bordeaux-colored soft leather. It looked more like a small comfortable recliner than a work chair, Andersson noted jealously as he squirmed in his uncomfortable chair.

Stridner straightened her glasses and looked down at the paper she held in her hand. She read directly from the page: "'Jacob Schyttelius's stomach contents showed the half-digested remains of a hot dog and mashed potatoes. He drank orange soda along with it. His last meal was consumed at around six o'clock.' Does that match your information?"

Stridner peered at Andersson over the edge of her glasses.

"Yes. The assistant at the hot-dog stand on Södra vägen got in touch with us. She remembers him. Apparently he was a regular and usually came around six o'clock, several evenings a week. She remembers that it was Monday, because the next day she had a backache and was out sick. And the owner of a men's clothing store on Södra vägen also phoned us. Jacob was there just before closing on Monday evening."

The superintendent became annoyed at himself when he heard how he blurted out his information, strutting to show that, by golly, he was in the know. A simple "yes" would have been sufficient.

Stridner nodded and looked down at her paper again. "Then I would like to place the time of the murder at between eleven o'clock and eleven thirty. I can't be more precise, since we don't know *exactly* when Jacob ate his hot dog with mashed potatoes.

"Regarding the parents' stomach contents, it's even more uncertain, since we don't know when they ate their last meal, which was salmon mousse and green peas. Based on the level of digestion, they probably ate six hours before the time of death. And drinks. . . ."

Again Stridner gave Andersson a sharp look. Unaware, he sucked in his stomach, which was hanging over his belt.

"Elsa Schyttelius had coffee and water in her digestive tract. Sten Schyttelius had beer and whiskey. His blood alcohol level was one point one. High, but he was only slightly drunk. The condition of his liver bears witness to a rather significant alcohol intake over the years."

"Was he an alcoholic?"

Stridner hesitated. "Alcoholic? . . . More like a regular heavy drinker. His blood sugar was also a bit high, and he was overweight."

She gave Andersson a meaningful look. He was terribly close to asking her what the pastor's blood pressure had been, but managed to stop himself. A sulky Professor Stridner was the worst thing you could confront. Instead, he said, "We've traced a phone call from the rectory to Jacob's cell phone. The call came at six thirty-two. That's the last telephone call registered to or from the rectory's telephone on the night of the murder. I wonder if one of the parents called Jacob to see if he wanted to join them for dinner. If I've guessed right, it means that Mr. and Mrs. Schyttelius ate around six forty-five or a little later. That would mean that they were killed as late as quarter to one. Fifteen minutes in each direction, but probably closer to one o'clock."

Stridner nodded. "That's possible," she said. She took off her glasses and tapped one of the rims lightly against her front teeth. "It was an execution," she said.

Andersson replied, "Those Satanic stars and all that damn . . . drivel were meant to suggest a ritual murder. But it doesn't really look like it. I mean . . . there aren't signs of any sacrifices."

"No. These are not ritualistic killings," Stridner agreed.

"Have you seen any Satanic murders?" Andersson ventured to ask.

"Yes. One. The Purple Murder. I had just started here in Pathology. Are you familiar with the case?"

"Yes. I remember it, but I didn't participate in the investigation."

"Then I don't need to go through the circumstances surrounding the case itself. The man was found dead in his apartment with his throat cut. But that's not all. Someone had carved a pentagram on his stomach. It wasn't very deep, but it had bled. The man was alive while the pentagram was being incised."

"Could he have done it himself?" the superintendent interjected.

"No. It was very well done, with the points all being exactly the same size. You wouldn't be able to do that to yourself. Not even if he had stood in front of a mirror. Besides, he was heavily drugged."

"What kind of drug?"

"LSD, which actually is a drug commonly used during Satanic gatherings, I learned. I discussed this case a few years later with a colleague at a conference in Philadelphia who had experience with three ritualistic murders with connections to Satanism. Very interesting! It was two young children and a teenage girl who—"

Stridner stopped herself. "But it was the the Purple Murder we were discussing. So the man had taken LSD, or someone had forced him to take it. Because of the drug, he probably didn't feel anything when the symbol was carved on his stomach. Aside from his throat being cut after the carving session, he also had five stab wounds in his body. The interesting thing about the stab wounds was that all of them were inflicted with the same knife, but not by the same person."

Andersson raised his eyebrows in surprise. This last was news to him.

"I didn't hear anything about that at the time. It was, after all, not my case, but you would think I would have heard something like that through the grapevine—"

"No. We chose not to spread it about, because the information wasn't supported. Rather, it was only a hypothesis."

"What did you base it on?"

"The man was alive when the pentagram was carved, and he was also alive when his throat was cut. The blood shot out in a cascade and he quickly bled to death then.

"The stab wounds on the body differed greatly. Two of them were only about a centimeter deep and located peripherally on his chest. One went straight to the heart and would have been fatal in and of itself, just as the fourth, a stab wound to the stomach which perforated the liver, would also have resulted in death. The last stab wound was, strangely enough, positioned directly above the pubic bone and slanted in toward the bladder. None of these knife wounds had bled much, which points to the fact that the man had been dead for a while before they were inflicted on him."

"I seem to recall that evidence of sexual contact was also found. . . ."

"Yes. We found vaginal secretions on his penis and sperm in his anus. So he had had sex with at least one man and one woman. If it had happened today, we could have done DNA profiles, but we didn't have that back then."

Stridner fell silent.

"You remember this case surprisingly well," Andersson ventured to say.

She replied dryly, "Yes. It was a case that stays with you. Unusual."

She straightened her glasses mechanically and looked down at the papers in front of her on the table. "The reason I started talking about that case is to justify my doubt that the killing of the Schyttelius family was a ritualistic Satanic murder. Firstly, we have the appearance of the crime scenes. No strange objects or utensils for Satanic rituals, only the symbols painted on the computers."

"There was an upside-down cross in Mr. and Mrs. Schyttelius's bedroom. . . ."

"Just to mislead. Nothing about the *bodies* pointed to ritualistic activities. They were simply executed in cold blood."

Andersson nodded and admitted that she was right. These were thoughts he had had several times himself. "So if it wasn't Satanists who murdered them, who was it?"

"A murderer without mercy. Familiar with guns and with a perfect aim. None of the victims were moved after the murders. He was sure they were dead."

Andersson thought about what Stridner had said. "The strange thing," he said, "is that the only ones familiar with firearms and who were expert marksmen, in the context of this investigation, are the victims, Sten and Jacob Schyttelius."

IRENE HAD started preparing for her trip to London on Tuesday evening. She ironed her navy-blue linen pants and matching blazer. The new low-heeled dark-blue pumps would be perfect, but what could she wear under the blazer? After a great deal of agony, she decided to go for a light-purple sleeveless top with a deep V-neck. The time between checking in and boarding the plane would be spent in the airport shops. There she would try to find a new lipstick and a new perfume. Her mascara was almost out, and—

The door opened and Katarina stormed in. "Guess what."

"Hello. What?"

"I've pulled out of the contest. I called the club where the final is being held on Saturday and said that I don't have time for that beauty stuff."

"What did they say?"

"They became, like, so angry. But I don't give a damn. Those idiots can run their competition any way they want." She disappeared into her room.

Why the quick change? Why didn't her daughter need proof any more that she was pretty enough? Was it out of fear that she wouldn't win? Or—?

Irene stopped her train of thought when she realized what the answer must be.

"What's his name?" she called toward Katarina's room.

Her daughter stuck her head through the door opening with a surprised look on her face. "He? How do you . . . ?" Then she broke into a sunny smile. "Johan." She ducked back into her room. Irene smiled to herself, feeling like a very good detective.

A little while later, when she was considering the Schyttelius murders, that feeling evaporated like a dewdrop in the desert. What if her trip to London was unsuccessful? Maybe Rebecka really didn't have the faintest idea about the motive for the murders or who the perpetrator might be. She hadn't lived in Sweden the last couple of years. She hadn't had close contact with her family. They hadn't found any letters or postcards from Rebecka to either her parents or her brother.

Then a thought struck her: computers. They had each had access to a computer. Maybe they kept in touch through them. Sent E-mail or chatted. . . . But they would never be able to prove it, since the hard drives had been destroyed.

But maybe something had been saved on removable disks? Irene stopped herself. They hadn't found a single removable disk, whether floppy diskette, Zip disk, CD/R, or any other kind, either at Sten's or at Jacob's. The investigators had assumed that they had stored everything only on the hard drives. But what if they hadn't? What if the murderer had taken the removable disks with him? How do you utterly destroy such a disk? She suspected that the answer was probably different for each kind. She made a mental note to herself to find out first thing the next morning.

RIGHT AFTER morning prayers on Wednesday, the telephone in Irene's office rang. She threw herself through the door and hurdled over the desk in order to catch it in time.

"Inspector Huss." She could hear that someone was breathing heavily on the other end of the phone but trying to calm down.

"Hello? Who's calling?" Irene asked.

She could hear the person at the other end clear his throat nervously. "Yes . . . I don't know if I really should, but this is Assistant Pastor Urban Berg in Bäckared."

"Good morning."

"Good morning. I was wondering . . . it happens that I've found out about something which may have nothing to do with the murders, but one never knows. . . ."

"Do you want me to come and see you so that we can talk, or is it okay to do it via telephone?"

"No, . . . I'm coming into the city today anyway. . . . Can we meet this afternoon? I would prefer if no one finds out that I've spoken with you."

"What time works best for you?"

"After two o'clock. Does that suit you?"

"Of course. Just announce yourself at the reception desk and they'll call me. I'll come down and meet you."

"Thank you." Relief could be heard in his voice.

What had Urban Berg found out that he couldn't tell her over the phone? Maybe this was the first crack in the case they had all been hoping for? But that was probably wishful thinking, she told herself.

IRENE DEVOTED the entire morning to administrative cleanup. She was very pleased with her efforts when she looked out over her bare desktop before she went to lunch just before one o'clock. The Insurance Office's cafeteria was offering an acceptable chicken stew.

She looked for Tommy both in the station and in the cafeteria, but she didn't see him anywhere. The Speedy investigation was probably moving along, which was more than could be said for the one she was participating in. Since she hadn't spoken with Urban Berg during the questioning a week earlier, it would have been good to learn Tommy's impression of the pastor before she met him herself. The only thing she remembered was that Urban Berg had said that Bengt Måårdh was a womanizer. It may have been true: Bengt was a stylish man and had a pleasant manner about him. Maybe his manner was a little too pleasant.

Irene remembered that she had viewed Urban Berg as reserved during the brief glimpse she had gotten of him in the Fellowship Hall. And, according to Bengt Måårdh, he had problems with the bottle.

What was it Tommy had called both of the pastors? Now she remembered: "petty gossiping pigs." They had tattled on each other. Probably because they were competing for the position of Schyttelius's replacement as rector. Bengt Måårdh had also happened to reveal Jonas Burman's possible homosexuality and that he saw himself as being extra religious and orthodox.

It was with a certain degree of anticipation that she took the elevator down to pick up Urban Berg. The receptionist announced him at two o'clock on the dot.

He stood glued to the wall of the waiting room right next to the bookshelf. The room didn't offer many hiding places, but the pastor had found the one that existed. With a stiff facial expression, he focused on three dark-skinned men who were sitting on the visitor's couch. He seemed to be slightly cross-eyed, since at the same time he was keeping an eye on a suspicious man who was sitting in an armchair and reading that day's edition of *GP*. Irene could have informed Urban Berg that the man in the chair was a plainclothes prison guard who was waiting for someone. She didn't bother. Instead, she opened the glass door and smiled welcomingly at the pastor. Relieved, Berg hurried toward her.

"I've been going back and forth about what I should do . . . but I've decided to tell," said Urban Berg.

He sat erect in Irene's visitor's chair and declined her offer of coffee. Irene left him for a moment while she retrieved a cup for herself. Based on what she could see when she came back, he hadn't moved an inch.

Now he looked Irene in the eye and repeated, "I've decided to tell."

He stopped himself. Irene drank her coffee and waited for him to begin.

"It was the Friday before the murders. Sten came over to my home in the afternoon, and we sat and talked. We had a very pleasant time and ate a little bit of food. Very pleasant. He said—"

There the assistant rector stopped and looked to the side. Irene got the feeling that he was terribly troubled. She wondered if she should ask how much they had had to drink, but decided that it was irrelevant. With the knowledge of both men's drinking habits, it had probably been a good deal. Berg cleared his throat and commenced again. "He said that he suspected that Louise Måårdh had embezzled money from the church association."

Irene was very surprised. Could Louise possibly have embezzled church funds? The beautiful, elegant . . . then Irene stopped herself and remembered the stunning pearl necklace and the exquisitely cut dress she had worn the week before. Irene had to admit that her impression of Louise also included the word "expensive."

"Did he have any proof of his suspicions?"

Troubled, Urban Berg squirmed before he answered. "I . . . we talked about how Bengt and Louise bought a new car again. It hasn't been more than three years since they bought a Volvo. Brand-spanking-new. Now they've purchased a BMW!" At the last piece of information, he opened his eyes wide, meaningfully. Apparently he viewed the BMW as clear proof of Mr. and Mrs. Määrdh's deceit. At first he looked disappointed when Irene didn't comment on the information, but after a short while his determination returned.

"Last winter they traveled to the Maldives, and last summer they were in Italy, and this summer they're traveling to Greece. Their sons study at the university without taking out any student loans, and they each have an apartment. And then, they've bought a bigger boat which is docked at Björlanda Kile. Stuff like that costs money!"

He couldn't conceal the triumph in his voice. Irene tried to choose her words carefully. "Did Sten Schyttelius suspect his accountant of embezzlement simply because of all of these expenses?"

A blush shot up from the pastor's throat and spread unflatteringly over his pale cheeks. "He . . . he thought, as I do, that it's very strange that they can afford all these things. Pastors in the Swedish Church are not well paid."

"But he didn't have any proof to base his suspicions on," Irene asserted.

"Maybe not directly. But this has been discussed in the association for the last few years. According to Sten, we aren't the only ones who have been curious."

Irene watched the man sitting upright in her visitor's chair.

She was inclined to agree with Tommy; Urban Berg was a gossip-monger. Yet experience told her that a grain of truth can often be found in a rumor. Maybe it was worth pursuing. But someone else would have to do it; she was going to London.

"I'VE SCOUTED the woods around Norssjön and the rectory in Kullahult. It isn't all that difficult to make your way through."

Fredrik had taped together the two map pages that the superintendent had torn out when he introduced the theory about the murderer taking a shortcut through the woods.

"The first hundred and fifty meters from the cottage are a bit tricky, but then you come to an area that has been cleared for power lines. It goes straight as an arrow toward Kullahult. In some places the power line goes over meadows and fields, but it never gets close to any houses, until you're almost at Kullahult. It wouldn't have been hard to sneak up to the rectory on foot."

Fredrik looked up from the map pages in order to make sure they were following along. Irene, Hannu, and Superintendent Andersson were sitting around the table, and they were paying careful attention. Encouraged, he continued. "The power lines continue across the large field that lies behind the rectory. If you go through that field, you come to the back of the church hill. There aren't any houses until here, on the other side, where the farm that owns the field is located. It's too far away for the people at the farm to be able to see if someone is moving near the church."

"So you can use a flashlight without any great risk of being seen," Hannu said.

"Absolutely. But in order to be on the safe side, you can keep to the edge of the field. I went out there last night around eleven and checked. I had no problem making my way without a flashlight by walking along the edge of the woods. The forest stretches all the way to the church hill, and then a stone wall takes over. If you continue along it, you come to the spruce hedge behind the rectory. And that's when I did what Irene's dog does."

Fredrik paused for dramatic effect and smiled.

"What the hell does Irene's dog do?" the superintendent asked, irritated.

"Follow the animals. And I followed the deer. They've actually made a passage through the spruce hedge. The fat tulips in the garden lure them. The opening was a tight fit for me, but it's possible to push your way through. I can guarantee that the murderer went that way."

The triumph in his voice couldn't be missed. The others sat quietly because this was Fredrik's performance, and he was playing it for all he was worth.

"I found a footprint and a red woolen thread inside the passage. I called the technicians before I pushed through the opening. They took care of the yarn and made a cast of a shoeprint. This morning I talked to Åhlén. They say that the yarn piece is the same type as the two that Irene and I found. My theory about the tasseled murderer still holds."

Irene giggled but realized right away that she was the only one amused. Hannu and the superintendent were completely absorbed. Knowing that he had his listeners' full attention, Fredrik continued. "The shoeprint was perfect; the rain hadn't gotten at it. The print came from a sturdy Adidas athletic shoe, size 11. According to Åhlén, it's a winter model, almost like a boot."

"Gore-Tex," said Hannu.

"Probably. Light, warm, and waterproof. The technicians are in the process of trying to find out exactly what kind of shoe made the print. It shouldn't be impossible."

"So we're still looking for a short guy with a tasseled hat who has big feet on which he wore Gore-Tex boots. He shouldn't be difficult to get ahold of," Irene said.

In her mind, she could see the little man in a tasseled hat

fighting his way through the woods, stumbling in his large boots. A second later, when she remembered what he had done to his victims, he didn't seem as comical any more.

"I also timed how long it took to go between the crime scenes. One hour and five minutes," Fredrik concluded.

Irene told them about Urban Berg's visit, and Hannu promised to check to see if there was any foundation for the accusations against Louise Måårdh. Covering up embezzlement could be a motive for murder. It would have had to be a great deal of money, thought Irene.

Chapter 12

It was quiet at Landvetter Airport at six fifteen in the morning. Irene had checked her small suitcase and stumbled, half asleep, toward the open café.

"Small cup, or large?" the smiling girl behind the counter chirped.

"Bucket," Irene croaked.

Her sunny smile unchanged, the girl turned and took out a ceramic soup bowl. She filled it two thirds of the way.

"Milk or cream? I can steam the milk if you want."

Irene felt a warm thankfulness over meeting a fellow human being who really understood her basic early-morning need.

"No, thanks. Just black."

Irene attempted a smile, but felt it was too great an effort: Her facial muscles weren't awake yet. She was moved when the girl behind the counter placed a napkin and an After Eight chocolate on her tray. It made her realize that she must look like the wreck she felt.

After finishing her bowl of coffee, Irene was ready for shopping. She went to the perfume store and starting selecting items for herself and for the twins, based on the list they had given her. Pretty soon, she realized that maybe ten percent of the basket's contents were hers; the rest was for the girls.

The plane landed at Heathrow after barely two hours in the air. Hail splattered against the body of the aircraft, then turned into a light drizzle as the passengers were leaving the plane and wandering down the stairs. It was windy, damp, and raw.

Several people were waiting holding up cardboard signs

outside Customs. One of them had "Ms. Irene Huss" on it. Irene realized this must be Inspector Glen Thompson. Her surprise must have been obvious, because Glen Thompson broke into a wide smile and then laughed.

"Welcome to London. I'm Glen Thompson."

His white teeth shone against dark skin. His hair was a shiny black, short and curly. He was slightly taller than Irene and a few years younger.

He held out his hand to greet her, and Irene managed to get her act together and squeak out her name.

Glen Thompson took her bag and said, "I think we'll go to the hotel first."

Outside the airport terminal, a pale sun now shone between the clouds.

"You have April weather," Irene commented.

Thompson flashed his teeth in a quick smile and nodded. He walked up to a black Rover and unlocked it, then politely held open the door on the passenger's side for Irene and threw her bag onto the back seat.

"We've had fantastic weather the last two weeks, then yesterday it turned. It rained all day. But it's going to be better today."

Irene couldn't hear the slightest bit of an accent when he spoke. If he hadn't been born in England, then he must have grown up here, she thought.

They drove past budding trees and greening fields. The cherry trees, too, were blooming, a month earlier than in Göteborg. When they drew closer to London and the first block of houses popped up, she saw yellow forsythia and magnolias in bud.

Traffic became thicker the closer to London they came. And everyone drove on the wrong side! Irene thanked her lucky stars that she didn't have to drive. Glen Thompson didn't seem to have any problems with the traffic. When Irene admitted that it was the first time she had been to London, he immediately said, "Then we'll take a longer route so I have an opportunity to show you the main streets. It's easier to orient oneself using them. And you'll want to walk around on your own without getting lost."

He talked and pointed out sights worth seeing without seeming to give his fellow road users the slightest bit of attention.

"I've booked you in at my sister's hotel. Our father started it after the war. He was Scottish and married late in life. My mother was in London with a Brazilian dance group and stayed on after she met the old man. He died a few years ago, and then my mother opened this restaurant a few blocks from the hotel. The restaurant was a childhood dream—look, there's the Marble Arch, and on the left side you have Hyde Park—and she manages wonderfully. You'll get to meet her tonight. The whole Thompson family will be eating dinner there, and we hope that you can join us."

"Thanks, I'd love to," Irene replied, dazed by her host's voluble friendliness.

"I called Rebecka Schyttelius last night. She had just come home from the hospital. She agreed to see us today, late morning," Thompson continued.

They surged forward in the heavy morning traffic, the green surfaces of Hyde Park behind the tall fence on one side, and beautiful stone houses with expensive façades on the other.

Glen Thompson turned in on a cross street. The contrast was striking. The road was relatively narrow, with little traffic. The houses were faced with brick or stucco, tall, but not as impressive as those lining the more magnificent streets. Small shops and restaurants with exotic names were squeezed onto the ground level. Irene also noted the striking number of hotel entrances.

"There are plenty of hotels around here," she noted.

"Yes. Some are really posh, but most of them are small family-owned ones."

They turned onto an even smaller street and stopped. A few

steps led up to a heavy door with lead-framed windows. Two columns supported a portico. Under the roof, there was a frieze with "Thompson Hotel" written in elegant gold letters. Through large windows on each side of the entrance, the reception area was visible. The façades of the neighboring houses adjoined each window. The tall, narrow property appeared to be newly renovated. The stucco shone white, freshly painted, and the window frames were newly trimmed in a soft light blue. Irene immediately liked the little hotel.

Glen Thompson held the door open for her and insisted on carrying her bag. Irene entered the bright lobby and was met by a smiling woman who, she realized, must be Glen's sister. When she smiled, Irene saw the family resemblance. She was a head shorter than her brother and had a somewhat lighter complexion. She appeared to be about the same age as Irene.

"Welcome to the Thompson Hotel. My name is Estelle."

She held out her hand to greet Irene, automatically brushing the other hand over her neck to smooth her chignon. Her golden brown short-sleeved dress matched her eyes. Irene realized that the woman in front of her had been a stunning beauty in her youth; she was still very attractive.

"Hello, Estelle," said Glen. "You can treat me to a cup while Irene gets settled in the room." He asked Irene, "Is fifteen minutes enough time?"

"Absolutely."

"Good. I'll be waiting on the couch."

HER ROOM was located on the top floor. For the first time in her life, she encountered a one-person elevator. It wouldn't have been possible to get anyone else inside the tiny cage unless they were tenderly entwined and didn't have any luggage. When the small elevator had safely rattled its way to the fourth floor and opened its doors, Irene decided that she would have to use the stairs from now on.

The room was surprisingly large, decorated in emerald green and golden tan. Everything was bright and new, from the carpet on the floor to the tiled bathroom. A graphic print with a theme from the Carnaval in Rio adorned the wall.

Irene hung up the few clothes she had brought in the closet and took the opportunity to use the toilet. Then she walked down the stairs to the lobby.

"Should we walk? It's only about half a mile from here," Glen Thompson said.

"I'd love to walk," Irene agreed.

The sun was shining, but it was still quite cold in the wind.

A surprising number of houses had scaffolding on the outside and several were already restored. Irene realized that Bayswater was a part of the city which was regaining its old character. As if he could read her thoughts, Glen said, "Quite a few immigrants live here in Bayswater but at the same time, we have an influx of English people who want to live in central London. Of course, other areas of the city are more fashionable, like Mayfair or Holland Park, but the houses there are terribly expensive. Yet even if Bayswater has become trendy, it's nothing compared to Notting Hill. That's where Rebecka Schyttelius lives. I don't know if you've seen the movie with Julia Roberts and Hugh Grant . . . ?"

"No."

"The movie had an amazing impact, and now it's fashionable to live in Notting Hill."

Irene noticed that they were headed west. Pretty soon, the houses became dirtier and more decayed. There was also a lot of scaffolding here, but the houses that were undergoing renovation hadn't originally been as beautiful as the ones in Bayswater.

"Notting Hill is a old blue-collar neighborhood. But there are a few really nice houses, like the one up there."

Glen pointed at a large white four-story house with a beautifully ornamented façade. The first floors had narrow balconies running along the whole width of the house, where flowers in boxes and pots were already blooming. The balconies faced a thickly wooded park surrounded by a high iron fence. The general public could only peer through the bars at the greenery, because a sign hanging on the gate told them that it was private.

They walked past a large Tudor-style red brick house, continued to the next cross street, and found themselves on Ossington Street. A pub was located at the corner which, according to the black sign with an ornate golden text, was called "Shakespeare." The building that housed the pub looked considerably older than the surrounding structures. It was low with small, lead-paned mullioned windows, painted a dull greenish-brown color.

Even here on Ossington Street, scaffolding dominated, particularly on one side. Most of the houses on the other side seemed to have been restored already. Glen Thompson stopped in front of a white stucco house with a bright red door. Two brass plates shone on the door, but the distance was too great for Irene to be able to read them.

"Here it is," Glen announced after checking the address on a piece of paper.

Irene noted that the next house and Rebecka's house looked identical, aside from the fact that the neighbor's door was bright blue. There were even two matching brass plates on the blue door.

A high stone stoop led up to the red door. "Datacons. Lefévre & St. Clair" read the larger sign. "Rebecka Schyttelius" had been engraved on the smaller one. So Rebecka lived at her place of work.

Glen Thompson pushed the shiny new brass-surrounded doorbell. There was a faint dingdong from inside the house. After a few seconds, they heard quick steps and the door opened.

For the second time in a few hours' time, Irene's jaw dropped when confronted by a man who didn't look at all like she had expected. Because, as far as Irene knew, this one had been dead for almost twenty years. His murder had been featured on the front pages of newspapers all over the world and on news programs around the globe. Now he stood before her, peering at Irene with brown eyes behind round-framed eyeglasses. His thick shoulder-length dark-brown hair was parted in the middle. A white cotton shirt with rolled-up sleeves was open at the neck and hung outside his faded jeans. On his otherwise bare feet were a pair of sandals.

His name was John Lennon.

But when he held out his hand and introduced himself, he claimed that his name was Christian Lefévre.

He smiled when he became aware of Irene's surprise. In a friendly way, he said, "I've won some look-alike contests. People are usually startled when they see me. It's actually become a fun thing. Especially since the Beatles are my idols, although I was too young during their golden years."

Christian Lefévre stepped aside to let them in. They took off their coats in the narrow vestibule and were shown into an airy room with a high ceiling. Sunlight entered through tall curtainless windows, filtered through the leaves of the large green plants. Colorful and expensive framed posters of various computers hung on the walls. The Beatles' "Yesterday" flowed into the room from concealed speakers.

Irene counted three laptop and four desktop computers, standing on wooden desks that had been covered with clear varnish in order to show off the grain of the wood. The thin metal rectangles, the laptops, were closed and rested together on a separate table. Only two of the computers were on.

"Unfortunately, Rebecka couldn't handle the tension before this meeting. I had to drive her to see Dr. Fischer this morning."

"Is she going to stay there?" Glen asked.

"Don't know. But she'll probably take a sedative. It won't be possible to speak with her today."

Irene didn't know if it was her imagination, but she thought there was a note of satisfaction in Christian Lefévre's voice.

Glen said, "Okay. Then we'll interview *you*."

That wasn't what Lefévre had expected. His surprise was apparent. "Me? Why? I don't know anything."

"Maybe, but we still want to speak with you."

"But I have a lot of work . . . now, since Rebecka hasn't been able to work for a while. . . ."

"It won't take long."

Thompson was adamant. Lefévre shrugged his shoulders in a very French way and walked toward a closed door. "We can talk in here," he said, opening the door and showing them into the room with a sweeping gesture.

It was a small kitchen that also contained an inviting sofa and chairs covered in soft black leather. A bright red rug covered part of the floor, a spot of color in the otherwise white and black room. The only wall decoration was an exquisite horsehead in red glazed ceramic.

"Coffee or tea?" Lefévre asked.

"Coffee," Irene answered quickly before Glen had time to decline.

He had had a break at the hotel but she hadn't, and now she was ready for coffee. Christian filled an electric kettle and turned it on. Irene realized too late that instant coffee was on its way. As long as it wasn't decaf, it would suffice, she comforted herself.

Lefévre took his time, setting out plastic mugs, tea bags, sugar, milk, and Nescafé. When the water boiled and he had poured it into the mugs, he couldn't stall any longer. He was forced to sit. There was no doubt that he didn't like the situation.

Glen observed him closely before he asked, "Why don't you want us to speak to Rebecka?"

Christian focused on his mug. The water, colored a golden brown from the contents of the tea bag, seemed like the most fascinating thing he had ever seen. It was a long time before he answered.

"I'm not trying to keep you from speaking with Rebecka."

"Yes, you are."

Christian fished out the tea bag and threw it into an empty mug in the middle of the table.

"Maybe you're right. I want to protect her. She doesn't have the strength even to think about what's happened, not to mention talk about it. She gets sick if you even refer to . . . what happened."

"How long has she been sick?"

He quickly looked up but then looked away again. "What do you mean? Since the murders—"

"No. She was depressed before."

"How do you—? September."

"Has she out sick since September?"

"No. She has been able to work quite a bit. It's been good for her, distracted her from sad thoughts and anguish. But sometimes she became unable. . . . Listen here, what does this have to do with the murders in Sweden?"

Irene interjected, "We don't know. We're looking for a motive. Did you ever meet Rebecka's parents, or her brother?"

"No."

"Did Rebecka say anything to you about someone in her family having been threatened?"

At first Christian looked surprised, then he said, vaguely, "No, she didn't say anything. But wasn't there something in the papers about a clue which led to Satanists?"

"The papers wrote that, yes. Has Rebecka said anything to you about Satanists?"

He sipped at the hot tea, while he appeared to be trying to remember.

"It was quite a while ago. Her father asked for her help in tracking Satanists via the Internet."

"How long ago was that?"

"Rebecka mentioned it in the fall, saying that he'd asked a year before that. So, more than a year and a half ago."

"And she never said anything to you about personally feeling threatened?"

"No. Never," he said firmly.

"Did she say or do anything unusual at the beginning of last week?"

"You mean before the murders were discovered?"

"Yes. On Monday or Tuesday."

"No. Everything was normal. Both of us worked all day Monday. It was probably a bit too much for Rebecka. She went to bed early, around five thirty, because she had a headache. I went to Shakespeare. That's the pub on the corner. A group of us usually meet there on Mondays and put together our betting pool for the week."

"What did you do afterward?"

"I went home."

"Did you see Rebecka?"

"No. She had gone to *her* place."

Glen couldn't contain himself any longer. "Don't you live together in this house?"

"Yes, and no. I've owned the house next door for some time, the one which now has a blue door. My office was located on the ground floor and I lived on the two other floors. The office felt too small, and I was looking for a new location when this house became available. I bought it and offered Rebecka the same living arrangement as I have, including breaking through the wall on the first floor and expanding the office. As you can see, it worked out very well."

"So you don't live together as a couple?"

Christian Lefévre glared angrily at Glen. "No. And I don't see how that has anything to do with your investigation."

"It does. Rebecka is the only surviving member of the

Schyttelius family. Everything which affects her life is important to the investigation," Glen told him.

It wasn't really true that everything was important, thought Irene, but it quieted the Frenchman, if he truly was a Frenchman.

Lefévre squirmed in his chair. Finally, he said, "If there is nothing else, I'd actually like to get back to work."

"I'm glad you said that. What exactly is your work? Are there other employees?" Glen asked.

Christian sighed heavily before he answered. "Here, in London, it's just Rebecka and myself. Andy St. Clair has moved up to Edinburgh and works from there. But he has a lot of other businesses to run as well. So it's mostly Rebecka and I who work together. We take on different projects from companies and organizations that deal with computers and networks. Right now, we're working on exponential and open networks. We look at security questions. Our client is a secret, but I can reveal that there's a military interest in this. The risk that terrorist groups could completely paralyze the Internet is actually quite high."

"But you can't paralyze the whole Internet! There are millions of Web sites that would have to be destroyed," Irene objected.

"Not at all. It's quite simple. The Internet is an open network. It's not sensitive to occasional problems, but it's sensitive to attacks against the important computers and servers that make up the backbone of the system. Through an attack directed at these servers, the interconnected Internet could be reduced to isolated islands."

"I've never heard that," Glen said. "What are exproportional networks or whatever they're called?"

Sincere interest and curiosity could be heard in his voice. Christian had relaxed as he spoke about the Internet. Apparently, he felt much more comfortable in cyberspace. "Exponential networks don't have any servers. All the computers are equally strongly linked to each other, peer-to-peer. This makes the network sensitive to occasional problems but protects it against attack."

"Does Rebecka also work on these things?"

"Yes. We're specialists on everything that has to do with different networks, where one's own organization's competence isn't enough."

"Is there a lot of money in this sort of thing?"

Lefévre treated himself to a smile for the first time since he had opened the door for them. Without attempting to conceal his satisfaction, he said, "Yes. Lots."

Glen rubbed his forehead thoughtfully. "Let's see . . . we've spoken about Monday. Nothing unusual happened on Tuesday?"

Christian's smile disappeared as if someone had shut off a circuit breaker. "No. Nothing strange happened on Tuesday. Except that I slept late in the morning. I guess I had too much beer and whiskey at the pub the night before. But I bought croissants and Danish pastry to make up for it. Rebecka had already eaten breakfast, but she took a Danish anyway."

"What time was it then?"

"Nine thirty, ten o'clock. Something like that." Christian threw his hands up as he shrugged his shoulders in a gesture of bafflement at their interest.

"Did you both work here during the day?"

"Yes. But I told Rebecka to stop at around four. Personally, I sat here until nearly eight o'clock."

"Did Rebecka receive any strange phone calls during those two days?"

"No."

"And as far as you know, there hadn't been any strange phone calls earlier?"

"No."

"And nothing via E-mail either?"

"I said no."

Christian couldn't hide his irritation any longer. He rose and started clearing the table. Irene remained sitting because Glen did. Neither broke the silence.

"Will you go now? I have a lot to do." Christian's self-control broke. He walked to the door and held it wide. His Adam's apple bobbed up and down as he tried to swallow his anger. "Get in touch if you have any further questions but right now I don't have any more time," he said as calmly as he could manage.

Irene and Glen walked through the impersonal white computer room with the beautiful green plants and on toward the dark entrance. John Lennon's voice in "Hey Jude" accompanied them out. Now Irene understood why the vestibule was so narrow. It was split by a wall and a door, which led to Rebecka's apartment.

"Are the apartments identical?" she asked Christian.

"Yes." His facial expression told her that he considered it to be none of her business.

"HE'S HIDING something. He seems tense. Maybe he really is only trying to protect Rebecka's weak nerves, but I doubt it," Glen said as they walked back to the hotel.

"Hard to say. But what would he be hiding?"

"Don't know. Maybe there's some threat that he doesn't want to reveal. Or maybe he really doesn't know anything. Then he is what he says he is: a young hard-working millionaire in the IT business who's trying to protect his business partner."

Glen had voiced something which Irene had been mulling over for a while.

"Don't you also think that he's very keen on his partner? I mean, he let Rebecka move into the house next door and he renovated it."

"True. But it could have been for simple, practical reasons. That part about expanding the offices. Space is terribly expensive in London these days. He's probably saving a lot by having his office at home in a building he owns," said Glen.

They walked through different parts of Bayswater than the ones they had passed through before. Here the streets were wider and people swarmed on the sidewalks. Commerce was in full swing in shops and restaurants. Irene started wondering what to buy as a souvenir. Yet again, Glen displayed a creepy ability to read her thoughts.

"If you want to do some shopping, we can go to Whitley's. It's nearby, all sorts of shops in one place. I usually take the wife and kids there when it's time for a shopping trip. They buy, and I sit in the pub on the top floor and read the paper."

He smiled his infectious smile and Irene was strengthened in her opinion that he was very pleasant. A man who willingly went along on shopping trips! Although he cheated a bit and sneaked off to the pub, he was still there.

They walked up to a building which looked like a shining white wedding cake in the sunshine, more like a grand cathedral than a department store. Glen stopped inside the colonnade but outside the large glass doors. "We'll meet here in an hour, then we can have lunch. While you're shopping, I'm going to try to reach Dr. Fischer."

Irene went in and out of the shops, realizing she wouldn't have time to visit a fraction of them. She determined that the Swedish krona wasn't worth much against the pound. At the same time, there were a lot of things which awoke her "must have" craving.

The most intriguing store covered two floors and carried only women's lingerie. She had been lured in by the display of wonderful garments in every imaginable color. She selected a light-blue bra and panties, each of which cost twelve pounds. She was standing there pondering as to whether it was expensive or cheap, when a young woman appeared in front of her.

"Let me take your measurements and I'll help you find the right size and model."

Somewhat skeptically, Irene allowed herself to be led into a fitting room and was measured around the bust and hips. The salesperson disappeared and quickly returned with four bras with matching panties. Irene decided in favor of two of them.

Holding the exclusive light yellow bag with its gold inscription, she walked back toward the entrance where she was going to meet Glen. Now she was starving.

To Irene's disappointment, Glen had chosen a restaurant called Mandarin Kitchen. She didn't want to eat Chinese food now that she was finally in London, since Göteborg has lots of Chinese cafés. But she changed her mind once the food arrived. They didn't serve half-manufactured food here. Everything was fresh from the market. Based on Glen's recommendation, she ordered the scallops with garlic, which smelled and tasted heavenly. The cool beer washed the exhaust fumes and dust of the big city from her throat.

Neither of them wanted dessert with coffee. Glen took out a pack of cigarettes and offered one to Irene, who declined. He lit a cigarette and took a sensual drag.

"I got in touch with Dr. Fischer. He spoke to Rebecka. She has agreed to meet with us at the doctor's office tomorrow if he's allowed to be present during the interview. Apparently it's okay with him. Does that suit you?"

"Of course."

"We decided on eleven o'clock at his office."

"That will be fine."

Glen smiled through the smoke, saying, "Now I need to get back to work. I'll drop you off outside New Scotland Yard; unfortunately, I don't have time to show you around. I have a meeting. I can leave you at the stop for the sightseeing bus. It's on Victoria Street."

"Great. I don't know much about London."

"Then a sightseeing tour will be perfect. Estelle will be waiting for you in the lobby at seven o'clock. You can go together to Vitória."

"Vitória?"

"Mamma's restaurant. My grandmother's name was Vitória. I'll see you there tonight."

NEW SCOTLAND Yard was an enormous building made of glass and concrete. It looked like it had been designed by an architect who was still in his Lego phase. On the other hand, the surrounding older buildings were beautiful and impressive.

"That's the Houses of Parliament, the seat of Parliament since the fifteen hundreds. And over there you can see Big Ben. It's not the tower but the clock itself which is called Big Ben," Glen told her.

He dropped Irene off at the bus stop near the Thames, not far from a bridge which, according to the signs, was Westminster Bridge. She realized that she needed a map. A friendly, white-haired lady in a kiosk next to the bus stop sold both maps and one-day sightseeing tickets.

"You can get on and off the bus wherever you want," the little lady said, smiling a sunny toothless smile.

Irene sat on the open top deck of the bus and buttoned her jacket tightly around her neck since the wind off the water was cold.

IT WAS five thirty when she dragged herself through the door of the hotel room. Her head was spinning and her feet ached. She was completely exhausted. She threw shopping bags on the bed and went into the bathroom, turned on the faucet in the tub, and started filling it with hot water. A bath was her primary need—right after caffeine, that is. Thankfully, she noted that the hotel provided a small water heater in each room. Next to the white ceramic cups, there was a bowl with tea bags, instant coffee in single servings, and sugar. Irene filled the flask with water, plugged it in, and poured the bowl's three packages of coffee into a cup.

She had gotten off at Oxford Street on the way home, just outside Selfridge's department store. A quick sweep of the floors had revealed that the prices were too high for her. To her glee she saw an H&M store a bit farther down the street, and there she found a nice light green sweater and a black top decorated with glitter. Attractive and cheap, since the sweater was on sale for half price. Irene was very pleased with her finds, but slightly embarrassed at the same time. To travel to London only to shop at H&M was really like crossing a pond to get water from the far side. If someone were to ask her where she had bought the sweater or the top, she decided to just answer, "In London."

She took the steaming cup with her into the bathroom and set it on the edge of the tub. It was heavenly to sink into the warm water and take a few sips of the venomously strong coffee. The caffeine rushed around her body and chased away her fatigue, at the same time as the heat from the bathwater increased her circulation. Her whole body started to feel pleasantly relaxed.

DARK CLOUDS gathered on the horizon and quickly closed in on the sandy beach. What had seemed warm and pleasant a little while ago, suddenly became cold and threatening. Irene was freezing but didn't know what she should do to get the temperature to rise. Her arms and legs were frozen stiff and refused to follow orders. Fear gripped her with its claws and she realized that she was paralyzed and freezing to death. The icy rain and cold were relentless; the tide would soon sweep her out into the sea. On top of all this suffering, thunder started roaring.

Irene sat up in the cold bath water with a jerk. The roar of thunder could still be heard. It took a moment before she realized that someone was knocking at the door. Shaking from cold, she stood and grabbed a big white bath towel. Shivering, she fumbled it around herself as she went to open the door. Estelle was standing outside.

Her hair was just as impeccably arranged as it had been that morning. She was dressed in a striking figure-fitting bone-white dress with matching shoes. Over one shoulder she had thrown a jacket. She smiled. "Hi. Are you almost ready?"

"No . . . I fell asleep in the bath."

"You poor thing. You flew in early this morning, and you've been busy all day. It's not surprising that you fell asleep. It's just a quarter past. I'll call and say that we'll be a little late."

She walked quickly away over the corridor's soft carpet without tripping or wobbling on her high heels. Some women know the art of walking in heels, others don't, Irene observed. Irene was definitely in the latter category.

In a flash, she showered in scorching hot water to get her circulation going. She didn't have time to wash her hair, but there was just enough to blow it dry with the hair dryer. She dived into the light-purple top and her blue linen suit. Two quick swipes with mascara over her eyelashes and a pass with the newly purchased lipstick, and she was ready to float down to Estelle, who had said she would wait in the foyer. At the last second, Irene had remembered jewelry, a present from Krister on her fortieth birthday. With quick movements of her hands, she exchanged the small silver balls in her ears for larger gold ones. Around her neck she hung the long chain with a beautiful oval golden pendant. Krister's cousin Anna, a goldsmith in Karlstad, had made them. They were the most expensive pieces Irene had ever owned, and she loved them. One glance in the mirror confirmed that she looked good enough for a London restaurant.

"YOU MANAGED it in twelve minutes. I'm impressed," said Estelle.

They walked barely a hundred meters down the street from the hotel. Vitória was located in a large brick house. They could hear South American rhythms out on the street, and a carnival atmosphere ruled inside. Some thirty people of all ages sat around a long table. Everyone sang along with the music and raised their glasses in toasts. Irene almost had to scream in order to be heard.

"Are you celebrating something?"

"Didn't Glen tell you?" Estelle asked, surprised.

"No. What?"

"Mamma is turning sixty-five."

"But then I shouldn't be—"

In her confusion Irene couldn't come up with the phrase for "butting in." Estelle said, "You aren't. It was Mamma's idea that Glen should invite you. She didn't want you to be all alone in the big city. Mamma loves to have people around her."

A plump woman in a fire-red dress came toward them with a big smile and wide-open arms. "Welcome! Now the party can really start, because everyone is here! A special welcome to Irene! My name is Donna!"

In the next moment Irene found her nose in a food-and-perfume-scented wave of gray hair, her arms locked at her sides in the woman's powerful embrace.

Donna gently pushed her back and looked up at her face. "If all police officers in Sweden are as tall as you, then I want you to send a male example, the right age for me. I love tall men!"

She smiled a glittering golden smile; for a split second, Superintendent Andersson's pale, flabby face floated by in Irene's mind. He could use someone soon to liven up his life as a retiree. Maybe she should send him here to Donna? He was about the right age, but a bit lacking in height. This vibrant woman would run him ragged in a few weeks; Irene was already feeling a bit exhausted herself.

Glen waved and hollered, pointing at two empty chairs on the other side of the table across from where he was sitting. Estelle made her way there with Irene in her wake.

"Hi, Irene! May I introduce my wife Kate and the twins, Brian and . . . where is Kevin?"

Glen got up and shouted at a group of children. While Glen

was trying to find his progeny, Irene met Kate. She was beautiful, with thick reddish-blond hair, big blue eyes, and a very pale freckled complexion. The dark, curly-haired boy at her side was joined by an identical copy whom Glen had managed to fish out of the pack of kids.

"I also have twins. But they are girls and they just turned eighteen. And they aren't—"

Irene stopped, again at a loss for a word. What were these twins called in English?

"Identical twins," Kate proffered.

A waiter came and served drinks from a tray. The dark sweet liquid that burned Irene's stomach was probably rum, but she wasn't completely sure. After a while, food was brought to the table. They ate shrimp and mussels with a spicy sauce into which you dipped wonderful newly baked bread. Then skewers of chicken and vegetables were served. The sauce that went with this course had a strong taste of chili. That's probably why the good red wine disappeared so quickly. As the levels in the glasses sank, the mood around the table soared. To her horror, Irene realized that there was more food coming when large, aromatic steaks were brought in. She was already stuffed. The meat was served with a red wine sauce and roasted potatoes.

"This meat is from South America, not England. No mad cow disease!" Donna trumpeted from the head of the table.

It tasted wonderful, but two more glasses of wine were needed to wash down all the food. Irene started feeling the effects of the wine. She told herself to take it easy. It wouldn't do to be hung over during tomorrow's questioning of Rebecka Schyttelius.

The warm mood—and the actual warmth—in the small restaurant increased. The guests cheered and sang for the birthday girl; since Irene didn't know Portuguese, she had to hum along as best she could.

A magnificent fruitcake was served for dessert, with coffee. Irene declined an after-dinner drink accompanying the coffee.

The guests talked, laughed, and sang, but the hour was approaching twelve and Irene felt that she couldn't stay awake much longer. It had been a long, eventful day. She went up to Donna, thanking her for the fun party and all the good food. Donna pulled her face down and gave her a smacking kiss on each cheek. "Promise now that you'll send me a retired police officer! A tall one!" Donna chirped.

Irene promised to do her best.

THE COOL night air felt pleasant against Irene's flushed cheeks. She took a few deep breaths in order to vent the smoke-and-alcohol-tinged air from her lungs. Glen had offered to follow her back to the hotel, but she declined when she saw that he was trying to corral the overtired twins. A taxi slowly crept toward her but continued past when she didn't hail it. It wasn't far to walk, and she could find her way.

The street was quiet and deserted. So when a car came up behind her, she heard it. She also heard it stop and a car door open, but she thought it was dropping off a passenger. She was completely unprepared when a pair of hands grabbed her upper arms from behind and thrust her through the open rear door of the taxi. She hit her forehead on the door frame so hard that she saw stars. She was roughly pushed into the car.

"Drive, damn it!" a hoarse voice muttered at her side in a London dialect. He had nauseating breath that stank from alcohol and rotten teeth.

For a second, Irene's brain was paralyzed from surprise and fear. She didn't have time to scream before he closed the car door. They had landed in a heap on the floor of the passenger compartment. She couldn't see her attacker, who was still behind and on top of her. She twisted her head using all her strength, but all she saw of the driver through the window between the rear and the driver's seat was a thick, shaved neck with a large black tattoo.

What did these men want? Who were they? The man who'd grabbed her started groping her breasts, and she was convinced that he was going to rape her, but when he tried to grab her golden pendant, she realized he was trying to rob her.

Then she became completely calm. He had released his grasp on her upper arms; his left arm was around her neck in a chokehold. Irene tensed her neck muscles and seized that arm with one hand. With all her strength, she rammed the elbow of her other arm into his stomach. The air was completely knocked out of him, and his chokehold loosened immediately. In a split second, Irene twisted out of his grip and struggled to his side. She was grateful that London taxis have generous legroom for passengers. Irene kept a steel grip on the man's arm, twisted it up behind his back, and forced him down onto his stomach. She locked his other hand by sitting on his back, driving her knee below his shoulder blades and holding his arm against the car floor with her free hand. The slightest move would increase the pressure on his back and inflict terrible pain. He lay completely still.

Everything had happened in a matter of seconds. The fat-necked guy in the front seat hardly had time to figure out what had happened, but something had: That much he understood. "What the hell are you doing?" he screamed.

He tried to turn his head and look down behind him at the floor of the taxi as he drove. Irene heard a half-suppressed curse, and then the car began to skid. It lurched and the tires screamed. Irene had a hard time keeping her hold on the man underneath her. The car came to a dead stop with a dull thud. The driver wasn't wearing a seat belt. His head struck the windshield, and he lay draped over the steering wheel.

The man under Irene didn't move either, and she was afraid that he had stopped breathing. Maybe she had unintentionally pushed too hard on his back when the car had stopped suddenly. It was a dangerous hold, and people had died previously after it was used on them. Irene leaned over, and to her relief, she heard the man breathing, but he appeared to be unconscious.

She managed to get the car door open and was helped out by a man who was hurrying toward her. He used one hand to steady her, and in the other he held a cell phone. ". . . crashed at the corner of Westbourne and Lancaster Gate . . . single-car accident . . . ran into a pole . . . a woman is uninjured but the men seem badly off . . . ambulance is probably best. . . ."

When the man turned around to find out what had caused the accident, the woman was no longer there.

Chapter 13

EVEN THOUGH IRENE HAD made up her mind not to awaken with a headache, that was exactly what happened anyway. It wasn't the fault of the alcohol she'd drunk, but that of the large bump on her head, which pounded and ached and was starting to turn blue. It was proof that last night's attack had really happened and wasn't a horrible nightmare. The bump, with a little scrape, was located right at her hairline and wasn't very visible when she brushed her bangs forward, although then the bangs stuck out oddly.

She had sneaked away from the scene of the accident. Feeling that she didn't have the energy for a night-long police interrogation, she had managed to find her way to the hotel and climb up the stairs to her room. Despite being shaken by the happenings of the previous hour, she had managed to fall into a deep and dreamless sleep. Maybe she had passed out?

Irene tottered down to the dark breakfast room in the hotel's cellar level and downed several cups of instant coffee. She was still full after Donna's birthday dinner. Half a cheese sandwich was all she had room for. Her headache eased and she could start thinking.

She had to tell the police what had happened. The only sensible thing to do was to try to reach Glen Thompson. They had decided that he would pick her up outside the hotel at twenty minutes to eleven, but now it would be better if he arrived earlier.

In her room, Irene took out Glen's card and dialed his work number. She was in luck; he answered right away. Irene tried to explain that something serious had happened the night before, but he interrupted her. "I'll come as soon as possible."

Irene went down to the lobby to wait. Estelle hurried past, chirped "Good morning," and disappeared quickly into the hotel's inner environs. She couldn't have slept too many hours, but you wouldn't have been able to tell by looking at her. Irene didn't fool herself; her reflection in the mirror had shown that her night had been difficult, but Estelle probably assumed that it was because of too much wine.

A black Rover turned in at the hotel entrance. Glen's sunny smile faded immediately when he saw Irene's face.

"Let's go up to your room," he said.

I R E N E E X P L A I N E D exactly what had happened. Glen didn't interrupt her. When she was done, he shook his head.

"Unbelievable! The question is, who had the worse luck: you, who were attacked your first night in London, or the attackers, who went up against an ex-master of ju-jitsu!"

He smiled but immediately became serious again. "I'm going to notify the police in this district."

Glen called from the telephone in Irene's room. He spoke a long time with different people. He was quiet for long periods, nodding and listening. Sometimes he glanced in Irene's direction and she thought that something flickered in his eyes; he almost looked frightened.

"Come on. It's time to go. I'll tell you all I learned in the car," Glen said, finally.

H E D I D N ' T start the car directly when they had gotten in, but looked at Irene gravely.

"You had incredible luck. Thanks to your knowledge of ju-jitsu, you avoided a terrible fate."

He turned on the ignition. The car started with a soft rumble, and he pulled away from the curb. "The taxi was stolen. The driver was found, with critical stab wounds having been robbed, on a small back street where they are in the process of tearing down some houses, just a few blocks from Vitória. He was gagged and his hands were bound with tape. He's in pretty bad shape and is in the hospital. The only consolation is that now both culprits are, as well."

Glen stopped to let an older woman with a walker cross the street at a crosswalk. When she had managed to make her way to the other side, he gunned the accelerator and continued. "The man in the back seat who attacked you is Ned Atkinson, known as Gravedigger."

He fell silent again. Irene's headache was pressing against the inside of her forehead. So she had fought with a man named Gravedigger. She tried to speak, but her tongue felt stiff and strange.

"Ned is an old lag and a drug addict. He was released a few months ago after completing a twelve-year sentence as an accessory to murder. His specialty is to assist in contract killings in the underworld and to get rid of the bodies. Hence the name Gravedigger."

Irene managed to coax her tongue to move and tried to reassure herself with a feeble smile. "Dare one ask what the other man is called?"

Glen gave her a long look before he answered. "The Butcher."

The Butcher. Irene decided not to ask anything else.

"You were lucky that he wasn't the one who pulled you into the car. The Butcher weighs about a hundred and thirty kilos and is incredibly strong. But he injured himself when he escaped from prison last month. They discovered a large infected sore on his knee when he was admitted to the hospital last night for his head injury. The superintendent I spoke with said that a normal person would hardly have been able to walk around with such an injury. The Butcher was forced to. He couldn't go to an emergency room: A nationwide bulletin had been issued for him."

They had passed Marble Arch and continued onto Oxford Street. Traffic was heavy and the sidewalks were jammed with people running in and out of the shops. Glen slowed down, turned onto a cross street, and continued. "He's being cared for in a special hospital for mentally ill criminals. He'd been in prison for a series of unusually vicious murders and rapes. Some were contract jobs, others he committed for pleasure."

Glen parked parallel to the sidewalk. When he had turned off the engine, he said softly, "Ned was without oxygen a little too long during your struggle. He's going to survive, but he'll probably have permanent injuries, although his brain damage may also have been caused by an overdose. They found high levels of morphine in his blood and he's a known heroin addict. His system is weakened by drugs and he's in overall poor health. The Butcher struck his head on the windshield and has serious skull injuries. His condition is critical. And Irene. . . ."

Glen paused and looked into Irene's eyes. "They found a large knife next to the Butcher. The same one he had stabbed the taxi driver with. It was still bloody."

Robbery. Rape. Stabbing, and maybe murder. That's what would have awaited her if she hadn't managed to get away. She couldn't keep her knees from shaking when she stepped out of the car. Despite the fact that it was thirteen degrees outside, sweat was running down her back.

DR. FISCHER had his practice in a beautiful stone house a little way from the bustle of Oxford Street. All of the houses along the cross street had been lavishly and reverently renovated.

After having spoken into the intercom to identify themselves, they were admitted. The vestibule was preserved in a Victorian style with a lot of marble and carved dark mahogany. To Irene's relief, the elevator was completely new and certainly large enough for two people.

A large man in his late fifties was standing at an open door waiting for them when they emerged from the elevator. He had thick steel-gray hair which was combed back over his high forehead, and a short gray beard. His light-gray suit was tight across the shoulders and back, but it looked expensive. His face was wide and powerful. His smile revealed large teeth, but couldn't compete with his penetrating gray-blue eyes. Despite his elegant clothes, Irene thought that he looked more like a big-game hunter than a doctor. He scrutinized them over the edge of frameless glasses.

"Officers Thompson and Huss, I believe. I'm Dr. Fischer. Come in."

He made them a slight bow, greeting them without shaking hands, and gestured toward his office. They passed through a dark hall and came to a small living room used as a waiting room. "Rebecka would like us to sit in here," said Dr. Fischer. He opened the door and stepped across the threshold first. It was furnished with antique furniture which harmonized well with the decorative plaster work of the ceiling and the lead-framed mullions in the top of the windows. There were Oriental rugs on the floor which looked genuine to Irene's untrained eye. Everything pointed to this not being your average clinic; the charges were doubtless above average as well.

Fischer approached a woman who was seated in an armchair next to one of the windows and laid one hand on her shoulder.

The light came from the side and fell on the right half of Rebecka's face. Irene could see that she was thinner than she had been in the pictures taken at the Christmas breakfast. She was dressed in a white cotton polo shirt and a black suit in a thin material which was beautifully tailored. As far as Irene could see, she wasn't wearing any jewelry. Her hair was longer than in the photos, and just as thick. However, it was completely dull, as if it hadn't been washed for quite some time. It suited her to have lost a few kilos. Her full lips and high cheekbones had become more prominent. Her eyes, looking large and empty in her pale face, betrayed her worry and anguish. Irene could see what it was that had made Christian Lefévre try to keep Rebecka away from them. He wanted to protect her against her own fear and pain.

She heard Eva Möller's voice again: "Rebecka is like her father. . . ."

"Rebecka, these are the police officers who want to speak with you," said Dr. Fischer.

Irene and Glen walked over, shook hands, and introduced themselves. Rebecka's hand felt limp and cold. Irene was unsure about how she should begin, so she said hesitantly, in Swedish, "I don't really know how I should express my colleagues' and my sympathy for you. What has happened to your family is tragic, and we're doing everything we can to solve the murders. But we need your help. There are too many questions we don't have the answers to. Do you think you have the strength to answer a few questions?"

Rebecka nodded almost imperceptibly without looking at Irene.

"My first question is, do you have any thoughts as to a motive for the killings?"

A brief headshake was the only response.

"Have your parents or Jacob ever told you that they had been threatened?"

"No," Rebecka replied softly and hoarsely.

"Have you personally ever been threatened?"

Another headshake, slightly stronger.

No one in the family had been threatened, but now three out of the four were dead. It sounded unlikely. Rebecka must know something, even if she didn't realize it, Irene thought.

"Do you know of anyone who could have hated your parents so much that he or she could have killed them?"

"No."

"And Jacob didn't have any enemy you knew of either?"

"No."

Neither Dr. Fischer nor Glen understood a word of their conversation, of course, but both of them sat perfectly still.

Irene would have given almost anything to hand the conversation over to Glen. After the previous evening's events, she was off kilter. But she had to conduct this interview herself. She decided to start another topic.

"We've heard that your father asked for your help in tracing Satanists via the Internet. Is that correct?"

"Yes."

"Did you find anything useful?"

For the first time Rebecka looked at Irene, but she turned away before she answered. "We found a lot of their propaganda. But Pappa wanted to find the ones who had burned down the church. There were just chat sites on the Web."

"Chat sites?"

"Yes. On one, someone congratulated them on the . . . 'successful raid against the enemy's temple by the sea.' Signed, 'Satan's faithful servant.' I managed to trace it to a computer at a high school in Lerum. That was it."

She spoke with a great deal of difficulty, and Irene saw cold sweat break out on her forehead. It was clear that this was hard for her.

"Do you know if your father managed to find anything during his own investigations?"

"No. I don't think so."

"You weren't home this past Christmas, correct?"

"No."

"So it has been a while since you saw your parents?"

Irene let the question hang in the air on purpose since she really didn't know how she ought to continue, but she was surprised to see Rebecka wince. She took a deep, audible breath before whispering, "Yes."

"When was the last time you saw them?"

Rebecka licked her dry lips. "Easter . . . one year ago. . . ."

"Did you notice anything out of the ordinary? An unusual or strange feeling? Someone who said something odd?"

Rebecka appeared to be thinking. "No."

"Did your father speak about the Satanists?"

"No."

"Did your mother say anything about Satanists?"

"No."

Rebecka sagged against the backrest. Her face was ashen, and Irene realized that she wouldn't be able to handle much more. The next question was sensitive, but it had to be asked. In a gentle voice, Irene said, "We found a book about Satanism at your brother's. It was hidden in the cottage. It was written by a founding figure within Satanism—"

"LaVey."

"You know the book?"

"I bought it. Here in London."

"Why?"

"He wanted it. I gave it to him as a Christmas present."

"Last Christmas?"

"No, the Christmas before."

"The Christmas when you were home?"

"Yes."

"Have you read it yourself?"

"No."

"The book was hidden in a space behind a wall panel in one of the bedrooms in the cottage. He also kept a rifle there. Did you know about that hiding place?"

"Yes."

"Did you know that he had a rifle behind the wall panel?"

Rebecka shook her head slowly.

"Who else knows about the hiding place?"

"Only our family. It was like a . . . safe."

Rebecka closed her eyes and leaned her head back. It looked like she didn't have the energy to hold up its weight any longer. Dr. Fischer started clearing his throat and twisting his large body in the chair he sat in. Irene thought feverishly. She realized that her time was almost up. Suddenly, she remembered something she had been wondering about.

"Someone said that you had been home last summer and that you had had your boyfriend with you. Is that correct?"

Rebecka looked like she was asleep but after a while she opened her eyes and looked straight at Irene. "It was Christian and myself. We were called to Stockholm . . . to do a job. Christian had never been to Sweden. We flew to Landvetter and rented a car. Drove up . . . so that he could see. We drove past Kullahult. They weren't home. Unusual."

"Did your parents know you were coming?"

"No. Short notice. I thought about surprising them. Idiotproof . . . they never went anywhere. And just that day, they drove to see Pappa's old school friend in Värmland. Went to a market, I think."

"Did you tell them later that you had been in Kullahult?"

"Actually, I don't think so. We just drove by."

"Did you see Jacob?"

"No. He didn't move down until August."

"When did you and Christian go to Stockholm?"

"The end of July."

"So Christian has never met your family?"

"No."

"And he isn't your boyfriend?"

Rebecka shook her head weakly in reply.

"Who were you going to visit in Stockholm?"

Rebecka turned her head away and didn't answer for some time. Finally, she whispered, "Save the Children Sweden."

Dr. Fischer hit the armrests on the chair firmly with the palms of his hands and said, "No. Now this is enough. Rebecka can't handle any more."

Irene saw that he was right. Rebecka lay in the armchair like a punctured balloon.

"Thank you, Rebecka, for helping me. I know how difficult

this has been for you," she started, but was interrupted by Rebecka mumbling something that sounded like ". . . no one can understand," but Irene wasn't completely sure.

Irene quickly took out her card and handed it to Glen.

"Glen, please write down the telephone number of the Thompson Hotel and your number in case she wants to reach me later in the day."

Glen did as she asked. Irene held the card out to Rebecka.

"You can reach me at the numbers on the back of the card until five thirty tonight. Then I have to fly home. After that, you can reach me at the numbers on the front. And you can, of course, always reach me on my cell phone number. Don't forget to dial the country code, plus forty-six, if you call my cell number."

Rebecka nodded. She let the hand with the card sink into her lap without taking a look at it.

"I HAVE a meeting at three o'clock. How about going to eat lunch now?" Glen suggested.

Irene thought that sounded like a good idea. Breakfast had been on the meager side.

"I'll pick you up at the hotel just after five thirty tonight. You can keep your room until then. Then you'll have plenty of time to grab a bite to eat at the airport before the flight home. What do you want to do on your own this afternoon?" Glen asked when they were in the car again, weaving their way through the heavy traffic.

"Actually, no idea. What do you suggest?" Irene said.

"Do you like old buildings, or shopping, or what?"

"Shopping I did yesterday, and old buildings really aren't my thing. Something fun that doesn't cost a lot of money," Irene concluded.

Glen thought about it for a little while. Then he brightened up. "I know! The Tate Modern. Then we can eat at a good restaurant nearby."

They drove over the Thames and turned to the left at the bridge abutment. Glen found an empty parking space where he managed to insert the Rover by a feat of advanced parallel parking. They went into a three-story building which turned out to be one restaurant on three levels. The top floor was, for the most part, made up of a terrace. A large sign explained that one could rent the entire top floor for large parties. The wind and gray weather outside didn't really inspire such use on that particular day. Irene preferred the delicious pub warmth of the bottom floor.

They found an empty table and hung their coats over the chair backs to show that they were taken. At all four corners of the table, a metal disc with an engraved number had been inserted. They had to go up to the bar to order, state their table number, and await table service. One didn't walk back to the table empty-handed, though: Instead, one carried a glass of beer.

Irene had chosen lasagna; Glen, potato and tuna salads. The servings were extremely generous and the food very good. The stereotype that Englishmen couldn't cook seemed mistaken to Irene. She had eaten well during her two days in this country. She actually hadn't eaten typical English food, though, but Chinese, South American, and Italian, consumed in the company of a dark-skinned half Scottish/half Brazilian named Glen. Nothing during her trip had really been "typically English." Maybe the beer would be.

"What impression did you get of Rebecka?" Glen asked.

"She's really sick; it's obvious. But I don't know if she's suffering from a normal depression or if she's simply overcome with fear. It seemed to me as if terror has sapped her strength. She was completely exhausted."

Glen nodded. "I, too, sensed that she felt anguished. But she actually spoke with you and answered your questions."

"Yes, she answered the questions. Not that it added much to what we already knew. But I have the feeling that she still hasn't told us everything. What is she afraid of? Who is she afraid of? Why won't she talk?"

"A lot of questions without answers," Glen said.

"I still don't know if she fears for her own life. She denied that anyone in the family had been threatened. Yet three of them have been murdered."

Glen looked at her thoughtfully. "Rebecka is a mystery. She fascinates me. She's beautiful, intelligent, but so frightened and isolated. You must speak with her again; you should wait a while but then you must get her to talk. One problem is that she doesn't want to hear about the funeral or that she should go to Sweden. It hasn't even been possible to bring it up," he said.

"How do you know that?"

"The pastor from the Seaman's Church who was with me when we first told her what had happened. He asked her to get in touch if she wanted help finding someone who could assist her, like a funeral director. I called him to find out if Rebecka had been in touch with him. She hasn't. He was concerned, because there are certain practical arrangements to be made as to funerals and estates."

"I can call him if you want. It might be a good idea to ask him to contact Dr. Fischer. He can raise the question with Rebecka when he sees that she feels a bit better and has the strength to discuss it."

"That might be a good solution."

Glen took out a notebook and flipped through it for a while before he found the number he was looking for. "Here! The Swedish Seaman's Church, Assistant Rector Kjell Sjönell," Glen read aloud.

Irene laughed when Glen tried to pronounce the Swedish *sj* sound. She wrote down Kjell Sjönell's number and his office hours.

THEY WALKED along the Thames and talked about the dramatic occurrences of the last twenty-four hours.

"I'm going to write down your account of the attack. I'll fax it to you so that you can read through it and sign it. I don't know yet if you'll need to come here again to testify at the trial against those villains, if they happen to recover enough for there to *be* a trial. I'll find out," Glen told her.

"Why do you think they chose me as a victim?" Irene asked.

"Well, they saw a woman leaving a restaurant alone, a restaurant that seemed to be quite lively. There was a good chance that she was intoxicated. A perfect robbery victim."

Suddenly, Irene remembered the taxi she had seen just as she'd reached the street. She had left her jacket open because it had been warm inside the restaurant. Gravedigger and the Butcher would have seen the reflection of their headlights on her gold jewelry. Instinctively, she grabbed the golden pendant which was hanging around her neck.

After a walk of about a kilometer or so, Glen pointed at a large building that rose up a short distance from the Thames. "That's the Tate Modern. It's an old electrical station that was converted into a modern museum. The ceiling height in the old turbine hall is thirty-five meters. But it's actually fun to walk and look around. Kate and I were there just a few weeks ago. There's a lot to see. And it's free."

"How come it's free?"

"Built with donations. From the Guggenheim Fund, I think."

Irene had never heard of that fund, but there appeared to be a lot of money in it if it could finance the massive building that rose in front of them. Of course, the fund hadn't built the building itself, but made sure it was renovated and filled with art.

* * *

IRENE SPENT several pleasant hours at the Tate Modern, among the works of some of the most famous modern artists. For the first time, Irene saw original paintings by Picasso, Monet, Dalí and van Gogh, Leger and Mondrian. She realized that most of the artists she'd thought of as "modern" weren't actually very recent: Most of them had been productive at the end of the nineteenth century and then up to the middle of the twentieth century. Despite that, they were known as the groundbreakers of modern art. Irene felt the power in the images and understood that they were about what had been "New" around the turn of the twentieth century, which had transformed art forever.

Wandering among the artworks felt instructive, but was also tiring for the feet. She finally ended up in the overcrowded cafeteria at the top of the building, on the seventh floor. She managed to find an empty barstool and order a beer. Sitting and looking at a mixture of people from all corners of the world was intriguing. If she grew tired of them, she could gaze out over London's rooftops and at the boats below on the Thames. Time flew by until she had to head toward the hotel and the airport.

GLEN DROVE her to Heathrow. Before they parted, Irene said, "I reached the pastor, Kjell Sjönell. He promised to get in touch with Dr. Fischer and then to contact me. We'll have to see if Rebecka recovers sufficiently to be able to come home to Sweden. Otherwise, I might have to return here once more."

Glen smiled. "It would be very nice if you could visit us again. But, of course, I hope Rebecka gets better. I've been thinking about her and her mystery. I think she holds the key to the truth. Whether she knows it or not."

Irene nodded. "That's exactly what I think as well."

Chapter 14

IRENE STORMED INTO HANNU Rauhala's office with Sunday's edition of *GT* in front of her.

"Hannu! Explain!"

He looked at the black headlines on the front page: **"Church accountant who was questioned in SATANIC MURDERS is suspected of EMBEZZLEMENT!"**

"Can't. I only saw it yesterday too."

Irene was so upset that her voice shook. "How could you talk to Kurt Höök about this?" Höök was GT's famous crime reporter, and he had his sources. If you had a tip about a criminal activity, Höök was the person you called.

"I haven't." Hannu leaned back in his chair and looked her straight in the eye. Irene knew he wasn't lying. Even if he might need money for the new house and the baby, he would never do something like that.

She threw the paper on Hannu's desk and sat in the visitor's chair.

"Honestly, I didn't think you had. But who else could it have been? Only you and I and Sven knew about these rumors. I've been in London. And Sven would never speak with Kurt Höök. They detest one another. By the way, did you find anything that might point to there being some truth behind the accusations?"

"Nothing. The auditor showed me everything, going back ten years. There have never been any suspicions of embezzlement."

"But this is still a catastrophe for Louise and Bengt Määrdh! It's going to take a long time before they're cleared."

"Who has something to gain if these rumors come out?"

Irene wrinkled her brow. "Urban Berg."

Hannu nodded.

Irene went into her office and did some serious thinking. She made her decision and placed a phone call. Later on in the day, she would make another, but it was still too early.

LOUISE MÅÅRDH bore obvious traces of the happenings of the last day. Her hair wasn't combed, and her only attempt at makeup was sloppily swiped-on red lipstick, which clashed with her rust-colored sweater. She was wearing a light green T-shirt with a damp coffee stain on the front. Her dark-blue jeans were wrinkled and her feet were covered only by slippers which were worn at the heel. With a tired gesture, she motioned for Irene to come in.

The Måårdhs didn't live in a rectory, but in a relatively new house outside Ledkulla. The house was decorated in pastels, which worked well with the modern furniture in light-colored birch. Bookshelves, filled with volumes, towered along the walls. The house had a soothing but sophisticated atmosphere. Even to Irene's untrained eye, the rugs and art appeared to be of exceptional quality. She understood why suspicions and jealousy had grown over the years. "How can they afford it? It can never add up." "She manages large sums of money. Think how easy it would be to let a thousand disappear from time to time."

Louise led Irene into the light, airy living room. "Please, sit down," she said dully.

Irene sat in a graceful armchair that was covered in light-gray suede. It was really comfortable. Louise sank down heavily onto the gray leather couch across from her. Irene felt uneasy and started, rambling, "I understand that this is terrible. We're doing everything we can to try to find out what might have happened. It was one lead among many others we were looking into. Just routine. . . . How GT got ahold of it, we don't know."

"I can't go to work. We've been hung out to dry in the press and already judged and found guilty. It doesn't matter if I'm cleared eventually. People will always whisper 'No smoke without fire' and the like. Anonymous calls have already begun. I don't even dare to go out and get the mail."

"Has the press called?"

As if in reply, the sound of a ringing telephone cut through the room. After two rings, it fell silent. Someone at the other end of the house answered. Bengt must be home, thought Irene.

"They call all the time. It's not that difficult to figure out which church accountant has been involved in the investigation of the Satanic Murders. There's just one. Me."

Her voice was still creepily toneless. But she couldn't maintain her self-control any longer. Heavy sobs were wrenched from her and tears ran down her cheeks. Irene managed to find a clean tissue in one jacket pocket; she held it out to Louise, who took it.

Irene's sympathy for Louise was mixed with growing anger. False rumors are evil, unpleasant, cruel . . . and impossible to defend oneself against. Resolutely, she moved next to Louise on the sofa. Anger toward the person who had caused all this unnecessary pain made her voice sound cold.

"Listen and I'll tell you what happened. Urban Berg came to see me at the police station and told me that Sten Schyttelius suspected you of embezzling money from the parish. Because this is a major homicide investigation, naturally we have to follow every lead we get. The risk of someone's being revealed as an embezzler would theoretically be a motive for murder—"

Irene didn't get any farther. Louise jumped up, her apathy and tears replaced by anger.

"Urban Berg! That drunken, hypocritical fool! I'm going to kill him!"

It probably wasn't the wisest choice of words under the circumstances, but Irene understood. However, Bengt Måårdh looked startled when he stopped, hesitantly, on the threshold to the living room.

"But sweetheart, who is it who's . . ." he said awkwardly. His brown eyes behind his glasses were helplessly confused.

"Urban Berg! That damned Urban! He's the one who's behind the whole thing!"

It took them almost ten minutes, using all their powers of persuasion, to calm Louise sufficiently so that Irene could explain.

"Listen, Louise. This is what I think we should do," Irene said at last.

THE FIRST thing Irene did when she entered her office was to call him. She had his direct number.

"Höök!" he answered briskly.

"Irene Huss here."

"Well, hello!"

He sounded sincerely happy and Irene felt a stab of guilt for what she was about to do. But for Louise and Bengt's sake, she had to pull herself together. None of this how's-it-going-let's-go-have-a-beer nonsense! Though it was usually fun to do that with Kurt. That would have to come later. First, he needed to make things right.

"Hello to you. I'm calling because you're going to do an interview."

A brief, surprised silence ensued. "I am? An interview with who?" he asked.

"Me."

The next pause was considerably longer. It was obvious that he was on the defensive. "Really? About what?"

"You're risking a prosecution for slander! And you'll lose."

"Wait a second, sweetheart. . . ."

"I'm not your sweetheart! You didn't check your source, and it has had disastrous consequences for the persons identified. Your information is based on pure lies and spite. Louise Måårdh has never been suspected of embezzlement or been the subject of a police investigation."

"But I called and checked with the auditor. He wasn't there, but . . . a person close to him confirmed that the police had been there and checked the accounts."

"That's correct. We checked out the tip. But we didn't find any irregularities whatsoever. Neither the auditor nor anyone else has any suspicions either. There's no official police report or even a decision to investigate, so there's no reason for prosecution. No one has ever put forth any valid suspicions about Louise Määrdh, just malicious slander and nothing else!"

Höök was silent. Irene continued, and in a pedagogical tone. "Assistant Rector Urban Berg tricked you, and me too. He came here and told me that Sten Schyttelius suspected that Louise Määrdh had embezzled money. No one else has ever heard anything like that and, as is commonly known, Sten Schyttelius is dead. Urban Berg probably thought it was safe to claim that a dead man had uttered suspicions about financial swindles. He lied to my face."

"But why? Who could conceive of a pastor who lies?"

"In order to get rid of his toughest competitor for the rector's position. Berg has two convictions for drunk driving. The only thing Bengt Määrdh has is a reputation as a ladies' man—and actually, now that I think of it, that charge also came from Berg. Even if it is finally established that the accusations against Louise are unfounded, the decision about the new rector will have been made: Urban Berg would have become the rector of Kullahult. We've been joking during the investigation and saying that the pastors in this case are 'petty gossiping pigs,' but Urban Berg is something else. He's a liar and a schemer."

Kurt sighed. "And what do you think we should do about it?"

"Expose Urban Berg. We're going to tell the public just what happened. I'm going to pull out the old drunk-driving convictions. I'm going to recount exactly what he said when he came to see me last week. Of course, we're going to make it very clear that Louise Määrdh is innocent. You're going to write the whole truth."

"Is there any foundation to the charge that Mr. and Mrs. Måårdh spent a suspicious amount of money in the last few years?"

Irene smiled as she replied. "Bengt told me that he and his brother inherited a large sum of money from a childless uncle a few years ago. Neither Louise nor Bengt told anyone else about this inheritance, so that there *wouldn't* be a lot of gossip."

"And I'll write that as well," Kurt determined.

"Of course."

"Poor Urban Berg. And poor me."

"No one feels sorry for either of you. The least you can do is try to make things right. Innocent people have been hurt. Remember, there must be bold headlines on the front page!"

"Okay, okay. I'll do it."

"WELL. TWO days in London at our expense, and the only thing you come home with is a bandage on your forehead."

Superintendent Andersson drummed his fingers on his desk-top. Irene had just finished her account of her trip to London. They were reviewing the case in the afternoon, since morning prayers had been cut short because the superintendent had had to go to a superintendents' meeting. With good reason, it could be assumed that this was one cause of his bad mood.

Another was that Jonny Blom had called in sick again. Since the unit was understaffed, if a single person was missing it was immediately felt. The ones who remained nearly collapsed under the requirements of the job. Work accumulated on their desks. Prioritizing was tough. It wasn't easy explaining to the little old lady who had been threatened with a knife and robbed of a hundred and forty-three SEK, when she called for the seventh time in three days, that this investigation didn't have the highest priority. For her, what had happened was a nightmare. For the police, it was yet another piece of paper on their desks. Maybe they would catch the culprit if there were further similar attacks in the area. If they were lucky, they might get a good description. If not, that report would just sink farther down under the pile of new cases.

"I actually think it provided us with a lot of new information. For example, I learned that Rebecka brought Christian Lefévre to Sweden last summer. They drove to Kullahult but never met her parents or brother. They drove up to Stockholm to discuss a job for Save the Children. Then they flew straight home to London again from Stockholm, without getting in touch with her parents," said Irene.

"She never told her parents that they had been by the rectory?" Fredrik asked.

"I asked, and she said no."

"What did they do for Save the Children?" Hannu wondered.

"No idea. That was the last question I was able to ask before she collapsed. Maybe we should contact Save the Children in Stockholm?"

"What the hell? They can't have anything to do with the murders!" the superintendent exclaimed.

It really wasn't one of his better days. Irene was overcome by a strong desire to send him over to Donna Thompson. Partly to get rid of him for a while, and partly because it probably would do him some good. But Donna would be disappointed. A pale and chubby bald superintendent with high blood pressure wasn't what she had wished for. It was probably better for all involved if Andersson remained at the station in Göteborg.

"I know that it may be a dead end. But we don't have any other leads, except for the computers, in this investigation. The only thing we know is that the computer screens were marked with bloody pentagrams. And that all the information on the hard drives was erased. Sten Schyttelius used computers. Jacob Schyttelius used computers. Rebecka works with computers at the highest level, as does Lefévre. The only one who didn't have anything to do with computers was Elsa Schyttelius."

"Where are the removable disks?" Hannu interjected.

"We haven't found a single one," Fredrik said.

"Exactly. There should be loads of them. Not least for back-ups," Irene agreed.

"What exactly do Rebecka and that guy do?" Fredrik asked.

"Lefévre was communicative when I asked about their work. Apparently, most of it has to do with Internet security questions. How to stop sabotage and things like that."

"What does that have to do with the murders?" the superintendent wanted to know.

"Perhaps nothing at all. But maybe it has to do with other things. When it comes to the Satanic lead, we've hit a dead end and can't get any farther. What if Sten Schyttelius came across something completely different when he was searching for the Satanists? Something that was threatening enough to one or several people that they decided to kill him? That would explain why Elsa and Jacob were also killed. The murderer didn't want to risk that Sten Schyttelius might have told the people closest to him about what he had found."

It became quiet in the room. Eventually, Hannu said, "Then Rebecka is still in danger."

"I'm afraid so. The murderer can't know if Sten or Jacob had time to reveal anything to her. She seemed to feel a great deal of anguish *and* she was very frightened."

"But why can't the chick spit out what she knows?" Fredrik asked.

"Rebecka is a private person. Maybe she has no idea what it's all about. Maybe she has a faint idea but doesn't want to admit it to herself, suppressing everything that's threatening. Maybe she's in denial. I don't know."

"If the murderer took the time to destroy the hard drives, then he may have also destroyed the diskettes or removable disks. But maybe he still has them, so he can use the information they contain. Maybe they're hidden somewhere in the area," Fredrik suggested.

"Or they're with the murderer," Hannu added.

It would have been meaningless to destroy the hard drives and leave any removable disks. All the important information that was on the hard drives would also have been backed up, unless they had neglected this step. Had they? Not everyone was conscientious enough to back up their data.

"Could we have missed a place in the houses where you can hide discs or diskettes?" Irene asked, without much hope.

"Hardly. The houses have been gone over with a magnifying glass. Remember, the technicians found the hiding place behind the panel in the cottage," Fredrik answered.

"The hiding place, yes. . . . Rebecka said that was used as a kind of safe. Who needs a safe in a cottage?" Irene asked.

"Maybe they feared a break-in. Break-ins at summer cottages are rising astronomically," the superintendent muttered.

"But it wasn't that far to the rectory. Why did they need a hiding place for important things at the cottage?" Irene persisted.

"Maybe he needed to hide the bottles from the wife," Fredrik suggested.

"But according to Rebecka, everyone in the family knew about the hiding place."

"What's the guy like?" Hannu asked. A certain confusion arose until they concluded that he meant Christian Lefévre.

"A John Lennon lookalike who's a thoughtful employer. He's very worried about Rebecka. Overprotective. He's tried to keep the police away from her. Having met Rebecka, I now understand him better. She really is in bad shape," said Irene.

"Is it possible that she's pretending to be sicker than she really is?" Andersson asked, with a hint of interest in his voice.

"No. She's terribly ill. And Dr. Fischer told Gl . . . Inspector Thompson that he had begun treating her for depression last fall. He seems to be a well-known doctor. Nice office."

"And Lefévre and Rebecka don't seem to have something going on?" Fredrik wondered.

"No. Not that I could tell."

"Irene has to go back," Hannu said, looking at the superintendent.

Andersson turned red. "That's not possible. Do you know what it costs?"

"Rebecka holds the answer," Hannu said.

"Possibly. But we'll wait. She's too damn sick to help us, according to Irene."

Irene decided it was appropriate to break into the conversation. "I've spoken with the pastor at the Swedish Seaman's Church in London. He promised to get in touch when Rebecka improves."

"Then we wait until then," Andersson concluded.

IT TOOK quite a while before Irene managed to get ahold of the right person. The one who had been most involved in the investigation was on Easter vacation in Idre but after a good deal of wandering about the telephone exchange, she was able to speak with an officer named Lisa Sandberg. Irene introduced herself and explained the reason for her call.

"My question, then, is what kind of work Rebecka Schyttelius and Christian Lefévre did for you at Save the Children."

"It's no secret from the police, even if I don't want you to spread it around. There are probably a lot of people who would like to see Schyttelius's and Lefévre's heads on a platter," Lisa Sandberg said seriously.

"The information will remain confidential. Only the investigation team will learn of it," Irene assured her.

"Okay. What happened was that, out of sheer luck, we received a tip about a network of pedophiles who were spreading child pornography on the Internet. They had created a Web community, which is like a closed club, on the Internet. We traced them but didn't have the ability to get into their archives of pictures and films.

"Then someone in our group mentioned Rebecka Schyttelius and that she worked with a very clever guy. They had done similar jobs for the WHO. We contacted Rebecka, and she and her partner came here. We gave them all the information we had, and they went back to London and started to work from there. They were able to get access to the group without being discovered. It turned out that there were fifty-seven people, from all over Scandinavia, in the community. They had a bulletin board and a chat site where they met at certain times and discussed pictures and fantasies. This is the largest child pornography ring ever identified in the Nordic region."

"I remember reading about it in the paper last winter. There were a lot of people who one wouldn't have suspected would ever be arrested for something like that."

"A professor of comparative literature who was about to retire, a female municipal commissioner who was a mother of four, a famous Danish furniture designer. . . . Well, there were a lot of surprises. But that's what we learned from this investigation: It's never possible to predict who's going to be obsessed with child pornography."

"How were you able to identify all of these people?"

"It was very difficult. Everyone used nicknames and anonymous E-mail addresses. It was Rebecka's and Christian's work that made it possible to locate so many."

"Was it possible to identify all of them?"

"No. Five remained unidentified: two in Sweden, two in Norway, and one in Denmark."

"What were the 'names' of the ones in Sweden?"

"Peter and Pan."

"Were Peter and Pan connected? It almost sounds that way. Peter Pan."

"No. We also thought that, but we found nothing to support it."

"So Rebecka and Christian made their way into this group, and then revealed the identities of those involved?"

"Yes. They followed the group's activities for a few months and collected evidence. For example, they found out when, where, and how the E-mail addresses had been used in connection with other activities on the Web. They systematically revealed who had hidden themselves behind nicknames. If I understood it correctly, they traced them through the computer. I guess there's something called an IP address number . . . I'm not very good when it comes to the technological aspect."

"No, I understand. That's why you asked Rebecka and Christian for help."

"Yes. They did a fantastic job. The pictures and films are of the worst kind and show violent assaults on children. A grown man having sexual intercourse with a three-month old baby; small girls and boys only five or six years old being raped in front of the camera; and so on. The network held visual documentation of thousands of sexual assaults on children. You could say that the admission ticket to the club was that you submitted your own pictures or films to the archive.

"We're in the process of trying to identify the children. It's a difficult job. The pictures came from all over the world. All of us who have seen them have been sickened. They're terrible images, and I've had problems sleeping and sometimes felt depressed—for no immediate reason—after viewing them. I realize that it's the terrible pictures that pop up in my head that are affecting me."

A thought struck Irene: Was it the work on child pornography that had triggered Rebecka's depression last fall? If seasoned investigators were disturbed by the evidence, it didn't sound too farfetched to think that Rebecka could have been affected even more. Was this something to bring up with Dr. Fischer and maybe Rebecka herself?

"Thank you for taking the time to tell me about this," said Irene.

"It's not a problem. It's Save the Children's mission to spread information about what's happening on the Internet. Sexual assaults on children happen every day, and pictures move with the speed of light and are spread via the global network. They're copied all the time on an unknown number of computers around the world. Naturally, also here in Sweden."

"It feels terribly . . . hopeless. What can you do?"

"That's difficult to answer. The Web has a life of its own. There are no limitations of time or space. But we must never give up, for the sake of the children. They don't have anyone but us. The average person doesn't want to know about what's going on and doesn't want to hear us talk about it. They cover their ears and pretend they don't know anything. We're talking about the majority of the adult population. But the thing is that if they do know what's going on, but don't do anything, they're accessories. That's my opinion."

Irene agreed with her. She had investigated a few cases of incest over the years. Strikingly often, adults near the vulnerable children suspected or knew what was going on, but didn't do anything to help them.

After she had hung up the phone, Irene sat for a long time and thought about things. Could Rebecka have come across information about someone she knew during the investigation of the child pornography ring? Had she told her parents and brother? Had they used that information? Perhaps in the wrong way, since all three were dead.

The only one who could answer the questions was Rebecka. Hannu was right. Irene had to go back to London after the coming Easter Weekend.

ON TUESDAY morning, a young ornithologist phoned Superintendent Andersson. During his bird-watching on Sunday, he had found the remains of a campfire near the north side of Norssjön. At first he hadn't looked closely at the ashes, but an impulse made him do just that before he left the area. He was certain that there had been fragments of computer diskettes in the remains of the fire. Thanks to the newspapers, everyone knew about the destroyed hard drives and the bloody penta- grams at the crime scenes. Still, it took him all day Monday to convince himself that his discovery might have something to do with the murders.

Andersson set up a meeting with him, so he could guide them to the site of the fire. Sven beeped Fredrik Stridh without get- ting a reply. Then he dialed Irene's direct line. She was in and promised to come by his office immediately. The superintendent gave her his information and asked her to bring a technician with her to the meeting place.

THE FIFTEEN-YEAR-OLD birdwatcher stood, stamping ner- vously, at the agreed-upon place outside the pizzeria in Kullahult. An expression of disappointment was visible on his acne- covered face when Irene drove up in her unmarked car and introduced herself as a detective inspector. The question was what disappointed him the most: that she was a female police officer, or that he wouldn't have a chance to ride in a police car with its blue lights flashing. Irene jumped behind the wheel again. Svante Malm sat in the back seat, a large technician's bag next to him. The youth introduced himself as Tobbe Asp. He sat next to Irene in the front passenger seat and directed them toward Norssjön. They stopped at a small side road a few hun- dred meters before the gravel road that led to the Schyttelius family cottage. The weather was beautiful, even if it was still chilly. Wiser now, after her earlier forest wanderings, Irene had brought along a pair of rubber boots. With the bird-watcher in the lead, they tramped down toward the lake.

At the edge of the lake, they found the abandoned campfire in a deep crevice in the cliff. With a naked eye, Svante Malm determined that there were remains of diskettes in the ashes.

While Svante took care of the remains and investigated the

area surrounding it, Irene drove the helpful Tobbe back to the pizzeria. He inquired if it would be possible to go along to the technical lab at the police station, like, follow the ashes he had found. Irene said conspiratorially that for reasons of procedure it could not be done, but that his discovery was invaluable. With that he seemed to be satisfied.

Chapter 15

"SHE WAS ACTUALLY THE one who suggested that I film her."

Tommy waved the videocassette he held in his hand. Irene, Superintendent Andersson, and Fredrik sat in front of the TV in one of the larger interrogation rooms, the audience for Tommy's movie premiere.

With a ceremonious expression, he inserted the cassette in the VCR and started it. The chosen audience could hear Tommy's voice when he announced the date, which was a bit unnecessary since it was also displayed in one of the corners of the screen. Then he continued, "Present are myself, Detective Inspector Tommy Persson; Prosecutor Inez Collin; and attorney Henning Neijlert. The witness who will be questioned is Mrs. Gertrud Ritzman."

The camera captured Inez Collin's profile. Her light hair was gathered in a neat ponytail. She was wearing a light-brown leather blazer and a toffee-colored silk top under it, with the pearl necklace she often wore around her neck. She unconsciously stroked the pearls. Irene noted long bronze-colored fingernails and a large brilliant diamond ring on her left ring finger.

Attorney Neijlert was a nervous blinking man, a bit past middle age. His hairline was almost at the top of his head, but the curly hair that remained was surprisingly thick and silver-gray. His pointy facial features made him look like an old poodle.

Previously, Tommy had told Irene that Gertrud Ritzman had just turned eighty. She looked it, but her haggard appearance was mainly a result of her illness, not of her age itself. Her claw-like hands shook when she pulled a light-blue sweater tighter around herself. The skin on the backs of her hands was spotted and wrinkled. It seemed too big for her almost transparent hands. Her lips had a bluish tinge against the pale-yellow skin of her face, and her breathing was heavy and strained. A large oxygen tank sat next to her. A thin plastic tube ran from it to her nose to provide her with extra oxygen.

"Mrs. Ritzman has asked me to videotape her testimony about what took place on the night in question, and early that morning. She believes she's ill enough that there's a chance she might be . . . gone . . . when the time comes for the trial of Asko Pihlainen," Tommy's voice said.

"I'm going to be dead. I should be already, but I'm tough." Resolutely, the little woman took the initiative and explained how she had seen Asko Pihlainen and his neighbor, Wisköö, pull up in front of the houses right across from her own on the morning in question. The time was almost five thirty. There was no way they could have been playing poker with their wives at around five o'clock, as they claimed.

Inez Collin asked a few questions in order to check how well Gertrud Ritzman was aware of dates and times. There was never the slightest hesitancy in her answers. Her memory was sound as a bell. The group asked a few supplementary questions. Toward the end, her clear gaze clouded somewhat and her voice shook noticeably between her wheezing breaths. She was completely worn out and wouldn't last much longer. Tommy must have realized this as well, because he finished the questioning with a pan shot of the people present in the room. Then the TV screen turned black.

Andersson broke the silence. "Will this hold up?" he asked.

"According to the prosecutors, it will hold up in court," Tommy replied.

"How is it going for Narcotics?"

"They are in the process of tracing some leads. Where the narcotics have gone after being brought ashore, and so on. But you know how Narcotics is: They don't say much."

"Okay. Keep in touch with them," said Andersson.

Irene asked permission to speak and told them what Lisa Sandberg at Save the Children had said. She finished by explaining her own theory. "Apparently, the pictures are terribly disturbing and those who have seen the material have not felt well afterward. Rebecka's depression in the fall started during her work on this pedophile ring. I'm starting to wonder if she came across something that threatened a certain person. Maybe she told her parents and brother. I think they revealed their knowledge to this person. Maybe they didn't realize that it could be dangerous. The person felt so pressured that he—or she—killed all three of them."

"But then why won't Rebecka tell us what it's about?" Fredrik exclaimed.

"I don't know. Maybe she doesn't know herself. Or maybe she's been frightened into silence."

"Hell, she wouldn't protect her own family's murderer!" Andersson exploded.

"I agree that it sounds strange. But that's the only conclusion I can reach."

Finally, Fredrik said, "Rebecka is the key to everything. You will have to try to talk with her again. She must be made to understand that she might be the next victim."

The superintendent drummed his fat fingers on the table. The color in his face rose and he moved his lips as he was thinking. Suddenly he slapped the palm of his hand on the tabletop. "Okay. Rebecka has to start talking, Irene. You'll have to get in touch and try to arrange a new meeting with her." He pursed his mouth thoughtfully. "There's something that doesn't add up about that girl. Could she have *done* it?" he asked.

Irene had just realized that Andersson's words meant that

she would get to go to London again. She was surprised by his follow-up question. The thought had never occurred to her. When she had recovered from the shock, she said, "No. Rebecka has an alibi. Christian Lefévre says that she worked all day. Then she had a headache and went to bed. And she was at work when Lefévre arrived on Tuesday morning. Jacob and her parents were killed during the night. No. There's no chance.

"And furthermore, I honestly don't think she could kill another person."

"And Lefévre?" Tommy asked.

"Hardly. He has never met Rebecka's family. And he went to his usual pub right after work and worked on a betting pool with his friends. That can be checked out."

"Check it, then," the superintendent decided.

The meeting was finished.

"HEY, GLEN," said Irene.

After many fruitless telephone calls, she managed to reach him. He sounded sincerely happy when she said that she would be coming back to London for supplementary questioning of Rebecka Schyttelius. Irene told him about the information that Save the Children had provided. Glen reflected on what she had told him.

"It's a possibility. In a way, I think it's more plausible than the Satanist lead. Or maybe the search for Satanists on the Internet got the same result as the search for the pedophiles. That is to say, that Rebecka found something troublesome about a person who absolutely didn't want it revealed."

"You mean we can't drop the Satanic theory?"

"Well, there were the pentagrams."

He was right. Irene thought the pedophile theory was likelier, since Rebecka's depression had started during the fall while she was working on that investigation. But then there were the bloody pentagrams. The murderer must have known about the Schyttelius family's Internet search for Satanists. A pedophile could hardly have known that. Unless he was close to the family.

Irene had to admit that they couldn't rule out the Satanists entirely.

They agreed that Glen would check Christian Lefévre's visit to the pub, just as a formality to placate Superintendent Andersson. Irene would get in touch with the pastor of the Swedish Seaman's Church, Kjell Sjönell. When she knew the dates she would be in London, she would contact Glen again.

"I ACTUALLY haven't had time to call Dr. Fischer as I promised. Since Rebecka is so sick, I thought there wasn't any hurry," Kjell Sjönell apologized.

"There isn't. But it's of the utmost importance that I meet with Rebecka again. You and I didn't have time to talk much, the last time I called you. How did Rebecka react when she found out about what had happened to her family?" Irene asked.

It struck her that she hadn't asked Glen about this either.

"I've thought a great deal about poor Rebecka. To deliver news of a death is one of the worst jobs I've had. And still I've performed this service many times." Sjönell's voice was filled with compassion.

"How did she react?"

"At first it seemed like she didn't understand what I had said. When she realized what had happened, it was as if ice-cold fear enveloped her and froze her."

"What do you mean?"

"All color left her face. She sat there with her mouth gaping, with a terrified look in her eyes. As if frozen in the moment. Nothing else happened. She just sat there, in the armchair. The question is whether or not that scream is still frozen inside her. I think it never came up out of her throat."

He was probably right. This man had seen a great deal and

met a lot of people at different stages in their lives. Irene sensed that he possessed a good knowledge of human nature. He was putting into words what she had suspected when she met Rebecka.

"Did you and Inspector Thompson meet her in her apartment?"

"Yes. She has an amazingly beautiful home. But it seems a bit minimalist. Don't misunderstand me: It's as consciously minimal as the decor in home design magazines. But I got a feeling of . . . loneliness. It didn't feel like she ever had large parties or entertained a lot of people in her apartment. If you know what I mean."

"Yes. You see Rebecka as a lonely person."

Sjönell seemed to weigh his words before he answered. "As a pastor, I often run into human loneliness. It's an illness in today's society. Yes, I think she's solitary. The only ones she seems to have faith in are the young man she works with and Dr. Fischer. She asked us to call Dr. Fischer when she finally managed to say a few words."

"So he came to her apartment?"

"Yes."

"Have you and Dr. Fischer had any contact regarding the practical details surrounding the funerals?"

"No. But I can call him this afternoon. I have a good friend who runs a very well-regarded funeral home in Göteborg. He can best help Rebecka with all the arrangements. Might it be better to postpone the funeral for a few more weeks? The possibility exists that Rebecka will become well enough to be able to travel home."

"Yes, it may be best to wait a bit longer," Irene agreed.

She didn't think Rebecka would ever be able to come home, but decided not to say anything.

A CERTAIN calm had fallen over the unit before the

approaching Easter weekend. It would probably last for a few days, then be broken by chaos on Easter Eve. Domestic disputes, drunks, assaults, rapes, murder; everything that usually went along with the celebration of a holiday would occur. If there was a murder, then the inspectors who were on duty would have to take care of it. For the first time in many years, Irene was going to be off duty the whole weekend. Four days free. It felt too good to be true. On the other hand, she had been on duty the whole Christmas weekend and would have to work over Midsummer, so being free for Easter was only fair.

"It seems appropriate to talk about ashes today on Ash Wednesday," said Svante Malm.

He had shown up around three o'clock in the afternoon to make a report. Irene suspected that he had smelled the coffee all the way down in the lab. Either that, or it was the smell of the freshly baked Tosca cake. It was Tommy's treat, since his birthday would fall on Easter Monday. The next day, Maundy Thursday, he was going to go with his whole family to Åre for the season's last ski-and-snowboarding trip. Irene didn't envy him. Four hundred and eighty miles in an old Volvo with two adults, three children ages nine to fifteen, and a lively dog—incidentally, a daughter of Sammie's—plus a lot of luggage, didn't seem like a dream vacation. Even if the car was a station wagon, it would be a tight fit. Personally, she was looking forward to a relaxing weekend off with her family.

"There were definitely the remains of diskettes in the ashes. But we also found remains of videocassettes. Everything was burned pretty badly. There isn't a chance of recovering what was on them."

He leaned forward and took out a thick transparent plastic bag filled with small black clumps and black powder. To Irene it looked like regular ashes.

"This is interesting," the technician said.

The gathered police officers tried to look sincerely interested.

"He—or she—had brought along charcoal with which to start a fire."

The superintendent looked blank. With a show of patience, in a pedagogic tone of voice, Svante Malm continued, "It was cold and it started raining during the night of the murders. It wouldn't have been easy to start a fire with the damp branches that were available in nature. So the murderer brought some charcoal, which is used in outdoor barbecues, in order to start a fire. We've also found traces of lighter fluid around the fire. Charcoal burns longer than regular wood. It becomes very hot and everything is thoroughly incinerated.

"Charcoal and lighter fluid. So the murderer had planned on burning the diskettes and the cassettes. He knew what he would find before the murders and what he would do with it," Tommy concluded.

"But, of course, he had a little bit of bad luck. The wind probably blew this out of the fire, because it was caught in a bush a few meters away from it. We think it's the cover from a match book. Advertising matches."

Svante bent and fished out a smaller plastic bag. At first, Irene thought it was empty; but then she saw a small burned piece of light cardboard in one corner. After yet another deep rummage in the roomy bag, Svante stood and leaned a large piece of paper against the flip-over notebook stand behind him.

"An enlargement," he said and stepped to the side so that they all could see.

Pu
Mosc

"Moscow. A Russian bastard who comes from Moscow," said Jonny Blom. He laughed to show that it was a joke. Nobody paid attention to his remark.

"'Pu.' Could it be, for example, 'public' or 'pub'?" Irene asked.

"Possibly. The edge of the paper ends right after the 'u' in 'Pu' and after the 'c' in 'Mosc.' I'm a bit uncertain as to whether there really is a small 'e' in front of the 'Pu,' but it looks most like an 'e.' It has a different appearance than the other letters. Old-fashioned script style."

"Gothic," said Hannu.

"If you say so. . . ." said Svante.

He nodded to himself as if he had gotten something confirmed. Then he continued, "The text is white on a black background, except for the gothic 'e,' which is gold-colored."

Something flickered at the very back of Irene's memory, but it was too faint for her to make out what it was. Had she really seen that writing somewhere? She let it go, since she wasn't sure.

She bought *GT* on the way home. The headlines proclaimed: **"Pastor with connections to Satanic murders bore false witness!"**

You're managing, little Kurt, she thought contentedly.

MAUNDY THURSDAY started beautifully. The weather service had promised fine weather for the entire weekend, but their promises were not very dependable. In Irene's opinion, you could put more stock in Eva Möller's crystal balls and spells, or magical formulas. Speaking of whom, Irene found herself wondering if she had been hypnotized or ingested some kind of hallucinogenic drug at that strange witch's place. But then she hadn't had time to eat or drink anything. Had what she thought she had seen and experienced really happened?

She thought about it when she put on her jacket to get the car and drive to work.

Running into Mrs. Bernhög at the gate felt like a confirmation of her thoughts. Little Felicia tumbled around on a thin pink silk leash.

"I'm teaching her to walk on a leash. Just a few minutes a day to get her accustomed," Margit Bernhög confided.

The apricot-colored furball sat and sniffed at a faded crocus.

Pollen in her nose made her start to sneeze. She was irresistibly cute, and Mrs. Bernhög tenderly picked her up. Irene couldn't help but pat Felicia on her back. Then the kitten peered up at Irene's face. Irene realized that she recognized the look.

"KJELL SJÖNELL, pastor, has called. You have his number," said a note lying on top of the pile on her desk. He's a morning person, this pastor, thought Irene. She felt completely exhausted, but she was going to have her Easter holiday soon. The long vacation loomed just ahead of her.

Morning prayers was quick and short. Annoyingly, Jonny Blom hadn't shown up. He hadn't called in, either. Irene was a bit worried, since she knew that he was down for duty for three days during the long weekend. There was no one else to cover for him, since both she and Tommy would be on leave.

Irene didn't find Kjell Sjönell at his work number, but he answered on his cell phone. He asked if he could call back later, because he was on the way to deal with a pressing matter. It wasn't a problem for Irene: She was planning on spending the day cleaning up her paperwork.

Sjönell called around eleven. "I apologize for not being able to speak with you when you called, but I had to deal with an attempted suicide. A young man on a boat made an attempt last night. He needed to talk." His voice sounded tired and sorrowful.

"No problem. I understand that you, too, need to work when needed," said Irene.

"Yes. Unfortunately, it happens. But I phoned this morning to tell you that I've spoken with both Rebecka and Dr. Fischer. Both of them think it's a good idea that I ask my good friend to take care of all of the funeral arrangements. He will even make an estate inventory. My friend will keep in touch with Rebecka and inform her about what is happening."

"It must be a relief for her not to have to worry," said Irene.

"Certainly. But she said something strange. I asked her if she wasn't concerned about the houses and suggested that maybe she should put in a burglar alarm now that they're going to be standing empty. She answered that she didn't want a single thing from either house and, more than anything, wished they would burn down. She lost her entire family, and you would think she would want some keepsakes."

"Strange attitude. But maybe the houses and the things would be a constant reminder of what happened."

"That's probably it. As I said, I spoke with Fischer and explained that you needed to speak with Rebecka again. He wasn't pleased, but I said that new information has come forward that only Rebecka can explain. Then he said that maybe the week after Easter would be all right. There's no point in trying any earlier."

That worked perfectly for Irene, and she said so. When they were about to conclude the phone call, Sjönell said, "I forgot to say that the doctor wants to be present during the meeting this time as well. Was he there last time?"

"Yes. We met Rebecka at his office."

"It seems as though he really cares about his patients. Either that, or he's very involved with Rebecka."

"That occurred to me as well."

Irene pondered after they had ended the conversation. When she had made up her mind, she called Glen Thompson.

"OKAY," GLEN said. "Check Christian Lefévre's pub visit on Monday night and look into the head-shrinker. Is there something in particular you're looking for when it comes to Fischer?"

"No. Just a feeling that it would be good to get to know him a little better. He is, as I said, unusually protective of Rebecka."

"I know. He's protecting her from us," Glen laughed.

"It feels that way," Irene admitted.

"When you visit next week, it would be better if you didn't

arrive on Tuesday or Wednesday. I'll be out of town and will return late Wednesday night. Thursday and Friday are better for me."

"That works for me."

Glen promised to book a room at the Thompson Hotel for Thursday night in case she was going to stay overnight.

"You can actually make the trip in one day. Even if that is a bit stressful," he said.

"It would be too stressful," Irene decided.

It was a matter of seizing her opportunity, now that she had a second chance at visiting London. Furthermore, it was critical that she speak with Rebecka in peace and quiet. She couldn't predict when during the day would be suitable for the lady. Just as well not to be pressed for time.

IRENE BOOKED the same flight times. She already dreaded the ungodly early-morning departure from Landvetter, but it was necessary if she wanted to have time to get anything done in London. The later flight didn't arrive until one thirty in the afternoon. Even if English time was an hour behind Swedish summer time, it would still feel like the whole day was over.

Louise Måårdh called in the afternoon to say thank you. "I have no idea how you managed to get that damn journalist to write his article. I think it's important that the same journalist wrote both. When he described how Urban manipulated and fooled the two of you, it felt great. I've gotten justice, even if we have to live with anonymous letters and phone calls a while longer. If Bengt doesn't get the position as rector, Urban won't either. That's the only thing that matters!"

It wasn't possible to miss her vindictive tone. Louise's overflowing gratitude left a sour taste in Irene's mouth after the she had hung up the phone.

She'd gotten interesting glimpses of church life during the investigation. Before this case had begun, she had had a faint

impression of pastors devoted to their calling of caring for souls;
but that picture had been altered. Pastors, she had found, are like
everyone else, with faults and weaknesses. The difference is
that they can conceal them behind their pastor's garb and people's inherited reverence for the church. If you lift the gold-
embroidered chasubles and scrape at the pious surface, then
you find everything from compassion to ordinary human feelings. It was a relief to meet a pastor like Kjell Sjönell. He seemed
sincerely interested in other people's fates and tried to be there
for his fellow man. But of course, this took its toll. Irene remembered how tired he had sounded on the phone.

ANDERSSON CAME into Irene's office just as she was leaving
to pick up Krister. Sven seemed washed out. His face looked like
it had been quickly put together out of dough. Irene was already
on her way out of her office; but when her boss sank into the visitor's chair, she sat back down as well. Andersson lifted his
reading glasses and pinched the flesh between his eyes with the
thumb and index finger of one hand.

"It's as if everything is going wrong. The Speedy case is moving forward and we've bagged the post office robbers in Lerum.
But in the investigation of the Schyttelius murders, we still
don't know much more than when the investigation started. It's
as if everything is fizzling."

"I think that feeling is pretty familiar. It always shows up at a
certain point in an investigation. It's supposed to work that
way." Irene smiled encouragingly at the superintendent, but he
didn't acknowledge it.

Instead, he continued. "And then Jonny's wife called a little
while ago. He's in the hospital. Something is wrong with his
stomach. She didn't know what it was."

He looked guiltily at Irene. "That means that we need to
divide his shift over the weekend. I already have Friday and Saturday, and I can take Sunday as well. Tommy is already on his

way to the mountains. Could you think about taking Easter Monday?"

There went her long weekend. Bitterness toward Jonny swelled within her. It was always something with that incompetent fool! Stiffly, she said, "Put me down for Sunday and Monday. You need to have time to recover as well. Jonny will have to rest up in his sickbed. His poor liver will need it. His 'stomach.' Call it what you want!"

"Liver? Oh, you think. . . ."

Andersson avoided making eye contact. He tried to feign ignorance, but everyone in the unit knew that Jonny had a drinking problem. Andersson didn't hesitate to go after people who in his eyes mismanaged their jobs, but he thought it beneath him to discuss personal problems. "Fuss," he would mutter and quickly start talking about something else.

He rose clumsily from the chair and started toward the door. Before he reached it, he turned and said, "It's nice of you to take Easter Sunday and Monday. This investigation is probably taking more out of me than I've realized. I actually met Sten and Elsa once, a long time ago."

His shrunken figure disappeared down the corridor. Irene was reminded of an old potato sack, shuffling around the house. Old. Andersson had really gotten old. It was increasingly evident that he wouldn't be able to head the unit forever.

The thought frightened her. Who would become boss in his place?

"So you're free on Good Friday and Easter Eve then? I work late on Easter Eve and all day on Easter Sunday. Easter Monday I'm free, but you're working. We'll have to aim for Good Friday," Krister concluded.

They sat in an endless traffic jam on Södra vägen heading toward Mölndal. They had realized too late that it wasn't a good idea to take this road toward Korsvägen, which was just one single chaos of roadwork and blockades. The idea had been to drive to Frölunda Torg and shop for the weekend. Irene would have preferred to avoid being squashed together with thousands of tired and stressed people on exactly the same errand; she would rather have driven straight home. But according to Krister, there was a threat of starvation in the pantry and refrigerator, so there was no choice.

Krister was driving. Irene leaned her head back against the headrest and closed her eyes. Thoughts swirled around aimlessly in her tired brain.

Her comfort level had suffered when Krister began to work full-time five years earlier. Before that, he had worked thirty hours a week and everything had run more smoothly at home. During the whole time the twins were young, he had had a reduced work schedule, since there were no part-time positions for detective inspectors and Irene hadn't wanted to take a desk job. The deciding argument had been that she earned more as a policewoman than he did as a cook. When he got the offer to take over as head of the kitchen at Glady's Corner, Irene had energetically supported him. It was his turn to focus on his career. She had regretted this many times since, but would never have told him so. He loved his work, even if he was often tired to the point of exhaustion when he came home. And who wasn't, thought Irene. The worst thing was that they didn't see each other very often. Now, with the twins living their own lives, it was more and more common that she came home to an empty house. Good thing Sammie was around.

They split up inside the shopping mall according to a well-rehearsed strategy. Irene had a list on which her husband had written what she should buy at the State Liquor Store. He went and botanized in the fruit and vegetable aisles, toured at the fishmonger, and rounded things off with a visit to the delicatessen. According to Krister, cheeses had to be tasted before they were purchased. He could stand and sample for fifteen minutes before he made up his mind. When Irene was doing the shopping, a plastic-covered Herrgård's mild cheese went right into the basket without further ado, or maybe a tub of soft cheese flavored with shrimp.

IT WAS almost seven o'clock when they finally dragged themselves and their heavy bags over the threshold of their row house. Sammie jumped and bounced around them, eagerly investigating what was in the bags. He stuck his nose into a bag and sniffed. Little wieners? Liver paté? Grilled chicken? Yes! Grilled chicken!

Irene tripped over him when he was fussing around her legs. With repressed violence, she shooed him away from the grocery bags and went into the kitchen.

She made sure that she remedied the threat of starvation by filling the cupboards. Krister had purchased fresh baguettes which were still a little warm, a piece of whiskey cheddar, and a perfectly aged Brie. The cheese was going to be enjoyed with the evening's salad. Because Jenny didn't eat meat or fish or anything of animal origin whatsoever, all members of the family got to make their own salads. A base of tomatoes, onions, corn, cucumber, black olives, lettuce, and fresh basil was set in the middle of the table in a large bowl. There were smaller bowls with feta cheese, chicken pieces, and Thousand Island dressing around it. The dressing was made light with crème fraiche, which was the reason Jenny wouldn't eat it but used vinaigrette instead.

Both girls were at home, and they helped slice the ingredients of the salad. Naturally, Jenny refused to involve herself with the chicken cadaver, so Krister had to do it himself. He paused in the middle of cutting up the chicken and said, "Girls. As usual, Mamma and I are working at different times this weekend—"

He was interrupted by Katarina, who exclaimed, "But you were supposed to have the weekend off!"

She looked at Irene accusingly. Irene knew full well that she worked too much, but with the occupation she had, there wasn't much she could do about it. When there was a lot of work to do, there was also a lot of overtime.

"Had you planned on being home?" Irene asked Katarina.

Katarina didn't answer, but merely shrugged. Recently she had turned eighteen, giving her the right to vote, the right to marry without parental permission, and the right to drive a car, but still sometimes she was just a child. At least she couldn't buy alcohol at the State Liquor Store yet, thought Irene.

"Katarina probably planned on driving practice. Just like me," said Jenny.

"We'll arrange it. When are you going to take the test?" Irene asked.

"In three months. There's a waiting list," Katarina said sulkily.

Both girls had had their learner's permit and had driven, accompanied by their parents, for more than a year. They were very good. The driver's test would certainly go well. But it would be difficult financially, since both of them were going to obtain their much-desired licenses at the same time.

Krister cleared his throat. "If I may return to what I was saying earlier, we're going to have Easter dinner on Good Friday. It's the only day both myself and Mamma are free at the same time. And I start work at five o'clock on Easter Eve. But I should have time for a smaller Easter lunch before I start."

Jenny stopped in the middle of chopping onions and said hesitantly, "Is it okay if I invite Martin?"

"Of course, sweetheart," Krister said, smiling wide.

Irene was pleasantly surprised. Katarina had dragged home various boyfriends over the years, but Jenny had never brought anyone home. There had been romances in Jenny's life, but nothing more serious ever seemed to develop. They had died and gone to glory at an early stage and quietly disappeared without leaving any noticeable marks on their daughter. Martin must be special.

"How long have you been together?" she ventured to ask, curious.

Jenny answered, "A few months."

A few months! Irene had heard about him for the first time last week.

"Grandma is coming, right?" Katarina asked.

"Oh, good thing you said that! I need to call and change the day. Otherwise she'll think it's Easter Sunday," Irene exclaimed, hurrying out of the kitchen to the telephone in the hall.

GOOD FRIDAY dawned with sunshine and a clear blue sky, even if it was cool. Irene and Krister devoted the morning to their sorely neglected garden. What did it matter if last year's leaves were raked up only at the beginning of April? Irene used to convince herself that it was healthy for the lawn to have a protective cover of leaves in case it was a cold winter. And some nutrients went into the ground when leaves decomposed. On the other hand, those were the only nutrients the lawn ever got. If you thought about it, their little garden plot was actually ecologically managed, completely without artificial fertilizer.

Krister started fixing the Easter buffet around lunchtime. He had started preparing the herring at the beginning of the week. He had finished the coriander-preserved salmon and the shellfish paté then as well. Now he was baking the chicken filets, which he was going to serve cold with various sauces. Irene had greedily circled him like a barracuda and noted a delicious mango chutney sauce and a crème fraiche sauce with fresh basil and garlic.

The seductive smell of Jansson's Temptation—with its spicy anchovies—came from the oven. It was Irene's favorite dish at both the Christmas and Easter buffets. As usual, a rootstock casserole stood simmering next to it. Jenny had told them that

Martin was a lacto-vegetarian. He wasn't orthodox in Jenny's vegan eyes, but apparently she could put up with this. She had also promised to make a large tomato and onion salad and chick-pea pilaf—red peppers filled with rice and chick peas, her specialty. The rest of the family also thought the chick-pea-filled peppers were delicious, and therefore the dish was included on the Easter buffet table. The obligatory hard-boiled eggs were cooling in cold water. Later they would be peeled and halved. The egg halves were decorated with mayonnaise, caviar, and shrimp.

The dessert had even been ready for a few days; Krister's punch parfait was in the freezer. He served it with his chocolate sauce made according to a secret recipe. Irene had managed to work out that it contained coffee, and she knew that he made it with dark chocolate of the finest quality. This was Glady's Corner's signature dessert, and if it wasn't on the menu, the regulars would grumble.

Irene's mother, Gerd, and her significant other, Sture, arrived at about five o'clock. The air was still warm enough that they could drink a glass of sparkling wine in the garden. They had to wear sweaters and over-shirts, but the air felt pleasant and spring-like. They were standing and chatting on the patio when Jenny and her Martin appeared in the doorway.

Irene quickly looked down at her right hand in order to make sure that her grip on her wineglass was firm. She understood why Jenny had looked hesitant when she spoke about Martin the day before. Conversation stopped completely, and everyone looked at the lanky figure in the doorway.

Martin was a few years over twenty. His shoulder-length hair was dyed black. His T-shirt was also black with a bright pink legend across his chest: "Fuck me, I'm famous!" He wore black jeans with large rips through which his pale knobby knees stuck out. A thick metal stud pierced his lower lip, and there was another in one eyebrow. He had used black eyeliner to draw heavy outlines around his eyes. A wide tattooed pattern encircled his neck in blue and red. He had taken off his shoes and stood uncertainly on the threshold in tattered black socks that his big toes stuck out of.

Irene's mother was the first to pull herself together. She smiled happily and walked up to the young man. "Hello! I'm Jenny's grandmother, Gerd."

Martin took her outstretched hand and said politely, "Martin."

Irene also went over to him to introduce herself and the rest of the family. Katarina didn't have her new find, Johan, with her. According to what Irene had discovered, he was in Norway with some friends, skiing. Despite this, Katarina looked beamingly happy. She introduced herself to Martin, who looked confused.

"Didn't you say you were twins?" he asked Jenny.

"Yes, but she's adopted," Jenny replied quickly.

The girls were used to this reaction. They smiled at each other in understanding.

"We have to leave by seven at the latest," Jenny told Irene.

"Why?" Krister asked before his wife had time.

As a craftsman in the culinary arts, he loved long enjoyable dinners and detested stress and haste during mealtimes.

"Martin's band is playing tonight."

Gerd opened her eyes wide in surprise.

"Do you have school dances on Good Friday these days?"

Then Martin smiled, and Irene saw why her daughter had fallen for this rocker. His blue eyes were mischievous but friendly. "It's been several years since we played at school dances. Tonight is bigger. More like a concert."

"Concert? Do you play classical music?" Sture wondered.

"Nah. It's got more of a beat to it, and it's really popular," Martin replied, still polite.

"But, hello! Don't you recognize Mackie in Black Thunder?" Katarina exclaimed and rolled her eyes.

A quick look at the gathered group of older relatives revealed their ignorance.

"They're huge! How many records have you made? Four?" she asked Martin, alias Mackie.

"Five," Martin answered and looked almost embarrassed.

"And it's going really well in Germany. They have a hit there now. Top of the charts with 'The Eagle Said,'" Katarina continued.

"Even if one is a rock star, might he want to have a glass of bubbly before dinner?" Krister asked, filling an empty glass that was standing on the tray. He didn't pour anything for Jenny, because she was absolutely drug-free and didn't even drink light beer.

"No, thank you. I don't drink alcohol," Martin declined.

Yet something else that united them, in addition to music, thought Irene.

"Okay. But you need food in your stomach. Especially if you're going to give a concert tonight. I suggest that we start eating," Krister said, gesturing toward the house.

Irene noted during the dinner that Katarina ate relatively little. Hadn't she also become much thinner in the face? The wide neck of her black cotton top showed considerably sharper collarbones than Irene could remember. It still seemed as though she was dieting, despite the new boyfriend and her decision not to participate in the beauty contest. She had to talk with Katarina about this. What was wrong?

EASTER WEEKEND was busy. The two biggest motorcycle gangs' feud about the division of prime drug and sex districts exploded into violence. On Easter morning, one of the gang leaders, and his girlfriend, were shot when they left a night club at about four o'clock. The gang had celebrated quite a bit on Easter Eve and, in their drunken state, their security precautions had slipped. A man from a passing car had loosed a rain of bullets from an automatic weapon at their leader. The driver pulled away before any of the drunken bodyguards had time to get their weapons out. Both the gang leader and the girlfriend had suffered life-threatening injuries.

Two hours later, a call came in about a car burning in a wooded area outside Gunnared. The car turned out to be stolen, and the police were pretty sure that it was the car the shooter and his driver had used. They had disappeared without a trace, having most likely had another car parked in the area.

At eleven o'clock in the evening of Easter Sunday, a heavy truck plowed through the tall wooden fence around the other motorcycle gang's headquarters outside Alingsås. The tarp was pulled off of the rear, and a grenade launcher began to toss its containers of death through the windows of the building. The man handling the weapon was right on target. The explosions laid waste to the old farmhouse. The whole thing was over in about a minute. The heavy vehicle backed out through the hole it had made in the fence and disappeared without having been fired upon.

Left in the ruins of the house were one dead man and three who were critically injured.

IRENE SPENT a difficult Easter as a result of the first attack. The investigation was one big mess; several units within the police department were involved. The toll increased from one to two as the gang leader died of his wounds around midnight, shortly after the grenade attack.

On Monday morning, Fredrik Stridh was to begin his weekend shift. He and Irene had been detailed to go to the scene of the grenade attack outside Alingsås. Irene wanted to fill him in before they drove out there.

She found him in his office, sitting in his visitor's chair with the back of his head resting against the wall. It looked like he was sleeping, and in fact he was. Irene had to punch him hard on his upper arm in order to get him to wake up. With an inarticulate groan, he straightened in the chair. He immediately grabbed his head and sank back against the wall for support. He closed his eyes again but to Irene's surprise, a smile tugged at his lips. It shouldn't have, if he was as hung over as he seemed.

"Hello! Time to start work! We're up to here in shit! The motorcycle war has broken out!" Irene yelled.

"Okay, okay," Fredrik mumbled and nodded. The satisfied smile still played on his lips, but his eyes started opening. Suspiciously, Irene leaned over in front of him and sniffed. No smell of alcohol. He was dead sober. She detected a contented gleam in what she could see of his eyes. Irene said with feigned harshness, "Young man, what kind of trouble have you gotten yourself into that has so completely sucked the life out of you?"

"How do you know it's something bad?" he asked, looking up at her teasingly.

"You look too damn satisfied."

Fredrick chuckled before he replied, "You're a good judge of character. But bad was the last thing it was. I've celebrated a late Ostara. They don't celebrate Easter."

"Ostara? What's that?"

"The vernal equinox."

He closed his eyes again. Celebrated the vernal equinox? Who does that instead of Easter? Suddenly the light bulb came on. "Well, I'll be damned! Have you been celebrating the Witch's Sabbath with Eva Möller?"

A delighted smile spread across Fredrik's face. It wasn't necessary for him to respond.

"THIS FEELS surreal. This is what it looks like in Bosnia or Chechnya, not in Sweden," said Fredrik.

Both he and Irene were unpleasantly affected when they walked around the remains of the farmhouse that had been one gang's headquarters. The technicians had worked the whole night and were far from being done.

"Where the hell did those bastards get a Carl-Gustaf?" Andersson's voice could be heard asking behind their backs.

He came zigzagging through the debris from the fire, his overcoat flapping. He couldn't stay away from the job when big things were happening.

"I have a feeling that it's only a matter of placing an order. These boys have big money. Everybody and everything can be bought. Even the military," Irene said in response to Andersson's question.

"You've met Hell's Angels before. Do you recognize any of the boys? They haven't been identified yet, neither the corpse nor those injured," Andersson continued, breathlessly.

Irene had met certain members of the Hell's Angels before, but she preferred to forget their confrontation.

IRENE DIDN'T get home until the wee hours of the morning. Krister had arrived before her and was asleep, snoring, on his half of the bed. Pictures from the scene of the fire flickered inside her eyelids as soon as she closed her eyes. It was impossible to fall asleep with them on her mind. She eventually got back up with a sigh, wrapped herself in her terry-cloth bathrobe, and pattered down to the kitchen. Sammie immediately took the opportunity to jump up and snuggle into the still-warm bed.

She lit a candle and set it on the table before pouring a glass of milk and spreading some Brie on a piece of hard bread. It felt really cozy to sit down in the flickering candlelight and chew on such a fancy late-night sandwich. In fact, it was so late at night that it was nearly a breakfast sandwich. As she looked into the flame, she reflected. Something she had pushed to the back of her consciousness during the drama of the last few days started working its way forward. It was something Glen Thompson had said during their latest conversation. Then she remembered what he had said and realized how important it could be.

She got up right away and went back to bed without brushing her teeth. Now that she had actually recalled what Glen had said, she didn't have any trouble falling asleep.

Chapter 16

"WE'RE UP TO OUR necks in this damn motorcycle war and then Jonny goes to the hospital and Tommy is skiing and Irene is going to go to London! The London trip has to be cancelled! Someone actually has to work!" Superintendent Andersson looked like he might have a stroke at any moment. He walked around the room, upset, and waved his index finger in the air in order to underline the seriousness of his words.

"Other units are already involved," Hannu reminded him.

The superintendent ended his fit of rage after a few seconds and glared angrily at the Finn, who calmly met his blood-shot eyes. As always, Hannu was right. What had happened during the weekend would have been too big for their unit to handle, even if they had been fully staffed. But Andersson felt frustrated. First a triple homicide, and now the motorcycle murders, all within a few weeks.

"It's important that Irene manage to interview Rebecka Schyttelius. Otherwise we'll never make progress in that investigation," Hannu continued, unaffected by the glare.

"You think so?" Andersson said, derisively.

"Absolutely."

Sarcasm didn't affect Hannu. The superintendent looked grim but thoughtful. His gaze wandered between Irene and Hannu. Finally, he shrugged and muttered something unintelligible like ". . . if you wonder who's boss . . . ," but he didn't say anything else out loud.

Irene breathed a sigh of relief and blessed Hannu in her thoughts. She, too, was convinced of the importance of meeting Rebecka again. If her new ideas turned out to be true, the investigation could take a dramatic turn. Then it would be even more important to get Rebecka's version of what had happened.

There was a knock at the door as it was opening. Lanky Svante Malm entered the room.

"Good morning. Was passing by and thought I'd provide some interesting facts about the fire and—" he started, before he was interrupted by Andersson.

"But it can't be finished yet!"

"Why not?" the technician asked, running his fingers through his tousled hair as he always did when he felt confused or unsure.

"Åhlén said that it would take several days! Those bastards blew the whole house to bits! As well as some of the lowlifes who got a taste of their own medicine."

The superintendent had an unmistakable tone of satisfaction in his voice as he uttered the last sentence.

To everyone's surprise, Svante started laughing. "I'm not talking about the grenade attacks. I meant the fire at Norssjön," he said.

"Oh." The superintendent sounded uninterested. Svante didn't let himself be belittled, instead pulling out one of his obligatory plastic bags from the pocket of his lab coat.

"We thought these small black clumps came from the videocassettes, but now we've analyzed them more carefully. They are six plastic buttons. And we've also found the remains of elastic bands."

To the rest of the group, the contents of the new plastic bag looked similar to all of the other bags of ashes he had shown them. The technician looked around triumphantly as if he had produced diamonds from the ashes. Since no one showed the slightest sign of understanding the importance of this discovery, he felt compelled to explain. "So we think the murderer also burned a rainsuit made of nylon."

It took a few seconds before the import of Svante's words sank in. Hannu was the one who understood the significance first.

"He was wearing it when he shot them, as protection against blood and gunpowder residue. Then he burned it."

"You have to admire his foresight," Irene exclaimed. "He brought with him a full-length nylon rainsuit which doesn't take up any room at all when it's folded up. It just needed to be pulled on over his own clothes, and it's easy to burn afterward. Not to mention the charcoal and the lighter fluid. Did he bring them with him too?"

"Right," Malm said. "I almost forgot about the charcoal. It probably came from Jacob Schyttelius's cottage. We found an outdoor barbecue and half a bag of charcoal under the glassed-in veranda. There was also an almost-empty bottle of lighter fluid. There aren't any fingerprints on the bottle; it was wiped thoroughly."

Svante's meaning was clear to all of them. Fredrik was the one who formulated it into one logical conclusion.

"He put the bottle back again, but he took the charcoal with him in a bag which he could burn. What a smart devil."

"Yes, he has been very cunning. But like all criminals, he's left evidence."

Svante's voice held more optimism than the detectives felt.

IRENE WENT to Hannu's office after morning prayers. He was on his way out, but took off his jacket and waited to hear what she had to say.

"Thanks for defending my London trip. Like you, I think it could be very important. Not least because of what occurred to me yesterday, or rather this morning."

She looked Hannu steadily in the eyes and said, "It's possible to fly to London and back in one day. You can take a plane at seven in the morning from Landvetter and return at seven thirty in the evening from Heathrow.

"But you can also do it the other way around and fly *from London to Göteborg* and back *overnight*."

Hannu raised his eyebrows and nodded in response. Irene clarified her statement. "You take the flight in the evening from London and return with the morning flight at seven o'clock. There are express trains and buses into London from Heathrow. It only takes fifteen minutes and then you're in the middle of the city. The flight itself takes less than two hours."

"And the car ride between Landvetter and Norssjön takes fifteen minutes at the most," Hannu thought out loud.

"Exactly."

"So someone could have flown here from London one evening, killed the Schytteliuses, and been back in London the next morning."

"Exactly."

Hannu looked at Irene thoughtfully and asked, "Do you suspect Rebecka?"

"Not really. She was sick even before the murders. But we can't rule anyone out at this stage."

"The Frenchman?"

"Lefévre isn't a good candidate either, since he doesn't have any personal connection to Rebecka's family. I actually don't know who or what I'm looking for. But it's mostly a feeling I have . . . a cop's instinct."

Hannu didn't smile at her last words, since he knew exactly what she meant.

"You want me to go through the passenger lists," he concluded.

"Yes, please. And maybe also the car-rental companies out at Landvetter. We know that our murderer had to have a car and that it was probably the one that was parked out in the woods during the night of the murder. Too bad the man with the dog didn't go any closer."

"This may take some time. I'll try to get to it before you leave," said Hannu.

Irene felt a huge sense of relief. If there was anything to be found in the lists, Hannu would find it. If not, she could let go of the thought and move on.

IT WAS with a great deal of discomfort that Irene took part in the interrogations surrounding the motorcycle-gang murders. The physical scars from her confrontation with a Hell's Angels gang a few years ago, which the superintendent had referred to, were less significant than her mental ones. She still woke in the middle of the night bathed in sweat.

The officers were usually alone when they questioned people at the police stations during regular interrogations, but these were far from ordinary; therefore, they put together teams with two officers on each team.

Irene and Fredrik were a team. They had three of the Alingsås gang's members allotted to them. The gang, Hells Rockets, had been members in good standing of Hell's Angels for four years. Because one of the ten club members was dead and three were in the hospital, there were only six left. The six of them were in various stages of intoxication and on the verge of thundering hangovers. None of them had been at club headquarters when it was attacked; they had been at a strip club in Göteborg. A plainclothes policeman at the strip club had recognized some of the club's members in the haze around two in the morning and contacted the station, which had been able to collect them for interrogation, but they hadn't come without a fight. The drunken bikers thought that they were going to be harassed for firing shots at "the Asshole."

"The Asshole" was the Hells Rockets' name for the gang leader of the Bandido-affiliates, The Devils. His real name was Ronny Johnsson.

The interrogation room at the jail was occupied. Irene and Fredrik decided to question the three at the station, after handcuffing them during the transport to and from the jail. There would be a guard present during the interrogation.

First up was Roger "Killer Man" Karlsson. Irene shivered involuntarily when, led by Fredrik and a prison guard, he appeared in the doorway. He was of average height but very stocky. Powerful arms with swollen biceps stood out from his body; he couldn't have pressed them against his sides even if he'd wanted to. Although it wasn't warm outside, he wore only a vest lined with leather and beneath it only a black T-shirt with the text "Hells Rockets" across the chest. His arms were bare to emphasize his muscles and multiple tattoos, some of which were real pieces of art, others just graffiti. There was a reason for his accumulation; Killer Man was thirty-eight years old and had spent sixteen of them in prisons.

His black hair was thin and tied in a small greasy ponytail at the back of his neck. Puffy cheeks were covered with reddish stubble, and his eyes were tinged with red as he stared angrily at the police and the guard. Irene could see his hangover hammering behind his eyeballs.

"I'm not saying a damn thing! Bring me my lawyer! You don't have the right to hold us, you bastards!" he yelled.

His breath stank of aged Danish cheese, tinged with rich amounts of garlic and alcohol. It spread throughout the room when he opened his mouth. His dirty shearling vest, with its sour smell of ingrained sweat, added to the aroma.

"Please, have a seat," Irene said. She forced herself to smile and made an inviting gesture toward the chair on the other side of the table. He sat down, not so much to obey her order as because his legs couldn't hold him.

"None of you have been formally remanded into custody yet. We brought you here this morning for practical reasons, so you could sleep off the worst of your drunkenness before we started talking about the events of the past few days."

In reply, Killer Man lifted one of his butt cheeks and let a big one go. He thought this was hilarious and started laughing. Maybe he thought that a female cop would give up before the interrogation had even started. But Irene was experienced and had seen a lot over the years, even if the air in the room had become stultifying.

Addressing the tape player, which was recording, she said dryly, "The interrogation will be on the defendant's level."

"Consider," she continued, but more in the direction of Killer Man, "that we're protecting you. One of your friends is dead and three have been critically injured. There's a threat hanging over the rest of you," she said, forcing a friendly tone of voice.

Killer Man shook his heavy head. Fredrik had been sitting at the end of the desk. He asked a question which both he and Irene had raised when they had heard about the gang's arrest. "How come the six of you went to a strip club when you knew that Ronny Johnsson had been popped? Didn't you realize that they would be seeking revenge?"

For the first time, a faint trace of interest could be glimpsed in Killer Man's eyes. He grinned and said, "The Asshole got what he deserved, but it wasn't *us* who—" He paused, and his mouth snapped shut.

"Please continue. 'It wasn't us who . . .'?"

Fredrik tried to get him going again, but Killer Man refused to say anything else.

Irene decided to get to the point. "Where were you around four o'clock on Easter morning?"

The gangster couldn't resist the urge to again try to shock a female police officer. "We had a hell of a smoker party out in the yard. Headquarters, and all the stuff you could want. I fucked a fourteen-year-old sometime in the morning." The look of sensual pleasure that crossed his face was corroboration enough of his story.

"Sex with a minor is, as is commonly known, punishable by law," she intoned.

"Suck me, baby!" he answered, smiling at her mockingly.

Irene was becoming provoked by his attitude. Maybe she had

better let Fredrik take over. She gave him a quick glance and he responded. "So you claim that you were in the yard around the time shots were fired at Ronny Johnsson. Was everyone in the gang there?"

At first Irene didn't think Killer Man would answer but to her surprise, he suddenly said, "Yes."

"No one from the gang was missing?"

"Nope."

"Why were six of you in the porn club the following night while four were left at what you call headquarters?"

"The others weren't up to coming, so they stayed and kept an eye on the house. The Easter party was, as I said, really cool!"

"Didn't you feel threatened? Didn't you know that Ronny Johnsson had been shot?" Fredrik continued.

A troubled expression passed over the biker's pasty face.

"We didn't know that they had popped the Asshole. The Easter party went on until late in the morning, then we slept the whole day. We started up again in the evening, but those who stayed at the house were too tired to tag along with us. It wasn't until we got there that we found out that someone had wiped the Asshole."

"Weren't you concerned? Afraid of revenge and retaliation?"

"Nope. It was a damn good reason to party harder!"

Killer Man grinned triumphantly again. Irene wondered if he really was as stupid as he sounded. Was he trying to buy time? Maybe get some information out of the detectives? That was the only reason Irene could give for him to speak with them at all. Could Hells Rockets really be innocent of the attack on Ronny Johnsson? That would explain why they hadn't been concerned when they learned of the shooting of the gang leader and his girlfriend. In a cold, expressionless voice she asked, "And who do you claim did shoot Ronny Johnsson?"

Killer Man hadn't been prepared for this question and he didn't like it. "I haven't claimed anything!" he screamed.

But uncertainty could be heard in his voice even if he was trying to conceal it.

"You say it wasn't you. And it could hardly have been the Devils themselves. Then it must have been someone else. Probably another gang. Which one?"

His gaze wandered as he tried to look derisive. "You're trying to pull a fast one," he said.

"Then I guess it was as our witness stated."

Irene didn't glance at Fredrik, hoping that he wouldn't betray them by looking surprised. It wasn't a big risk, since Killer Man's bloodshot eyes were pinned to her face. Slowly, with emphasis on every syllable, she said, "There's a witness to the shooting of Ronny. The car the suspects were riding in was a red Mustang. Do we know anyone who has a car like that?"

Furious now, Killer Man jumped up from his chair and screamed, "What the hell! Some bastard is trying to nail me! My car was in the barn! None of us—"

He stopped abruptly once more and squinted at Irene. "Wait a minute. You're trying some sort of dirty cop trick. You cunt."

He was right. The car that had disappeared from the scene of the attack was described by the only witness as a red Saab 9000, and it was also one of those that had burned outside Gunnared. But in the midst of all the excitement and in the dark, the witness might possibly have been mistaken. And Irene could always say that she had misunderstood what car model the witness had mentioned. She lied because she had seen a shiny red Mustang parked in the undamaged barn. There was no doubt about who it belonged to: "Killer Man" was written in silver paint on one of the front doors, the other reading "Hells Rockets."

She shook her head in response to his accusation. Fredrik continued, "That's why we can keep you in custody. We don't know who was driving. Or who was holding the rifle. We don't even know if they were shooting from your crate. The technicians need to go through the car. As far as the prosecutor is concerned, you're all murder suspects. The investigation is going to take some time, during which all of you will remain in jail."

Killer Man's self-assurance faltered. He was a tough, used to keeping his mouth shut and denying everything, but it was difficult for him this time as he didn't know what had actually happened. Not to mention his hangover. . . . Even if he was used to being in prison, he didn't look forward to sitting in jail for an unspecified period of time. Especially if the guilty ones were free and able to take over the territory of The Devils or Hells Rockets before they got out. Irene could hardly believe her ears when he started to rat. "There's a gang . . . the Outsiders. They are in contact with the Brotherhood."

Neither Irene nor Fredrik had heard of the Outsiders, but they didn't show it. They tried to press Killer Man for more information, but he realized that he had said more than he had to and remained silent during the rest of the interrogation.

The two other members of Hells Rockets didn't add anything to the investigation. Neither of them could have, even had he wanted. One sat half asleep, still heavily intoxicated, and the other appeared to be subnormal mentally. He was the youngest member of the gang, barely twenty years old; his older brother lay critically wounded in the hospital. It was soon clear to Irene and Fredrik that the biggest thing—the only thing—in his life had been his acceptance as an aspiring member of Hells Rockets a year earlier. His only comment, which he repeated like a mantra, was: "You don't squeal."

LATER THAT afternoon, Irene telephoned Leif Hansen, the superintendent of the intelligence service for the county police. He laughed when Irene described the questioning of the Hells Rockets members.

"I know those boys pretty well," he said.

"Killer Man mentioned another gang that might have instigated this wave of violence," said Irene.

"Really? Who does he blame?"

"The Outsiders. Who are they?" Irene asked.

When Hansen replied, there was no amusement in his voice. "The Outsiders. Did he really say that?"

"Yes."

"Then we have big problems. We had suspected that it would happen, but not this soon. . . . The Outsiders are a prison gang based on an American model, similar to Hell's Angels and The Brotherhood. The gang accepts members of different nationalities. What they have in common is their violence. We've known of the Outsiders for almost ten years, and recently they've grown. What you've told me supports a rumor that has been circulating during the past few months. And it would explain the events of the last few days."

Irene waited impatiently for his next words. Her relief felt physical when he continued. "Rumor has it that a couple of Serbs from Bosnia have joined the Outsiders. And these aren't just any old hoodlums. They've been trained, members of the Special Forces. What they don't know about killing people isn't worth knowing. Special Forces educates specially chosen soldiers in murder, sabotage, infiltration of the enemy, and all types of operations. They become masters of the arts of war on land and sea. The smartest, strongest, and most cold-blooded soldiers are selected for this training."

"Why would they join the Outsiders?"

"Some of the Serbs literally feel homeless in Bosnia. They have been driven out of the country, and there are rotten eggs even amongst the others in Special Forces. With what the army has taught them, they can make money. Their expertise is invaluable to gangs like the Outsiders. If these boys have taken over the leadership of the Outsiders, the happenings of the last few days make sense."

She asked, "Can you explain what you mean?"

"The shots fired outside the nightclub were fired by an expert.

The car the criminals were traveling in was stolen and later burned. The driver and shooter disappeared without a trace in another car. Hells Rockets' clubhouse was shot to pieces from the back of a truck by a grenade launcher. Everything was over in a minute. They disappeared, and the truck hasn't been found yet. How do you hide a truck? We'll probably find it in some warehouse or barn. In any case, if you analyze these two attacks, there's one thing that's clear."

He paused for dramatic effect.

"Military precision."

He was right. A lot pointed to military planning and execution.

"Why are the Outsiders doing this?" she wondered.

"To take over certain criminal activity areas: sex trade, drugs, extortion . . . everything that brings in the big bucks. They have to damage their competitors, to weaken them as much as possible, preferably by playing them off against each other. What's better than shooting the leader of one gang and decimating the other by a grenade attack?"

Irene pondered the scenario he'd outlined. She said, "I think you're right. Can you confirm that these Serbians from Bosnia really exist?"

"Previously, they were one rumor among many. Now, I think we have to take it seriously. If we can't get at the truth, then the Hell's Angels gangs and the Bandidos gangs all over Sweden, and maybe all of Scandinavia, will start fighting each other. Gang wars have a tendency to spread. A lot of old grudges may be dug up. If we can prove that the Outsiders are behind these incidents, maybe we can calm everything down before it even gets started."

"Will you keep us posted? I'll be gone on Thursday and Friday, but I'm going to inform my colleagues of this possibility. You should speak with them. It's probably best if you talk to Sven Andersson or Fredrik Stridh. They've been working on this investigation," said Irene.

"I'll be in touch as soon as we have the rumor confirmed."

IRENE REPORTED on her phone call with Leif Hansen during morning prayers the following day. Now she wasn't the only one who had this information. Despite the fact that she spent the rest of the day with the ever-more irritable members of Hells Rockets, she felt as though she had left that investigation. Mentally, she was already in London.

Chapter 17

AT HEATHROW, THE WEATHER was as overcast as it had been when the plane took off from Landvetter. The only difference was that the air was slightly warmer in London.

Glen Thompson was waiting at the same spot. A lukewarm drizzle began as Irene and Glen walked to his black car.

As usual, he talked about everything and everyone. First, he said that the Butcher was still in the hospital. According to the doctors, his brain injuries were permanent. Gravedigger had regained consciousness but was in critical condition. Glen cleared his throat with difficulty before he asked, "You weren't injured seriously during the car crash?"

"No. Just bumps and bruises," Irene answered, surprised.

"Good. He's HIV-positive. AIDS is developing. I was thinking about contacting you when I found out, but since you have to wait at least eight weeks before you can be tested. . . ."

He finished the sentence with a shrug. It was unpleasant to think that the man she had fought with suffered from HIV, but as far as she could remember neither he nor she had bled after the crash.

The taxi driver who had fallen victim to the two robbers had also been allowed to leave the hospital.

"He has healed physically but is unwilling to drive a taxi any more. Doesn't surprise me. They had to pump almost three liters of blood into him! He was very close to death from exsanguination. There'll probably be some legal proceedings, but since the defendants aren't in good shape it will take a while. According to my boss, it's not likely that you'll have to testify in person. I've made a final copy of your statement. Read through it and sign at the bottom."

"Can I take it home with me and read it in peace?" Irene wanted to have an English-Swedish dictionary at hand.

"Of course."

Glen also told her that Estelle had gotten a lot of bookings through a new partnership agreement with a large travel agency representing Scandinavian tourists who wanted to stay near the central city, comfortably and cheaply. This had given the small, well-run family hotel in Bayswater a big boost.

He and Kate were considering taking the ferry over and driving through Sweden during the summer, probably the last two weeks in July and the first week in August. The boys were fired up with enthusiasm about living in a tent, but Kate refused to wake up in a soaking-wet sleeping bag; she preferred staying at a bed and breakfast.

"Are there bed and breakfasts in Sweden?" Glen asked.

"Yes, but they're not as common as in England. However, we have hostels. They maintain very high standards and are economical.

"But in Göteborg, you'll stay with us," Irene said firmly.

Glen smiled. "If we accept the invitation, we'll have the twins with us," he warned her.

"They are more than welcome. Neither Jenny nor Katarina will be home during those three weeks. Katarina is going to be traveling by boat in Greece, and Jenny is going with her band to practice new songs and record a demo."

"Aren't you and your husband going on vacation?"

"Yes. We're going to Crete, but not until the middle of August."

"We want to see the midnight sun. Is it really light all night long during the summer months in northern Sweden?"

"Yes. The sun never sinks below the horizon. But don't forget the converse: From the end of November to the middle of February, they don't see the sun at all up there. Then it's eternal night."

They found the car and started driving toward London. Summer greenery had taken over outside the car, and the gardens they passed were dazzling with flowers. Irene could understand why the English are crazy about their gardens. The pains they take are amply repaid when the gardens start blooming so early. In Sweden, the frosty nights at the end of May, when the temperature drops to freezing and all the tender newly planted plants freeze, postpone the blooming season. Irene had lost count of all of the tomatoes and marigolds that she had had to throw out after the night frost had transformed small sprouts into dead sticky piles.

Glen changed the conversation. "I checked out Lefévre's alibi for the night of the murder. The pub owner confirmed that Christian was there on that Monday night. There's a group of five guys who meet there every Monday to organize their betting pools for the week. Despite the fact that there were a lot of people at the pub, the owner says he would have noticed if one of the guys hadn't shown up. It rarely happens. And he remembers that he and Christian talked for a while before the others came. He was the first one there on that particular Monday."

"Which leaves Rebecka, who was lying alone at home with a headache. Not much of an alibi," Irene determined.

"No."

"Have you had time to check out Lefévre or Dr. Fischer?"

"Of course. Whom do you want to start with?"

"Lefévre."

"Okay. He's almost thirty, born in London to an English mother and French father. The parents divorced when he was five years old. He and his mother moved up to Edinburgh, to her sister who lived several miles outside Edinburgh. The sister was married to a rich Scot. He owned large tracts of land and many different businesses. Christian's mother took a job at one of her brother-in-law's companies as a financial manager. She had a degree in finance. The sister had a son who was the same age as Christian. They grew up like brothers, since the cousin only has a half-sister who is slightly older. His father, George St. Clair, had been married but was a widower."

"St. Clair! Christian's company is called Lefévre and St. Clair. Then Christian's cousin must be the 'business partner' who moved up to Scotland."

"Exactly. With IT, you aren't limited geographically. It's easy to live in Scotland and network with a partner in London. They've worked like this for more than two years. Andrew St. Clair took over his father's business when his mother died, a few years after his father's death. Today he's one of Scotland's richest men."

"And he also gets an income from the computer company."

"Yes. But when Andrew moved up north, his interest in the computer company waned. He still owns a part of the business, but his other investments take up a lot of time. That's probably why Lefévre started looking around for a new partner. One who was very skilled. And he found Rebecka."

They fell silent as Irene digested this information. She asked, "Why did Christian stay in London? And why did Andrew agree to this?"

"London is where the big clients and the money are. And London has always lured young people. Both cousins had an early interest in computers and were proficient even when they were young. They moved to London and started their business almost nine years ago, and they have been very successful. Even from the outset, they were recognized as one of the best in the business."

"That means that Rebecka must also be outstanding," Irene remarked.

"Of course. Maybe that's why Lefévre takes such good care of her. He knows that she's unique. He wants her to get better so she can work again."

"And he thinks that as long as she isn't worried and is protected from people like you and me, she'll get better faster. He's wrong. She'll never get well if she doesn't talk. Have you spoken with her?"

"I've spoken with both Rebecka and Dr. Fischer. Rebecka is still very sick, and Fischer is concerned about her. He has increased her medication dosage, and he wants her to be admitted to the clinic again. I got the impression that he's angry with Lefévre, that he thinks the guy is interfering too much."

"I agree. When can Rebecka see us?"

"At eleven o'clock. Same place as last time. But I really had to insist. Neither Fischer nor Rebecka was particularly cooperative."

"Why this opposition?" Irene asked.

"It seems Rebecka is much sicker than we realized. The doctor can't say exactly what's going on, because of confidentiality and so on. . . ."

Glen didn't continue his line of thought since he was trying to make his way through a heavily trafficked roundabout. Irene hadn't noticed that they had taken a different route from the airport this time. Now they were entering Bayswater from the north.

"There's Paddington Station. The train to Heathrow leaves from there. A train leaves every fifteen minutes in each direction, and it only takes fifteen minutes to get here from the airport."

Irene saw people streaming in and out of a large stone building. No one would remember any particular individual. She saw, when she looked at the tourist map, that the station was located only a kilometer from Notting Hill.

"Do you think that Rebecka could have gone to Göteborg and carried out the murders?" Irene asked abruptly.

Glen pondered the possibility for a moment before he shook his head. "No. She has been sick for quite some time. There isn't any . . . strength in her. Is she at all familiar with firearms?"

"Not that we know of. Her brother and her father hunted. But we should ask her."

"Is there no one else with a motive?"

"We don't have a single suspect. But we have the theory concerning the Internet job for Save the Children. That's the most important subject I have to cover with her."

Glen glanced at her. "You believe that theory's behind the murders?" he asked.

"Yes. Because it's the only reason we have. The alternative is that a crazy person murdered them, that they were random victims. But that doesn't hold up, because they weren't killed in the same place. And then, the pentagrams were left at both sites. So we'd have to postulate a crazy Satanist!"

"I understand that the murderer also seemed to be familiar with the surroundings and acquainted with the family."

"Yes. That's the strongest argument against the murderer being a maniac. The murders were well planned. There's nothing haphazard about them."

They had arrived at the little hotel, and Glen parked. Irene took her dark-blue bag and walked up the steps to the entrance. Estelle was standing behind the reception desk, a pair of frameless reading glasses on her nose, as she typed information into the computer. She looked up from the screen and smiled when she recognized Irene.

"Welcome back! You have the room next to the one you had last time. I hope that's okay. They're identical."

She handed Irene a key and quickly returned to the numbers on the computer screen.

The room next to the one she had had before. Then she had to trudge up the stairs again. Irene tried to reconcile herself by recalling that such exercise prevented blood clots from forming after airplane flights and that it was good for one's all-around physical condition.

The room was the mirror image of the one she had occupied

previously; otherwise they were exactly alike. Irene hung up the few items of clothing she had brought with her—the same things she had packed the last time—and went into the bathroom. It struck her that she had forgotten to turn on her cell phone after the flight.

She heard Hannu's voice on her voicemail. His message was just for her to return his call.

She called him back, but he didn't answer. Perhaps he was questioning some of the motorcycle hooligans. Irene shivered with joy when she thought about having gotten out of that chore.

She clattered down the narrow stairs in high spirits. Glen sat in the hotel lobby, smoking a cigarette. He put it out when Irene reached the last step.

"Estelle is serving coffee and tea in the breakfast room. We should put something in our stomachs before we drive to Fischer's office," he said.

Irene agreed. She was hungry, because the airplane breakfast hadn't been much to cheer about. But the coffee had been tolerable and she had gotten as many refills as she wanted.

GLEN FILLED her in as to the information he had received about Dr. Fischer during the drive to Oxford Street.

"John Desmond Fischer, fifty-seven years old. His parents moved here from New York when he was four years old. They were very well-to-do. He has worked as a psychiatrist for almost thirty years and he has had his private practice for about twenty-five. He has a very good reputation and is the 'in' doctor for people with mental problems. And he's expensive! Not for the riff-raff," Glen said.

She understood that Christian Lefévre had probably arranged that Dr. Fischer take Rebecka on as a patient.

Glen continued, "He has been through three marriages and is now on his fourth. He has a newborn daughter. He has seven children altogether. The oldest daughter is thirty-two years old and has two children herself. His new wife is twenty-four.

"He was in hot water about eleven years ago. An eighteen-year-old girl who was one of his patients accused him of having sex with her. Fischer wormed his way out of it when several of his colleagues testified that the girl had delusions about sexual assault. The investigation was closed. The girl hanged herself shortly afterward."

"Where did you get this information?" Irene asked, amazed.

"Press archives. The gossip columns. I haven't found anything else of interest. But maybe it's worth thinking about."

Irene concluded, "He has a thing for young women. He's a conqueror."

Glen nodded. "What do they see in that fatso? You're a woman, you tell me," he said.

She started to shrug, but then she remembered Fischer's charisma, his air of virility and strength. The thick hair, the piercing eyes and smile.

"Power. He has power. A. . . ."

She searched in vain for the English word she wanted, and couldn't come up with it. Eventually, she said "aura."

"I understand. An aura women feel. Maybe men as well. But his women are young. Why are they drawn to him? He's not particularly good-looking."

"No. But, as we said, he has power . . . and . . . an aura. Maybe his profession makes young women feel safe with him. He understands them. He can listen and speak with them. But he also has social status. And economic status. You said yourself that he was rich."

"True. I realize that I've chosen the wrong profession," Glen said and smiled.

Irene looked at his attractive profile and noted the tiny dimple in his cheek. He had everything he needed to get women to fall for him without having a fortune. And they would never care whether or not he had a lofty position.

IT WAS harder to find a parking place this time. They had to leave the car in the vicinity of Grosvenor Square. The advantage was that they got to walk to Dr. Fischer's office.

The rain had stopped, and the thin cloud cover started breaking up. The air felt warm and damp despite the fact that it was only a relatively comfortable twenty degrees Celsius. The car-exhaust fumes hung in the air like an oily haze between the houses. Irene took off her jacket and walked in her short-sleeved blouse. Her shirt was clinging to her back by the time they arrived at the doctor's office.

The cool stairwell felt like liberation. John Fischer stood in the doorway waiting for them, just like the last time.

"Good morning. This mustn't take long. She's in bad shape," he said without any introductory remarks.

To Irene, who had already been on the go for seven hours, it felt strange to say "good morning," but she did. They quickly passed through the waiting room and went into the same room they had been in last time.

Rebecka sat in an armchair by the window, exactly as she had before. She was dressed in the same black suit. The white polo shirt had been exchanged for a shimmering white silk top. Despite this, Irene had a shock when she got closer.

Rebecka seemed to have aged ten years in the two weeks since their last meeting. Her hair hung, dirty and dull. Her skin was a grayish yellow color. Her eyes seemed enormous in the ever-thinner face. The worst thing was the look in her eyes. The last time, Irene had seen an anguish fluttering at the bottom of them. Rebecka had shown feelings. Now they were completely dead, empty. It felt as though a thick gray veil enveloped the woman in the chair.

The feeling became even more evident when they tried to

speak with her. No words penetrated her cocoon, nor was she able to reach out. Rebecka was turning into a puppet in front of their eyes.

"Rebecka is not feeling well at all. I'm not happy about your visit," the doctor said icily.

He ran a hand through his short beard. Glen and Irene looked at each other, at a loss as to how they should proceed. Rebecka hadn't reacted when they tried to greet her. Irene took her hand in an attempt to attract her attention, but it was limp and cold. Irene maintained her grip on Rebecka's hand and, for lack of words, she carefully started massaging it. Hesitantly, she started speaking to her in Swedish.

"I know that you're burdened by a lot of terrible images. I've spoken with Lisa Sandberg at Save the Children. She told me about the fantastic work you and Christian did when you exposed the pedophile ring. She also said that many of those who had been heavily involved in that investigation have had anxiety problems afterward. The pictures were apparently some of the worst they had ever seen."

Irene felt Rebecka's hand tremble, but the movement was so faint that it might have been her imagination. Encouraged, Irene continued, "So you aren't alone in having experienced the pictures and films as unpleasant. It's not strange at all—"

Irene stopped when Rebecka pulled her hand back. She gripped it with her other hand and pulled it against her chest. Her gaze was focused on the floor, at a point next to Dr. Fischer's elegant shoes. She sat in that position, catatonic, without blinking. Silence fell over the room. Irene became desperate. Rebecka seemed impossible to reach. Would the whole London trip be wasted? For lack of a better idea, Irene decided to continue speaking in Swedish.

"I think that you may have told your parents about what you and Christian had seen on the Internet. Did you also tell Jacob?"

Irene paused on purpose to allow Rebecka to react.

At first it didn't seem like Rebecka had heard. She sat immobile. Irene looked at Glen and raised her shoulders in a dejected gesture. Then Rebecka moaned hoarsely. Irene bent forward and tried to make eye contact with her. It was impossible; she stubbornly kept her eyes downcast. But she made an effort to move her stiff lips. With difficulty, she said, barely audibly, "No."

Her lips were completely dry and covered with sores. Thick yellowish-white saliva coated the corners of her mouth. Her tongue was sluggish in her bone-dry mouth. Irene frantically tried to decide what to say that would not scare Rebecka back into silence. Carefully, she asked, "When you say no, Rebecka, do you mean that you didn't tell your parents or Jacob anything?"

"No," she answered softly.

Just to be sure, Irene clarified, "So you didn't tell your family anything about the pedophile ring?"

"No," she whispered again.

Rebecka hadn't moved during the conversation, but now she turned her head toward Irene. Their eyes met, and Irene felt her heart stop for a few seconds. There was bottomless darkness in Rebecka's.

"No," Rebecka repeated.

In vain, she tried to swallow non-existent saliva. "She was . . . sick. I had to . . . protect her," she finally managed to say.

Wheezing shook her body and she covered her face with her hands. She rocked back and forth while mumbling, "My fault. Everything is . . . my fault."

Irene felt completely powerless.

"This is enough. Even you must see that this is cruel and futile," Dr. Fischer said.

Irene looked at Glen, who was at a loss. Rebecka continued to rock slowly back and forth with her hands over her face, but she had stopped wheezing. Irene was ready to give up questioning Rebecka today.

A large gray-haired woman materialized in the doorway.

Despite her size, Irene hadn't heard her come in. She carried a thin beige summer jacket as if she had come from outside. Apparently, she had the key to the office.

"Good, Marion. We'll drive Rebecka directly to the clinic," said Fischer.

Without saying a word to the police officers or even favoring them with a look, Marion stepped up to Rebecka. She wore sturdy jogging shoes, and Irene realized why she hadn't heard her footsteps. She put Rebecka's arm around her own neck and helped her to her feet. Rebecka was so tall that the woman could get her shoulder under Rebecka's armpit. By placing her other arm around Rebecka's waist, she managed to drag her loose-limbed body toward the door. Without turning her head, she said to the doctor, "The car is outside the door."

"I'll be there right away," he said.

He gathered together the few papers that were on the otherwise bare shining desk and put them in a thin briefcase of tancolored soft leather. He looked at them and gestured toward the door. "Please." He ushered them out and then hurried out himself, passing them on the stairs.

What was this man's relationship with Rebecka? As he at least sometimes had an interest in young women, could there be a sexual relationship? But surely Rebecka's condition precluded this? A thought struck Irene: Was Rebecka heavily drugged? Had the doctor given her psychotropic drugs?

Such thoughts buzzed in Irene's head the whole way down the steps in the cool stairwell. She discarded them, one after the other. A black car pulled away just as they emerged from the building. Irene glimpsed Rebecka's pale face. Next to her in the back seat was John Fischer.

Glen had gotten the same impression as Irene: Rebecka was really sick, but her doctor was certainly acting strangely.

Irene was about to suggest going to lunch, where they could

discuss their impressions, when the Marsellaise started chiming in her jacket pocket. She quickly pulled out her cell phone.

"Irene Huss."

"Hannu here. I tried to get hold of you earlier this morning, but you were probably on the plane."

Irene mumbled in order to avoid admitting that she had forgotten to turn on her phone after her plane landed.

"I've found something."

Irene realized that she had been holding her breath.

"There wasn't a Christian Lefévre or a Rebecka Schyttelius on the passenger list. I checked all the departures on Monday and Tuesday with all of the airlines. But one person spent the night in Göteborg. He left Heathrow at seven twenty on Monday evening and returned at seven ten on Tuesday morning. Furthermore, he had reserved a rental car at Avis, a dark-blue Volkswagen Polo."

Irene was in suspense. The decal on the back window of the car that the dog owner had seen could very well have been an advertisement for Avis.

"What was his name?" she croaked tonelessly.

"Andrew St. Clair."

Hannu gave her the information he had gotten from the airline. Irene pulled out her little notebook and wrote it down.

Glen was looking at her curiously when she hung up.

"Good or bad news?" he said.

She looked at him and answered, "Don't know. Or maybe. . . ."

She pulled herself together to explain what Hannu's investigation had turned up. For once he was quiet for almost a minute.

"Andrew St. Clair. One of Scotland's richest men . . . why would he fly to Göteborg and murder Rebecka's family?"

They ended up at a small Indian restaurant not far from Whitley's. It would have been fun to walk around the large department store again, but shopping was the last thing on Irene's mind now. She hardly noticed how good the tandoori smelled and tasted.

"The personal ID number on the list from the airline matches that of Andrew St. Clair. He's almost a year older than Christian," said Glen.

He looked thoughtfully at the paper where Irene had scribbled the information she had gotten from Hannu, and then he brightened up.

"Now I remember something from my studies of the gossip columns! He's going to be married soon. There was a big article about the upcoming wedding in which it was referred to as the Society wedding of the year."

"That doesn't explain anything. Why would a rich Scot go to Göteborg and shoot three complete strangers?" Irene asked.

Glen looked at her for a while. "Do we know that they were strangers to him?"

Irene thought about this before she answered, "No. Actually not."

"There's only one thing to do," Glen said firmly.

"What?"

"Ask him."

Irene would have to look after herself during the afternoon. Glen had to discuss how they would carry out the remainder of the investigation with his boss. Before they split up, they decided to meet at Restaurant Vitória at six o'clock.

During her first visit, she had told Glen that she wasn't interested in old buildings, but there actually was one in a tourist brochure that had appealed to her. Her idea was that she could wander around in a large, quiet building and use the opportunity to collect her thoughts. At the same time, she would be able to learn about some interesting cultural history.

She felt she was being brave when she decided to take the subway, the London Underground. The only subway she had ever taken before was in Stockholm. She found it surprisingly easy to orient herself using the electronic signs, and after several minutes the train she was waiting for came. She got off at the St. Paul's stop without any problem and walked up into the daylight to visit the cathedral.

St. Paul's Cathedral had been described in her brochure from the hotel as "impressive." She had to agree. She soon realized, though, that she could forget about devoting herself to tranquil contemplation. People swarmed everywhere. The magnificent domes, arching shockingly high over her head, made her feel like an insignificant miniature.

She dared to sneak into a group that had an English-speaking guide. He recounted the cathedral's history. The first building had been constructed as early as 604 a.d. by King Ethelbert, the first English king to allow himself to be baptized. A cathedral was added, but in 961 the Vikings burned it down. Irene had guilt feelings on her forefathers' behalf. The buildings were affected by several later fires through the centuries; and during the Great Fire of 1666, St. Paul's was consumed by the flames. That gave Christopher Wren the chance to perform his life's work: the new St. Paul's Cathedral.

Irene walked around for several hours admiring wall and ceiling paintings, statues, and carvings. She admitted that she was both overwhelmed and fascinated. She bought a stack of cards from a souvenir seller whose booth sign stated that profits from sales went to the upkeep of the church.

It was time to head back to the hotel. She wanted to freshen up before she met Glen and Donna. This time she wouldn't fall asleep in the bathtub.

DONNA WELCOMED Irene as warmly as the first time. She was magnificent in a bright turquoise tunic with a low neckline, worn over an ankle-length black skirt. A beautiful necklace of turquoise and silver glimmered against her dark skin. Her steel-gray hair was swept up in a fluffy pouffe on her head. And dangling earrings matching the necklace hung in her ears. Donna was a very feminine woman.

"And what have you done about my tall, stylish policeman?" she asked and winked at Irene.

"The only one I know who's going to retire soon is my boss. He isn't particularly tall or stylish," Irene apologized.

"But is he somewhat healthy?" Donna said, and her voice sounded sincerely interested.

"Not really. . . ."

"Send him here anyway. At my age, you can't be too picky," Donna laughed.

A distinguished man at the bar turned around and looked at Donna. The look told Irene that Donna could still afford to be *somewhat* choosy.

Glen arrived a few minutes later. They ordered before beginning to talk, vodka martinis as a starter drink, and then both chose crayfish soup and grilled lamb kebabs with salsa and potato wedges. Irene asked for a half carafe of red wine, Glen, a large beer.

"Naturally, my boss went crazy when I told him that Andrew St. Clair had popped up in the investigation. Bosses get cold feet as soon as big fish are involved. But he understood that it has to be followed up, so he called St. Clair. Or rather his secretary. St. Clair is busy with foreign businessmen all morning tomorrow, but he could meet with us after lunch. My boss gave his secretary my cell number, but neither she nor St. Clair has gotten in touch with me yet. You and I are booked on the morning plane to Edinburgh. We'll have to head back to Heathrow at five in the afternoon. Then you'll make the evening flight back to Göteborg."

Something clicked when she thought about what he had just said.

"Have you checked if St. Clair flew from Edinburgh to London?"

"Yes. He wasn't booked on any flights. He may have traveled by car."

Chapter 18

THEY LANDED AT EDINBURGH International Airport, west of the city. Because they had a few hours left before they were going to meet St. Clair, they stopped to grab a bite to eat there. Warm croissants and coffee tasted heavenly after the Spartan airplane breakfast.

They had barely been seated when Glen's telephone started ringing. The conversation was short but very polite. When he had hung up, he said, "That was St. Clair's secretary. We're very welcome for lunch at one o'clock."

"Where?"

"At his home, Rosslyn Castle."

"He lives in a castle?"

"Of course."

He smiled. With a pompous air, he took a piece of paper from his jacket pocket and cleared his throat as if he were about to make a speech.

"Kate has helped me do some research. We have several books at home about Scotland's history and the Scottish clans. She wrote down the relevant information, but I've only had time to glance at the paper. I didn't want to read it on the plane in case we might be spied on. We're to use the greatest possible discretion, the boss said several times yesterday."

He took a big bite out of his croissant and washed it down with coffee, squinting at the paper as he read it. After a while, he said, "The St. Clair family can trace its ancestors back to the fourteen hundreds. They are descended from the great Earl of Orkney and Sir William St. Clair. The earl built the castle and Sir William built a famous church. The family still owns large areas of land in the Pentland Hills. Andrew's father, George, had a head for business and invested in the Scottish oil industry from its incipience. Earlier, they made their fortunes from the wool and tweed trades."

"Have they been weaving their own plaids since the fourteen hundreds?" Irene asked.

"This tradition, that each clan has a special tartan, is said to be genuine. But actually it was a weaver from Lancashire who popularized the idea in the eighteen hundreds. Distinguished ladies sat in their drawing rooms and chose a pattern, which they named after their family. Probably they had to place a large order to obtain exclusivity. The whole world has gone along with it!"

Irene smiled but felt disappointed. Like most, she had thought the Scots had fought for freedom wearing their clan plaids like in the movie *Braveheart*. But one of the soldiers in that film had actually been wearing Nike running shoes when he was fighting in one of the countless bloody battle scenes, and she thought she had seen a glimpse of a pair of white Jockey underpants under one of the kilts. Hollywood films weren't always historically correct.

"Was your father from Edinburgh?" she asked.

"No. He was from Ayr, on the west coast. But we rarely came up here to visit. His relatives didn't like the fact that he had married a black woman. Even less that they had children."

Irene understood that it was a sensitive topic.

"Andrew St. Clair's half-sister is married to a Spanish nobleman and is incredibly wealthy. Of course, she also inherited money after her father died. Otherwise, Andrew is the only heir and runs the whole empire. He's probably getting married this summer in order to secure the lineage."

"Probably."

They wandered over to the Avis counter. Glen had reserved a Rover. They were assigned a red one, a change from his usual black.

"Do you want to take a spin around Edinburgh?" he asked.

"Absolutely."

EDINBURGH TURNED out to be a fantastically beautiful city. Well-kept buildings, nice streets, and open squares climbed up the high hills. Many of the streets were wide, and there were a lot of unexpected descents and stairs. They drove up toward Edinburgh Castle, which towered over the city on a high cliff. They parked outside the castle.

Glen said, "This is the Esplanade. A long time ago, people were executed here but these days it's used for the popular Military Tattoo. In August every year, they have a festival here which involves parades with bagpipe players in kilts and the whole deal. The tourists love it."

They walked around for a while, enjoying a magnificent view of the city. They were lucky with the weather, as it was sunny and clear, but the wind howled in their ears and was bitterly cold. Irene was thankful that she had her lined jacket with her, but she could have used a thicker shirt. After a turn in the biting wind, she was thankful to sit in the car again.

"How far is it to Rosslyn Castle?" she asked.

Glen unfolded the map they had been given at Avis.

"Between twelve and eighteen miles," he said. He pointed at a spot south of Edinburgh. "We drive down toward Penicuik. Maybe we should start now and take a look at the castle's surroundings," he suggested.

"Let's do it."

Irene didn't have a clue what Penicuik was, but she didn't care as long as she didn't have to walk in the wind for a while.

ROSSLYN CASTLE was also located on a hill, though it was not as high as the one on which Edinburgh Castle stood. Extensive fields and meadows spread out beneath the hill. They were already bright green, and flocks of sheep grazed in the meadows.

Behind the castle, the Pentland Hills stood as a backdrop.

Before reaching the avenue that led to the castle, they passed a beautiful old church with a sign that identified it as Rosslyn Chapel.

Glen pointed out the chapel's thick stone walls and richly adorned facade. "That's Sir William's Church. Ten St. Clair barons lie buried in their armor in the church."

If he ever grew tired of the police force, he could become an excellent guide, thought Irene. But she was glad to have come across a colleague who wanted to tell her about the sights, because she never would have learned so much about London and Edinburgh in her short stays if she hadn't had Glen with her.

A tall coniferous hedge rose up to mark the avenue's start. It ws pierced by ornate iron gates, through which they glimpsed a large stone house. Glen braked and backed up. "Come," he said and got out.

Puzzled, Irene followed his orders.

He stood before the gates, pointing at a brass mailbox. "Lefévre" was engraved on it in elegant letters.

"This must be Christian's childhood home," Glen said.

He grasped the handle of the right-hand gate and pushed it. The gate swung open on creaking hinges.

"Well, we won't arrive unannounced," he remarked dryly.

The grounds inside the hedge were unexpectedly large. They passed a forgotten rake leaning against a fruit tree, and someone had placed a large basket of woven osier a bit farther along. The driveway leading to the front door was covered with coarse gravel, which crunched under their feet.

The gray stone exterior and black slate roof made the mansion appear gloomy. Small windows added to that impression. Thick ivy climbed the walls and enlivened the dark façade.

When they were almost at the door, it was opened. A figure could be glimpsed in the opening, and a female voice asked, "Who are you?"

"Detective Inspectors Huss and Thompson," Glen said. He smiled his most charming smile and, at the same time, waved his police ID in front of him.

"We're actually here to meet Andrew St. Clair but since we're a bit early, we thought we would look around first. Are you Mrs. Lefévre?"

The opening of the door grew wider and a woman stepped out onto the stone landing. Irene was surprised at how young she seemed. She must have been over fifty, but her figure was slender and she was short. Her attitude was apprehensive. Though she stood very straight, she barely reached Irene's shoulder. Her hair was short, a dark reddish brown color, and the woman's almond-shaped eyes were dark brown. Her coloring and the expensively tailored dress she wore did not meet Irene's expectations of a Scotswoman. She recalled that it was the woman's ex-husband who had been a Frenchman; she was English. But she looked out of place here in front of this gloomy house, in the bitter Scottish wind.

The woman crossed her arms over her chest, either for protection against the wind or against them.

"Yes. I'm Mary Lefévre. What do you want with me?"

Glen smiled again. "Actually, nothing in particular. This is my colleague Irene Huss from Sweden. She's investigating the murder of Rebecka Schytellius's parents and her brother."

The dark brown eyes wandered from them. Glen asked, "May we ask you a few questions?"

"I have a flight to catch . . . I was just here to get my bag," Mary Lefévre said. She didn't make any attempt to hide her reluctance to answer their questions.

"We're going to meet with your nephew at one o'clock, so there will only be time for a few questions," Glen said firmly, but still with a smile.

With a resigned shrug, she opened the door and let them in. They found themselves in a large, dark wood-paneled hall, whose white ceiling two floors above them was covered by dark beams. A wide stone stairway near the door led up to the second floor. Its railing continued, forming a balustrade which stretched around the whole hall. From the gallery, a person could observe everyone who entered or left through the front door. Irene peered up at the second floor. Closed doors could be glimpsed behind the balustrade.

At the end of the hall was a vast granite fireplace. It was so large, a person could have stood upright inside it. It was obvious that both Irene and Glen were impressed with the fireplace or maybe Mary Lefevre was anticipating this reaction, because she said, "It really is magnificent, but I never use it. It just eats up wood and doesn't provide any heat. The space heaters are much more effective. There's one in every room. Plus, I have central heating. Otherwise I would freeze to death in the winter."

Irene could easily imagine how cold the house must be in the wintertime when the storms whined around the eaves. The windows were so small to allow them to keep the house warm.

Mary showed them into a surprisingly bright and pleasant living room. Light entered through the tall french doors to the terrace and the large picture windows, which must have been installed in recent years. The furniture was pastel-hued and modern.

"Please, sit down," Mary said, but she remained standing with her back to the picture windows. She had her arms crossed over her chest again. Irene and Glen were forced to sit on the rigid white sofa, which faced the window.

Glen made a vague gesture encompassing thee surroundings. "This really is a beautiful old house."

"Yes. Building was begun in the seventeen hundreds," Mary replied.

"It's a fantastic environment for children to grow up in. Does Christian visit often?" Glen continued in a casual tone.

"Sometimes."

"When was he here last?"

Mary thought for a moment before she replied. "In March."

"Have you ever met Rebecka Schyttelius?"

They couldn't observe the expression on her face, which was shadowed, but Irene could see her slender figure stiffen. "Once. This past Christmas."

"So she and Christian are a couple?"

"No," she said sharply.

Glen lifted his eyebrows meaningfully, which had the intended effect. Mary Lefévre felt that she needed to explain.

"She had been sick during the fall and didn't have the strength to travel home to Sweden over Christmas. Christian didn't want to leave her alone in London, so he brought her here."

"I understand. What impression did you form of her?"

This time the silence lasted quite a while.

"She was so quiet . . . it was difficult to reach her."

"That's exactly the impression we also received. She really is quite sick. The murder of her family has naturally worsened her condition," Glen said seriously.

Then he smiled and showed his charming dimple. He does it deliberately as part of his strategy, thought Irene.

"By the way, what's the name of Christian's girlfriend?"

The silhouette against the window froze. Her voice was tense when she answered. "I don't know. You'll have to ask him."

"We will."

He was still smiling, but his tone was more serious. "It's about time for us to head to the castle. Thank you for letting us intrude. Here's my card if any questions should arise or if there's anything you would like to tell us."

Glen rose, still with a friendly smile. Irene followed his lead. Like a sleepwalker, Mary Lefevre began moving toward the front door. She didn't look at Irene or Glen. Her movements were stiff as she opened it. She seemed afraid, almost shocked.

Why? Glen's questions had taken them into sensitive territory, but her reaction seemed exaggerated.

When they were about to leave the house, Glen held his hand out to say good-bye, but either Mary Lefevre pretended not to see it or she really didn't notice. Irene couldn't decide which it was.

"WHY DID you want to speak with Christian's mother?" Irene wondered.

They were in the car driving down the avenue that led to the hill that was topped by the magnificent castle.

"Because she's Christian's mother," was the laconic answer.

There was a certain logic in that, Irene realized. It had been a brief but thought-provoking interview, which they would need to analyze on their way home.

They drove through the open gate in the stone wall, ended up in a courtyard, and parked the red rental car next to a shiny new silver-colored Porsche. The cobblestones in the courtyard had been worn smooth by hundreds of years of trampling feet; they felt slippery. The castle towered on three sides of the courtyard. The main building lay straight ahead; the side buildings were like wings. The whole structure was made of gray stone, the roof of slate. There were walled, round towers in the outer corners, topped by turrets, reminiscent of Sleeping Beauty's castle. The sturdy ivy on the walls added to the effect. A few splendid trees and large rosebeds gave a little life and a touch of greenery to the otherwise barren stone surroundings.

The main building, straight ahead of them, was a bit taller than the wings. A substantial door of massive wood didn't look very welcoming.

"Here you need a sledgehammer to knock on the door," Glen observed.

They were walking toward it when someone yelled, "Hello! This way!"

Both of them stopped in their tracks trying to locate the source of the voice. Irene saw a man in the door to the western wing. He beckoned to them. They had only taken a few steps when Irene stopped again. They had gotten close enough that she could see Christian Lefévre standing before them in the doorway. But when she moved forward and got even closer, she realized her mistake. It wasn't Christian. The cousins looked very much alike.

Andrew St. Clair was a bit taller and somewhat larger than Christian Lefévre. But he had the same dark hair, worn in a ponytail. His dark-brown eyes behind rounded glasses blinked nearsightedly at his visitors. The cousins could very well have passed as brothers, both dark-haired and brown-eyed, despite the fact that they were English. Irene had expected that a Scottish nobleman would be red-haired, with ears sticking out and an overbite, the stereotype in Sweden of a Scot. There had been quite a few times during this investigation when her assumptions about how Englishmen—or Scots—would look had been proven wrong.

St. Clair was dressed in a bright red knitted woolen sweater with a little symbol on the chest, which Irene recognized but couldn't remember the name of. A white collar could be seen in the V-neck opening and a tie with bright red and blue stripes. His checkered pants of thin wool were of the highest quality, just like his expensive shoes.

"Everyone goes the wrong way their first time. Welcome to Rosslyn Castle," said Andrew St. Clair.

It sounded as though he really meant it. He shook their hands before he showed them into the house.

It was unexpectedly warm and cozy in the large hall, which was similar to the hall in the Lefévre house but significantly larger. St. Clair took their coats and hung them in a large cabinet with carved doors illustrating some form of a hunt, with dogs and running deer.

"Only this part of the castle is occupied. Everything is modern and comfortable here. I've kept the fireplaces and tile stoves, but on the ground floor I had the stone floor taken up and I installed heating under the floor. Then I replaced the old stone slabs."

The pride in his voice couldn't be missed. Irene realized that it was justified. It must have been a time-consuming job. But something told her that Andrew St. Clair had not actually done the work himself, even if he described it that way. As he walked in front of them, he chatted about the castle's history and made them feel like long-awaited guests. Meeting people was easy for him, and he was friendly. That was the big difference between him and his cousin. And his aunt, too, for that matter.

"The wing across from this one is the oldest part of the castle. It was built at the end of the fifteenth century, but was rebuilt after a fire two hundred years later. In the late sixteen hundreds, the main building was constructed as well. This portion was built at the end of the seventeen hundreds, at the same time as the gatehouse at the beginning of the avenue. My grandfather started its renovation, and my father and I have finished it. But we've been very careful about maintaining the castle's style."

He led them through large rooms with gold and red silk striped wallpaper and large tapestries covering the walls. Light filtered in through beautiful stained glass in the high windows, which showed images from the family's history and family coats of arms. Andrew St. Clair enthusiastically described the picture in every window they passed. Gloomy gold-framed portraits stared down at them. Shields and old swords were hung between the portraits. Here and there, suits of armor stood ghost-like along the walls. There were also large heavy cabinets in dark wood decorated with carving and gilded fittings. All the furniture they passed seemed very old. Irene felt as if she were in a museum as their footsteps echoed desolately on the stone floors. As if in response to her thoughts, their host continued, "I've had the finest and oldest furniture moved to the State Room. Wooden pieces don't do well in unheated spaces, and I don't heat the uninhabited portions of the castle."

They had reached their destination. He opened one half of a set of double doors and motioned for them to enter an enormous room. Almost the entire far wall had been glassed in.

"Come and look at the view," he bade them.

They crossed the endless floor, covered with Oriental rugs, to the glass wall, which extended all the way to the edge of the cliff. The view over the meadows and fields up toward the Pentland Hills was striking.

"It is very beautiful," Irene said, sincerely.

With a satisfied expression, he asked them to sit on the soft leather sofas which were turned to face the view. Irene realized that all the sofas and armchairs were placed so the occupant could enjoy the view.

"Food will be served in a few minutes in the Hunting Room. I think it's more pleasant to eat there. The dining room is too large for three people."

Irene didn't have any trouble imagining what the dining room must be like. A gloomy room with armor along the walls and even more ancestral portraits staring down from the walls. And, of course, the table must be colossally long, with fifty chairs around it. And there Andrew and his future wife were supposed to sit and yell to each other from their respective ends of the table and. . . .

She suddenly became aware that both men were looking at her. One of them must have asked her a question. She smiled uncertainly. "Excuse me. I didn't quite understand . . . ," she said.

"I asked if you had been in Scotland before," Andrew said, looking at her curiously.

"No. I've never been to Scotland before," Irene replied.

She was rescued by a door being opened at the far end of the room. Andrew stood and said, "I see lunch is served. Please."

They waded away over the sea of floor and stepped into what was called the Hunting Room.

Irene stopped abruptly on the threshold. Unprepared, Glen bumped right into her back.

"Oops," he said. At the same time, he took the opportunity to give Irene a nudge in the right direction. She stepped into the room.

Here, too, the outer wall had been removed and replaced by an enormous bay window. A table and eight chairs had been placed inside the alcove, which had glass walls on three sides. The table was set for three people. No one had to tell Irene that the furniture was antique. The beautiful wood carvings on the chair legs and backs spoke for themselves. But it wasn't the furniture that had surprised her when she stepped over the threshold.

Even though the room had been referred to as the Hunting Room, she hadn't expected it to be filled with weapons. Naturally, there were stuffed animal heads and birds that glared at them with glass beads for eyes, but the room was dominated by weapons. Swords and daggers, along with old pistols and rifles with decorated butts, lined the walls. More weapons could be glimpsed inside the glass doors of high cabinets. Three of the cabinets were fitted with metal doors and heavy locks.

"I thought my weapon collection might appeal to you as police officers." Andrew smiled.

He started guiding them to the exhibits on display, but was interrupted by a door opening and a serving cart being rolled in. An older woman in a black dress waited with the cart until they were seated. She served them cold poached salmon with a caper sauce and steamed vegetables, and cold beer, dark or light as they preferred. Irene chose a light English ale, while Glen and Andrew asked for a darker Scottish beer.

"I thought it just as well to have you here to lunch since you wanted to speak with me. I'm busy with important clients, but I've put them on a plane heading up to the oil rigs. Then they'll take a helicopter out to the platform itself. My right-hand man is taking care of them, and they won't return for several hours. But at three o'clock I must be in Edinburgh. Can we finish here by two thirty at the latest?"

It was a polite question, but he left no room for negotiation.

Thankfully, Glen was also a good talker, and he cleverly managed to maneuver the conversation away from unpleasant but unavoidable questions. The men established rapport quickly. Both were loquacious and interested in history. And Scots. Andrew only lifted one eyebrow when Glen told him that he was half Scottish. Between mouthfuls, he and Andrew were soon involved in a discussion about Scotland's bloody history. They were both in agreement that it was a pity their forefathers had been forced to capitulate in 1707. The union with England and Wales had never been good for Scotland.

Glen and St. Clair had to wash down their rebellious patriotic feelings with large gulps of dark beer. Irene, listening, was amazed at how engaged the two were in Scotland's history. She realized that these national sentiments hadn't cooled over the years, but were still alive. It wasn't farfetched to dwell on old wrongs, committed in 1295, here.

They had chocolate cake with whipped cream and coffee for dessert. Afterward they headed back to the living room. Their host walked over to a beautiful glass cabinet and took out a bottle.

"The family's whisky, from our own distillery. Among the finest there is. Very exclusive. It can only be purchased in certain shops. Aged twenty years, of which three are in sherry casks," he said proudly.

A black label with St. Clair in silver gothic type adorned the rounded bottle.

"I'm driving," Glen mumbled.

"Just a wee taste," Andrew declared.

He took out three beautifully polished shot glasses and poured in some of the golden liquid. With an expression of pride, he handed a glass to Irene and one to Glen. Sensually, he sniffed the aroma from his own glass, and the police officers followed his lead. He raised his glass.

"*Slainte!*"

"*Slainte!*" Glen replied and raised his glass.

"*Skål!*" Irene said in Swedish.

In the company of these two men, she had to assert her own ethnic identity and highlight her temporary exoticism. Even if neither of the two looked like a Scotsman, their hearts and souls were Scottish.

The whisky was distinctive, without the slightest hint of sharpness. It rolled nicely on the tongue and left a long finish with a hint of sweetness from the sherry. It was really a very fine drink. Irene realized there wasn't any point in her asking if she could buy a bottle to take home with her for her husband, because she would never be able to afford it.

They sat again. Andrew leaned back in a leather armchair. "I know that you didn't come here all the way from London just to have a pleasant chat. I also know that you want to talk about my cousin and the terrible murders in Sweden. It affects poor Rebecka the most, but he's certainly affected as well since they work so closely together."

Glen decided to take the opportunity to proceed.

"New information has surfaced in our investigation. May I ask how well you know Rebecka?"

"We've met a few times in London and at Christmas she was here for two . . . no, three days."

"Hasn't she been here more than once?"

"No. Just one Christmas."

"How often is Christian here?"

"About every other month. More often during hunting season."

"Is he interested in hunting?"

"Members of our family are born with weapons in our hands.

Christian and I grew up together, so he learned to shoot at the same time as I did. He's a devoted hunter. A very good shot, and knows almost everything about weapons."

"Then you have only met Rebecka in person a few times, if I understand you correctly."

"Yes."

"Did you become close?"

Andrew raised his eyebrows in surprise. "Close? Absolutely not. We have done some computer jobs together. But these days it's mostly Christian and Rebecka who do this kind of work. She's very skilled, when she's well."

"Do you have any idea why she became ill?"

"Not a clue. Christian says that the depression is hereditary in her family. Her mother has . . . apparently had it as well."

"Have you met her family?"

"Her mother and father? Her brother? The ones who were shot? No, never. I don't think they ever came to visit her. It makes you think. That's a bit strange."

"Have you ever been to Göteborg?"

"No. Only to Stockholm a few times. It's a very nice city. And there are a lot of computer-savvy people there, with IT-expertise. That's why I went."

Irene saw that Glen was thinking intensely about his next question. To buy time, he put his nose over the edge of the whisky glass, spun it around, and sniffed the aroma with noticeable pleasure. He took a small sip of the contents.

"We've tried asking this question of Rebecka and Christian, but neither of them has given a clear answer. That's why I'm asking you. Do you think—or know—whether they are in a relationship?"

Andrew raised his eyebrows again, but several seconds passed before he responded.

"I don't think they are in a relationship, a sexual relationship.

But they're close to each other. Christian worries a great deal about her, now that she's sick."

Glen nodded. "Do you know if Christian has a girlfriend right now?" he asked.

"Christian has always had a lot of girlfriends. But right now I actually don't know. He hasn't spoken about anyone special."

"When was the last time he spoke about a girlfriend?"

"It was probably a year ago."

Glen carefully placed his glass on the table before he sought to make eye contact with the man in the leather armchair and ask the question they had come for.

"Have you ever been to Göteborg?"

Andrew scrutinized Glen intently. Irene could see his intelligent brain going into overdrive.

"Is that the crux of this matter? So this whole thing is about me?"

Before Glen had time to respond, Andrew answered him. "No. I have never been to Göteborg."

"You are listed as being booked on a plane from Heathrow to Göteborg the night Rebecka's family was killed. You're also on the passenger list for the morning plane back to Heathrow from Göteborg the next day."

All jovial warmth had disappeared from Andrew's eyes. "Heathrow? Why would I go to Göteborg?"

"That's one of the questions we've asked ourselves," said Glen.

Andrew rose from his chair and walked up to the glass wall. He stood there, looking out over the landscape. With his back to the police officers, he started speaking.

"I certainly have an alibi for the days at the end of March when Rebecka's family was murdered. I remember when Christian called and told me what had happened. It was on Wednesday. I had just driven my future parents-in-law to the airport. They were here, together with my fiancée, the entire weekend and through Wednesday. I had taken off work and shown them around the estate, as well as Edinburgh. They are from Leeds and had not been here before. We were together for most of the time during those five days. The night between Monday and Tuesday, when according to you I was in Göteborg, I spent with my fiancée here in my bedroom. And we were awake until the early hours."

Andrew turned and looked at them.

"There may be an explanation. My passport was stolen during a break-in sometime in March. I don't know the exact date of the break-in because I didn't discover it right away. It's been reported to the police."

"When did you discover the break-in?"

"April first. I actually was asked if I was joking when I called the police."

"Did the burglars leave any traces?"

"No. Nothing. The police don't have any explanation as to how he, or they, got in and out."

"Did they take anything in addition to the passport?"

"Yes. A Beretta 92S, with ammunition, and a very valuable antique dagger. I had just purchased it, and it was unique."

"I assume the staff was questioned regarding the break-in?"

"Naturally. Altogether, there are six people who take care of me and the house."

They had no problem realizing that it would require *at least* six people to look after this portion of the castle. When one had finished cleaning one end of the house, it was time to start again at the other. Irene saw the benefit of growing old in a one-bedroom apartment, with cable TV as the only luxury.

"Is there any theory about how the thief or thieves got in?"

"No. When I'm not home, I always close the gate at the port arch. You probably didn't notice it when you drove in, but it's there alongside the wall. It closes automatically from inside the house. At night it's always electrified. As are the wires at the top of the wall. All windows and doors are equipped with burglar alarms. Despite that, he got in."

"There is no one you suspect?"

"No."

But when he replied, his eyes shifted away from them. Both Glen and Irene saw it. Glen looked at her quizzically. Oh yes, she had a question she wanted answered.

"When was Christian here last?" she asked.

Andrew jerked. Maybe he was surprised that she had spoken instead of depending on her English colleague. He made a noticeable effort to think before replying. "He was here in March."

"When in March?" Irene continued relentlessly.

His gaze wandered. "In the beginning or the middle . . . I don't remember."

"Can you find out?"

Now Andrew was staring at them, and they could see clear fear in his face.

"But . . . you can't seriously be thinking that Christian. . . ."

His inspection of the police officers convinced him that they were serious. He sank back and said, almost inaudibly, "In the middle of March. Aunt Mary's birthday is the eighteenth, and he came home on the evening of the sixteenth. It was a Friday."

"He stayed at his mother's house, right?"

"Yes."

"Was he here at the castle at any time?"

Andrew nodded. "We ate dinner here on Saturday evening. Christian, Aunt Mary, my fiancée, and myself. John couldn't come. That's Aunt Mary's boyfriend."

He smiled a bit at the last sentence. Apparently, John wasn't a boy any more.

"Did Christian know where you kept your passport?"

"Yes. He knows the house as well as I do. We grew up here, after all."

He sank down into the armchair again, as if all of the strength had been sucked out of him. Irene continued, "Did he know where you kept the gun and the dagger?"

"Of course! I had just shown him—"

He stopped and stared helplessly at Irene.

"You had just shown him your newly purchased dagger. Correct?" Glen added.

Andrew nodded. Suddenly he sprang to life. "But this is unbelievable! You're getting me to imply that Christian stole my passport, my gun, and my dagger. And then that he flew to Göteborg and shot Rebecka's parents and her brother. He has never met them! The whole idea is absurd! In the first place, he couldn't have gotten the gun through Customs."

"The victims were shot with Rebecka's brother's rifle. Both the rifle and the ammunition were found at the scene. All a person familiar with weapons had to do was load and shoot," Glen said.

The wild look in Andrew's eyes disappeared. He leaned forward and took off his glasses, leaned his elbows heavily on his knees, and hid his face in his hands.

"This cannot be true," he mumbled.

Fumbling, he put his glasses back on and looked at the clock. "You'll have to excuse me, but I need to leave for Edinburgh," he said, pulling himself together.

They stood at the same time. Glen and Irene thanked him for the wonderful lunch and the whisky. They walked together in silence through the museum-like rooms and into the enormous hall. Andrew went up to the carved cabinet and took out their jackets, as well as a plaid scarf in the same pattern as the pants he wore, and began to wind it around his neck. Irene couldn't keep from exclaiming. Andrew stopped, and both he and Glen looked at her.

"Excuse me. The scarf. Is it yours?" Irene got out.

Andrew looked even more surprised. "Yes, of course. It's the St. Clair plaid."

Irene stared as if bewitched at the scarf, which was bright red, blue, and green. Fringe hung along its edges. The pieces of yarn that Irene had found in the bushes at the cottage could well have come from the fringes of this scarf. And later Fredrik had found yet another tuft of yarn in the spruce hedge at the rectory which could also have come from the scarf.

"Is there something in particular bothering you?" Andrew asked, a little irritated.

"Yes."

Irene explained about the finding of the fragments of yarn. With a tired gesture, Andrew took off the scarf saying, "Here. Take it. Analyze it, or do whatever it is you do. But I promise that this scarf has never been in Göteborg."

He handed the scarf to Irene.

"There are other scarves that might have been in Göteborg. I gave all my customers, employees, friends, and relatives one of these as a Christmas present last year. Rebecka also has one, since she was here last Christmas. And Christian, Mary . . . every one of them has a scarf like this," Andrew added.

Glen nodded and said, "But only one has been to Sweden."

"Not mine," was Andrew's final reply.

They walked out to the courtyard and to their respective cars. Their red Range Rover looked middle-class and boring next to Andrew's silver-colored Porsche. He was in a hurry and threw himself into the sports car with a quick "good-bye," then disappeared through the gate.

"I understand why he became upset," said Irene.

"Me, too. He seems to be a nice guy. But we have to follow—" He was interrupted by his cell phone ringing. He took it out of his pocket and answered it. After a few abrupt "Yesses" and "I understands," he ended the conversation. He stared at Irene before he said, "Now things are happening. That was my boss. Christian Lefévre has kidnapped Rebecka. No one knows where they are."

Chapter 19

IRENE CALLED SUPERINTENDENT ANDERSSON on her cell phone. It took quite a while to explain everything that had happened, but in the end he understood. After many protests, he finally gave in. Irene had permission to stay in London and keep an eye on the new developments in the case.

"As soon as we send you out, there's always so damn much fuss," he grumbled.

Irene became angry and said, sharply, "I've only been abroad for work once before!"

"Exactly. And don't you dare say that there wasn't any fuss that time!" Andersson exclaimed triumphantly.

She had no good response. But the superintendent's criticism was unfair. She had not *caused* any of the developments in this investigation. But maybe the questions she and Glen had asked had provoked a reaction?

She ended the conversation and asked Glen, "What happened at the hospital?"

"According to my boss, Christian came to the clinic during regular visiting hours, between one and two. There are always more people moving about then, so it took nearly a half hour after visiting hours were over for the staff to discover that Rebecka was gone. At first they searched the ward and the clinic. When they couldn't find her, they contacted the police."

"Did he remove her by force?"

"We don't know for sure, since no one saw them leave the clinic. But there's nothing to indicate that he used force."

"Have they searched their apartments? And the office?"

"Of course. That was the first place they went. They aren't there."

"Where can they be?"

"No idea."

They were approaching the airport, and traffic increased. Irene wondered who might know where Rebecka and Christian were. She took out her wallet and, after some rummaging around, found the note she was looking for. It was worth a try, she thought, as she punched in Kjell Sjönell's cell phone number.

Irene quickly explained the situation to the pastor and asked him, "Do you have any idea where they may be?"

"No idea. But why would Christian kidnap Rebecka? There's no ransom money to ask for. What is his motive?"

"We don't know. But a great deal of evidence points to Christian having murdered Rebecka's family. And now he has taken her."

"Good Lord! Is he crazy?" Kjell Sjönell exclaimed.

"Possibly, although the impression he gave me was that he was mentally stable. What was your reaction when you met him?"

"The same as yours. Obviously, he was upset and concerned about Rebecka, but that's only natural."

"Have you any suggestion to offer?" Irene asked.

Glen had parked the Rover in front of the Avis office and gotten out of the car, but Irene remained to finish the conversation.

"Call each of their friends and every family member that you can come up with. Maybe one of them will have an idea about where they might be. Otherwise, the only advice I can give is to wait and hope that they'll get in touch somehow."

Irene realized that he was right. It felt frustrating to have to accept it, but she thanked the pastor and hung up.

Glen had already called Estelle and arranged for a new room for Irene. Irene called home, but there was no answer. She reached Krister at the restaurant. He calmly accepted the news of his wife's extended stay in England. "Take care, honey."

AFTER ENDURING bumper-to-bumper rush-hour traffic, they finally made it to the Thompson Hotel. It felt like coming home to Irene. A young girl with spiky red hair stood behind the reception desk and smiled in welcome. Irene explained who she was and was given a key. To her joy, they had given her a room on the second floor this time. Two fewer floors to climb. She threw her bag down and went to the bathroom before she rushed to the lobby again.

Glen was sitting on the sofa with a cigarette in one hand and his cell phone in the other. He looked up and smiled when Irene came up to him.

"I have been looking for Andrew St. Clair, but I haven't managed to reach him. His secretary has promised that he'll contact us as soon as he has a chance. But I did speak with Dr. Fischer. He was furious. I hope we find Christian before he does."

"Did he have a theory about where they might be?"

"No. Not the faintest idea."

Irene sat down on the sofa next to Glen. Together they tried to think of another person who might know where Rebecka and Christian could be. Glen had asked Andrew's secretary if she knew at which company Mary Lefévre worked as financial manager. She knew; but when they telephoned the company, the Edinburgh Tweed Company, her male assistant informed them that Mrs. Lefévre had just left on a business trip to Germany and wasn't expected back until next Wednesday. Unfortunately, he didn't know which airport the plane would land at. According to him, she was going to spend the weekend with German friends, but he didn't know what their names were or where they lived. He promised to contact the companies Mrs. Lefévre was going to visit and leave a message for her to contact Glen Thompson right away.

"We have to find Andrew. He may know who his aunt is going to visit in Germany," Irene exclaimed.

"Perhaps. But there isn't much we can do right now. Let's go to Vitória and eat. Kate and the boys are also coming," said Glen.

AS USUAL, Donna was ebullient. She pulled Glen and Irene into her plump arms and chirped how happy she was that they had made it home safely. She acted as though they had been wandering around the Scottish heath for several weeks, rather than having been gone just part of one day.

Kate and the twins arrived soon after, and it became a real family dinner with very good food. To be on the safe side, Irene and Glen didn't drink any wine, just beer. When coffee and ice cream with exotic fruits were brought in, Irene sensed that her fatigue was about to overwhelm her. It had been a hectic and eventful day. She had arisen extra early two mornings in a row, and she was starting to feel it. Thanks to four cups of strong coffee, she started to revive. It was just after nine o'clock.

Kate gathered together her sons, kissed her husband and mother-in-law, and gave Irene a hug. "If we don't see each other again before you go home, then we'll be in touch about the summer vacation. I am looking forward to seeing the midnight sun."

Kate and Glen probably don't realize how big Sweden is, Irene thought, nor how far it extends from north to south. Nor did they realize how many mosquitoes there were in Norrland. And, even worse, that one never falls asleep there in the summer: Who can sleep when the sun is shining in the middle of the night? Still, she remembered her family's vacation in a rented trailer in Norrland as the best one they had had. That was almost ten years ago. The trip had taken three weeks, and they had seen a great deal of Sweden.

Irene was telling Glen about her own trip to Norrland when her cell phone started ringing.

"Irene Huss," she answered.

"This is Christian Lefévre. Where are you?"

"At a restaurant. I've eaten dinner."

She gestured at Glen and pointed at the cell phone. She mouthed, "Christian."

"Are you alone?"

She was uncertain whether she should lie but decided not to. "No. Inspector Thompson is here as well."

"Good. How long will it take you to get to Ossington Street?"

"Well . . . maybe fifteen minutes. Is that where you are?"

Glen leaned forward and tried to hear what Lefévre was saying. Irene pulled the phone a little away from her ear so he could hear better. While he was eavesdropping, he pulled out his own cell phone and started looking for a number in the address book.

"Forget about where we are. You won't find us. Be at the office on Ossington Street exactly fifteen minutes from now. The key to the red door is under a cement block beneath the steps. Lift the block and you'll see it."

"How is Rebecka?" Irene asked, trying desperately to lengthen the conversation.

"She's okay. Fifteen minutes, starting now." He hung up.

"We have to be at Ossington Street in fifteen minutes," she told Thompson.

He spoke into his cell phone as they rushed out. That conversation ended before he started the car and began to drive fast to the computer company's office.

"They may be able to trace that phone call. It will take a little bit of time, but they may be able to tell which area the call was placed from," he said.

Traffic was rather light, and they got there in just seven minutes. Irene had one eye glued to the clock on the car's instrument panel. When they turned onto Ossington Street, Irene caught a glimpse of the sign above the old pub on the corner. She couldn't keep from exclaiming, "Glen! The matches came from Shakespeare!"

"Impossible. He died in the sixteen hundreds." Glen grinned. "Not him. The pub!"

She pointed at the black sign written in gothic script.

"But why did it say 'Mosc' under 'Pu'?" she asked, confused.

"Because the pub is located at the intersection of Ossington Street and Moscow Road."

The tires squealed when Glen parked at the curb. Irene jumped out of the Rover before it had completely stopped and rushed over to the stairs leading to the bright red door. Just as Lefévre had said, there was a light concrete block under the steps, perhaps forgotten after the renovation of the house. The key was lying exactly where he had said. She and Thompson raced up the stairs and unlocked the red door.

It smelled stuffy inside, as if no one had been there for a few days. The door to the office was half open, and they walked into the white office. The green plants drooped in their designer pots. It was silent and close. Irene and Glen split up and quickly looked through all the rooms of the office. When they met again, in the large room, they shook their heads. Irene was just about to suggest that they make their way into the apartments above when one of the computers turned itself on.

After a moment, Christian Lefévre's face appeared on the screen. Although the picture was small, he was clearly visible.

"Webcam," Glen said softly to Irene.

In the background they could glimpse a bookshelf with book spines neatly arranged in a row, nothing else. Lefévre looked straight into the camera. He dialed his cell phone; a second later, hers rang. Hastily, she fumbled it out of her jacket pocket.

"Irene Huss."

"Are you in place?"

"Yes."

"Do you see the picture on the screen?"

"Yes."

"Good."

He ended the conversation with a click, which Irene confirmed by a glance at the screen. Glen searched his own coat pockets and took out a pocket tape recorder. He turned it on and set it in front of the computer speaker.

Lefévre sat erect, looking straight at the camera. He cleared his throat before speaking.

"Now I'm going to tell you what actually happened. It's important that this should conclude in the right way. And it's just as important that you know why Sten and Elsa Schyttelius had to die. Not to mention Jacob."

When he spoke Jacob's name, his expression hardened and Irene thought she could detect pure hate in his eyes. In the next moment it was gone, and he continued. "I know that you've asked Mamma if Rebecka and I are a couple. She denied it because I asked her to do so. But she's the only one who knows the truth. When she called me, she told me that you were on your way to interview Andy. So I know that you're getting closer . . . and I've decided that it's time to bring this to an end. There's no happy ending for us. But first everything must be ready."

Christian cleared his throat again and took a large gulp from a tumbler, which he set down on the table again with a bang. He grimaced slightly, which might mean that the drink was strong.

"Rebecka and I love each other. Once in your life, you may be lucky enough to meet a person who speaks directly to your heart and you know that it's forever. Rebecka is that person for me. Almost exactly a year ago, we realized that we were in love with each other. That summer was the most wonderful time of my life. We traveled to Sweden. Rebecka wanted to show me where she came from. But she didn't want us to meet her parents. That's why we chose exactly those days when she knew her parents wouldn't be home. I didn't understand then why she didn't want us to see them, but I accepted her explanation that they weren't on good terms with each other."

He fell silent and glanced to the side. Irene and Glen heard a low mumbling.

"Rebecka." Glen's whisper in Irene's ear was barely audible.

Suddenly, Rebecka's pale face popped up next to Christian's. He shifted to the side, out of the picture, to make room for her. Her hair hung, dirty and disheveled, around her sunken face. Her eyes were vacant. In vain, she tried several times to form words with her dry lips. Ultimately, she managed to speak.

"I shouldn't have . . . told. . . . Everything is my . . . fault," she stuttered, in Swedish. "My fault . . . could never tell . . . anyone," she whispered, still in Swedish.

For a long time she stared into the camera with a blank expression.

They could hear Christian mumbling, but it was hard to tell what he was saying. Rebecka turned her head and rose. Her clothes rustled as she disappeared from the picture. They could hear her sit heavily in a chair very close to the camera and the microphone.

Christian's face reappeared on the screen.

"When we were in Göteborg in July, Rebecka showed me the house where her parents lived. There wasn't any problem getting inside, since they always left a spare key under a pot next to the steps. She showed me the weapons cabinet and the rifles. Of course, she was aware of my interest in hunting. I also saw where her father had hidden the key to the summer cottage. She took it out. We drove out there. It was a warm day, so we went down to the lake and bathed. She told me how close the rectory was to the cottage if you went through the woods. She had done this many times. Later, in her apartment here in London, she showed me a map of the exact area where the houses were located. I took it with me when I. . . .

"But first I'm going to tell you about our visit to the cottage. Here, too, we found the key under a pot by the steps. Then we went inside. And there she showed me the secret space behind the panel. A rifle with cartridges was hidden there. Rebecka told me that her brother was in the process of moving into the cottage and that the rifle was probably his. He had brought down a load of things a few days earlier. He was going to come again the next day, but we weren't going to stay that long.

"We continued toward Stockholm in the afternoon and had a nice drive through Sweden. And our days in Stockholm were also completely fantastic. Neither of us realized that that was the beginning of the end."

Christian fell silent and swallowed hard. When he started speaking again, his tone was neutral, almost a monotone.

"We met with the representative of Save the Children. They initiated us in the problems surrounding the largest pedophile ring that had ever been discovered in the Nordic countries. Our assignment was to collect information and uncover the identities of the participants. We really discovered all but two but to the Save the Children people, we said that there were five whom we hadn't been able to trace."

Rebecka said something that was inaudible to Irene and Glen, and Lefévre turned his head in her direction. They heard him answer her soothingly, as if he were speaking to a child, "Yes, sweetheart. It's necessary. They need to know everything. I promise that it will only be the two of them. No one else."

Neither Glen nor Irene had time to think about what he had said before he turned back to the camera and continued.

"We began our work and penetrated the pedophile ring without being discovered. In the beginning I didn't notice anything, but after a while Rebecka began to change. She . . . became sick. I got in touch with Dr. Fischer. He said that she had developed depression and that it ran in the family. Before this, I hadn't known that Rebecka's mother suffered from depression. Naturally, I wondered why she had become sick. I had a feeling that it had to do with the job we were doing for Save the Children.

We talked about it one night, and Rebecka started to tell me everything."

A faint outcry was heard from Rebecka, but Christian just said, "Yes, sweetheart." He looked quickly in her direction but continued. "As an admission ticket to the pedophile ring, each participant had to submit some of their own material. Films or pictures. One of the participants who we didn't officially reveal called himself Peter and offered this film."

Christian typed on the keyboard in front of him and the screen flickered to life.

Irene began to feel queasy. They saw a grown man force himself on a small girl from behind as she crouched on all fours. Of course, he didn't show his face. She was only seven or eight years old. The girl kneeled there, immobile, like an animal about to be slaughtered. Only the man's sexual movements made her body move. She turned her head and looked straight into the camera.

The realization of the girl's identity struck Irene like a blow to the head. She had a hard time breathing. Before she had collected herself enough to say anything, Christian stopped the film, reappeared on screen himself, and confirmed what she had known for a few seconds: "The little girl in the picture is Rebecka. The man who is forcing himself on her is her father. The camera operator is her brother, Jacob."

His face on the screen looked as if it had been carved from stone. His voice was completely toneless.

"Rebecka was eight years old when this film was made. Jacob was fourteen. Both he and his father had been sexually assaulting her for three years, since she was five years old. Sten Schyttelius lost interest when she turned eleven, because she reached puberty early. However, Jacob's interest didn't fade: just the opposite. He abused her systematically until he was drafted by the army, way up in northern Sweden. Rebecka had to have an abortion when she was thirteen. Pappa Pastor drilled into her that if she told anyone, God's wrath would descend on her. She would be breaking the commandment to honor and love your father and mother. That, of course, included her brother as well."

Christian's voice, broke from anger or sorrow, but then he started speaking again.

"Rebecka's mother knew what was going on but didn't do anything to help her. In her depression, she hid from the truth. And Pappa Pastor didn't forget to tell Rebecka that if she didn't cooperate, her poor, sick, frail mother would have to. Little Rebecka was forced to make herself available to the men of the family."

Without changing his expression, Christian took a drink from his glass. Tonelessly, he said, "Now we come to 'Pan's' contribution. That's the Internet name he adopted."

The screen flickered again. This time they saw a white man having sexual intercourse with a small African girl. Her eyes were just as large and afraid as Rebecka's had been. They were bright from tears, but she wasn't crying. It was appalling to see the fear and pain in her wide-open eyes. She was very thin; she was perhaps seven years old. They lay in a narrow bed, with only a pillow and a sheet. A mosquito net, glimpsed over the headboard of the bed, had been pulled away so that everything could be filmed.

The film stopped and Christian returned to the screen.

"Pan was Jacob Schyttelius. Rebecka understood right away that Jacob and her father had abused the children they were supposed to be helping when they were in Africa in September touring children's villages. This film showed up on the pedophile ring's Web site just a few days after they returned home, and Pan was then accepted into the group."

He made an ironic grimace, which was replaced by a sorrowful, resigned expression.

"That was the last straw for Rebecka. She became very sick. That was when she was admitted to the hospital for treatment the first time. After that . . . nothing was the same as it had been. She couldn't have sex, she couldn't even touch me . . . she retreated from me. In some periods, she was better and could function but between us . . . it didn't work any more. Of course she loved me . . . but I couldn't reach her any more. She had enough to contend with, dealing with the demons that had come to life when she saw the films. As she described it, I understood that she had managed to repress most of what had happened. She hadn't wanted to remember, and then she didn't. But everything rose to the surface after she saw these films. She never told Dr. Fischer what lay behind her illness; he suspected one thing and another.

"Fischer said that I should be patient, but the months passed. Understandably, she didn't want to go home at Christmas, so she called and said she had the flu. We drove up to Edinburgh, and it went pretty well. But she wanted to return home—to London, that is—again after three days. She couldn't keep up the appearance of normality. During January and February, she continued to get worse. I realized that she would never recover. That's when I decided to kill those damn pigs. They deserved it. I took their lives, but they had already taken Rebecka's. When she was little, they were supposed to protect her from evil, but they were the ones who destroyed her."

Rebecka was moaning audibly, but Christian seemed not to hear. He stared right into the camera without blinking.

"I decided to kill them. I thought she would get better again if they vanished. That she would feel some sort of . . . revenge fulfillment. I didn't want to travel under my own name, in case some smart cop, like you, came up with the idea of checking the passenger lists for the days in question. So I stole my cousin's passport when I was at Rosslyn Castle in March. We're enough alike that I could pass through Customs with it, especially if I put my hair up in a ponytail rather than leaving it down like John Lennon.

"I tried to make it look like a stranger had broken in, so I also took a dagger and a Beretta. They're hidden in Mamma's basement, behind the hot-water heater. I decided to do it on a Monday. I planned to create an alibi, with help from the guys in the betting pool. This particular Monday, Rebecka was feeling better and had the energy to do a little work. But she went up to bed at about four o'clock. I packed a regular shoulder bag with my light boots, a pair of thin leather gloves, a small flashlight, a compass, a map of the woods I would have to go through, a toilet bag, a thick sweater, nylon raingear, and plastic covers to pull over my shoes. And the most important thing: the diskette containing the software with which to erase their hard drives. The day before, I reserved a car at Avis at Landvetter via the Internet. I had already ordered the ticket for the evening flight."

He drank greedily from his glass. The drink was amber-colored. A whisky? Maybe St. Clair's.

"I was at Shakespeare's early, just before five thirty. I spoke for a long time with Steven, the owner, so he would remember that I had been there. The other guys dropped in around six, and we drank beer and discussed the week's tips. I treated everyone to a round of whisky. At six thirty, I mumbled to Vincent that I was expecting an important phone call and had to go home. It was noisy and crowded around the bar, and I don't think anyone noticed that I left a little earlier than usual. I raced home and grabbed the bag. It took barely a minute. Then I rushed down to Bayswater Road and hailed a taxi. We drove to Paddington, and there I took the train to Heathrow. At five minutes past seven, I picked up my ticket and boarded as the last passenger. I took my shoulder bag on board as hand luggage. Then I had to grab it and make sure I was the first person off the plane so I wouldn't lose time. The car was ready at Avis and I had taken care of all of the paperwork via the Internet. It is barely a fifteen-minute drive from the airport to the cottage."

He took another mouthful from the glass and continued. "I had already decided on where I would park the car. In reality, finding the trail in the dark was a bit more difficult than I had expected, but at last I managed. Then I took off my coat and put on the sweater and the boots, and the rainsuit over them. The hood made it less likely that anyone would recognize me and decreased the risk that I would leave any hair I might shed. I put the gloves and plastic covers in my pockets, with the flashlight, compass, and map. I'm used to moving in the woods, but it was pretty difficult to make my way to the cottage.

"Luck was on my side: Jacob hadn't come home yet. If he had been there, I had planned on killing him with an axe from the shed. There had been one in the chopping block when we were there in July, and it was still there. I put on my gloves and brought it in with me but as I said, I didn't need to use it. I returned it to the block afterward. Since he wasn't home, it was just a matter of opening the door with the key from under the flowerpot, putting on the shoe covers, pulling out the rifle, and loading it. Then I inserted the disk-formatting software and started running it. While it was running, Jacob came home. He opened the door and stepped into the hall, and I shot him."

Rebecka started moaning again. Christian didn't seem to notice. His expression was rigid, his voice a monotone, as he described the crimes in detail and at length. Neither Irene nor Glen had changed their positions during the whole time the computer had been on. They still stood, bent slightly forward. Now Irene felt that she needed to sit. She pulled an office chair toward her and sank onto it.

Christian had fortified himself with another swallow from the glass and was ready to continue. "I had plenty of time to erase his hard drive completely. I also found several diskettes and a few videocassettes in the hiding place behind the panel. I put them in a plastic bag and found charcoal and lighter fluid under the patio, which I took with me. I knew that there would be cassettes and diskettes at Pappa Pastor's as well. Everything had to be burned, since there might be more tapes with Rebecka on them.

"In that secret space I also found a book about Satanism. Then I had an idea. Rebecka had told me how her father and brother had searched for Satanists on the Internet. With respect to what these two gentlemen had been doing, I thought it appropriate to mark their computers. So I dipped a pastry brush from the kitchen drawer in Jacob's blood and drew a pentagram on the screen. And that's why I turned the crucifix in the bedroom upside-down when—"

He stopped to finish his drink, then filled it up again.

"I made my way through the woods to the house, even though it was difficult. Along the way, I planted some fibers from the scarf that my cousin had so graciously bestowed on me as a Christmas present. I wanted to implicate him, in case the airplane passenger list was followed up. I wanted it to seem that he had been there; to confuse matters.

"The rectory was dark when I got there. The key was still lying under the pot, and after putting on the shoe protectors and gloves, I went in and sneaked into the bedroom. Both of them were sleeping. First I shot the pastor, and then his wife. They never woke up.

"I erased the hard drives and took all the diskettes and videotapes I could find. There were lots of disks, but only three cassettes. Because I had drawn a pentagram on Jacob's computer, I drew one here as well. But I used both the mother's and the father's blood. It felt . . . appropriate. They were both responsible.

"Well, then I went back through the woods again. Oh yes, I burned the videotapes and diskettes. And the rainsuit and gloves and shoe covers. I kept the plastic bag to put my dirty boots in when I got back to the car, so that I wouldn't soil the inside of my carry-on bag. I packed my sweater in the bag, and I put on my coat again and the clean shoes that I had left in the car. I drove out to the airport, went into the bathroom, washed up and shaved. No one could tell that I had just murdered three people.

The plane left at seven twenty Swedish time, and it landed at eight twenty English time. I didn't sleep at all on the plane, because I wasn't tired. Rather, I was elated. I've never regretted that I shot those bastards, but sometimes I wonder if it was worth it. . . ."

He turned his head in Rebecka's direction. Not a sound could be heard from her.

"She understood right away that I had killed them. But she didn't want to talk about it. She feels that it was her fault they died, that she shouldn't have told me about what she had suffered. They had managed to break her and brainwash her."

He laughed a short joyless laugh and took another swallow of whisky.

"Now you know everything. I've rigged both of these computers. Everything will be erased from them. There will be no way to rebuild them. You two report what I've said. Rebecka and I have made up our minds. There's no future for us. We've come to the end."

He disappeared from the picture. A shot was heard and then, a few seconds later, another one.

Irene and Glen sat as though made of stone, watching the neat bookshelf and the upper part of a black armchair. The screen went black and the computer shut down.

Neither spoke for a long time. In the end, Glen stretched out his hand and turned off his tape player.

"Lucky I had this with me. Everything he said is on this tape."

Chapter 20

THE TECHNICIANS HAD MANAGED to trace Lefévre's cell-phone call to Mayfair, to the area around Berkeley Square. They couldn't pinpoint it more exactly. At first, Irene had speculated that Rebecka and Christian might be in Fischer's office, but that location was too distant.

"Has any Mayfair address come up during the investigation?" she asked.

Glen shook his head.

They were still in Lefévre's office, trying to figure out where to start searching.

"That bookshelf was well-stocked and made of a light type of wood," said Glen.

"Could you read any of the titles?" Irene asked.

"No. The distance was too great."

They had tried to start the computer again, but it appeared to be completely dead. Glen called a computer expert at the Metropolitan Police, who patiently guided their attempts to restart it. When all attempts had failed, the expert concluded, "He must have placed a bomb in it."

"A bomb!" Glen exclaimed.

"Don't worry, not that kind of bomb. I mean a computer virus which erases all information on the hard drive. It can lie dormant, to be activated at a later time or on a certain occasion or command. The computer cannot be started again. Or, technically, the computer itself is not damaged and can easily be started up from a different disk but everything on its internal hard disk is gone forever."

"So there's nothing to do then?" Glen asked.

"Nothing."

Dejected and at a loss, Glen looked at Irene. "What do we do?"

"Try and get hold of Andrew St. Clair. He might know where Christian is."

She was interrupted by Glen's cell phone ringing.

His expression brightened as a voice on the other end spoke. He waved at Irene to come closer and said, "Good evening, Mr. St. Clair. Yes, we've been trying to reach you all evening . . . via the local police in Edinburgh . . . I understand. Yes . . . there are very sorrowful circumstances that have made it necessary."

Calmly and methodically, Glen gave an account of the afternoon's and evening's events. At first, St. Clair refused to believe his story. When Glen came to the end and reported the two shots, Andrew was silent for a long time.

When his voice was heard again, it shook. "You say that the phone call came from the area around Berkeley Square. I still have my apartment in London. It's located on Hill Street, which leads into Berkeley Square."

"Could Christian get into your apartment?"

"Yes. He has a key."

THE SCENE that met them and the technicians from the Metropolitan Police at the apartment was expected, but unbelievably tragic.

Rebecka sat, leaning back, in a high-backed white leather armchair. Her eyes were closed. Just above the bridge of her nose, there was a black hole between her eyes. The backrest behind her was drenched in blood.

Christian sat on the floor in front of her, his head resting on her lap. He had shot himself in the classical way, through the temple.

The gun was a Magnum, and the large-caliber bullets had been deadly, tearing away portions of their skulls on exiting.

For an instant, Irene had a vision of the ending of a Greek tragedy, or maybe a variant Romeo and Juliet. But here it had been neither a strict father nor an old family feud that had thwarted the young lovers, but rather crimes committed long ago, which had led to new crimes. It was difficult to tell who the victims were and who the criminals in this story.

The apartment, a trendy loft with an open floor plan, was located at the top of an old Victorian house. Everything was unbelievably expensive, both in terms of materials and craftsmanship. The decor was extremely modern, with a lot of stainless steel, light natural wood, and a black and white color scheme. It was in striking contrast to the museum in Scotland that Andrew St. Clair nowadays called home, thought Irene.

The chair Rebecka sat in was turned toward a square stove with glass doors in all directions, standing in the middle of the floor. A large sofa and four armchairs covered in white leather were gathered around it. On the floor was the largest Oriental rug Irene had ever seen. Aside from two colorful paintings, the rug provided the only spot of color in the room, glowing in ruby red and steel blue. The paintings seemed to have been painted by the same artist. One was completely red, the other blue. Irene immediately associated them with Rebecka and Christian's front doors on Ossington Street. Both canvases had been slashed. On the red one, there was a tear in the middle; on the blue one, it was in the lower right-hand corner. Irene recognized the style of a painting she had seen at the Tate Modern, but she couldn't recall the Italian artist's name.

Andrew's work corner, under one of the sloping windows, was the size of Irene's living room. Two computer desk tables stood at an angle to each other, a computer on each table. Desk chairs in black leather, small comfortable armchairs on wheels, stood in front of each computer. The wall behind the desks was covered by a built-in bookshelf made of light birch, like the computer tables. A webcam was mounted on one computer, the one that faced the wall lined with books.

An opening in the wall of bookshelves led to a short corridor with two doors. A large bedroom lay behind one of them; behind the other was a bathroom tiled in Mediterranean blue. Irene noted the Jacuzzi, meant for several people.

She returned to the main room and found Glen in front of the computer. His efforts to start it up were in vain. It was just as unwilling as the one they had given up on in Lefévre's computer office.

"There's a bomb in this one as well. Damn it!" he said.

One of the technicians bending over the dead bodies jerked and turned his head in their direction. When he saw their expressions of resignation, he returned to his work.

Chapter 21

WHAT WAS HAPPENING ON the other side of the North Sea? What was the motive of that chap Lafayette—or whatever the hell his name was—for kidnapping Rebecka? What was that supposed to solve? It was typical, when you let Irene loose. The strangest things happened. But she usually managed to get it together in the end; that, Andersson had to admit. But an extra day—maybe several—in London would be expensive.

They should have brought Rebecka Schyttelius home to Sweden right after the murders. Maybe she would have had to be escorted by that headshrinker and some police officers, but she should have been forced to come home. Then the Frog and the doctor wouldn't have been able to hide her from them. She couldn't have been so sick that she couldn't talk. She had given them a statement earlier in the investigation. And it would have been a lot cheaper.

Sven Andersson hadn't bothered turning on the lights, despite the fact that the darkness was creeping in on him. He sat in the dusk and enjoyed his well-earned can of ale—in all honesty, the third he'd had this April Friday evening. And that wasn't anyone's damn business, in his opinion.

When the doorbell rang, initially he was terribly upset. He automatically glanced at his watch and noted that it was almost nine o'clock. His first impulse was not to open the door, to pretend he wasn't home. On the other hand, it was very seldom that his doorbell ever rang. Sheer curiosity propelled him out of his recliner and to the door.

To his surprise, his cousin Georg was standing on the front step. He was alone, without the ever-cheerful Bettan. There was nothing bad to be said about her, but sometimes she could be rather trying.

"Hey, Sven," said Georg.

Andersson noted that his usually self-confident cousin stood and rocked uncertainly, teetering from side to side.

"Hi. What do you want?"

Georg licked his lips nervously and forced a smile. "Could I come in for just a minute?"

Again, curiosity took hold of the superintendent. Maybe his police instincts were awakened. That's what he preferred to think, but old honest curiosity had also led to the solution of cases.

Sven backed up so he could let his cousin in. With one foot, he discreetly pushed away the boots which were lying where they had been thrown, just inside the threshold, when he got home from the previous weekend's fishing trip. He had spent the only day he had taken off during the whole Easter weekend pursuing his hobby, fishing. His other hobby was gardening, but he hadn't told them about that one at work.

He became aware that it had been a while since he had cleaned his little house. "You'll have to excuse the mess, but a lot has been happening. The Schyttelius murders and the motorcycle gang war that broke out over Easter . . . I've had to put in a lot of overtime."

That would have to do as an explanation. If it didn't, Georg could pull out the vacuum cleaner and clean up himself. It was Sven's mess, and he was content with it. But right now it was probably worse than usual.

So that the layer of the dust on the furniture wouldn't be visible, he only lit one lamp.

"Do you want a beer?" he asked.

"No, thank you. I'm driving."

Of course he was driving. He and Bettan lived in Billdal, on the other side of Göteborg. Andersson suppressed a sigh, but at the same time he was pleased. He only had three cans left in the fridge.

"Coffee then . . . ?" he inquired, halfheartedly.

"No, thank you. Nothing. I just wanted to talk about . . . something."

Georg sat gingerly on the outer edge of the green sofa. He may have been worried about his light-colored suit. The sofa was quite faded and soiled after all these years. Several times, Andersson had thought about buying a slipcover to conceal these imperfections, but he had never gotten around to it. Andersson himself sank down into his well-broken-in leather armchair. It was a fiftieth birthday present from himself. His half-consumed beer can sat in front of him on the stained teak table.

"Okay. You want to talk about something. Go ahead. You're among friends," Andersson said jovially, smiling at his own joke.

Georg didn't seem to have understood that this was an attempt at humor. Troubled, he cleared his throat, hesitated, then spoke. "It's about Jacob Schyttelius. Naturally, this has nothing to do with his murder. Both the girl's father and I thought it was best to let everything go . . . to die with Jacob, so to speak. If we started digging into things, it would only cause more damage. And Jacob is, after all, dead. He can't defend himself. And for her, it's probably best the way things are. So that she can forget all about it. Children forget quickly."

Confused, Georg gave his cousin a desperate look. Andersson only felt bewildered. For lack of a better idea, he picked up the can and drank a gulp. What was it Georg was trying to say? Something about Jacob Schyttelius and a child. Thoughtfully, he put the blue can down.

"How about taking it from the beginning? And preferably in some sort of chronological order."

"Of course. Certainly." Georg straightened the permanent crease in his well-pressed pant leg and cleared his throat again.

"I think it feels good to tell you about this . . . it has been gnawing on my conscience, ha ha . . . even if it doesn't mean anything to the investigation itself of. . . .

"Right. To the point. The Monday Jacob was shot—but of course it was much later in the evening that *that* happened—one of our students' fathers came to me. The truth is, he was waiting for me outside my office when I arrived that morning. He was terribly upset. It's understandable, if what he said was true. But we just don't know. *They* come from another culture where the relationships between teacher and students is much more strict and authoritarian. They may have misunderstood the slightly more informal relationship between students and teachers in the Swedish school and—"

Andersson had sat up in his chair. "Where do 'they' come from?" he brusquely interrupted his cousin.

"Syria. They are Christian Syrians," Georg answered.

"Why was the father upset?"

Georg squirmed. Clearly, he wasn't happy, with his seat or the situation.

"He claimed that his little eight-year-old daughter had a breakdown over the weekend. She said that Jacob had made her do 'bad things.'"

"What kind of bad things?"

"The father said that Jacob had shown her his 'thing' and forced her to undress completely. Then he supposedly . . . touched her."

"Where did this supposedly happen?"

"At school. After regular school hours. Jacob apparently offered to give the girl extra help. She has difficulty with the language and is quiet. She had fallen behind in math."

Andersson looked at his cousin in his elegant suit. Finally, he said slowly and with emphasis, "You stupid shit!"

Georg jerked back but didn't say anything.

Upset, Andersson got up from the armchair and started walking around the room. "Do you realize what you've done? You've withheld important facts in a murder investigation! It's prosecutable! Damn it, you've gone and kept to yourself a motive for murder!"

Andersson had to pause to catch his breath, and Georg tried to defend himself: "But Jacob denied the accusations. He protested his innocence and said that the girl had misunderstood his kindness. She was the one who wanted to sit in his lap. He had had to turn away her affectionate impulses. Maybe she had imagined more than there was. Or maybe she simply wanted revenge."

Andersson glared at his cousin. "An eight-year-old?" he asked dryly.

"Well . . . kids lie."

"What did Jacob say about forcing her to take off her clothes? And the accusation that he had exposed himself?"

"Naturally, he was horrified. He swore several times that he was innocent. He was terrified of an investigation. What would his parents say? Think of his father, being a rector."

"And a good friend of yours. Did you believe him?"

"Yes . . . he seemed trustworthy."

"And there never was an investigation into the accusations?"

"No. He died. That night."

"What a relief for you. No unpleasant publicity for the school. No fear of loss of subsidies. No fear of the parents complaining on behalf of other children. Everything works out."

Andersson's voice dripped with sarcasm, and he did nothing to conceal it.

Georg rose from the sofa. He was almost a head taller than his cousin. In an attempt at retrieving his dignity, he said, aggrieved, "I came here to inform you about what happened on the morning of the murder. Actually, I shouldn't have bothered, since it has nothing to do with the murders. . . ."

With three quick steps, Andersson was at Georg's side. He

craned his neck back and stared up at his cousin. "How do you know it doesn't have anything to do with the murders? How do you know that the girl's father or uncles, or whoever the hell else is in that big family, didn't shoot Jacob and his parents?"

"Why . . . why would they have done that?"

All of Georg's arrogance disappeared. He glanced away and tried to brush a non-existent spot off one of his sleeves.

"Ever heard about a thing called vendetta? They dispose of the whole family to get revenge. We were stymied for a motive in this investigation for a long time. This is actually a serious motive," Andersson said.

Georg tried to tough it out and said formally, "It was a mistake for me to come here and take up your precious time with these unimportant details and—"

"Deep inside, you've known the whole time that they were damned important. Otherwise you wouldn't have driven across the whole city in order to ease your delicate Christian conscience!"

In the dark room, the two men stood and measured each other. Georg turned away first. Stiffly, he said, "I'm going now." He turned and hurried into the hall.

Andersson heard the front door close behind him with a bang. Sighing, he walked over to the coffee table and grabbed his beer can. He made a gesture with the can at the closed door and said loudly, "You do that. And say hello to Bettan!"

Chapter 22

IRENE LOOKED AT HER colleagues. The last shot had just been heard on the tape that she had played for them. They had sat, mesmerized, for a whole hour while she described the events that had taken place in England and Scotland. It almost seemed as though no one wanted to break the silence. But Superintendent Andersson finally cleared his throat.

"Georg Andersson . . . the director of the school where Jacob worked . . . got in touch on Friday. There I was, up to my neck in motorcycle shit, and then he comes and finally decides to talk. . . . Started blabbering about his conscience."

Andersson stopped and Irene saw the color in his face rise. She wasn't completely unprepared when he slammed his fist onto the table in front of him and bellowed, "If that ridiculous jackass had only said something! We would have solved this a lot faster! But he was worried about the school's reputation, and since Jacob was dead, then it wasn't necessary to drag events into the daylight! Both he and the girl's parents thought it was best not to say anything. Load of crap! I told him a thing or two."

It was clear that the superintendent's cousin had gotten into hot water and was on the minus side when it came to brownie points, but the reason for his having fallen into disfavor was still concealed. Irene finally ventured to ask what the superintendent meant.

"On the morning of the murder—so, on Monday—a student's father came to the principal's office. He was sad and angry, and that can be understood. His eight-year-old daughter had told him, sobbing, that her teacher had several times forced her to perform different sexual acts. Guess who the teacher was."

"Jacob Schyttelius," several of the officers answered at the same time.

"Exactly! Georg called Jacob to his office and told him what the girl's father had said, but he flatly denied it. Said that people from other cultures could get hold of the wrong side of the stick, might not understand our Swedish openness between students and teachers in a Swedish school. The girl's family are Syrians, I believe it was. So I checked with the police in Norrland, where Jacob was a teacher before his divorce."

The superintendent waved a pile of faxes in the air. "These came a few hours ago. That damn Jacob had been forced to quit his job after he was suspected of making sexual advances toward students! Or he resigned voluntarily, rather. Then he moved down here, and proceedings against him there came to a halt. Up there in Lapp hell, they were just happy to get rid of the bastard!"

Irene remembered the sad, intimidated Kristina Olsson, the ex-wife who had moved to Karlstad. Her unhappiness had an explanation. But she hadn't said anything either.

"If only someone had said something!" Andersson exploded.

Thoughtfully, Irene said, "I've been thinking quite a bit about something Svante Malm remarked. He said that the devil is inside us all. Where the devil clearly manifests himself in heinous crimes, it's easy to see him. Murder, sexual abuse, and rape are definite and clear manifestations of evil that we can fight. But it isn't so easy to fight against glass devils."

"What the hell kind of nonsense is that?" Andersson hissed.

Irene continued, "A glass devil is a person in whom evil becomes transparent. People simply don't see it, despite the fact that it's there all the time. The side of himself that the devil shows blinds people. No one saw the devil in an old clergyman who wore a silver cross around his neck and donned gold-embroidered chasubles. And who saw the devil in a handsome young teacher who was so friendly and well-liked by his students? No one. And no one *wants* to see him, either."

Andersson glared at Irene as if he couldn't believe his ears. "Seriously. . . . Maybe this has been too much for you?" he finally said.

"No. I've actually learned a great deal during this investigation. The glass devil's victims remain silent because they know no one will believe them, and for fear of even worse. Rebecka asserted until the end that it was her fault her family was killed. The father's prophecy was fulfilled; if she told even a single person, terrible things would happen to both her and the family. And that's exactly what happened."

SUPERINTENDENT SVEN Andersson's thank-you speech at his sixtieth birthday party:

"As you know, I'm no speaker but since you have given me such a fine present—not to mention this party—then I have to say thank you. I was at a loss for words when, in his speech, Tommy started talking about me not getting a present but an *experience*. I thought that sounded suspicious. . . .

"—Yes, thank you! Pour it in! You only turn sixty once in your life!" he said as someone offered him more champagne.

"Where was I? Right, an experience. It will probably be a fun experience to see London again. I was there at the beginning of the sixties . . . '61. We took the boat over and damn, was I seasick!

"It will be much better flying, I hope. That . . . what was his name again? Where is the paper? Glen Thompson! He seems like a nice fellow. He's going to meet me at the airport and he has his own hotel . . . what did you say, Irene? Oh. His sister's hotel. I'm going to stay there three nights, and he's providing all my dinners at a restaurant in the area.

"And I've received a card from the lady who owns the pub. She writes that she's going to take care of me in the best way. I think this sounds promising. Donna is her name. Maybe she's a small blond Donna? Ha ha.

"So I can tell you now that I've applied for an exemption to permit me to stay on for another year as superintendent of this unit. Now you're supposed to look happy! And actually I was wondering what kind of coup Irene and Fredrik were whispering about. I heard everything! Hey, Irene! I'll find out later. . . . Well. No one tells me anything. But I guess that's the way it should be when it's your birthday. Thank you all for a really great party and the wonderful present . . . er . . . experience. Cheers!"